SEE ME

BOOK 1 IN THE NOVUS PACK SERIES

M. JAYNE

Publishers Note

See Me – Copyright September 2018 by M. Jayne for Big Dog Publishing

Cover Design by Fiona Jayde

Editing by Delilah Devlin

Proofreading by Susan Panak, Susan O'Sick Cambra, Wanda Adams

Medical Advisor: Joy Smoll-Adams

Author's Assistant and Professional Hand Holder: David Panak

Printed in the United States of America

First Edition

ISBN E-Book: 978-0999642122

ISBN Print: 978-1724636362

CONTENTS

All of the dreamers, for I am one.
The people who feel like they want more, dream about more.
Those who wake each morning feeling like they should be doing
something different.
Keep Dreaming.

AUTHOR'S NOTE

Welcome to the world of the Novus Pack.

I've been a part of Novus since 2009. The story has changed over time but the theme has stayed the same: a human female thrown into the Lycan world.

It took me three tries and the deletion of a hundred thousand words to write this book. I needed to grow into it as an author, to do Novus justice.

Now for some housekeeping- This book contains violence. A human female is injured in this book. A teen is killed. In flashbacks there is a sexual battery. There is build-up to these events so if they are triggers, be aware.

Remember…

Cum Nobis aut contra Nobis
With us or Against Us

CHARACTER LIST

Raider Black—Novus Packleader, known as "The Black" or Laird

Theodora Morrissey—Seer to the Novus Pack, Human, Raider Black's lover

Conal MacGregor—Second in the Novus Pack, Mated to Solle, Novus Board Member

Solle MacGregor—Mated to the Second, Changed Human, Doctor

Tex —Novus Board Member, Changed Human, Tech Genius, D.J.

Onyx— Novus Board Member, Pack Historian and Counsel, Theodora's Tutor

Glass—Novus Board Member, In Charge of Novus Guards and Training

Lorenzo Barducci—Son of a Seer and Packleader, Mass Murderer, Spy for Novus Pack, Theodora's Tutor, Loner, known as "Lore"

Other Characters
Novus Guards—Issa, Wale, Asher, Sarita

Basil—Novus Employee, Black's Administrative Assistant

Brian—Solle's Medical Assistant

Clifton—Majordomo of the Packhouse

Siobhan Dolan—Future contracted Mate to Raider Black

ONE

THEODORA MORRISSEY

"*C*hild you must wake."

The voice seemed to vibrate through my heavy body. My very cold and, now that I thought about it, aching body.

What the fuck?

I reached for consciousness like a swimmer fighting to break the surface after a deep dive and let's face it, this was a crappy dream. I was freezing. "*Wake up*," I commanded, but my eyes didn't want to open. However, my senses were stirring, and Goddamn, my cheek was on fire.

I swallowed hard and tried to get my bearings. I attempted to lift my head. Christ, I hurt. Not just the burning in my cheek that felt like someone was jabbing it with a hot poker, but my entire body felt as though I had just left the octagon.

Where? My eyes flew open as I searched for an answer, any answer. It was…dark, and yet, it wasn't. I used my knee to wrench my body over onto my back.

"Focus."

Again, that unnatural voice that seemed to be in my head and all around me sounded. It was feminine, maybe. Well, it wasn't exactly male. I caught a sense of concern in the tone.

Had I been drugged? I didn't touch them because of my mom's history, but this was a freaky trip. I tried to recapture the last few hours. Hazy images of feeling anger and hopelessness washed over me.

I hated feeling weak or out of control, so again, I closed my eyes.

This has got to be a dream. My eyes were having difficulty focusing, everything was dark and hazy. I hoped that the next time I woke up I would be in my own bed, or rather, Allen's.

"No. You must not rest." Definitely female, but it held a timbre that I'd never heard before.

Something wet landed on my face. Again, I opened my eyes to examine my surroundings and I was looking straight up into…the moon.

It looked huge and full. I thought that if I reached out my arm, I might be able to touch it.

The what…? I took in a deep shocked breath that sent a shooting pain throughout my body.

When I could breathe again without the pain making me want to pee my pants, I tried to break down what I was experiencing calmly and rationally. I'd always had very realistic dreams. The kind that caused me to wake up confused and disoriented. My mother had ordered me never to talk about them. She'd done so with so much intensity that she'd often scared me and made me cry. This had to be one of those dreams. *Time to wake up, dumbass.*

Another freezing drop of moisture landed on my chin. *Take stock*, the rational part of my brain ordered. I was very cold and I couldn't ignore the pain. I tried to wiggle my toes, and then my feet. Something was wrong with my right ankle, or maybe it was my foot, but moving it sent a white-hot shot of pain up my leg and into my belly.

Not good. I continued doing a body check. My left arm was numb, I didn't know if that was because I had laid on it or if it was damaged, too.

This was different. Before, when I realized I was dreaming, I'd wake. Plus, I'd never felt so much pain before. I prepared to open my eyes one last time, hoping I would see that ugly Picasso print Allen had hung on the far wall of our bedroom. The thing always made me uneasy with what looked to me like a giant eye watching me. *Okay, here goes...on the count of three.*

Shit! That definitely was the moon in a velvety dark sky. She was almost a perfect circle. I'd always thought the moon was female even though most used the term, the man in the moon. For some reason, she had always given me a measure of comfort.

I tried to shift my body to find a comfortable position on the hard surface. This definitely wasn't a mattress. *Wait, why would I be lying outside on a mattress?*

"Child, you need to seek shelter, now." This time the voice definitely caused my body to pulsate, like when the bass of a sound system is turned up, and it feels like your heart is trying to match the pounding beat.

I blinked several times trying to piece together what was happening. "What the fuck?" Shock sent me into a sitting position, which made me cry out. I was outside and it was...snowing hard. I looked around. *How the hell?*

My body wanted to collapse back onto the hard surface, but I couldn't do that. "What? How?" I sputtered. I didn't know where I was or, worse, how had I gotten here?

I stayed still and listened as I tried to force my brain into action. Christ, I knew that sound. I grew up in the Ohio Valley on a farm, miles from neighbors. The utter stillness was of isolation. "Hello?" I called hopefully. "Help," I tried a few more times, but I knew instinctively that no one could come.

I was alone.

"Okay," I told myself as if speaking aloud helped bolster my confidence. "Can't stay out here." Why was it so hard to think?

A wave of hysteria rose up and enveloped my body and mind. I needed assistance and no one had answered my calls. What did I have to lose? "Uhm, Lady?" A crazed giggle escaped my lips. Hopefully my insurance covered a stay in the looney bin—if I got out of this alive. "Hey, uhm, Lady who was talking to me earlier, I could use some help," I yelled while looking up at the moon.

"Finally."

The voice made my body vibrate with her exasperation. I was definitely going to be moving into one of those special facilities with secured doors. I felt her presence, and yet, I knew that she wasn't really here. "Yeah, uh, sorry about before."

"Daughter, you are in a dire situation."

No shit. I didn't speak my first thought, not when this hallucination might be able to help. "Can you call someone or send for some help?"

4

"The wolves are on their way."

"Wolves!" The thought of stealthy predators made me react. I rolled over so that I was on all fours while trying to ignore the pain, praying that my adrenaline would kick in and mute it soon. "I don't think a wolf is going to be much help." My voice came out in a pant. I had to get to my feet. I was prey, weakened prey.

"You are near shelter. Follow my voice," her tone urgent.

I fought to get to my feet, but my ankle wouldn't support me. I fell to my knees with my arm bent under me. "Jesus, fuck, ouch," I cried in a panicked voice. I sucked in some shallow breaths. "I, uh, I can't walk."

No response.

I needed to move, or I would die. "I'm going to try again," I announced. Somehow, saying it helped. Maybe I could coach myself through this?

I ended up doing a modified crawl. Progress was slow. My good hand was bleeding by the time I saw a building illuminated by the silvery light. She hadn't lied. "I-I see it." I started to cry, maybe from relief or the pain. I honestly didn't know.

"Trust in me, my daughter."

It felt like a farewell. "Don't leave me," I screamed. I didn't want to be alone.

Silence.

I continued crawling to the side of the building. There, I noted a window about shoulder height. I didn't consider looking for a door. I just wanted in. There was a downspout running beside the window with a metal drum right under it. I could climb up on the barrel and through the window.

5

I crawled closer to the metal downspout and used my good arm to pull my body until I stood. I leaned heavily onto the barrel's lid, not putting any weight on my ankle. At the best of times, I wasn't in great physical shape, no way could I pull up my one hundred and sixty pounds—okay, one-eighty—with both arms, let alone only one.

I started to sob. "So close, so fucking close." I looked around, hoping that some other opportunity would present itself. "Please," I begged. "I can't, I need…" W*hat?* "Lady please, I'm so close."

Everything went bright. If neon white made a sound, it would be what echoed through my head like a microphone's feedback. I felt dizzy and dazed. Closing my eyes against the brightness, I made a grab for the drain pipe before my good knee gave way. I felt my stomach drop like I'd just survived the first big hill on a rollercoaster.

I was breathing heavily and sweating in the cold. Slowly, I opened my eyes to find that I was looking into the window while standing on the barrel. "Don't think about it," I ordered myself as I kept a death grip on the drainpipe. This was all too much. "Thank you," I yelled. I laughed shrilly at my good manners and my self-diagnosed insanity.

I glanced down at my feet, and then at the window. I wanted to kick it in, but I knew my bad ankle couldn't bear my weight. I leaned my hip against the window, slowly released my grip on the drain pipe, and did my best to balance. I was going to have to use my elbow to break the glass.

"I'd make a terrible burglar," I mumbled as I pulled back my elbow and forced it through the glass with the entire weight of my body. The glass cracked and gave way. I tried to grab onto the side of the window casing but, instead, fell through the opening, landing on the glass-covered floor.

"Not good." I'm not sure if the words even came out as I crawled to the first object that could shield me from the now unprotected opening. I couldn't go on.

TWO

CONAL MACGREGOR

Whitehite Zombie's *More Human than Human* blasted through my Yukon's sound system. The song always made me smirk. If only the world's populace knew. I drove easily on the icy road. My heightened reflexes would handle any skid expertly. I hit number one on my phone. I also didn't have to worry about multi-tasking while driving.

She answered on the second ring. "How are the roads?"

My mate still thought like a human at times. "Babe, a little snow won't be a problem."

"Eighteen to twenty-four inches is *not* a little snow," she corrected in that superior tone that always got me hard.

"Not much traffic and the roads are still passable." The hospital's bright lights came into view. "Happy?"

"I'm glad people took the warnings seriously. I've checked with my three expectant mothers, and they seem fine. Things here are quiet and I'm hoping they'll stay that way."

I could picture her ticking off her list on her tablet. Solle was very efficient and thorough. "I'll be at the door in one."

"One? I need to grab my coat and check in with Titus. He's on duty tonight." She wouldn't leave the hospital until everything was done, checked, and rechecked. We both knew that.

"Take your time. I'll be waiting for you." I ended the call.

The SUV was parked under the overhang protecting the Emergency Entrance. I relaxed back into the heated leather seat. After we got home and ate whatever the housekeeper had left for dinner, a run sounded good, then…. Well, that sounded even better.

My cell vibrated on the dash where I had tossed it. The screen showed "Control Room" as the caller. "What?" I snapped in a form of greeting. I'd been gone exactly thirty-seven minutes.

"You need to get laid," Raider Black's deep voice rumbled in my ear.

Immediately, I sat up straighter, out of habit. "Fuck you." We'd known each other since we were young. Our bond was eternal, as was my pledge to guard his life with my own.

"I'm going to tell Solle that you said that. It would only serve you right if she decided that she wanted to watch."

I could hear the subtle teasing in his voice, which was becoming so rare. He took his responsibilities as our leader very seriously. "What's up?"

"Maybe nothing, but it could be something…" He let the rest of his thought hang.

"Where do you need me?" The Laird wasn't asking, but we both knew that he'd called me to handle this job.

"Dispatch got a call from Cora Bransky. She claims a plane used the southwest strip."

"Nothing's scheduled." I pictured the list in my head of our current jobs and nobody was scheduled to fly in for two weeks.

"And in this weather…" he grumbled.

"Questionable decision to land on an untreated strip with no lights." It was a terrible risk, but desperation made people stupid.

"Tex is heading that way."

"I'll meet him there," I promised. "I'll keep you updated."

"I'll be in the Control Room tonight."

"Try not to scare the kids too badly." Our Packleader didn't share his sense of humor often. If he was working with that shift tonight, the wolves were probably terrified they might make a mistake or need correcting by the fierce Lycan.

"Now, where's the fun in that?" he drawled.

See? The man could be funny.

I sensed Solle's approach. She threw open the back door and placed her medical bag behind her seat. After she climbed in and closed the door, she leaned over the console and kissed me. "Hmmm, nice."

This would never get old. I didn't care if I did live forever; I'd never take her touch for granted. "Good day?" I started the engine.

"Quiet, except for the storm prep." She buckled her seatbelt even though our kind's human form could take a great deal of damage—short of decapitation or incineration. Her doctor's training and being born human still played a part in her actions.

"I'm going to drop you off and then I need to go check on the southwest airstrip."

"I'll go with you," she said with a grin. "You might need back-up."

I didn't laugh out loud. My mate was just over five feet tall and I was six-three and doubled her in weight, but Solle could be fierce. "I'm supposed to meet Tex there."

"Then I'll back up Tex," she told me firmly.

My first impulse was to turn the direction that led to our home, but I'd learned that my mate didn't want to be stowed away safely. Further, I doubted that we'd encounter anyone at the site. I made a mental note to check on Mrs. Bransky more often. She'd been widowed for a year. Perhaps she wasn't well. Her family had been in service to our kind for centuries, she'd been marked as an Article since birth. She was a human under the pack's protection. "I'm sure Tex will appreciate having your help."

"Ass," she muttered as one side of her mouth lifted in a smirk.

I laughed as I drove on the deserted road toward the southern part of our county. As we neared the unmarked entrance to the drive, I asked, "See any signs of him?"

Solle lowered her window, unbuckled her seatbelt, and got onto her knees. She leaned on the passenger side door with her hips as she stuck her upper body through the window. After a few beats, she answered, "Yes, there." She pointed sharply to her right.

I continued down the drive for a quarter of a mile

and stopped. Three minutes later, a tall, bearded male approached my driver's side window. I gave him a nod. "Tex."

"You see anything?"

Although Tex had left the lone star state almost a hundred years ago, that slow drawl could still be heard in his voice. "Nothing," I said. "I passed two trucks ten miles back. You?"

"Quiet. I think that old woman has finally tossed a brick." He bent lower and sent a smile to my mate. "Evenin', Doc."

Solle wrinkled her nose and glared at the male. "Tex, you leave Cora alone. I'm sure she saw something."

Tex looked up at the moon, and then back at us. "I dunno...taking a risk in this weather. You'd have to be familiar with the set-up."

That was the next part of the problem. If indeed we found evidence of a plane, the location of this airfield was not widely known. Whoever directed the plane to make an unauthorized landing would be in trouble with Novus and that would not bode well for them. Our specialty was highly sought after by a select few, and those people knew few specifics. "Get in."

I didn't use my headlights as I kept the SUV moving slowly down the drive. The full moon's reflection on the snow made it a very bright night. As we neared, I could clearly see the maintenance barn.

I glanced at Solle. "You stay here while we do a perimeter check."

"That's not fair—"

"Solle," I cut her off. I was the Second to the Leader of the Novus Pack. My orders were followed without question.

She frowned, and her eyes flashed with frustration. "Understood," she huffed.

I stopped the SUV, got out, and checked my Glock. Not that a bullet would stop our kind, but a well-placed shot could slow a Lycan in either form. When I verified that one was in the chamber, I slid out of my jacket and left it on the hood. I nodded at Tex, and we headed toward the building quickly and silently.

As we neared, Tex stopped and lifted his nose to the air.

I smelled it, too—fresh blood. Someone or something was injured near our building. At the corner, we took our defensive positions, Tex against the building and me behind him. I stepped wide around the corner with my gun raised. The scent of blood was stronger. We hugged the side of the building, and I think we both saw the shattered window at the same time.

Tex gestured that he would go through first. After he crawled inside, I tucked my gun into my holster and dove through, close on his heels. Once inside, the smell made my wolf stir. We separated, I went to the right and he the left.

I saw him go to his knees. "Get Solle." I started to cross the room when the front door flew open.

"I smelled the blood." My mate knew how to make an entrance. She stalked in with her medical bag in hand.

"Over here." Tex's voice carried a note of concern.

I moved to cut in front of her. I wanted to assess the situation before my mate neared.

A woman lay in a pool of blood.

Solle dropped to her knees beside the stranger, going into doctor mode. "Hello." She lightly tapped the woman's exposed cheek. "I'm Solle, and I'm a doctor," she continued as if the woman was conscious.

She moved over the woman's chest to unzip the light-weight leather jacket. "I'm going to check for injuries."

The woman's eyelids fluttered then opened.

My body tensed; I was ready to intervene.

The woman didn't move, but her blue eyes never left Solle's face. She whispered, "Are you a wolf?"

Tex moved first. He thrust his hands under the unfamiliar woman's shoulders and lifted as he went to his feet. She was against the opposite wall, hanging from his grasp before Solle or I could stop him. "What did you say?" he demanded. His face was a mere inch from hers.

I grabbed Solle's shoulder and pushed her behind my body. This woman was a stranger to me.

The woman cried out in pain and fear. Her eyes were so wide I could see their whites.

"She said tha...that the wolves would come."

Her head dropped, I didn't need to be a doctor to know she was unconscious.

"Easy, Tex. Right now, she's not a threat." Solle shouldered her way around me and headed to the woman. "We need to get her to the hospital, or she's not going to make it."

"I didn't think." Tex was looking over Solle at me.

"Who's the 'she' that she spoke of?" I asked of no one in particular.

"We can figure all of that out later," Solle said over her shoulder. "She's suffering from severe blood loss, exposure, and probably a list of other injuries. I need to keep her alive so she can answer your questions. But right now, she isn't in good shape."

I moved to the old wooden desk that stood across

15

from the door and tore the top off. "We'll use this as a stretcher."

When the woman was positioned to Solle's liking, we headed to my SUV. Solle rushed ahead to lower the back seat and open the back gate. She climbed in after we slid the woman and the wooden plank inside. "I'm guessing road conditions aren't great, but I don't think we have much time." She flashed me a meaningful look.

THE JOURNEY to the E.R. took about thirty-five minutes. As soon as the staff opened the back hatch, Solle barked orders. She'd already called in with her observations.

Tex and I followed the E.R. team into the large bay. One of the nurses started cutting away the patient's clothing and dropping the items onto the floor. Titus Mohr, the lead surgeon, rushed in and gave additional orders. I leaned against the wall by the door, out of the way of the chaos, but I stayed focused on the patient.

"I'm going out to call Black with another update," Tex told me as he left the room. We'd placed the initial call to the Control Room as soon as I'd started the engine.

Titus had been a healer before the word doctor was invented and, later, attended human medical school. Solle believed he was a fantastic surgeon, but an even better diagnostician. Our people were lucky to have a total of five doctors in the area. "Diminished breath sound on right side," he stated without looking up.

Solle paused in her exam of the woman's arm. "I witnessed her back make contact with a wall, so there could be damage."

Between them, they rolled the woman onto her belly in a well-choreographed move.

Titus continued listening with his stethoscope. "Pneumothorax. Possible flair chest. I need a—" He took a jerky step back.

I moved instinctively toward the table. "What?" I demanded looking first at the doctor, who wore a shocked expression on his face and then at the patient. "Titus?"

"I…ah, I've never seen one, only drawings." He took his gaze off of her back and faced me. "I thought it was a myth." The old wolf looked mystified.

"Doctor, what's happening?" Solle asked sharply.

He pointed with his gloved finger. "There," his voice full of reverence, "the Lady's Mark."

The "mark" looked like a bruise, but as I approached and leaned in closer, I saw that it was round in shape and blueish, like a fading bruise in color. I whipped out my cell and started snapping photos.

"Have you ever seen the mark in person?" Titus whispered.

"No. I met two that were marked when I was with the Council Guard, but I never saw their marks." I realized that I too was talking softly, respectfully.

"What the hell is happening?" Solle was giving Titus an angry stare. "Her lung, doctor."

She had moved around the table. Part of the staff was staring at the woman's side in fascination.

Titus went back into doctor mode while I spoke to my mate. "The Lady blesses us with those who carry her mark."

Solle's eyes widened. "You mean, this woman?" She looked back down at the human.

I squared my shoulders and took control. "Nobody leaves this room, and nobody," I looked at the six people attending the patient, "says a word about this." I added in a threatening tone, "I need to get Black here." I turned on my heel but paused at the door. "Don't let her die."

Her survival meant everything to our pack.

THREE

NOVUS

RAIDER BLACK

B eing the Packleader meant I was the final word and responsible for the pack, every member and Article. My decisions were law, I answered to no one. Sure, there was the Council, that oversaw all Packs, but by the time they acted, I could destroy the continent. For some, ruling a Pack was too much power. The Council had or was in the process of dismantling those kingdoms. I didn't want that to happen here or to my people. I hoped the safeguards I had set in place would stop any decline into that type of despotic behavior.

One such safeguard was that I worked beside my people, which was why I sat in the Control Room tonight. It made good sense, because any decisions made would ultimately be mine. Currently, this human found on our property was a mystery, but I was sure my team would soon get answers.

I took Tex's call, hoping for a fact-filled update. From the initial report, I didn't believe she'd come willingly.

She wasn't dressed for a Nebraska snowstorm, and from the preliminary list of injuries, she'd put up a fight.

Tex's manner of speaking was unhurried. Some thought him to be mentally slow, but they were wrong. The man was a technological genius; he was focused and loyal. That was why he held a position on my Board. I relied on his advice and his ability to learn secrets. "No I.D. and no phone on her," he said.

"Someone went to a great deal of work to dump her." I leaned back in my chair and rubbed the space between my eyes. I was tired. I needed to run. That always cleared away the tension that pulsed throughout my body.

"She appears to have been in good health. Her clothes were good quality, not designer but also not cheap. No tattoos or scars that I could see. Maybe her prints will turn up in one of the databases but if not, we'll have to wait until she can tell us who she is and why she's here."

"And who she was with," I added.

"In the past two years, twelve non-pack pilots have used that airstrip. In my estimation, only four have the skill-set to find it during a storm."

Tex's recall was foolproof. "Get me those four names," I ordered.

"Three are based on the west coast. I've already forwarded the names to Lore, and Sarita has the other."

"Good." My agents, or as some called them, spies, out in the field would find answers. "Now, what do the doctors say?" I wanted to know how soon the woman could be questioned.

In the background, I heard Conal's voice say clearly, "I need to speak with the Laird, immediately."

20

Tex must have handed him the phone because Conal's voice blasted in my ear. "I'm sending you photos from my phone. You need to look at them and tell me if it's real."

I pulled the phone away from my ear and waited for the photos to appear. I tapped the phone's screen and studied each picture closely. I drew a deep, silent breath. I returned the phone to my ear. "Where did you get these?" I asked cautiously, as if my words could jinx what I'd just seen.

"The woman." Conal's bitten-off words told me that he, too, was being careful. "Titus saw it and froze. He thought it matched old drawings."

"You and Tex stay with her. Do not leave her alone." I was already on my feet.

"I'll stay with her," Conal assured me.

"I'm on my way." I ended the call and was heading down the hallway when Asher fell in behind me.

"Going somewhere?" My guard asked with a flash of a smile as we took the steps at a run. He liked to fight and be in the thick of things.

"Hospital, E.R."

"Taking the truck or on foot?"

I called to my wolf and changed. At my age, it was instantaneous. I was a man one second, and the next, I was a werewolf. My clothes gone, like my human form. I didn't even break stride.

Our kind were made of magic, blessed by our goddess, The Lady.

With my heightened hearing, Asher's utterance of, "I guess that answers that," voiced his excitement. We hit the exit door and as soon as he threw it open, he changed.

21

As we made our way across town, I wondered what this meant. A Marked human dropped upon us. It seemed too good to be true. I was always suspicious of gifts. This seemed too easy, and as far as I knew, there hadn't been a recorded gift from the Lady in the last century. I would have to ask Onyx whether that was true. As I'd aged, my sense of time had become warped. Surviving over a thousand years would do that to a Lycan.

At the hospital entrance we changed into human form. Asher walked two steps in front of me through the automatic doors.

Tex met us. He swept out an arm to guide me. "This way Laird. Titus had to inflate her lung, but they believe she'll survive."

Asher pushed open the door to the examination room, and I gave a quick look around. There were two doctors and four others in the room, plus Conal. As a group, they spoke their greeting, "Laird." Some bowed their heads, but they all stopped what they'd been doing.

"Continue," I ordered. I wished for the millionth time that some of the old ways could be done away with. My pack was considered progressive. There were still pockets in the old country where they dressed as if Louis the Fourteenth was going to visit. A pack in northern Canada still lived in a castle and its grounds. When time means nothing, change comes slowly to some.

Titus stepped away from the table, peeled off his blue Latex gloves, and dropped them onto the floor. "The patient has an anterior shoulder dislocation, along with an ankle that will require surgery to repair. Three ribs were fractured, and we had to inflate her lung. She received a serious blow to her left cheekbone and, finally,

I'd put her concussion at mid-grade level with minor brain swelling."

I only understood about half of what he'd shared. "And?" I bit out in my impatience. Older Lycans were always difficult about sharing what they knew.

"Barring any serious infection, she should recover."

I appreciated his briefing, but I wanted to see The Mark. "You know why I'm here."

"You four, out." Conal's voice seemed to echo in the room. He pointed at everyone but Titus and his mate. "Asher, take them to a room and keep them there."

"Yes, sir." The guard motioned for the three women and one man to precede him through the swinging door.

I moved to the area at the foot of the examination table. The human looked to be of medium height, early thirties, with pale skin and dark hair that fell past her breasts. "What else can you tell me about her?"

"She's a fighter." Solle was also studying the woman's face.

"With those injuries, it couldn't have been easy climbing up to break the window in the cold," Conal continued Solle's thought.

"She wasn't dressed for the weather." Solle raised her gaze to mine. "Her boots were low-heeled, but they weren't made for snow, and her jacket was fall weight." She smoothed the woman's hair back from her lacerated cheek. "I can't imagine how scared she must have been —cold, hurting, and all alone out there."

I turned to Tex who was still leaning against the far wall. "Did she have an accent? Use odd words?" I didn't know what I was searching for, but I needed some bit of information.

"She surprised me by asking if Solle was a wolf." Tex

23

widened his eyes as he finished. "I was so shocked that I, well, I rammed her against the wall."

Solle frowned. "That could have been a hallucination. The brain can do amazing things to shield us from the reality of the danger. Add into that the pain and concussion, she might believe she heard a voice."

"But no Laird, I didn't hear any type of accent, she said only a few words… but they weren't oddly phrased." Tex shrugged. "I should have listened more closely."

I nodded, but none of that explained the wolf part.

"Would you like to see The Mark, Laird?" Titus's tone held a strong note of respect.

"I would."

He and Solle rolled the patient onto her stomach and repositioned her arm so that it was lifted over her head.

I felt the pull immediately. When I had become Pack-leader, The Lady had gifted me with certain additional powers. I now recognized the source of the low level buzz that I'd felt when I'd entered the hospital. I moved closer to look at the area where Titus's index finger pointed.

When I was young, I'd served the Council in Edinburgh. I'd seen several who'd carried The Mark. The humans were sheltered and guarded at all times, their interactions limited. I'd been too young to be assigned that important post.

"So, what does it mean?" Solle's impatience came through in her tone.

"Your mate has been remiss in continuing your education." I used a firm voice but did that more to tease her than to chastise Conal.

"Noted." Conal moved to stand beside me. "They're so rare; I didn't think to mention them."

I shot him a smirk. The couple was still in their honeymoon phase, although they had been mated for... Damn, was it over thirty years? No matter, they fucked all of the time as if they'd just discovered one another.

I needed to research the ritual that would activate The Mark's gift. The details were buried in one of the ancient texts I kept in my personal library. "I want some answers first."

Conal's eyebrows rose. "Before you know for sure what she is?"

"A Healer or a Seer would be a welcome addition to the Pack. A Patterner, you know that we would be compensated, but she'd be moved to Edinburgh." The Council claimed that a Patterner would assist all Lycans. Therefore, they served in Scotland under the Council's watch.

"What do we want her to be?" Solle asked in a quiet voice.

"A Marked Healer would be a help to you and the hospital staff. Their skills are for more than tending the ill. They are said to help with volatility, especially when our young go through their first change and work to find their place in the pack," I shared while thinking aloud. "Having a psychic could be beneficial, if she can learn to harness her ability."

"Don't they go insane?" Conal asked.

So, he remembered the stories.

Titus cleared his throat. "Some do, the ones who don't learn how to control their gift. There's a legend about a Seer who kept her Pack alive during a war and helped strengthen their position in Asia. It's said that the pack members still honor her grave."

"She's already proved she's strong," Solle muttered as she attempted to comb her fingers through the woman's matted hair.

Conal needed to start planning for a child. With her huge heart, his mate needed someone else to care for. "Titus, you will be rewarded for recognizing this. I thank you, as does the Novus Pack."

The doctor stood straighter. "Thank you. I proudly serve Novus."

I nodded once. "Tex, arrange permanent guards. Let me know when she wakes." I motioned to Conal to follow me into the hall.

We moved to the end of the corridor.

Conal walked beside me as was his place as my Second. "What are you thinking?"

"I want to know who dumped that woman and why. There is something about this find that is causing my senses to warn me to be suspicious." I ran my hand through my hair. "This could be the beginning of a series of fortuitous events for Novus, or did somebody arrange this, and is there going to be a demand for repayment of this gift?"

He rocked back on his heels. I rarely spoke about my enhanced senses. "So, she's the real thing?" He fought a cheeky grin. "The Lady has smiled upon us, the pack filled with outcasts and ruffians?"

Novus has been described that way many times. "Yes." When it had been decided that I would be given the Packleader title and my subscription to start up a new pack in the New World, I'd known then that I needed Conal, not only for his brilliant mind but because his easy-going temperament was complimentary to my intensity. He was my brother in every way except for blood.

His smile grew. "We'll solve the puzzle, then there'll be much to celebrate."

I gave my best-friend a slight smile. "The Pack does like to celebrate."

"Indeed, we do." Conal chuckled.

FOUR

THEODORA MORRISSEY

"Ooooh. Oohhhh, *oooohhhhh.*" *Christ, who is making such a racket?* I was trying to sleep.

"Oooh." *Whoever was making so much noise needed to shut up. They were working on my last nerve.* I tried to roll onto my side and—*ouch.* My eyes flew open as a moan escaped from my dry lips. *What the hell?*

It took my eyes a moment to focus, like I'd been sleeping hard for a long time. This wasn't my bedroom. The lights were dim, yet I could see a woman sitting in a well-padded chair facing me. She held a tablet up like she was going to take my picture.

The flash blinded me. "Hey, stop that," I ordered curtly. My voice was hoarse, and my throat ached.

"Hang on. Just one more."

When I could see again, she was tapping on the screen.

"What...?" I paused because I didn't even know where to start. Plus, I realized that my head was pounding, and my leg and my shoulder… Hell, my entire body hurt.

The woman wedged the tablet between her hip and the arm of the chair. "You're probably wondering what's going on, am I right?"

I nodded and squeezed my eyes together tightly as the roar of pain thundered through my head.

"Moving isn't the greatest idea right now."

"Ya think?" I grumbled. After a few moments, I opened my eyes and looked at her.

"Feisty," she commented dryly. "I'm Solle MacGregor, one of your doctors." She rolled her big brown eyes. "Yeah, I know, I probably should have kept my own last name, but he convinced me…" Her smile turned sweet as though she was reliving a moment. "Anyway, I'm glad you're awake. You were in pretty bad shape when we found you. You're in the hospital, if you couldn't tell. I can give you the rundown of your injuries, or we can skip that part right now, and you can tell me who you are."

"Hospital?" I slowly turned my head from side to side. The space did look like a hospital room. "Where?" I tried to figure out what she was talking about. Sensory memories flooded my mind—cold, dread, and pain. I squeezed my eyes shut as I tried to slow the information down. It was overwhelming. I blinked several times and realized I was breathing hard from the effort. "I'm in the hospital?" None of this made any sense.

"Yeah, I just said that." She continued looking at me expectantly; however, her eyes sparkled, so I thought she might be teasing me.

"Where am I?"

The door opened, and the overhead lights came on,

causing me to want to shield my eyes from the brightness.

"She's awake?" A very deep male voice sounded.

"She is."

"Has she talked?" His voice was closer this time.

I wanted to answer, but some inner voice told me to be quiet and stay still.

"She's still getting the good juice, I don't know how clearly she's thinking at this point," my doctor said.

"I know that you're awake."

His voice was close, and I knew without opening my eyes that he was leaning over me. I slowly opened my eyes. He had golden-blond hair, light blue eyes, and a ruddy complexion—and he was big. "Hello," I rasped.

He straightened, and yeah, he was tall and thick with broad shoulders. One side of his mouth hitched upward. "Uh, hello."

I took the half-smile as a good sign. Still, this was the type of man you didn't mess around with.

His gaze swept my face. "Who are you?"

It was a demand. I felt like he wanted more than my name. "I'm Theodora." I tried to clear my throat, but that made things worse. I started to cough because my mouth was so dry.

"I'll get you some water." The woman pushed up from her chair. "Stop scaring her," she chided the man before she walked out of the room.

He watched her walk away. Clearly, he liked what he saw. When his focus returned to me, his eyes went cold. "We are no place near the scary part," he added.

I knew that he wasn't kidding. My eyes went wide. I wanted to shy away from him, but I also didn't want to show him how badly my body was damaged. My

31

instincts had gone on high alert. My inner voice was screaming for me to be still. *Cooperate, and maybe he'll go away.*

"So, Theodora, do you have a last name, or are you famous and only use one, like Bono, or Cher?" He might be scary as hell, but his voice was nice, deep with a hint of an accent.

"No, I mean, yes." I was out of breath, and my brain was in hyper-drive. I was terrified, and I didn't know why. I tried to swallow once, and then again, as I organized my thoughts. "No, I'm not famous in any way. And yes, I have a last name. It's Morrissey." I suddenly wished the doctor would come back.

"Spell your name for me." He pulled his phone from his back pocket.

I did and waited for his next question as he typed my information into his phone. In reality, I should be asking him a few questions, like why was I hurt and…where was I? He hadn't shown me his badge yet. Weren't police officers supposed to do that? Should I ask to see it? *God, this was exhausting.*

The door opened again. I wanted to see who was coming in, but I couldn't look away from the man furiously typing. The speed of his big fingers on that small screen, it was mesmerizing.

The doctor moved to the other side of the bed. "I'm going to raise the top part of your bed. Let me know if it hurts too much."

I heard the motor before the bed started to move. I could feel pain in my torso, but I gritted my teeth together so that I wouldn't complain. Thankfully, the movement stopped.

"I'm going to hold the cup and place the straw

between your lips. Sip slowly." She sat on the side of my bed and leaned in closer. Her movements drew my gaze. I felt the room grow tense.

"Solle," he growled.

Yes, his voice was low and rumbly. I swear I felt my body begin to tremble.

"Shhh, she's fine." Solle glanced at the man, but then her gaze returned to mine. She had really long lashes, and I wondered whimsically what brand of mascara she used. "Take it easy now." Her voice had gone soft as she placed the straw between my open lips.

That felt...intimate? Too close? Definitely unsettling.

She gave a low laugh.

The water tasted so good. I think I smiled, but I kept the straw in my mouth.

"Not too much." She pulled away the cup.

I licked my lips, hoping to catch a few more drops. "Thank you," I whispered. "Better."

"Now that she's hydrated, maybe we can continue?" the man said, his lips tightening with impatience.

I focused on him.

The doctor started to slide off the bed.

"No, please." I tried to reach for her hand to stop her, but my arm was attached to the tubing giving me drugs and it hurt when I moved it. "Don't leave me."

"Conal, you're upsetting her," she admonished the giant. She made a calming sound as she turned back to me. "It's going to be okay, I promise."

I wanted to believe her. I gave her a long pleading look, and once I was sure she wasn't going, I turned back to the man who was called Conal.

"Ms. Morrissey, why are you here?" He slowly sank his bulk into the chair Solle had vacated earlier.

With him seated, some of my anxiety abated. "I don't know." I answered slowly because I really didn't.

One eyebrow arched. "You don't?" Clearly, he didn't believe me.

"I mean, I, uh, I don't know where I am." I glanced at the doctor. "I mean, this is a hospital, but I don't know which one." My words came more slowly as the impact of my words hit me. My eyes ping-ponged between the two as my heart started to pound. I really didn't know.

"Wolfsbane, Nebraska." By the intensity of his stare the name should mean something to me.

"Nebraska?" I tried to picture the map of the U.S. in my head and when I couldn't immediately locate Nebraska, I closed my eyes and sighed. "How?" I wheezed. I was on the verge of crying. Nothing made any sense.

"We are using the working theory that you arrived by plane. I was hoping you could fill in the details."

I tried to think, but the panic and effort it took not to sob seemed to be blocking my mind. "I, uh, I…" Nothing came to mind. Nothing. *Fuck*. I lost it. The first sob tore through my body, and it hurt. The second one hurt more, but I couldn't stop.

Instantly, Solle moved closer. "Don't cry. Please don't cry. You're hurting yourself." Her voice rose, but I couldn't stop.

I was terrified. I didn't know these people, and I definitely didn't know anything about Nebraska. How could this have happened?

"Theodora."

His sharp tone cut though the haze in my brain. I forced myself to stop crying. I immediately choked.

Solle gently stroked the back of my hand. "Theodora's a very pretty name," she crooned as she continued to try to keep eye contact with me. "You've had trauma to your head. You've been unconscious for a while. Sometimes, it takes a bit for things to start clicking again."

"Are you sure?" I tried to grab onto her hand. I needed that to be true.

"Be patient. It will come," she promised.

I closed my eyes because I was so damn tired and lost.

I WAS in that place where everything is fuzzy and warm, not fully awake. I didn't want to leave, but I was curious if that entire Nebraska scene had been a dream. I tried hard to listen, but I remembered that our apartment was pretty quiet. However, I didn't hear Allen's light snoring, nor did I sense him in bed beside me.

I slowly opened my eyes. Light was streaming in through the windows. I was lying on my side and I could see the blue, very light blue, sky.

"Are you with us, again?" The voice was deep, but not as deep as Conal's.

Slowly, I prepared to roll over to see who was talking to me. It still hurt to move, but I did manage to get onto my back with only a grimace. I took in air through my nose and let it out through my mouth several times. Once the pain was manageable, I turned my head to the side to see who was with me, watching me sleep, which was creepy.

I didn't know this woman. If I did, I would definitely remember her. She, too, was big. Her hair, which looked to be light, was closely cropped to her skull. She had alert green eyes. I doubted that she missed much. I guessed she had Native American blood, her high cheek-bones were wide and somewhat flat.

She sat still as if she was allowing me to study her. I realized I was being rude...or at least, I thought I was. "Hello, I'm Theodora."

"So I've heard." She crossed one leg over the other.

We stared at each for a few long beats. I grew uncomfortable. "And you are?" I tried to soften my question by widening my eyes.

"I am Glass."

What kind of name was Glass? More silence. I realized I hadn't been dreaming. I was in the same hospital room, so I must be in Nebraska. Nervous now, I licked my lips. This wasn't good. "Could you tell me what day it is?"

"Is that important to you?" she countered, tilting her head as she stared.

"Maybe," I blurted. "How long have I been here?" This time I didn't strain. I tried to figure out what I remembered. I'd gone into the office, there had been a stack of notes on my desk. No. That had happened a while ago.

"It's Thursday."

Thursday?

"You've been here for eleven days." She raised an eyebrow, silently questioning me.

"Eleven!" I opened and closed my mouth several times as I tried to formulate my next sentence. "So long?"

"You slept so long the doctors were becoming concerned."

That struck something in my memory. "Cold. I was

really cold," I said, not sure if I was looking for confirmation or approval for remembering.

She nodded. "The snowstorm had begun."

I was getting used to her speech pattern. I sort of liked that she kept her sentences short. A picture was starting to form in my mind. "It was nighttime, but the moon..." There was something important about the moon. I could feel the thought, but it wouldn't formulate. I strained for it to come into focus. "So much white," I recalled.

Glass's entire body shifted in the chair. For someone so big, she moved gracefully as she faced the door. One moment later, Solle walked in.

She nodded at Glass and walked around my bed. "Good, you're awake." She smiled warmly.

I liked her. I don't know why, because she was a stranger. I felt like she cared about me, and right now, I needed an ally. "Dr. Solle, right?"

Her smile increased in warmth, "Well technically, it's Dr. MacGregor, but Solle is fine." She studied my face. "You're better. I can tell by looking into your eyes."

I didn't say anything as she poked and prodded and asked a series of questions. "I guess it's a five? It still hurts," I responded when asked about my shoulder.

"Hungry? Thirsty?" she asked.

"Both," I blurted. I never turned down the offer of food.

Solle pulled a tablet from her white lab coat's pocket. "Well, before you say that, you might like to know that it'll be Jell-O and a clear soup."

"The answer is still yes." Suddenly, I was starving.

"I'll send in the order." Solle ran her finger over the

tablet's screen. "If you feel like it, I'd like to see you sitting up for at least thirty minutes."

"Okay." She was already reaching out to press the button on the side of the bed.

Glass cleared her throat. "Aren't you forgetting something?"

Solle ignored her frowning glance. "No, I'm not."

I tried to relax my body as the upper part of the bed moved. I was stiff from being inactive. *Eleven fucking days?*

Solle continued talking. "Seeing to her medical needs take priority over your questions. She isn't going anywhere, so let me do my work and then you all can do yours."

Glass made a "hmph" sound before she spoke. "Conal won't like the delay."

"You leave Conal to me," Solle assured her.

Glass smirked at the doctor. "This time I don't think a blow job will take care of things."

My eyes rounded at the crudeness of the suggestion, but the doctor didn't seem to take any offense.

Her eyebrows waggled. "You'd be surprised."

Then Solle giggled and I was surprised when the other woman joined in.

THE NEXT TIME I opened my eyes, it was dark outside my window, and the man, Conal, was in the chair at my bedside.

"What time is it?" I rasped.

He glanced at the watch on his wrist. "Almost midnight."

I slowly lifted my free hand and rubbed it over my face. I ran my fingers through my hair. Yuck, I needed a shower; I felt dirty. Then I cringed, *did I smell?* I needed to stay awake and ask a nurse or Solle if I could bathe.

"How do you feel?" His eyes were studying my face.

I thought before I answered. Something about this man made me cautious. "Much better, thank you," I added politely. I looked down at my bed in the very dim light. If we were going to continue, I wanted to sit up. I searched for the control.

He pointed. "It's on your other side."

"Oh, thank you." I frowned as I tried to figure out how I could press the button and not pull the I.V. in my arm.

"Would you allow me to help?" he asked, his tone formal.

Relieved by his offer, I prepared for the bed's movement. "Yes."

He pressed the button, and when I was sitting up, he settled back into the chair. "I would like to ask you a few questions."

I nodded.

"You are Theodora Morrissey. You live in California. You're thirty-four, never been married."

Somebody had been doing their research. "Yes." I waited for him to continue, but he simply watched me, which made me feel the need to share more. "I actually live in Thousand Oaks."

He gave an approving nod. "With an Allen Ledderly."

"Has he been looking for me? Did you tell him I was okay?" I drew my brows together. Wait, something wasn't right about Allen. I blinked several times quickly as I chased the impression in my mind.

"No, we've had no contact with Mr. Ledderly, nor has he filed a Missing Person Report with the police."

It took me a long moment to understand the importance of that fact. I opened my mouth and closed it. I pressed my head further into the pillow and looked up at the ceiling.

"You work with Mr. Ledderly," he said, his voice even and uninflected.

I closed my eyes and tried to picture Allen in my head. We were in...in an airport. Everything clicked. "We were in New York City," I whispered. I felt the anger, frustration, and disappointment sweep through my body—and then the terror. I exhaled in a whimper. "They-they left me to die." My gaze met the man's, and I read affirmation.

"Your memory has returned."

"Why?" I cried. "Why would he let that happen?" I needed an answer. I turned my head and stared straight ahead, trying to make sense of this all. Reeling from the betrayal.

The man handed me a cup from the table between us. "Perhaps I can help?"

My hand was shaking too much for me to hold the cup, so he did. I took three pulls on the straw as I tried to put the pieces of the puzzle together.

He returned the cup to the table.

"I'm sure you and your...the others...have done so much," I started a little rockily. I suddenly felt very alone.

"We are very interested in how you came to be left on our airstrip, but also why?"

I knew he wasn't going to leave until he got answers. Taking a few moments to order my thoughts, I tried to find a good starting point. "I work for Allen's company.

We acquire commercial real estate, rehab it or hold it, and then resell it."

"You are a carpenter?" He gave me a quizzical look.

"No." I let out a small chuckle. "I'm terrible with a hammer. I did things like payroll and made sure the permits were in order...a lot of administrative work."

He said nothing while waiting patiently for me to continue.

"We've had some success...luck, really." I bit down on my lip. This part was going to sound strange. At the time, I had thought it odd that a multi-millionaire and big player in the L.A. market would be interested in our little company. "Allen and I were on a business trip in New York City."

"Just the two of you?"

"No." I shook my head once. "The President of a big company flew us in."

He nodded once, while his gaze remained on me, studying me.

I shook my head, frowning at the memory. "I told Allen it didn't make any sense that Pedestrian would even notice us."

"Pedestrian?" The man leaned his elbows on his thick thighs.

"Pedestrian Holdings. They're a big deal in the L.A. area." I watched the man closely. He was familiar with Pedestrian. I couldn't explain how I knew; it was another one of my feelings. "They flew us to New York City to talk business. Like I said, it didn't make sense to me, but Allen was thrilled. He'd dreamed about playing with the big boys. So, he was all in, and I went to see what was really going on." We'd fought about the meeting several times.

"You were suspicious?"

"Pedestrian probably spends more on business lunches in a week than we pay out in a month." I tilted my head to the side while I searched for an explanation. "It felt odd," I answered weakly.

Again the man nodded. "And you trust your feelings?"

Something about the way he said those words made my body go on alert. I fumbled for a response. "Of course, don't you?" I tried to play it off.

FIVE

NOVUS

CONAL MACGREGOR

The woman's fumbled reply was very telling. I waited for her to continue.

She let out a deep breath. "The Pedestrian Group didn't include me in their meetings." She scowled, and her eyes narrowed. "But I didn't have to be in there to know they wanted the company."

"And you would be out of a job." I was trying to understand where this was going.

She gave me a half-smile. "I want to go back to school. I've been saving. So, if my job was gone, it wouldn't have mattered. I knew I could go back to waiting tables or whatever." She frowned. "The company is Allen's. He used a loan from his father to get started. What I didn't like was the way that trip went down..." She looked away from me.

I knew she wasn't telling me everything. Theodora was giving me just the basic facts, only expanding when I pressed. I leaned forward, my gaze drilling into her eyes.

"Allen did something unforgiveable." She shifted in the bed and crossed her arm over her chest protectively. "I mean, how stupid can you be? A strip club. It's a cliché." She let out a loud puff of air. "When he didn't come back after the business dinner, I figured the men went out for more *entertainment*." She spat the word. "But then, I started getting alerts about the business accounts... That was something totally different. I mean, he was messing with other people's lives." Her deep blue eyes flashed with anger. "I wasn't going to ignore that."

"So, your boyfriend went to a club and spent some money?" I was starting to get the picture.

"He's not really my boyfriend anymore," she muttered. She looked at the ceiling, and then closed her eyes and let out a loud sigh. "Would it be all right if I called you Conal?" Her voice was flat. She sounded defeated.

She was still stalling, but I was willing to work with her. "Only if I can call you Theodora."

"Allen called me Teddi." She made an angry sound deep in her throat. "I hated that name." She looked back at me and gave a slight shrug with her good shoulder. "I didn't love him. He might have cared about me at one point, but it was really all about the business."

"Theodora, men don't keep women around because of business," I corrected her. She was attractive; "lush" was how my mate had described her.

She shook her head. "The business was very important to him. I helped him pick properties. I'd look at the financials, maybe go see a property and, sometimes, I'd get a hunch that it might be good," she said with a sheepish shrug. "It paid off a little."

Bingo. If her ability was that strong, then we would be truly blessed by her gift. "I'd guess your intuition paid off more than just a little." I gave her a speculative look.

"We did okay. We grew the company to twenty-two employees." Her gaze fell away. "Fuck," she breathed.

"What happened?" I made my voice gentle.

"Allen, he took the money. He spent it. *All of it.* In one weekend." Her voice increased in volume. "The overdraft protection kicked in, so he cleared out both accounts. Gone."

"You're telling me that your…" I quickly corrected his title. "The business owner cleaned out his accounts?"

"Pinch me." She held up her forearm. "Because this is so insane, it has to be a dream." She dropped her arm. "But I know it's not." She frowned as she looked around the hospital room. "I pulled up the accounts and I saw a list of the transactions. When Allen finally showed up to our room, I gave him hell."

I was starting to get the picture. Pedestrian Holdings was a successful business, but it was an even more successful front for a drug cartel. If their leader wanted something this small business held, Theodora was lucky they hadn't killed the owner. "Allen…he didn't like you confronting him." I knew the answer by the way she was touching the cheek that had been fractured, with a cut so deep it would leave a small scar.

She frowned. "He reminded me that it was his business. Which I knew, bu-but payroll was due on Wednesday. How were we going to pay our people?"

Interesting, she didn't seem to mind that her man stayed out all night at a strip club, but she was upset the employees wouldn't be paid.

"I was already packed. I couldn't stay in the hotel room with him a minute longer. I went to the lobby to wait." She rolled her eyes dramatically. "I didn't think that far ahead. *We* had to fly back on their private jet, so while we waited for the plane to be readied, or whatever they do, hanging out in this special lounge, another alert came through on my phone. I showed it to Allen." She paused to lick her lips. "I guess I was hoping it would occur to him what he'd done. But instead he got shitty with me, and I gave it right back. I was tired. I mean, I'd been up most of the night."

"You were worried about your man and what he'd been doing," I reminded her.

"He hasn't been my man for a long time, okay?" Her dark blue eyes turned even darker. "Don't paint me to be some simpering girlfriend, crying because her boyfriend might be out cheating with a stripper," she said angrily. "He could have fucked as many strippers as he wanted, six ways to Sunday. I was upset about the business."

"I apologize and stand corrected." She was sharing and I didn't want that to stop. Plus, I liked her fire. I was gaining some insight into her personality.

She sighed again. "No, I…I think I'm overwhelmed by all of this. I didn't mean to snap."

"You've been through a great deal." I found that I was starting to like her a little.

She sighed. "I kept at him, and the other men were watching us. I guess…I, uh, I embarrassed him, and he…he…" Her voice broke.

"He struck you." I didn't like it. And I really didn't like that she seemed to shoulder some of the blame for his actions.

"I didn't know what to do," she murmured, sounding as though she was still in shock.

"That was the first time he hit you?"

"Do I look like the type who would stand for that shit?" She glared at me for a second, and then she laughed.

I didn't understand what she thought was so funny.

"God, you just met me. You don't know what I'm like." She rolled her eyes again. "I think I'm rambling."

When she licked her lips, I motioned at the cup of water.

She shook her head once. "So, on the flight back, I didn't want to talk to him. I was trying to figure out what I needed to do, or more to the fact, what I *could* do." She bit her bottom lip again. "Allen sat down beside me and started to give me excuses that were so lame. I didn't want to hear them. So, we fought some more."

I could smell her frustration and anger. She was telling the truth.

"I guess, Mr. Peters, he owns Pedestrian, had had enough, because he told me to 'shut the fuck up'." She shook her head. "I didn't take that very well. I mean, this guy didn't have clean hands. They've been involved in some shifty land grabs." She shot me an exasperated look, perhaps to see if I knew what she meant. "He grabbed my head and I think he punched me."

My gut tightened. Romero Peters would have no problems striking a woman. He'd done worse many times. "Go on," I said, fighting to keep my voice calm.

"Now, this part is kind of hazy. I was out for a bit. The next thing I remember was being dragged by my feet." She narrowed her eyes as she thought. "I think Allen was yelling for the guy to stop." She rubbed her

47

nose a few times. "I tried to grab onto something, anything, but the guy, he was strong. I fought him. I…I knew something bad was going to happen."

"They left you on the air strip."

"I don't remember that part," she admitted slowly, "just that I was freezing when I woke up." She looked up at the ceiling and let out a long breath. "And I think I had a hallucination."

I fought the urge to press. I was very interested in this part. "You had a concussion."

"Conal, I heard a woman's voice," she told me with a confused look on her face. "I mean, it was like the voice surrounded me and was in my head. It wasn't natural."

Holy Fuck. I kept my expression neutral. "Do you remember what the voice said?"

Her eyes turned an even darker blue. "At first, she urged me to find shelter. She spoke very, uh, formally. She called me 'child'." She shrugged slowly. "Then there was the wolves thing…"

I couldn't stop myself. I leaned closer. "What wolves thing?"

"Yeah, I thought it was weird, too." Theodora narrowed her eyes as she seemed to strain to recall. "She said, 'The wolves are on their way.' That freaked the shit out of me. I wouldn't stand a chance against one, let alone a pack of wolves."

Was The Lady watching over this woman? She did carry her Mark. This was amazing.

"So, I was found, right? I just remember flashes… like a metal barrel, a desk and…and I know this didn't happen, a huge black wolf at the end of my bed." She shook her head once. "That had to be wrong." She looked at me for confirmation.

48

I couldn't help myself. I looked directly at the camera that was streaming the live feed from the hospital room. There was only one black wolf in the States, and it was our Packleader. Theodora had never seen him in his wolf-form. Hell, she couldn't know that he was referred to as The Black or Black. "You did manage to find the storage building. You climbed up on a metal barrel and broke a window. We found you unconscious, under a desk, but there was no black wolf there." I didn't lie. I simply chose my words carefully.

"I climbed up on a barrel?" She sounded shocked. "How did I manage that?" She looked down at her legs. "I don't really know what to say."

"Your will to live is very strong. There are hundreds of stories of people doing extraordinary things in order to survive." The scent of her confusion and sadness were filling the room.

"I guess," she said softly. She relaxed back into her pillow and closed her eyes. "I probably should call somebody and figure out how I'm going to get back to Cali."

"Are you going back to that man?" My protective instincts kicked in before I realized she wouldn't be going anywhere.

"No. Are you nuts?" She opened her eyes and gave me a one-sided grin that faded. "I guess I need to see what happened to the business. If anybody needs anything?"

"And your things…" I played along.

"I don't have a lot. I've never needed much. Just my books and my laptop, and my …" She was out.

I watched her sleep until my phone vibrated.

"Laird," I answered.

"Meeting in fifteen." His words were clipped.

"Can we make it twenty? I want to check in with Solle."

"Twenty."

"What do you think?"

"She is…unique."

Yes, Theodora was, and we were just getting to know her.

SIX

NOVUS

RAIDER BLACK

"So, we are agreed, five days." I was tired of waiting. Ms. Morrissey's injuries and recovery were becoming tiresome, and I dealt quickly and efficiently with inconveniences.

"Conal, you've spent the most time with her when she was awake. What do you think?" Tex asked without looking up from his tablet.

My Second leaned back in his chair. They were custom-made to accommodate our size, and they all tilted back. "My nose tells me she's been truthful so far, but, to what degree, I don't know."

"She's highly educated." Glass's expression was neutral.

"In an obscure subject," Onyx scoffed.

Conal arched a brow. "Yet, I find it interesting that she studies folklore. Researching and amassing local stories about the odd, or what some might call, the supernatural." One side of my Second's mouth hitched upward. "Perhaps she studied us?"

"Tex, have you managed to locate any of her submitted work?" I waited until the redhead made eye contact.

"Only a few papers from her advanced studies. I sent copies to Onyx, but I can send them to you as well."

He sat very still. I didn't like that he still anticipated physical violence from his Packleader. "A brief summary will do."

Onyx steepled his long fingers. "She has researched ghostly sightings, especially those of family members returning from the dead to foretell or warn those of upcoming events." His tone clearly broadcasted that he didn't think much of the subject.

Glass rolled her gold pen between her fingers. "Interesting that she has studied foretelling. Do you think she somehow recognized her gift?"

Tex pointed at the wall. "Her explanation of her job was interesting. I think her hunches helped her man choose properties successfully." Tex had marked select passages from Conal's interview on the large projection screen that hung from the ceiling in the Novus conference room.

My wolf stirred. I cast my senses to check but found nothing to cause him to wake.

Conal abruptly leaned forward in his chair. "I would caution against mentioning the man, Allen Ledderly. Her emotions spiked when speaking of him, especially when I used terms linking them romantically."

"And still no Missing Person Report?" I glanced at Tex.

He shook his head as he ran his index finger over the screen of his tablet. "None."

"Send in Lore," I ordered.

"What about Peters?" Conal growled.

"I expect that Mr. Ledderly, the non-boyfriend, will be able to clarify who dictated the usage of our airstrip," I answered, keeping my tone even. "The transgression will be addressed with Peters at my discretion." The drug kingpin thought much of himself, but he had no idea what this act of trespassing on Novus land would mean to his business and his life.

"Why antagonize?" Onyx asked in his icy-calm way.

"Good question," Glass uttered with a frown. "We have had no issues with their runs."

"Could they be pushing to see if we respond?" Tex mused. "What are we willing to overlook, or what won't we protect?"

"That kind of push could result in something permanent," Conal stated with finality.

"My guess is that Romero Peters was still in a celebratory mood. The weekend garnered him his prize, for what end, I don't care. Perhaps, he thought at some point Ms. Morrissey would be helpful, but her outbursts or attitude became an annoyance." I tried to put myself on that plane with the group. "In his position, I would have killed her, but I doubt the humans would have wished to travel with a body for the rest of their journey."

"By dumping her, a concerned human could convince himself the woman would find help. No one on Peters' payroll would ask, and the...er, Mr. Ledderly could be monitored and controlled," Glass reasoned.

"Is there a message directed at us, or was it simply a question of right time, right place?" Tex pondered.

"If Ledderly doesn't know the answer to why she was

left here, then we'll work through everybody on the plane."

"The Lore will find out," Conal said with a chuckle. "I hope he takes photos."

My spy could be a ghost or, if he chose, he could be obvious. I had no doubt he would get the answers and send a message. Novus was not to be trifled with.

With that topic closed, I turned to my Second. "So, Solle will be fine with a guest moving in?"

"She has agreed," Conal answered slowly. "I think she's looking forward to helping the woman transition to our ways."

I considered that. "She was the last human changed in Novus."

"She's already making a list for instruction," Conal said with a smile.

"Her education is my responsibility." Onyx bit out each word.

Glass snorted. "You are going to educate the human about social interaction?"

My Historian gave the table a haughty look as he adjusted the snow-white cuffs of his pristine shirt. I caught the briefest glint of the golden sheen of his cufflink.

"She has much to learn. Dealing with our society is not a priority."

"I disagree," Glass stated calmly.

I had made a rule that there would be no physicality in my boardroom. With Lycans, many disputes were settled by claws and jaws. In here, we used words instead of strength. I did it for efficiency's sake, and it also kept my workload down. Replacing furniture was time consuming and costly.

Challenges happened within the Novus Pack, but compared to other packs, we had very few. I was a strong leader, and so was Conal in his enforcer role. I trusted my "brother" implicitly. Most challenges occurred amongst the newly changed or newly pledged. Too much aggression and bravado were the biggest contributing factors. The older wolves got that way by choosing their battles carefully. As Packleader, I helped by making sure there were ample opportunities to make money and to channel aggression. During my time with the Council, I'd studied pack histories and had learned that those that struggled financially also did so internally. Money bought security. Stability was the foundation of comfort. So, I made sure our holdings were diversified, and that we made money.

I tapped the table. "She will interact with the Pack, eventually. I trust that you and Solle will help her greatly." I glanced at Conal. "And you," I said, looking at Onyx, "will see to her schooling. Everyone will contribute eventually."

"Yes, Laird," they answered.

I stood, signaling the meeting had ended.

Conal fell into step beside me as I exited. As soon as we left the boardroom, today's guard, Issa, fell in two steps behind us.

Conal glanced back at the deceptively diminutive female. "What are you wearing?"

I, too, looked at the guard.

She glanced down at her shirt. "What? I like pink."

"Issa, it's a kitten." Conal sounded dismayed.

"Just because I like pretty things doesn't mean that I'm not skilled, Second." She was giving him a cheeky look. Like many of my female warriors, Issa was an expert with weapons. When I'd been in the process of establishing my pack, Glass had applied for a guard position. She'd soon become the trainer of the guards. She didn't exclude females from training. Her reasoning was sound: we were a new pack and needed every opportunity to stay strong. As many had learned, size and bulk did not always mean victory. I personally believed the smaller the wolf, the meaner.

Conal shook his head as we traveled the short corridor to my office.

The Novus office building was four floors, in a solid block. It housed the Pack's business concerns. Each Board member had an office and staff. As well, there was a gymnasium used for training, locker rooms, and a cafeteria. To the human world, we were a very successful security business based out of Nebraska for geographical reasons.

Conal followed me inside. Issa closed the door and remained outside to guard it.

I pointed at the well-stocked bar on the far wall and raised an eyebrow in question.

"Beer." He took a seat in the huge wing-chair that he favored.

I poured myself two fingers of whisky for myself and carried the beer bottle to my friend. "So, what do you really think about her?"

"Two things stand out." He took a long pull. "The first being that, although she mentioned calling someone, she hasn't brought up the subject again, nor has she asked to use a phone."

"She hasn't been awake for long stretches," I pointed out.

"I don't think she has anybody. We know there are

cousins in Ohio and when she spoke of Adderley, I sensed no feelings of affection. If there are friends, they're not close, because they haven't noticed her disappearance."

"And the non-boyfriend?"

"She spoke of her concern regarding the employees. She was infuriated there would be a problem with the payroll." He took another pull on his beer. "Her emotions intensified over her worry for them."

Our eyes met. "How do you interpret the two?"

He didn't respond right away. Conal always considered his answers. "I think she recognizes that she has a talent. She might not have understood it, or maybe she was made to feel odd because of it. So, she doesn't seek out friendships. She chooses instead to study occurrences that might be tied to her skill. There are no records of any marriages or offspring. She's attractive, yet seems to be very alone." He paused and frowned. "However, she cares deeply for her co-workers and is outraged on their behalf."

"You like her." Conal was a protector to the core.

"So far," he answered cautiously.

"And your mate?"

"Solle has talked to her more. She claims that Theodora smiles easily and worries about causing extra work for the staff. She has deemed her 'a good person'."

"They've spoken only a few times when the woman has been awake." I frowned.

Conal shrugged. "You know Solle. She connects with her patients. I'd say that, at this point, she has the best understanding of the woman."

I nodded. "I look forward to her updates."

We sat in silence for a few minutes.

"Her eyes... They are startling," he said in an off-hand way.

"On the screen, they appear very dark."

"Like the sky at dusk." Conal gave me an appraising look. "I wonder what you will sense when you speak with her."

"I'll have to remember that I'm dealing with a woman of this time. She'll get prickly about my actions," I grumbled. The few times I'd recently mixed socially in the human world, I'd said little. It was hard to keep track of ever-changing social etiquette.

"She doesn't like being called Teddi and I imagine we'll have to institute certain rules that she might disagree with."

"She has no say," I stated plainly.

"I might suggest that we not start with that statement." He held up a halting hand when he saw that I was going to object. "Solle says that people, but she really means herself, would rather be asked with a short explanation instead of ordered."

I made a low growl, grumbling over the need to be nice.

"We'll know more once she's installed in our home. I'll be able to closely observe her."

"Her intelligence is concerning. I've found that smart women can be tiresome." I frowned and stretched out my legs. I needed to run more.

"Solle is smart," Conal drawled.

"And she has no problem telling me when she believes me to be wrong." I paused and then smiled.

"You don't like being wrong." Now, he was smiling, too.

"I'm often wrong. I just don't like the fact being brought to my attention."

Conal made a toasting action with his bottle. "The mentioning of the black wolf that she believes is a hallucination...what do you make of that?"

I had spent hours pondering that statement. "I don't know." I sipped my drink. "If she sensed my wolf while unconscious then she has a very strong gift."

"If that is true, then I hope she can learn to handle it."

"I do too." I didn't relish having to kill a true gift from our Goddess.

SEVEN

NOVUS

THEODORA MORRISSEY

"Another blanket?"

Solle was fussing over me. "I'm fine, really." My hostess seemed to always be worrying about my comfort. "I told you that you don't have to fawn over me." I wasn't used to another caring for me. Even when I'd had a nasty bout with the flu last year, Allen had been scarce. He'd moved to the couch and had basically left me to suffer alone.

She took a seat at the other end of the huge sectional. "I know how tiring it is at first, until your strength returns." She rolled her finger in her long brown hair and made a corkscrew curl.

"You and Conal have been so kind. I feel like I should be doing something to help you." I'd been at their house for three days. When I'd been ready to be discharged from the hospital, Conal had told me that I would recuperate in their home. I tried to argue, but he wouldn't have it. Secretly, it was nice not to have to worry for a little bit longer. I had no idea what I would find when I returned to L.A.

Allen was too lazy to box up my stuff. He'd probably continued on or maybe he'd moved that admin from down the hall into his condo. She'd been giving him not so discreet looks for a couple of weeks. I didn't really care. Maybe there was something wrong with me? I enjoyed the companionship of living with him, but when it came to romance or sex, I was...blah.

I liked being held, and kissing was okay, but when it came time for his mouth or cock to be inside me...nothing. If I knew Solle better, I'd ask her about it. According to magazine articles, I was supposed to be in my sexual prime, but I wasn't. For a long time, I'd been sort of fumbling along, as if I was waiting for something...

"You aren't thinking happy thoughts," she said.

"I was wondering what was happening in L.A." I'd filled her in on the fight, and my feelings, or rather *non*-feelings, for Allen. "It's not going to be pretty." I frowned. I should make that call to Allen, but I wasn't ready...yet.

"Then don't go back."

My eyes widened. "What? I...I couldn't do that."

"Why not?" She turned her body to face me and curled her legs so that they were crossed in front of her. "I mean, the business is done. Your rela...I mean, your whatever," she corrected herself with an eye roll, "is over. So, until you figure out your next step, why not stay here?"

"Oh, I couldn't," I repeated quickly. "What would I do here?" I'd only seen a glimpse of the town on the ride from the hospital.

"You could stay with us. We have plenty of room." She nodded a few times encouragingly.

She and Conal lived in a five-bedroom two-story with a finished basement. I hadn't made it down there yet. Next week, I was getting a walking cast so I would be more mobile. My shoulder and ribs were healing, but using crutches was painful. So, Conal carried me up and down the stairs when he was home. I was basically sedentary. "You wouldn't want that. A stranger around, underfoot all of the time."

She waved a hand. "You're no trouble."

"I'm a ton of trouble. Are you kidding? I have to be carried around. I'm another mouth to feed, and I'm like a lump, either on the sofa or in my room." A part of me was warming to the idea. It was nice to be wanted.

L.A. had never been home to me. I'd moved there because I'd wanted to establish state residency so that I could go back to school. I'd taken a temp job and met Allen. Starting the business had been fun, working with him to make his dream a reality, but to me, it was just a job. Not my dream.

"Then don't be a stranger," she continued. "I'd like for us to be friends. I thought we were...sort of."

Now, I'd hurt her feelings. "That's not what I meant. I, I..." The words tumbled out. "I'd like to be friends, too. But doesn't it feel weird having me here? I could be a killer and murder you while you're sleeping."

She giggled. "Believe me, that's the last thing that I'm worried about."

Well, she was right. Conal exuded the "don't fuck with me" attitude, so I bet he could take care of their safety. I wasn't really clear on what he did, but it had to be some kind of law enforcement. He was the one to ask questions. Although he hadn't done it formally, like at a desk, he had interviewed me. To this day, he hadn't let up with the questions. "I'd need a job," I added weakly.

"Don't worry about that. You need to decide what you *want* to do and somebody will hire you," she said with brazen authority.

I guess doctors didn't realize that unemployment was rampant. After all, college graduates were working in food service because they couldn't find jobs in their chosen careers. When I had been studying for my Master's at Washington State, another student had dropped out to go to nursing school. She'd said that she "needed to eat."

"But you'll have to heal first," my doctor used that steely tone I'd come to recognize as the part of doctor's orders that nobody messed with.

I blew out a breath. "I don't know. My degree isn't very marketable." I wasn't embarrassed that I loved to study and learn. Usually, I was shy around strangers, but when I went out to interview subjects for my research, I had a blast.

"But you told me that you loved hearing the stories." Solle tilted her chin like she was questioning whether I'd told her the truth.

"I do, *really*." I emphasized the last word. "It's the only time I feel like I'm doing what I'm supposed to do."

"What does that mean?"

I thought for a moment that my eyes were playing tricks on me. It seemed like she'd gone still as though she was analyzing everything around her. Or I could have imagined it. Maybe I should mention this to my doctor-friend? Was my concussion causing me to imagine that her stillness was a little strange?

I decided to wait and see if it happened again. I'd already told them about The Voice, so that was enough crazy from their houseguest. "Oh, it's dumb." I dropped my gaze and stared at the tip of my foot that was propped up on a pillow on the coffee table. I wasn't used to anyone taking so much interest in what I had to say. I usually took the role of listener rather than talker.

"So far, dumb is not a word I would use to describe you," she said with a rueful grin.

"Going after my ego now?" I smiled at her. Yeah, I'd like to be friends. "Okay, but it might not make any sense." I paused to try to find the words. I didn't want to make this a big deal. "Ever since I can remember, I've had this feeling I was going to do something important." I felt my cheeks heat with embarrassment. I looked away. "I know it's really silly. I'm not talented or that smart." I shifted and pulled the blanket higher on my shoulders.

Solle's voice was full of warmth. "I truly believe our feelings are never dumb. They're important to who you are, to who you want to be."

I swallowed hard as I considered her insightful words. "When I was a kid, I tried to sing. I'm okay but not awesome. I do okay in school, but I have to study. It's not that I mind having to work hard, but the feeling... I don't know." I shut my eyes as I tried to summon that particular inner knowledge. "It's like, it should feel so natural, not something that I have to work so hard to master." I glanced at her sideways to see how she was responding.

She got to her feet, which seemed a little bit abrupt. "Maybe it's about timing." She gathered my half-filled glass on the table. "I'll fill this up, and I need to call Conal." She headed to the kitchen.

Grandma was right. I shouldn't talk about my special feelings. Voicing them made things awkward.

I FELL ASLEEP AFTER LUNCH. Lately, I'd be chugging along, and then suddenly, I was exhausted. I was working up the enthusiasm to ask for assistance to trudge slowly to the bathroom down the hall, when a loud knocking sounded at the front door.

Solle hustled down the steps. "Stay there," she said as she moved to the door.

Like I was going anywhere? I ran a hand through my hair that was now in a messy braid and wiped around my mouth. I'd been horrified to learn that when I was heavily drugged, I drooled.

"Now?"

In the distance, I heard Solle's raised voice. A low mumbling followed that I couldn't make out. I wondered whether I could make it to the bathroom without being seen by the new arrival. I didn't have any clothes. It wasn't a big deal right now, because I couldn't really go anywhere. Solle had purchased several nightgowns for me and underpants. I'd borrowed one of Conal's zip-front hoodies to wear over the silky gown. Add the one tube sock that I wore on my good foot. I was quite a vision.

I was in the process of lifting my casted leg to the floor when I saw movement in my peripheral vision. Someone was entering the room. I looked up to see Glass—and a man I felt like I should recognize.

"Hello, Theodora Morrissey." Glass sort of smiled. Or at least I thought she was trying.

"Hey Glass, I told you that you don't have to use my last name." The tic was kind of endearing.

"Thank you." Solemnly, she dropped her chin.

"Ma'am," the red-haired man said in greeting and he also did the chin thing.

The mood of the room was serious. Solle looked unhappy, and my inner sense cautioned me to move slowly and to consider my words. The pregnant pause made me jumpy. "I was going to …" I looked down the hall. "You know, take care of things." I looked pleadingly at Solle, hoping she'd get my drift.

"Theodora you are to come with us," Glass announced.

"Go where?"

"With us. That is the order," Glass told me in that weird emotionless voice.

"Right now?" I looked down at my clothes and back at the hall.

"Raider Black sent us," the man said with authority.

That meant nothing to me. "Okay…? I don't know who you are, or this Random Black, but I can't go anywhere until I use the bathroom." I didn't like being crass, but my need was starting to become more of a demand. I wanted to cross my legs to prove my point.

Solle stepped around the coffee table and sat down on it facing me. "You'll have to go with them." Her tone was resigned.

"I don't understand," I whispered, fighting the urge to glance at the two interlopers.

"You just do." She widened her eyes and tipped her head a tiny bit, urging me to do as they said.

I knew that I wasn't supposed to argue. I nodded to show that I got the message. Again, I looked at Glass and the man. "I'll come. It's just that I have to use the bathroom. It's become a priority." I made my eyes big to emphasize the point.

Suddenly, Glass was beside me, picking me up. I didn't even see her move, but I was too busy grabbing at the blanket and praying that I could keep a tight hold of my bladder in all of this excitement.

"Her room?" We were already on the steps when Glass asked the question.

Solle was right behind us. "Turn left at the top of the stairs."

Glass acted like I didn't weigh a thing as she easily climbed the stairs. A part of my brain was fascinated by how she maneuvered my body. She carried me right into my bathroom. When she gently set me on my feet, I didn't even stop to worry about peeing in front of these women, my need was so great.

When I was done, I looked at that the women expectantly. "I think I can take it from here." I wanted them to go.

They didn't move.

We did the stare-down thing for about thirty seconds. And still, they didn't get the hint.

So, I slowly and very ungracefully got to my feet. I hobbled to the sink and started the warm water. "I'm going to freshen up. Solle, do you think you can find something for me to put on. Maybe some sweatpants?"

"You are covered," Glass told me.

"I'm wearing a nightgown," I countered.

"It does not matter," she proclaimed.

I checked the water temperature. It was warm enough. I washed my face and brushed my teeth. I quickly unbraided my hair and looked around for my brush.

Solle came up beside me. "I'll help." She gently brushed my hair while trying to communicate with her eyes in the mirror.

I wasn't getting it. I ended up giggling.

"Why do you laugh?" Glass looked from Solle to me. "Meeting the Laird is an honor. It is serious." She sounded haughty.

I don't know if I was reacting to her words or her confusion, but I laughed harder. "He's Scottish? Does he wear a kilt?"

"What is taking so long?" The man's voice boomed from the first floor.

"Tex sounds ready to go," Solle said haltingly.

"Is this really okay?" I asked Solle as I fingered the silky skirt of the lavender gown. I took a good look in the mirror. The damage to my cheek still looked ugly. Solle had promised that, eventually, the scar would be hard to detect. My skin was pale and I really could use some lipstick. Even though the hoodie was huge on me, I needed the support of a bra. This was a disaster. I didn't even have a bra. I felt my eyes start to burn. I was a mess.

Suddenly, Solle gripped the hand holding my gown and linked her fingers with mine. "Don't be stupid. Think before you speak," she said, her words and expression taut with intensity.

"Solle." Glass's voice sounded low, almost like a real growl.

"I'll be okay," I told my friend. Her nervousness was upsetting me. I didn't want her to worry about me.

I watched her let out a deep breath. "Of course, you

will be." That seemed to bolster her, because she went up onto her tip-toes and kissed my uninjured cheek.

I tried to smile reassuringly, and then I glanced at Glass. "I'm ready." I was pretending. If I wasn't going into some meeting wearing a nightgown like an invalid, I'd wear it like a damn five-thousand-dollar Chanel suit.

Glass again carried me down the stairs and out the front door to a SUV. Solle followed with a blanket to wrap around my legs.

She stood on the side of her driveway and watched us back out and pull away.

I felt like it might be the last time she'd see me.

The man, Tex, drove, and Glass sat in the backseat next to me. I thought it was a little bit of overkill. I mean, it wasn't like I could run away, but I kept that thought to myself. These people didn't seem to have much of a sense of humor.

After five minutes, the silence was getting to me. I was tired of looking at the countryside. "So, where are we going?" I tried to sound conversational, not nervous.

"To see the Laird," Tex answered. "We told you that." The last part was said like I was slow.

I shifted a little to my right so that I could see around the driver's seat. Something about the way he'd said that was very familiar. "You were there," I realized.

Glass shot me a questioning look, "Where?"

Memories came flooding back. "In that building. You...you found me."

"I did." He looked back at me in the rearview mirror.

When he didn't continue, I felt like I needed to say something. "Thank you," I offered weakly.

That was the extent of the conversation.

The SUV pulled into a drive that led to a modern office building with a sign that read, "Novus". It was out of place amongst the snow-covered fields but apparently, this Laird dude was very important to this business. Tex pulled up to the main entrance.

"Wait here." Glass opened her door.

"You can't carry me in there. I'll walk." Well, hobble, anyway. I tried to put as little weight as possible on the ball of my right foot and step with my left. With each step, more pain would shoot up my injured leg. Movement was slow, uncoordinated, and loud.

"You are not heavy," the woman told me.

"I can't be carried into a meeting. I mean, that's...." I didn't know what it was. This entire situation was insane. I was wearing a nightgown and wrapped in a blanket. I looked like I'd just rolled out of bed. "It's not very professional."

"I don't care how you do it. Just get into the building," Tex ordered.

Christ, the lobby was huge. The bank of elevators was still so far away I regretted my decision to do this on my own. I was breathing heavily and gritting my teeth. Pride was a terrible thing.

Tex huffed a breath. "Stop."

I looked around for something lean on, but strangely, this lobby didn't have any chairs. I guessed Novus didn't want people to hang around.

Glass wrapped her huge hand around my bicep. "You tire easily."

I wanted to say, "Ya think?" But the woman wasn't being snarky. I doubted that she'd appreciate my sarcasm. "I didn't realize it would be so far."

"You do not know your weakness, but Solle says it is

71

temporary. It is good that you challenge yourself. That is respected."

Wow, that was the longest I'd ever heard Glass speak.

I nodded although I didn't understand. I was watching Tex approach the woman who was seated at what must be the reception desk. She was a beautiful African-American, who was studying the man's approach with a cat-like smile. I could tell that she liked what she saw.

The man pointed at her seat. "Give me your chair."

The woman stood immediately.

Tex grabbed the back of the chair and lifted it, resting the arm on his shoulder, and then he grunted. "Thank you."

"Anything, Tex."

I had a feeling she was talking about more than office equipment, but the redhead seemed oblivious.

He moved back to us, and when he was about three steps away, he placed the chair on the tile. "Sit."

I did as he asked, although technically he hadn't, but I wasn't going to argue. It felt too good to take the weight off of my ankle.

He pumped the chair higher so that my feet didn't touch the ground. Then he pushed me toward the elevator bank.

Once in the elevator, I asked, "So, is this guy like the President or the Mayor?"

Glass nodded. "Yes."

Note to self—no more yes or no questions. They got me nowhere. I'd have to wing this meeting, sort of like I'd been doing with every encounter since I'd woken up in the hospital.

The elevator doors opened, and we exited into what

clearly was the executive floor. The carpet was thick, and the walls were painted a rich slate blue. The hallway I rolled down was quiet with many office doors open, but I saw no one. At the end of the hallway was a man sitting behind a glass-topped desk.

As we neared, he stood and walked around his workstation. "Well, hello," he drawled dramatically. He was tall and slender with a dancer's build. All muscle under the expensive suit. His head was smooth, and he was wearing eye-liner and if I wasn't mistaken, a bit of lip gloss that flattered his café au lait coloring.

I admired his artistry. His lashes were incredibly thick and long, and the arch of his eyebrows was a work of art. "Hi," I smiled. I liked his outrageousness amid the business-conservative environment. "I'm underdressed." I glanced down because the man was staring.

He frowned, but it was in jest, "Interesting choice of transport, but since you're in a cast, I won't hold it against you." He gave me a huge, bright white smile.

"I'm Theodora." I was stalling. I wasn't sure I wanted to meet the boss.

"You'll be fine, Theodora." He read my dread easily. "I'm *Bah*-zil." He stressed the first syllable so I would know.

Glass made a scoffing sound. "It was Basil until he went to Miami."

The man turned up his nose. "I can be whomever I want."

I suddenly wondered if Basil would look different the next time I saw him. He seemed like the type that would have no problem dressing to suit his mood. "It's nice to make your acquaintance, Basil." I pronounced his name his way.

Tex interrupted, "You done?" He moved from behind me and knocked on the door to Basil's right.

I felt my heart rate increase and I tried to wipe my suddenly sweaty palms on the front of Conal's hoodie. I needed to focus and God only knew what lay beyond those doors. Clowns, dancing hippos, a firing squad?

Glass moved behind me and I knew I needed to walk into that room. I couldn't appear weak. Granted, I was, but I needed to show that while I might be in a cast, I wasn't fragile.

"Hang on." I started to stand.

Basil appeared at my side. He took my clammy hand, wrapping it around his elbow as if he was escorting me to my seat at a wedding. "Allow me, Theodora." His kindness helped settle my nerves. We entered the conference room—very nicely appointed, I noticed immediately. I recognized that the furniture was expensive and that the rug sitting atop the carpet was antique. My escort guided me to a large conference table. "Gentlemen, Theodora Morrissey." He sounded like he was announcing a member of a royal family, not me.

I spotted Conal sitting next to an open chair at the end of the table, and seated on the opposite side was a black man. I mean, his skin was that dark. His suit rivaled Basil's in tailoring, and his skull glistened in the overhead light.

Another man stood looking out the windows with his back to us. His long dark hair hung unbound midway down his back. He, like Conal, was dressed casually in faded jeans and a dark thermal shirt. Nobody needed to tell me. I knew that this was "the Laird". Power emanated from him.

I hadn't realized that we'd stopped, because I was so involved watching the man who still hadn't turned around or even acted like he knew we were there. However, I sensed he was aware of my every move.

"Sit." Conal's voice was near my ear.

I jumped at his closeness. One thing I'd learned while staying in the hospital, these people had no respect for personal boundaries. They came in close to talk, to carry, or to simply sit. It was weird, but I didn't know how to say something about it. "Oh, yeah," I looked up at him and smiled, taking the chair he offered.

I hadn't realized Basil had unwound my hand from his arm and must have left because I heard the door close softly.

"You walked?" Conal's voice seemed very loud in the silent room.

I glanced at him and shrugged my good shoulder.

The man in the suit leaned onto his forearms that were resting on the table's top. "You do not follow your doctor's orders?"

How to answer?

Glass came to my rescue, well in her own way. "She thought being carried was unprofessional." She shot her version of a smile in my direction.

The suit was eyeing my outfit. His eyebrows rose. Clearly, he was horrified.

My head swiveled at the sound of Conal's chuckle. "Because that matters here?"

I had no clue what that meant, so I scooted back into the surprisingly comfortable chair and dropped my stare down to the table. I hoped that I'd pasted a calm expression on my face. I'd read somewhere that staring off into the middle distance at nothing was correct in a corporate meeting. It was considered polite, yet non-threatening. Not that anyone in this room thought me a threat. Even the well-dressed man would be able to do damage to me without breaking a sweat. It was a terrifying realization. I didn't know these people. Hell, I didn't really even know where I was.

One step at a time, I told myself. I slowly counted my breaths, trying to calm down. It felt like those in the room were focused on my every move, a blink, or an involuntary swallow. If their attention was unintentional then it was unnerving, and if it was planned, it was terrifying.

After God knows how long, the boss turned around. I thought that this meant it was time to start our conversation, but I was wrong. He stared at me, cataloging every inch of my body. I felt my nipples harden, and the muscles in my upper thighs flex. It was like I was aware of him as a man, and my body was responding to him. He wasn't as tall as Conal, but he was still over six feet, with a powerful build that somehow seemed to be natural, not created in a gym. His face had character, prominent cheekbones, a stubborn chin, and eyes that, at first, I thought were a pale blue but as I stared into them a beat too long, I realized they were gray, like the horizon on one of those dark, snowy days. He was too masculine; I could feel his strength. *Animal magnetism,* the term thundered in my head. I'd never really understood what it meant until this moment.

My secret skill clicked on. I knew he was the most dangerous man, not only in this room, but that I would ever meet. He was totally in control and comfortable with that power. Plus, he knew he was attractive and that I found him very much so. I dropped my gaze and used my hands to shift my casted leg. The action was overkill, but I needed to do something to stop looking at the man.

"Does it pain you?" His voice was like hot caramel, rich and warm.

I felt like I was slowly lowering myself into a hot tub on a cold day, feeling the warmth travel over my skin. I wanted to relax and luxuriate in him.

Wait! *No.* He was dangerous.

EIGHT

RAIDER BLACK

The woman froze at the sound of my voice. I think her heart skipped several beats. I knew because my wolf had awakened the moment she'd exited the elevator onto my floor. With the addition of my other half's heightened senses, I knew everything except the exact words she was going to speak.

Theodora Morrissey interested me. Our research had painted a woman who lived a quiet life. The company car she drove was a modest Honda, her banking and spending history demonstrated that she tried to hold onto every dollar. However, she spent money on books. She had little contact with her remaining family in Ohio and had no close friends. I had studied Conal's interviews with her numerous times, I concurred with his conclusion that she held no romantic feelings for Ledderly. She was a loner. Tex had hacked into Peters' files and found that he had that same information, and that was why he'd had no problem disposing of her.

From the list of her injuries, I was surprised to see her limping into the room. However, it pleased my wolf. Her show of spirit would bode well for her with my pack. I watched her peculiar blue eyes widen as she glanced at her cast, and then slowly at me again. "Pardon?"

"Your ankle, are you in pain?" I enunciated each word.

I could almost feel her thinking, trying to form the answer. My wolf stirred. If I was in that form, I would have lifted my nose and sniffed the air. I could do that now, but I would keep up the pretense of being human for a while longer.

"It's manageable." Her voice was a little huskier than before when she'd spoken to Basil.

She was in pain, but I appreciated that she was not going to admit it to me or the room. Perhaps it was her inner sense that caused her to be cautious. She was still watching me, but not in a challenging way, which my wolf approved. "I am Raider Black." I remained in place although I could be on top of her in one leap. She wouldn't even see me coming.

"You know Conal, who is my Second; Glass handles the guards and training; Tex, technology; and," I nodded in his direction, "Onyx, who acts as historian and counsel to Novus." I'd learned that humans listened to our titles and assigned their own meaning to the positions.

She nodded once, but asked no questions. Then she returned to staring at the edge of the table, sitting very still.

"Your studies encompass the supernatural. Are you a believer?" Perhaps this was an abrupt introduction, but

80

her silence and lack of questions suddenly irritated me. I wanted to shake her up. I wanted a reaction from this human who appeared detached.

Her gaze was steady as she answered. "I know that some of the people I've interviewed believe very strongly in what they told me."

"But you don't?" I raised one eyebrow to goad her.

"Mr. Black, I personally haven't experienced anything—I'll use your word—supernatural, so I can't really say. I am a recorder of stories, not a judge." The tilt of her chin displayed a tiny bit of challenge.

"You've been asked all of this before?" I realized her answers were canned responses. I wanted—no, I demanded her honest reaction.

She smiled pleasantly, but didn't show her teeth. "I have. I think everyone in my area of study has."

Not satisfied, I pressed. "And if you experienced something that could be termed supernatural, what would you do?"

This time, her smile relaxed. She rested her shoulders against the back of the chair. She thought this was a game. "I need you to be more specific. The term 'supernatural' encompasses a wide range."

I found that I was enjoying myself, despite my frustration. Her politeness held an edge. I wanted to see her eyes flash again. I briefly dipped my chin. "My apologies. Let's say a shapeshifter, isn't that what they're called?"

"You mean a being that is human in appearance that can change into another form?" Her eyebrows drew together as she asked for clarification.

"Yes." I tried to match her smile. I appreciated her thoroughness. "Perhaps an animal?"

She dropped her chin and looked at me under her

lashes, the look both demure and flirtatious. "Well, I would probably run away." She raised her head and bit down on her lower lip. "Which would be bad considering that in animal form, he would most likely give chase." She gave a small, one-shoulder shrug. "I *should* say that I would stand my ground and study the being, but I guess it would depend on what type of animal I encountered. I mean, if it was a were-bunny, I think I would stay, or maybe a were-duck?" She chuckled and widened her eyes with glee.

Was she serious? A were-duck? That was outrageous. I moved around the table, so that I stood between her and Onyx, who was trying but failing not to show his revulsion at her example.

"What if I told you there are those who can change forms?" I offered enticingly. I couldn't wait to see her reaction. A were-duck, indeed.

Her look was incredulous. "Okay…" She didn't hide the rolling of her expressive eyes as she leaned toward me.

"You don't believe me?" It was fascinating to watch her inner student war with the suspicious human.

She glanced around the room. Her gaze rested the longest on Conal, hoping one of my people would give her a hint. "Then I must say, 'Tell me where they are.'" Her confusion was at war with her bravado, but she was curious.

I let her see me trying not to smile. "Here."

Surprisingly, she didn't respond right away. Again, she looked at each person, until finally, her gaze returned to me. "In this room?" She wasn't mocking me. I could feel her trying to ascertain if I was serious. The buzzing against my skin intensified as she used her senses.

"Yes," I answered simply.

Her smile vanished as she considered my words. She chewed on her bottom lip as she studied me intently. "I can't run in this condition." Her voice was very quiet as if her words were meant for me alone.

My wolf growled at her appeal. I could feel the vibration low in my belly. He would protect the weakened woman.

"Don't ever run from a predator," I said, my tone matching hers, "that makes you prey."

Her chest rose and fell several times. Her eyes widened in understanding. "Wha...what are you?" Her hands were now gripping the arms of the conference room chair.

So intelligent, or was it...sensitive? She knew I was telling the truth. "You would say 'wolf'."

She stared intently into my eyes for one, no two beats. Then she turned to face my Second. "Conal?"

We didn't like that she looked to another for her answers. My wolf growled in anger as I snarled a simple command, "Conal, change."

With the extra push I added to the command, Conal could do nothing else. I didn't really believe he would question me, but in the moment, I only wanted her to see I wouldn't lie to her.

I felt the magic, a strumming of sound. A learned man had once used physics and biological terms to explain what he believed happened when we changed. I preferred the much simpler term. In less than a second, Conal's human form was no longer, and in his place stood a wolf the size of a pony.

Somehow, the woman used her feet to push off the floor and propel her body so that she stood on the seat of the chair. She was unbalanced. If I had not grabbed her waist and pulled her body into mine, she would have fallen backward.

She breathed heavily as she studied the Lycan, blinking several times as if she couldn't believe her eyes.

With my arms looped around her waist, I told myself not to notice how good she smelled. Inside, my wolf calmed, enjoying her proximity.

She whispered, "Ca—," then cleared her throat, "Conal?"

The Lycan turned his massive head to look Theodora in the eye.

She shifted in my arms and leaned closer to the wolf.

I had to adjust my hold or she would fall. She had no concern for her safety as she focused on the giant wolf. I readjusted my hold, and the backs of my hands brushed the undersides of her large breasts.

More, my wolf told me. We both appreciated her lush body.

She turned her head back to me. "Can I pet him?"

Tex snickered. No self-respecting wolf would approve of the term.

"That term is offensive, but yes, you may touch him."

"Oh, sorry." She turned back to my Second and lifted her hands slowly. "Conal, may I run my hands through your coat?"

I didn't have to look around at the members of my Board; I could feel their silent laughter.

Conal nudged the hand closest to his head with his nose.

She stroked her hands down his back, scratching him at the base of his tail. "Oh my God, he's so soft." She sounded amazed. She continued stroking and scratching him. Again, she looked at me. "I can't believe something so fierce can be so soft."

The others could no longer hold back their mirth.

I laughed loudly. Theodora was charming me. Her reaction was not what I had expected.

Conal changed back into his human form.

"You-you aren't naked?" She looked him up and down while she relaxed her body into mine. She was oblivious to the fact I still held her. As for my part, I told myself she needed to take the weight off of her injured appendage.

Conal looked down at his long-sleeved shirt and jeans. "Yup, I'm clothed."

"But the stories, they always say that when you change back, you're naked..." She leaned even more weight into my body, muttering to herself, "They were wrong."

Conal shook his head. "Theodora, you weren't even scared." He gave her an incredulous look.

She stiffened in my arms a little as she considered his censure. "Well, I mean, you all can do that right?" She looked around at each person ending with her face very close to mine.

I saw her eyes widen in surprise at our closeness. She tried to move away from me. I wasn't ready to let her go. This felt...good. "You are correct."

"Well, I wouldn't stand a chance, Conal," she said, her glance moving back to my Second. "I mean, if you were going to hurt me now, why did you keep me alive? That seems like a huge waste of resources."

I couldn't argue with her logic. My wolf was amused. The human was funny in a very rational way.

"The Novus Pack doesn't like to be wasteful," Tex said solemnly, although his eyes were sparkling with humor.

She sighed. "A wolf, wow. Just wow."

She was energized and thrilled. I knew that we all could identify the signature scent to those emotions.

"Maybe you should sit back down. I don't think Solle will be happy if you have to have that ankle reset," Conal murmured.

Her body tensed. "Oh, right." She shifted her weight, and the chair moved.

I tightened my arms so she wouldn't fall. "We prefer to be called Lycans by humans. Wolf is reserved for pack members."

Her hands gripped my forearms. Not to remove them, but to hold them.

I lifted her and gently placed her on the floor.

Her cheeks were pink when her ass was again resting in the chair. "Thank you."

"No problem," I assured her. I took several steps away from her. My wolf disagreed; he liked the feel of her body.

She sat primly in her chair, with her hands clasped in her lap. She wasn't looking at anyone, which I found interesting. It was as if she knew that direct eye contact could be interpreted as a challenge.

"Ms. Morrissey, do you have any questions?" I was curious about what she would do next.

She blew out a puff of air so hard it billowed her cheeks. Then she smiled hugely, and her eyes sparkled. "About a million." She ran her fingers through her hair, pulling it back from her face. "I don't even know where to start." She scooted her chair closer to the table and rested her arms on the glass-covered surface. Her mood turned serious. "What do you want from me?"

Conal's gaze sought mine. Time and time again, this woman demonstrated that she relied on her inner sense. She seemed to accept things at face value, but then circled around to the absolute truth. I continued to stand. My wolf wanted action. He was excited and anticipating the upcoming event. "That is an interesting question," I said softly.

Now, she was giving me a measuring look. "You want something. That's why you've kept me here," she said slowly, "and showed yourselves."

I could almost feel her trying to put the puzzle pieces together. Now was the time to see how cooperative she would be.

She looked at Conal. "And been so nice to me." Her dark eyes flashed with an emotion I didn't understand. Could it be disappointment?

"You are correct," I said, drawing back her gaze. "We do want something." I could feel the mood of the room become tense. I had veered from our plan of simply holding her down. "In our world, there are humans who know of us."

Her eyes narrowed minusculey as she processed that information.

"They are protected as long as they abide by the agreement."

"Not to tell." Her voice was low and strangled. She felt the atmosphere now, too.

"Come now." I gave a slight grin. "That goes without saying." I could hear the pounding of her heart, but I did admire her fortitude. She didn't shift nervously or measure the distance to the door. She kept watching me. "Humans serve. They are known as Articles."

"S-serve?" she stammered. She started to turn her head to look at Conal, but jerked it back in my direction.

She feels our power, my wolf stated. "Of course." I saw Glass stand and move to the bag that she'd placed on the floor by the credenza in front of the far window. "Humans have assisted Lycans throughout the centuries."

Her hands were shaking. She hid them from view under the table. "I'm going to serve you."

"The Pack," I corrected, "Novus."

"New," she mumbled the Latin translation.

"That is the name of my pack."

Glass moved to stand beside her. She placed her bag on the table. "Usually, they are one and the same. The Pack is Novus."

The woman looked up at Glass, as if she was trying to discern whether there was an extra message in that statement.

"Please give me your right hand Theodora." Glass worded it as a request, but it was a demand.

"Why?" She turned her attention back to me.

I noted that she always returned to me. "All Articles carry the symbol of their pack affiliation."

She didn't volunteer her hand. "So that other... Lycans will know."

"You will learn to recognize our kind. The symbol will grant you safe passage, or if there is a problem, you will be returned to Novus."

"And the symbol makes you part of our family." Glass had removed her instruments.

The woman glanced at the tools Glass had placed in

a neat line. "What are those for?" Her pale skin had turned even whiter.

Conal scooted closer to her other side. "She is going apply our brand. Think of it as your formal welcome into our world."

"A brand!" she exclaimed. Finally, her control cracked. She feared pain.

My Second dropped his muscled arm around her shoulders and secured her to his side. "You really don't have a choice," he said sagely.

Onyx cleared his throat. "Brand or die. That is your choice, human."

She looked at me again as if to verify the man's words.

My wolf didn't like Conal's arm around her. I was not in the mood to explain that Conal was no threat. Not that I was interested. Well, I did notice that she had large breasts and a voluptuous body, a keen mind—however, I had no time for a dalliance. If I desired a fuck, I would choose from one of the willing females that paraded past almost hourly. Humans were so...breakable.

"Where?" She breathed the word in surrender.

"Inner wrist," Conal said.

Slowly, she pushed up the arm of her too-large sweatshirt.

Glass took over. She pulled the sleeve up to the woman's elbow. "This will hurt, but it helps if you try to relax." She tore open an alcohol wipe package.

NINE

THEODORA MORRISSEY

*W*as she fucking serious? She's going to burn a permanent *mark into my flesh!* I watched as she applied the small bit of cotton to the skin of my delicate inner forearm about two inches above my wrist.

"Look at me," Conal's deep voice sounded close to my ear.

I did as he said.

"Don't watch. It'll only make it worse."

His expression was calm, yet I knew that he didn't like that it was going to hurt me.

I heard shuffling and clicking, but I forced myself not to turn my head. The boss, Raider Black, was out of my sight, and that made me uncomfortable. However, Conal was right. I didn't want to see this happen. A part of me wondered why I wasn't fighting? Not that I could have gotten away, but to sit calmly while being burned...this wasn't me. This couldn't be my life. *It's a small price to pay.* My inner voice told me.

I felt the heat near my arm. I tried to pull away from

Glass's iron-like grip. Conal's arm around my shoulders tightened as the heat seared through me. White hot pain traveled up my arm and throughout my body. "Oh, God." I moaned and squeezed my eyes shut.

"Theodora, look at me," Conal commanded.

"Ittt hurtttsss," I sobbed not caring that I was in a room filled with strangers.

"Five, four, three, two, one," Raider Black counted down.

I knew that Glass had pulled back the fiery iron, but my skin was still burned. The nerves going haywire, my body felt weak, and I squeezed my eyes shut. I wanted to pass out. That would be so easy, but that would leave me alone and vulnerable to the predators, real predators.

I fought to stay conscious, starting to count slowly in my mind while trying to focus. I also prayed that I hadn't or wouldn't pee my pants. Jesus, these people had just branded me like I was….theirs.

When I felt more in control, I glanced at my arm. Glass had placed some kind of jelly over the angry mark and was now applying a pad as she prepared to tape it into place.

When she had replaced her tools almost reverently into the black leather case, she returned to her place at the table.

"Theodora Morrissey, you now serve the Novus Pack," Raider Black said, his voice richly toned, fully ceremonious. "Welcome."

The others clapped their hands in unison.

I didn't know what the proper etiquette was, so I didn't say anything. I knew there was more, that they weren't done with me.

"We found you in a pool of blood under a desk on

our land." Raider Black's voice was filled with intensity. His odd gray eyes almost seemed to glow in the waning afternoon light. "During your medical treatment, a discovery was made. It was very fortuitous for you, since you had no ties to Novus and were trespassing on our land."

I shivered at his words. I had wondered many times about their reaction to finding me. Why had Solle and Conal been so kind? But I had no access to a phone. I didn't even have anyone to call. Since I'd awakened, I was never really alone. I'd done the only thing I could. I'd waited. A part of me knew something was up. People weren't that nice, taking me in, pretending to like me, and wanting to be my friend. That part hurt the most. I took in a deep breath and let it out slowly. "What discovery?" My voice shook.

"You carry The Lady's Mark."

Da-dum, I heard the cheesy organ music in my head. None of this meant anything to me. "I do?" I asked cautiously. This group seemed really concerned with marks, brands, maybe even tattoos. Fancifully, I wondered what happened to their tattoos when they changed.

I needed to pay attention.

"You told Conal a woman spoke to you." Black paused dramatically. I got the impression he was a bit of a showman. "A mysterious voice on a dark, snowy night in the middle of nowhere...it was The Lady."

Yeah, he was enjoying this. "It was a hallucination," I countered because this was insane.

"She told you that the wolves would come, and they did." He raised one eyebrow questioningly. "Did they not, Theodora?"

93

I hated when people arched their brows because I couldn't. But I liked how he said my name.

Fuck.

I swallowed hard while I told myself to concentrate. Okay, what he said was right...but it was...unbelievable.

And true.

My gaze flew to his. This was happening. This was really real. I ran my tongue over my dry lips as I tried to formulate a coherent question. "You say that I carry a mark. Wouldn't I have seen it? I mean, I've been in this body for thir...a long time." I wasn't going to accept all of this just because *he* said it was so. I wasn't some sheep, following the leader blindly. Because you know, wolves ate sheep. Yeesh! I shook my head trying to get rid of that thought.

"To your human eyes, it would seem ordinary." He answered as if he were trying to calm me. "Very few Lycans have seen one. The doctor treating you recognized it from old drawings." He paused as if he wanted me to digest that factoid. "Finding a Marked is very rare."

Not knowing what being "marked" signified, I accepted that they thought it extraordinary. I wasn't sure I wanted to be special—not if it drew this much attention. "And I'm supposed to be this...this special person?" I wanted to laugh, but something about all of this felt right. However, I wasn't sure. It was so outrageous. "Dude, I'm so ordinary. I think that your doctor's wrong," I said, fighting a growing panic because they all looked so intense.

"You do not address the Laird as 'dude', human," the guy in the suit thundered.

"Onyx," the Laird growled in a low voice.

94

"She must learn our ways and, apparently, some manners," Onyx groused as he sent me a superior look.

I didn't like that. I had manners. Usually, I was too polite, but this was overwhelming. I glanced at the Laird, and then down at my bandaged arm. "Really, I'm very ordinary." A part of me was a little disappointed; it might be nice to be special.

"Your instincts," the Laird spoke, but now he was next to me, leaning on the edge of the conference room table, facing me. "Some might refer to it as a sixth sense. You have relied on it, correct?"

I felt the hairs on my arms stand on end in warning. "It's nothing." Instinctively, I downplayed the skill. Damnit, why had I told Conal?

"Your mark identifies you as a gift to our people." He leaned closer to me.

I jumped to my feet. I felt like I needed to run, but I didn't even get to take a step. Suddenly, I was face down on the table. I tried to fight off the hands that were holding me down. Too much was happening at once. I heard the tear of fabric, and cool air on my now revealed back. I arched up to see what was happening behind me.

Someone jerked up my good arm, exposing my armpit and twisting my body a little, which made my ribs very unhappy. Black landed on the table beside me in a squat. I swear his features were part man, part wolf. I screamed in fear and frustration.

I knew when he touched my skin. His hands were warm, but it was something else. Like, I felt safer. Which was crazy, because *I was not*. I started to fight again.

"Goddess, we have located your daughter. We thank you for the gift." His voice filled the room and it carried

95

something more that I couldn't identify-- some special energy. "I, Raider Black, Leader of the Novus Pack, ask that you acknowledge your child."

I swear it was like a bolt of lightning struck inside the room. I was blinded by the bright light as my body seized. I bowed backward in an unnatural arc. I wrenched my arms free and made a grab for the boss. He would save me. He was the only one who could.

I needed him. He was the cure to the pounding in my head that made me feel as though my brain was going to explode. He pulled me into his arms as I tried to scream. Suddenly, I was blind. Everything was black and silent except for a pulsating roar that was pounding through my body. It was like the time I'd tried noise-canceling headphones on a plane; a weird, muffled white noise sounded in my head.

Another onslaught of pain hit. I wasn't me any longer. I don't know how I knew, or even how I could grasp what was happening, but it was true. I was running. I could feel my muscles compress and stretch. I felt so…free. The colors were brighter—and the smells! I could smell everything—the air, the snow, the crispness of the wind. It was *amazing*. I glanced down to see what I was. I knew that I wasn't a woman. Solid black fur covered the legs carrying me over the land.

I was with the black wolf.

I started to panic. How could this be? I was a woman, not an animal. I tried to stop this…this dream. *Oh God, oh please. I'm so scared. Make. It. Stop.*

TEN

RAIDER BLACK

The woman survived the ceremony. She had reached for me as her body bowed in a too-sharp angle. She had convulsed in seizure after seizure.

I pulled her into my arms, hoping to provide some level of comfort as power flooded her system. The others felt the Goddess's touch as they changed involuntarily. For one moment, it was as if the woman and I had merged. I could feel her terror and the agonizing pain.

When it finally ended, although in reality it only lasted a few moments, I looked around the room half expecting the walls to have come down around us. The others were changing back to their human forms.

"What the fuck was that?" Tex ran a hand through his wild hair.

"Maybe we should have done this outside?" Conal looked around as if he too had expected the room to be in ruins.

"Is she dead?" Glass stared warily at our Marked.

"No, she lives." I could feel her breathing against my chest.

"What's next?" My Second was back to business.

I shifted her body and studied the mark on her back. Now it was clearly a circle containing an eye. "Tomorrow the Seer's training begins." I glanced at the silent Onyx.

He straightened his tie. "I have reserved several hours each morning,"

"How do we know it worked? That she has the ability?" Glass stared at the woman's unconscious form.

We could easily send for an injured Article or child for her to heal, if she was marked a healer, but this gift was trickier.

"I am uncertain there are any official tests," Onyx muttered.

"We have faith," I told them, "that The Lady's gift will benefit us all."

"The texts say that each Seer has different talents and degrees of talent," Onyx cautioned.

I didn't verbalize my opinion that this woman would be strong. I knew it. I'd felt the power while I'd held her in my arms. "We'll know in time." I watched her for a few moments. "Now, she'll sleep. Go. We'll know more soon." I motioned with my head toward the door.

Conal stayed behind. "I'll see to her." He started to reach to take her from me.

"No," I snarled, immediately correcting my tone. "She's no bother. I want to speak with her when she wakes." I slid my other arm under her knees and stood.

Conal got the door and led the way during our short walk to my office. I took my usual seat on the large sofa sectional and adjusted the woman so that she rested against my chest with her legs draped over the padded arm.

"Need anything?"

My tablet was on the table beside me. I could work while she rested. I ignored the question as to why I didn't place her on the cushions beside me. "I believe we're comfortable."

He threw back his head and laughed. "Aren't we all with a beauty in our arms?" The look he gave me said that he wondered if I kept her for another purpose.

I narrowed my eyes. "I will deliver her later."

"I'm sure that Solle will still be up. She'll be concerned." Conal's tone always softened when he spoke of his mate.

"Go to her and assuage her worries." I wanted quiet. It was rarely, truly quiet.

"I'll post a guard and order that you be left alone." Conal nodded his good-bye and left.

As if the woman sensed we were alone, she shifted and nestled closer to my body.

My wolf was pleased by her proximity. He hummed his approval and settled. I stared appreciatively at her bare breasts. Her silky gown had been no match for my strength when I'd torn the sweatshirt from her body.

She shifted again, crossing an arm over her chest to grab onto my shirt over my heart.

This was an intimate hold that I found I enjoyed. Not that I didn't always appreciate women. I craved sex, but years ago, I'd entered into an agreement to join with another packleader's daughter. There was no agreed-upon date for our union, for at that time, I'd been working hard to establish Novus. In the intervening years, I'd enjoyed many partners, but only for fucking. I could only hope that, over time, my promised mate Siobhan and I would grow to feel affection toward one another.

Theodora sighed deeply as though she was content in my arms.

I scoffed at my thought. I was never a romantic; I left that nonsense to Conal. He'd known from a very early age that he would find his true mate. I was happy for him. Solle was smart and loving, plus as the smug smile on his face attested, she pleased him. Hopefully soon they would ask The Lady to bless them with young.

I wondered if I would have offspring. Our Goddess had made adjustments to our mating ritual almost a thousand years ago when battles and challenges had resulted in so much death. Our numbers thinned. A Contracted Mating came into being so that Lycans could be joined and young born. Not every wolf could meet their soulmate as Conal had. The agreed-upon matches were as real as the fated. I knew many couples that seemed very content.

I needed to do some work, to take my mind off such silly thoughts. I didn't have time for romance nor the right to enter into such a relationship, even though it would be short-lived. I was promised to another, and I always kept my vows.

I opened the cover to my tablet and started to read a financial report.

Two hours later, I felt her stir. I placed the tablet on the end table and glanced down into her now open deep blue eyes. I saw and sensed her confusion and caution.

"What?" She slowly turned her head. There was only the soft glow from my desk lamp in the room. Our kind had night vision, but to her the room was probably shadowed.

"How do you feel?" I asked slowly, keeping my volume low.

"Like I got hit by a truck," she continued to look around.

"I suppose in a way, you did."

Her gaze swept over her bared chest. She immediately turned her breasts into my chest, shielding them from my view. "Really?" She used an exasperated tone.

"They are nice breasts." I smiled not feeling guilty at all.

She shook her head. "I guess it doesn't matter if it is a man or a Lycan, the sight of bare breasts always entrances." She glared at me.

"I am male." I shrugged and continued to grin. Her breasts were large, full, and heavy. She had a woman's body, softer than a female Lycan's that were more muscular.

One side of her mouth tipped up. I knew she was fighting a smile. "So, all of this," she paused, "it really happened?"

"It did," I told her gravely.

She covered her breasts with one arm and used the other to scoot upward into a sitting position.

I placed my hands on her waist to assist. I kept one there, telling myself it was to help her balance. "If you wish, we can discuss it now."

"I feel like my head exploded and was put back together. Could we, uh, talk about it tomorrow?" She looked around the room again. "What time is it?"

I checked the antique clock hanging on the far wall. "Just after ten."

Her eyes widened. "I've been out a long time."

"I'm sure you needed rest."

"I am a champion sleeper," she quipped then sobered. "I'd like to go home. I mean, to Conal's, please." She started to wiggle down from my lap.

I liked that she thought of Conal's place as home. Sometimes, our casual statements were most telling. I helped her to her feet. "I'll drive you." She took a few steps away, and I stood. Of course, she didn't understand the importance of my driving her. As Leader, my guards drove me. It was considered a very high honor for the Leader to drive a member. I headed to my desk to grab a set of keys. It was too cold for us to take my bike.

"I need a...some clothes."

I looked up from my desk, puzzled.

"I can't go out like this." She looked down at her shredded gown.

"No one would question your dress." Except for the few guards that were posted, we most likely wouldn't encounter anyone.

She continued to coverer her breasts with one arm, the other was holding up what remained of the skirt of her gown, but I could see she prepared to give me attitude.

Her chin lifted. "Okay, I get that you all might not have an issue with being naked, but I do. I'm not wandering around like this." Her eyes sparkled with defiance.

She was so funny in her acceptance of us. I was sure she didn't realize she was already adjusting to our ways. I gave an exaggerated sigh. "I have a closet here. Perhaps you can find something you feel is appropriate. Or I can call Conal to have something delivered."

"No," she cried. She moved gingerly to follow me to the closet that was built into my private bathroom. "I don't want to bother them."

I moved slowly so she could keep up. I turned on the overhead light as we entered the room.

"Whoa." She paused and rested her weight against the door frame. "This place is awesome."

I had never really considered the room. Onyx had spearheaded the building and office design. I knew that the bathroom was roomy, the shower was large, and the water hot. I moved to open the walk-in closet doors.

She followed slowly. Her injured leg was giving her pain.. I could smell the emotion as she worked to ignore it.

"Do you live here?" she asked as she moved to the wall that held shelves.

"No, I have a house. I have clothes here for meetings or when I need to dress for appearances," I explained as I watched her pull out a black sweatshirt that would cover her from her shoulders to her knees.

"So, you can't just summon a change of clothes?" She shook out the garment, primly turned her back to me, and slowly pulled on the shirt. She had to use her good arm to dress her other arm and when she turned around, the remains of her gown pooled around her feet. "You're going to have to replace Conal's hoodie." She gave me a steady glare.

I nodded solemnly. "I will address that with Conal when I take you home." I approved that she was concerned about my Second's belongings.

She limped back into my office.

"Tomorrow, you will be assigned an office, and your studies will begin."

"Hold on." She held up one hand in a stop sign. "That's not going to happen tomorrow."

"Of course, it will," I countered, watching her with hidden incredulity. I wasn't used to others disagreeing with me so openly.

She shook her head. "It's not happening for two reasons."

I held my tongue, curious where she was going.

She held up one finger. "One, I don't have any business clothes. Well, technically, I only have a couple of nightgowns and I'm not wearing those into work."

"It doesn't matter how you're dressed," I said angrily, although I didn't like the idea of others seeing her in a silky gown with her breasts bobbing enticingly.

"Yes, it does," she argued.

"Ms. Morrissey, I will forgive you this one time for disregarding my wishes. I am the leader of the Novus Pack. My word is law." My voice took on a growl. "If I say that you will report tomorrow, then you will."

The speed of her breathing increased, and she dropped her chin. "I apologize." She did sound genuine. She raised her head again, "I think that if I am...what you say I am...someone who's going to help...serve the pack, I should look professional, or at least not like I just rolled out of bed."

The idea of how she would look in bed with a sheet threaded between her lush thighs, a light sheen of sweat blanketing her body flitted through my mind. *Gah*, I pushed aside the distracting thought. "That's a valid point. Tomorrow, Solle and Conal can begin your education while appropriate clothes are procured."

"Thank you," she answered softly.

"And the second issue?"

She pointed at her leg. "I need to be mobile. Next week, I'm to get a different cast."

"You can be carried if need be."

"No, I can't," she argued. "It's weird."

I didn't understand that at all. "Your guard can easily carry you."

She straightened as if she could make herself grow taller. "I don't want people I don't know carrying me." She tilted her head to the side. "It's disconcerting to have a stranger so close and for them to touch me so, um, much."

My wolf agreed. I considered her feelings. "I will consult with Solle, and we will decide."

"Perfect," she smiled, "I need to use a computer or a phone, probably both."

I didn't need to think. "No."

Her hand went to her hip, and her eyebrows lowered. "What do you mean no? I need to call my bank and make arrangements to get a credit card. I'll also need a new I.D. I don't have anything." She looked at me expectantly. "If I had a phone, I could shop and move my money."

All of those things were security risks. However, I didn't think this was the time to relate those reasons to her. "The Pack will purchase anything you need, within reason," I added quickly. "Tex or Conal will attend to your other needs."

"I have money," she told me haughtily.

I knew the amount in her accounts. Tex could easily transfer it to one that I set up for her. "Of course, but consider this the duty of the Pack, for your service."

Her eyes narrowed as she considered my response.

"It will be handled tomorrow," I said swiftly, and with authority.

She frowned. "But—"

"Theo," I said sharply, "do not get into the habit of arguing with me," I said, my tone justifiably imperious. She must learn that, although she held an elevated position within our pack, she was still my subject.

She dropped her gaze to signify that she'd heard me. After a couple of moments, she lifted her chin and headed to the door. "I'm ready to go now."

With her head held like a queen, she moved slowly and carefully. When I could take it no more, I swooped in close and picked her up.

"You don't—"

I cut her off. "Your leg is hurting. I want Solle to examine it." I continued to the elevator. I usually took the stairs, but I worried about jarring the much more fragile human.

"This makes me look weak," she said, her dismay telling.

"You are." After receiving another glare, I added, "Your injury makes you more so."

She was silent as I made my way to my SUV. I doubt she noticed the guards as we passed. They stuck to the shadows as they trailed behind us. At the door to the garage, Wale stood at our approach.

"Laird?" he said briefly, asking if he should accompany me.

"No need, Wale," I said, and he returned to his post.

Once we were on our way out of the garage, she cleared her throat. "I didn't even see that guy."

She sounded mystified. "Then he's doing his job."

She didn't speak for a few blocks. "Are there others like me?"

I didn't believe there was any other like her. She was unlike any human I had ever encountered. However, I knew she yearned to hear something positive. I'd studied the human's books on management styles and psychology. "Yes. My Pack has seventy-two Articles that are active," I said, proud of the fact so many chose to serve.

"Okay, but I meant, uhm, are there more like me... Marked." Her tone was much more tentative this time.

"There have been Marked recorded throughout our history. There are those who can heal, and others who have the gift of sight. The Council, our governing body, knows the exact number."

"But not many?" she continued.

I considered my answer carefully. I didn't want her to be overwhelmed. "No, not many." I didn't want to tell her the legend that Seers tend to go mad. Eventually, they got to the place where they couldn't discern reality from their visions.

"So, I'm the only one around here?" she asked.

The concern in her tone made me wish I could reassure her. As far as I knew, there had been a healer in one of the Canadian packs, but he'd been sent to Scotland in the mid-1900s. "That is true. We are honored to have you."

"Oh..." She didn't sound pleased.

As I pulled into Conal's driveway, the front door opened, and both Conal and Solle strode down the walk to where I would come to a stop.

Theodora watched the pair. "She looks upset."

One second after I stopped and hit the unlock

button, Solle opened the passenger side door. "Are you all right?"

Theodora unclipped the never-used seatbelt and offered a small smile. "I'm tired but, yeah, I'm okay."

Solle hugged the woman tightly. "I was so worried."

Theodora accepted the hug and used one arm to hang onto the woman. "I'm sorry. I hate that you had to go through that."

Solle pulled back. "Conal told me you were okay, but I needed to see for myself."

Conal circled his arm around his mate's waist. "Why don't you let her come into the house?"

I opened my door. "I'll carry you." I didn't need to look back to see the look of sly consideration on Solle's face. "I think you'll need to look at her leg. She has used it too much."

"Of course, Laird." The doctor cleared the doorway.

I carried Theodora into the house and placed her gently on the sofa. Solle busily wrapped a blanket around her shoulders and put a pillow under her casted leg.

"Solle, you don't have to fuss," Theodora said, trying to calm her hostess.

"We saved dinner for you. Are you hungry?" Solle asked, pausing in her ministrations.

"Not really." Theodora looked up at me, "Thank you...Laird. I appreciate your kindness." She dropped her gaze as she finished.

Although I felt some reluctance, I knew I must leave. "Welcome to our Pack, Theodora Morrissey." I moved toward the front door.

Conal was waiting on the porch. "She okay?"

"She's coherent and communicative." I felt a grin

spread across my face. I was surprised to find that I'd enjoyed my time with the human.

"I call it subtle feistiness. She goes along with you, and then gently slams on the brakes." Conal was now grinning, too.

"And she's funny, but she doesn't know it."

"I wouldn't recommend pointing it out, either." He chuckled.

"No. I agree, she wouldn't like that."

We both quieted so that we could listen to what the women discussed.

"So, you're one of them, a Lycan," Theodora said quietly.

"I was human," Solle said.

"But you aren't now?"

"I met Conal in 1980. He says that he knew the second he saw me that I was his mate. To me, I only knew that he was hot," she recounted. "We dated. I tried to slow things down; I wanted to go to med school, so I didn't have time for a man, but he was soooo..."

"Yeah, I can totally see it." Theodora added in a low voice.

That voice was alluring, and a part of me wanted to lean against the door to be closer to her. I could picture her flashing a conspiratorial grin.

"He convinced me to make a visit to meet his family. By then, I knew there was something different about him. Some of his answers to my questions, or I should say his non-answers, didn't make sense, but I was in love with him. He promised that once I was in Nebraska everything would make sense."

"And you're still here," Theodora added dryly.

"He went with me to Indiana for school. The Laird

made arrangements with that area's pack, so we could stay there with no problems."

"I imagine the packs are territorial," Theodora theorized. "My grandma loved books and movies about werewolves. Sometimes, if they weren't too gory, I'd watch them with her."

Solle snorted. "Oh honey, we aren't your grandma's type of wolves."

I glanced at Conal and burst out laughing.

ELEVEN

THEODORA MORRISSEY

Those movies and paranormal books that grandma had devoured were very wrong.

So much had happened. Every night before I went to my room, Solle, and sometimes Conal, made me recite what I'd learned that day. I felt like a kid and wanted to roll my eyes at them, but I instinctively knew from the moment I awoke in the Laird's arms, that I needed to learn everything I could, and fast. A misstep could mean grave consequences, like my funeral. Lycans had a thing about respect and challenges to them. I had to keep that in mind, all the time.

My education was exhausting and fascinating, with a good dose of terrifying thrown in. This was my new life. I didn't get a say. The Laird set the rules. His word was law. I'd learned that fact the hard way a few days later when I'd tried to use the phone.

It embarrassed me that, while shopping online, Solle used her credit card to buy my bras. I'd made my own money since I was fourteen. I hated owing people, even when they paid for my coffee. So, by the time we were done shopping, I was frustrated and that made me reckless.

Solle had left me alone, and the cordless was sitting on the end table within my reach. I picked it up and dialed the number to the main switchboard at my old office. I was told no one had filed a Missing Person Report, but in this day and age, I wondered whether I could really disappear and have no one notice? I wasn't super close to anyone there, but I knew all of their first names, their partners', and most of their kids. After three weeks and a missed payroll payment, wouldn't someone question where the fuck I was?

Further, I didn't know these people, er, Lycans. I had to consider that they might be lying. I needed to find out for myself. It was time to stop drifting and take back my life. I hit the send button.

Shelly answered, "Hell—"

And that's all I heard as the handset was wrenched from my hand and thrown across the living room, shattering into a million pieces against the wall. A male was standing over me and his eyes were flashing. He grabbed my shoulders, lifted me from the sofa, and began yelling.

Solle returned and was screaming. My brain was trying to catch up.

That scene ended with Tex and Conal storming in, and then me enduring a lecture from an enraged Conal that left me so scared I burst into tears.

Immediately, Solle came to my defense and yelled at Conal and that only made me cry harder.

Later that night, the three of us came to a kind of understanding. Solle acted as an interpreter, of sorts. Although Conal didn't like that I questioned their veracity, he did come around to seeing my point of view...a little.

Since that day, the Laird punished me by ignoring me, or at least that was what my gut told me. I hadn't seen him in a week. I wasn't sure if I was happy or sad about that, but let's just say, I was aware. The lesson had been learned. Two days later, Glass let me listen in when she called my old office and asked for me, only to be told that I was no longer with the company in a clipped tone.

I guess I'd been forgotten by my co-workers, or maybe I'd never been noticed? So, I made the decision, throwing myself into my studies and trying to figure out my role here.

Some of it was easy to accept and incorporate. Yes, the Lycans had two forms; they could change, but the transformations had nothing to do with the moon. There were Alphas and Betas. As with humans, it took all kinds to make up a pack. The Alphas were the take charge type, the ones who jumped in with both feet, while the Betas had a more think first, act second temperament. However, both were predators and dangerous when riled. Many seemed to hover on edge of violence all the time.

The majority of Lycans belonged to packs. There were some who chose to be alone, but most seemed to thrive when they were among their own kind. So far, I'd gathered that the Novus Pack was the newest pack in the Lycan world. Raider Black had been the Leader from the start. He was considered to be progressive because he and the pack attempted to change with the times. Many of the current Novus pack had petitioned to become members when the pack was first chartered. They'd been wolves unhappy with their circumstances or who'd wanted something different. The Laird treated males and females equally, in human and wolf form, which seemed to be a revolutionary idea.

That night, after he had touched my mark, I had a really weird dream. I was visited by myself. Well, it was a different me. She was stronger and quicker. She wasn't Lycan, but she wasn't entirely human. She was wearing a blood-red dress and her eyes were bright, too bright, as she warned me, "Think before you speak. Some will wait before they strike. Always consider your words, and never share all that you can do." I woke up freezing and sweating, so much that I shucked off my nightgown.

The next time I opened my eyes, the sun shone between the slats in my blinds. I wasn't alone; I sensed the presence of another. I thought about what the dream "me" had said, so I slowly rolled to my other side. Sitting in the floral upholstered chair against the wall was a woman. She was thumbing through a Vogue magazine.

"Hello." I hoped that my tone came out somewhere in that middle ground of "I don't know you," and "I guess you're supposed to be here."

"Hello, Theodora Morrissey, Seer to the Novus Pack." She closed the magazine and let it fall to the floor. "I've been waiting forever for you to wake."

"I'm sorry," I apologized without thinking. "I had a busy day and late night."

"Everybody is talking about you. Asher and Wale are jealous that I was selected to guard you today." She curled her jeans-clad legs under her.

I knew she was Lycan, but I would never have guessed she was a guard. She had pastel pink hair that brushed her shoulders and wore a huge white bow as a headband. Her top was black with a hot pink Minnie

Mouse outlined in sequins. I blinked as I considered her appearance and words. "I don't think there'll be much excitement," I warned her. "I'm really very boring."

The woman looked crestfallen, like I'd just kicked her puppy. "But you are Marked by The Lady, right?" She studied me intently.

Now, I knew how a mouse felt when cornered by a cat or, maybe, what a sheep felt when a wolf was near. I could feel her power. She was a killer and she enjoyed that role. I considered carefully how to answer her question. "The Laird and the Board think so." I started to stretch and realized I was naked, except for my panties. I pulled the blanket tight to my breasts. "I think I'm supposed to get my leg x-rayed today."

"Yes, and then we shop," she said with a smile.

Oh God, I hoped I wouldn't be outfitted in cartoon character T-shirts. "I'm sorry, I don't know your name."

"I am Issa," she said.

"Nice to meet you, Issa. Um, I don't know all of the 'guarding me' rules, but I need to go to the bathroom and shower. I'm not á big fan of public nudity." I was getting better about stating my needs. Otherwise, Solle would have stripped and followed me into the shower to continue a conversation.

"Why? I've seen many women." Her eyebrows drew together in puzzlement.

Internally, I sighed. This was going to be my life from now on. "We just met and, um, I don't feel comfortable being that open in front of you." I felt good about that answer.

"You would feel vulnerable." Issa nodded as if she understood that confession. "Solle warned that you would and that I should respect your feelings, since you are a weak human."

And that was the type of conversation I had with each of the Lycans who pulled guard duty. I tried to set the boundaries as they related to my weaker human status.

I started classes with Onyx three days later. We met four days a week at the Novus building. I couldn't say I liked the teacher, but we didn't have to be friends in order for me to learn. He was different from the other males. I don't mean because of the urbane look, or the beautifully tailored suits he wore each day. What made him different was that he made me very uncomfortable. In him, I sensed a violence that was barely contained and my flight instinct pinged constantly.

Onyx thought it was important that I learn the history of the Lycan race. I tried to grasp the intricacies of the different ruling packs and the practice of Contracted Mating, in which Pack Leaders basically sold off their children to strengthen ties with another pack. When you can live forever, memory is very long, and one can hold a grudge, well…forever.

I frustrated Onyx in many ways. I couldn't recall intricate family trees and I had yet to have a psychic breakthrough.

However, I loved learning. The texts were so old that I wore a protective mask because I feared that I might inhale some ancient dust or mold. Sometimes, I wore gloves so that the ink would not mix with my body's oils and cause any further deterioration. The drawings were amazing. In order to see such magnificent works, I gladly endured Onyx's constant censure.

Solle and Conal were in charge of trying to teach me

about the proper etiquette and the social niceties of this world. She'd made me practice for three uninterrupted hours how to present my brand to the Laird. Finally, I did it "prettily" enough to suit the tyrant.

Conal had mentioned that at some point Glass would want to evaluate my fighting and weaponry skills. I hoped he would forget that idea. The woman was over six feet tall and all muscle. She would pulverize me in a minute.

So, all in all, I was surviving. I took the good with the not so great and hoped that everything would be better tomorrow.

This day, Onyx was particularly cutting during our session when I yawned for the third time. I couldn't help it, Solle and Conal's *activities* had kept me awake until the early hours of the morning, again.

I couldn't say anything. I mean, they would know I was listening. Plus, it was their house, and they were very good to me. They'd followed the Laird's rule, removing the door to my bedroom. In all honesty, I don't think the door would have muffled the noise that much; the solid wall between our bedrooms certainly hadn't.

Something needed to be done. My brain and body required sleep. I knew that if I said anything to Solle she would tell Conal and, even worse, they would try to change their behavior.

No matter how many times they assured me they liked having me in their home, it had to be hard. I was always around. I couldn't even go outside without my guard. I didn't care if what they said was true, that it was an honor for me to be there; it still had to be odd.

I got to my feet before the thought had fully gelled in my head. I needed to talk to the Laird. I'd caught a few glimpses of him walking past my office, but we hadn't spoken since that night. Of course, I often heard, "The Laird said," or "The Laird requests" but he never spoke to me directly. I stepped out of my office into the hallway. Asher was right there in front of me.

"Where are you going, Seer?" The man towered over me. He had Asian features and long, shiny hair. The females had to go crazy for him. He was sexy as hell and had a cheeky sense of humor.

"I'm off to see the wizard."

He gave me a puzzled look. "I know of no such person." He pulled his phone from his pocket and I was certain he was going to make a call to ask someone who the wizard was.

Damn, I had to remember that pop-culture references meant nothing to these people. "I'd like to see the Laird." I hoped my voice sounded firm.

"Did he request a meeting?"

"No, but it will only take a moment." I was starting to lose my nerve. I shifted my weight from foot to foot, but I didn't lower my eyes.

"We will check with Basil." Asher didn't take my arm, but he somehow herded me down the hallway. Tricky wolf.

Today, Basil wore a red suit with a matching fedora. Now, that was something I'd never seen before, but on the admin, it looked spectacular.

"Theodora Morrissey, what brings you by?"

"Hello, Basil. I love your suit," I gushed shamelessly. "And I'm sure that you know, not just anyone can wear a hat and look so debonair."

"Thank you." He leaned back in his chair. "Now,

what can I do for you?" He was looking me up and down and I suddenly felt underdressed.

The boxes containing my belongings had arrived one afternoon, unceremoniously. I was glad to have my clothes and my books, but Conal was decidedly closed-lipped about how or who had retrieved them from Allen. Today, I wore a light blue silk blouse with a navy skirt that hit me at my knees, and one navy ballet flat.

I cleared my throat. "I was wondering if there might be time today to speak with the Laird."

"You don't have an appointment." Basil was now in gate-keeper mode.

"Well, yes, that's true." I told myself not to back down. "But, you see, I didn't know I needed one." I could tell that he was going to dismiss me, so I quickly continued, "Or I'd be happy to make one. I think I need about three minutes."

That caught his attention. "Three minutes?"

"And, um, when I'm done, I wondered if I could talk to you about my…" I was now making this up as I went along, "my hair." I flipped my ponytail over my shoulder.

He jumped to his feet. "I've been dying to do something with your hair since the day you first showed up." Suddenly, he was beside me and combing his fingers through my brown locks.

"I need…help, you know?" Suddenly, I liked this idea. Basil's look was loud, but he wore gorgeous suits, and his make-up ran the gamut from subtle to full-on drag.

"Darling girl, you go right in," he said, pointed a finger toward the Laird's office door, "and when you're done, we'll sit down and discuss." He practically danced a jig as he led me to the door. He knocked once, dramatically threw open the door, and announced, "Theodora Morrissey, Seer to the Novus Pack, Laird."

I peeked inside and saw that the Laird was sitting behind his desk, holding a file in one hand. He slowly got to his feet and walked around his desk. "Enter."

I tried to disguise my limp as I clomped in and hoped that all of the rehearsing that Solle had demanded paid off. I stopped about three steps in front of the man as I dipped my chin and eyes. I grasped my right wrist, sliding up my sleeve to display my brand.

"Theodora," his deep voice sounded very loud in the quiet office.

Still keeping my gaze downcast as taught, "Laird." I heard the office door close.

"Why are you here?"

So the social niceties were over. I didn't raise my eyes but I did lift my chin, so that I was looking at the general area of his chest. "I need to buy something."

"So? Tell Solle." He sounded dismissive.

"I can't." I bit my lip because I sounded a little desperate, and I now looked at him.

"Conal, then." Definitely dismissive. He gave me an unhappy look that caused the hair on my arms to stir. The muscles at the side of his jaw flexed. "I believe I already explained that the Pack would cover any expenses, within reason."

"I, uh, I understand that. It's just that I don't want to explain why I need it." I hated that I sounded hesitant.

"You're not making any sense." His gray eyes narrowed a little as he finished his thought.

"Look, can you just get me some headphones? The noise-canceling ones." Why did this have to be so damn difficult?

His eyebrows lowered. "Why would you need those?"

"I just do." I felt my cheeks get warm. I hated that I was blushing.

Now, he glared. "Theo, my time is valuable."

"I don't know who else to ask. I need the damn headphones…sir." I realized too late I was standing with my hands on my hips. Not exactly a deferential stance.

He raised one imperious eyebrow.

"Can you get them? Please?" I gritted out the last word.

"Not until you tell me why."

I thought I saw the hint of a smile. "I really don't want to." I let my gaze fall away.

"That is the price."

I let out a deep sigh. "They wake me up." I made my eyes wide and tilted my head a little to the side. "You know." God, I hoped he did.

"No, I don't."

Fucking man, er, wolf. "You know their…um, nightly and sometimes early morning activities…they get loud, and you won't let me have a door," I added accusingly. "So, they wake me up, and …." I had to look away because I was blushing so hard thinking about what I'd overheard the other night.

"I believe that you are a prude," he accused.

"I am not," I exclaimed. Too late, I realized he was teasing me and I'd totally fallen for it.

His laugh was deep, and I liked it. "Let me get this straight, Conal and Solle's sex life is too loud, and it's keeping you up?"

"Shhh, don't say it so loud," I cautioned him. I was still getting used to the Lycans' acute hearing.

He stopped laughing. "Or does it get you hot?"

"What? Noooo." Well, not all of the time. I couldn't take any more of this mortifying conversation. "Okay, you win. Just forget it." I stomped to the door and threw it open.

"Theo," his voice thundered.

I turned on my heel to face the man.

"I did not excuse you." There was censure in his tone.

Fuck. I made myself stand still waiting for his words.

"Have a good afternoon, Theodora."

"Thank you, Laird," I choked out. I stomped past Basil's desk, our appointment forgotten. Nor did I pause to see if Asher was at my back. Raider-fuckin'-Black frustrated the hell out of me. I made one, *one* simple request and he had to make it into a big deal. I had blushed like a teenager. Damnit, I wasn't a prude. I just wasn't used to others having relations so close. I mean, it was almost like I was right there.

"Where are we going next, Theodora Morrissey?" Asher's voice cut through my haze.

I hadn't been paying any attention, I was so mad. "I don't know. I just need to walk." I needed space and to get far away from that man.

"You are angry," he observed.

Great, now everybody would know. I stopped and turned around, taking in a few deep breaths. "At myself, Asher. Sometimes, I am an idiot." I shook my head. "Do you think we could grab my coat and maybe walk around outside for a minute? I need some fresh air."

"Of course." We turned to head back to my office.

TWELVE

RAIDER BLACK

I avoided that end of the hallway. I told myself it was because the Seer unsettled my wolf and that made it difficult for me to concentrate. I didn't need to check in with her. Everyone submitted reports. Plus, she was the topic of every casual conversation. I couldn't escape her. The woman was so…appealing, interesting, and sexy.

I pushed that thought away. No, she was frustrating. The way she'd curled into my body, resting her hand on my chest as she'd slept made me wonder, *what if?* How she stood up to me, just enough to push, but then backed off with that seeming innocence, widening her amazing eyes. She tied me up in knots. My wolf stirred every time she came near.

The time she'd invaded my office without an appointment was a perfect example. She could easily have asked Basil to make the purchase. Instead, she'd dropped by and forced me to pry the information out of her that she couldn't sleep because Conal and Solle were fucking too loudly. She'd looked so cute, blushing a bright pink. When I'd ascertained that the sounds turned her on, she'd stomped out of my space. Then I'd had to contend with my assistant, who'd grinned like a madman after he caught me watching her round ass in her tight skirt.

Basil stood at my doorway. "I ordered three different options, that way she can try them out and decide which works best."

"One would have done," I said, trying to cover my growl.

"True, but *I'm* not your average admin, and *she,* is not your average woman."

I responded by motioning for my non-average employee to close my door.

Today, she'd made another request. This time, she'd contacted Basil for an appointment. To throw off her game, I decided to pay a visit to her office. It was of medium size. She wasn't seated at her desk, or on the sofa against the wall, although her scent was strong, and my wolf knew that she was near.

Where could the human be? I stalked deeper into the room and followed my nose. I walked around her desk to the side that didn't face the door. She was sprawled on a bean bag chair with a book propped up on several throw pillows. She wore white gloves and a ridiculous mask over the bottom portion of her face. And she was singing a Rolling Stones classic.

"What the fuck?" I growled.

I watched as she slowly lifted her head from the book and craned her neck around the desk to look at me. "Oh." She closed the book and placed it gingerly on the floor, pushing up off of her belly to a sitting position.

"How long have you been there?" She was talking loudly because she still wore the blasted headphones.

I tapped my ear twice to signify she was still wearing her headset. She ripped them from her head and looked at them questioningly, as if she hadn't known they were there.

"Sorry," she mumbled as she rushed to show me her mark.

"Seer," I answered in greeting. "What is all this?' I pointed to her nest on the floor.

She looked at her space then back at me. "I was studying."

"Does the desk not suit or the sofa?"

She studied the desk and the seating area. "They're fine."

The stupid mask muffled her words. "Why are you wearing that?" I took one step closer and pulled the mask from her ears, dropping to her slender throat by the elastic band.

She started to jerk away from my touch, but I both saw and felt her fight off the instinct. "It's for the books," she explained as she pulled one glove and the other from her hands. "They are very old texts and I don't want to damage them."

"Damage them?" I hated that she made me repeat words.

"The oils from skin... Over time, they degrade the ink and the gold leaf. I gave Onyx some information about how to care for these books. I mean, they are treasures."

I didn't know quite what to say. She thought our books treasures?

She motioned toward the sofa and wingchair seating area. "Would you care to sit down?"

I took the chair as she chose the far corner of the sofa. I again looked from her desk to the doorway. "You prefer the floor to a cushioned chair?"

She didn't look at me as she answered. "Sometimes, I get tired of being on display."

"Theo, you make no sense."

She chewed on her lip for a moment. "People stand outside and watch me, or they slow down and glance inside. I tried smiling and inviting them in, or I even got up to go out to meet them, but by then my guard would send them on their way."

"The pack members, you mean?"

She rushed her words, "I don't blame them. I'm curious about them, too." She paused as if to see how I took that information. "It's just that I'm starting to appreciate how a tiger feels at the zoo." My confusion must have shown because she continued, "You know what a zoo is, right?"

"Of course, I know," I bit out, making sure my frustration showed on my face and in my tone.

"Hey, I didn't want to upset you. Don't you find the thought of an animal living in a cage distasteful?"

I shut my eyes briefly. "Just get to your point."

She stared pointedly. "I get tired of being stared at."

"So, you hide…"

"I guess so… It's different for me." She spoke slowly as if she was putting a lot of thought into her words.

I kept quiet. I wanted to see where she was going.

"I'm either the princess or the prey. Most of the time, I'm both." Her blue eyes had gone a shade darker with her strong emotion.

My wolf stirred, *"Protect her."* I considered what she'd shared. She was correct. "That leads me to your latest request."

She scooted forward on the sofa and grasped her hands together tightly. "I was thinking it would be a good way for me to meet the other pack members, since, they don't, er, *won't* come in to meet me."

I didn't respond. It was entertaining to watch her squirm.

"It would only be a few afternoons at Solle's office and I'd be at the receptionist's station. Just saying hello and making appointments..." She frowned. "I'd study in the evenings. I think Conal's going to set up a place in the basement. That way, I'd be helping Solle, and at night, they'd have some alone time."

"Has Conal or Solle said something to you?" Both had told me they enjoyed Theo, and that she was no bother.

"No. They're really nice. It's just, well, they should have some time without me hanging around." She shifted on the sofa again nervously.

I nodded.

"Your people—the Pack, I mean—they, uh, know about me, but they don't know how to approach me. If you want them to, that is..."

"Of course, they should meet you." I tilted my head so that it rested against the back of the chair. I hadn't considered how to introduce the Seer to the pack. There'd been so much going on. "Do you want to work at Solle's practice?"

"I do." She again bit down on her bottom lip.

"I'll make the call."

When she smiled, I felt lighter, as if a little bit of tension had left my body.

"Thank you."

I got to my feet. "You are welcome." I should ask Onyx if the texts said anything about Seers possessing witchcraft. This visit somehow made me feel better.

I called Solle later that afternoon. "So, you wish for our Seer to work for you?"

"She studies all the time. I didn't spend that much time with my books when I was in med school."

"You had your mate with you," I reminded her.

"That's true, but she's been a little lonely and I know she's tired of being stared at like a freak. Not to mention Onyx complaining that she hasn't done anything yet." Solle sounded irritated.

"What do you mean about Onyx?" Although Solle was not a member of my Board, I trusted her opinions.

"I shouldn't have said anything. Maybe he's acting on your orders…" She paused, and I imagined that she was considering if she should continue.

"Has he done something to upset the Seer?"

"Upset no…pressured….possibly." Solle sighed in my ear. "Look, I don't know how this 'Marked' thing works. But I think she's feeling like she's doing something wrong because she hasn't had a vision."

"There is no timeline," I answered off-handedly.

"You might want to remind your man of that," Solle said, her tone a little huffy.

"Is she distressed?" Suddenly, I cared.

"Look, she didn't say that. In fact, she's very careful about what she does say. She's never critical and is careful not to complain. I'm getting all of this from her questions to Conal."

"She confides in your mate?" I wondered how that affected their dynamic and why the thought made me feel a spark of anger.

"Don't go getting your undies in a knot. Conal and I are fine." She made a snorting sound in my ear. "Conal is good with her. Gentle, maybe a little coaxing at times, but she needs someone she can confide in. I think he's trying to be her champion."

"And it doesn't bother you that her champion is your mate?" Perhaps I should look for other housing. I wouldn't want to upset my friends.

"Not everything has to do with sex. He can spend time with her and not want to fuck her," she said primly. "I get upset and too protective, or so he tells me, so she probably doesn't share with me as much as she could."

"Is having her there, in your home, a problem?"

"No. I like her, Black. You should get to know her."

"I know enough."

"You know what your reports tell you. That isn't the same. She's funny and so beautiful, but she doesn't realize it. The other night, I commented that Wale was flirting with her, and she was shocked. I mean, she just doesn't have a clue."

"My guard was hitting on her?" I thundered.

"Oh, come on, you know the guy, he flirts as easily as he breathes. The point I was making is that Theodora was oblivious. She has no idea that men and some women are interested in her."

"What men and which women?" I growled as I started to pace.

Solle's laugh was low. "Did I touch a nerve?"

I sputtered, not liking where she was leading this talk.

"I don't want her to…" Hell, I didn't know what I wanted. Except her. A part of me wanted her.

Solle's laugh continued in my ear. "You'll figure it out. You're a smart guy."

For some reason, I thought that she meant exactly the opposite.

THIRTEEN

THEODORA MORRISSEY

I t had rained for the last three days. I was tired of the grayness, the chill in the air, and everybody's grumbly mood, mine included. I couldn't seem to concentrate. I felt jumpy, like I was over-caffeinated. Plus, I was tired of this damn boot. I wanted my ankle to be healed. Yesterday, I'd snapped at Onyx when he'd grown impatient with me.

"Just give me a damn minute." I threw myself back into my chair and closed my eyes. My head pounded and I needed a break. I knew which part of France the Duchene Pack ruled. I tried to picture the map in my aching head.

"We went over this last week," he said, his tone growing more impatient.

"I know this," I muttered. "The Pack was given a charter when a female from the Di Alberto Pack was contracted to the Duchene male."

"And..." he prompted unimpressed.

I opened my eyes and grimaced. My head hurt

worse. "And they went on to build one of the most powerful packs on that continent. A Duchene sits on the Council today."

"Correct," he said begrudgingly.

"I memorized all of those families," I frowned, "and I don't know why. It seems like unnecessary information."

"Are you questioning me?" He lifted his chin a tiny bit.

"Not you, just...just all of this." I pointed at the books spread across the top of my desk. "I don't understand how this is any help to me. Now."

"The Laird appointed me to be your tutor. Do you think I don't have other work to do? That I volunteered to teach you?" His eyes flashed angrily.

I dropped my gaze as I clamped my jaws together. Onyx had made it clear from the start that he wasn't impressed with me.

He stared at me. "No response?"

"I understand it must be taxing to have to deal with extra work." I fought to keep my voice respectful. "And just so you know, it's frustrating for me, too. The waiting for a vision or a feeling, or whatever is supposed to happen..." I ran my fingers through my newly styled hair. Basil had taken me a salon and I swear he'd supervised each snip of the scissors. My hair was now to my shoulders and I had a deep side part with sweeping bangs.

Damnit, I needed to focus. "I'm sorry, sir. I have a headache and I'm not myself today. Could you give me my assignment, so we can cut short my lesson?" I was tired of Onyx's constant scrutiny. I was tired of his never-ending fixation on my learning the founding families. I wanted something different.

He checked his diamond-encrusted watch. "We have two more hours."

I squeezed the bridge of my nose. "Look, I don't feel very well. In fact, I think I need to go home and go to bed." I closed my notebook and opened the drawer on my left.

"You do not decide when our lesson ends."

Something in the air changed. I felt it. The change made my senses come alive. "I can't concentrate, not today." I stood and started walking. I grabbed my jacket from the coat tree that stood in the corner by the door and I headed out, ignoring Onyx's expression, which was tightening with fury. I saw Asher standing in the hallway. "I need to go home."

"As you wish, Seer." He fell into step beside of me.

"Theodora." Onyx's raised voice was coming from somewhere behind me.

I didn't stop. I kept walking. I felt Asher's gaze on me. "Keep walking," I muttered.

"As you say, my lady."

"Ms. Morrissey!" This time Onyx didn't mask his discontent.

I stopped and abruptly turned around. My guard had to step to the side to avoid colliding with me. "We will resume tomorrow, Onyx." I used my most authoritative tone. I needed to lie down and close my eyes.

The dark-skinned man's eyes went big for a brief instant.

I didn't hang around to see what would happen next. I'd never before openly defied or questioned my tutor.

"Asher." I continued to the stairs, feeling like I'd won that round.

This day, I was again in my office, revisiting the first families. My head wasn't pounding, but I still felt antsy. I shifted in my chair for the fifth time in the last ten minutes.

"Moving to what is now known as Asia, name the packs." Onyx had started our session in a snippy mood and his disposition hadn't improved.

"I'm thirsty. Onyx, do you want something?" I stood to go to my small refrigerator. My throat was dry and, suddenly, I was burning up.

"You cannot avoid this work."

"I need a drink." I continued on my quest.

"You need to concentrate," he countered.

I stopped and snapped, "What I need is for you to get off of my ass." I think we were both surprised by my outburst. The next thing I knew I was flying through the air until my back collided with the wall.

Onyx's face was one inch from mine. "Do you really think, little girl, that I wouldn't hurt you," he spat. "The Laird would be angry, but it would almost be worth it."

I struggled against his hold. My feet barely touched the floor and his hand on my throat was almost crushing. Recklessly, I challenged him. "Do it." At that moment, I was tired of constantly having to learn, to be aware, and of being watched. Maybe it would be easier to end it all.

His laugh made my blood turn cold. "Perhaps, I would be doing us all a favor."

I kept my mouth shut. Instead, I struggled and kicked the man's shins.

"What the fuck are you doing?" Conal rushed into the office.

"She is insubordinate," Onyx explained but did not loosen his hold.

"*Onyx.*"

I felt the power before he'd completed the word. The Laird stalked into my office. His eyes were flashing and I swear he snapped his teeth at the tutor.

Onyx released me and my legs were so weak that I fell to the floor with a thud.

Conal was immediately by my side. "Are you injured?"

My hand went to my neck. "My-my throat," My voice came out in a whisper.

"Explain your actions," the Laird demanded.

His voice sounded inhuman. I turned my head to see what was happening. The Laird had Onyx pinned against the opposite wall with a fur-covered, clawed hand covering his heart.

For a moment, I was sure he was going to rip the organ from the man's chest. I spoke without thinking, *again*. "He's right, Laird. I-I wasn't paying attention."

The Packleader turned his head, focusing his eerie gray eyes upon me. "Is that true?"

Suddenly, I couldn't breathe. His anger suffocated me. I reached out to grab hold of Conal's arm, I felt like I was going to pass out. "Yes sir." Darkness was clouding my vision and my voice sounded weak.

"I need to get her to the clinic," Conal said.

I gave in and closed my eyes as I felt Conal slide his arm under my knees.

"I'LL BE FINE," I assured Solle for the tenth time. "You

two don't need to cancel your plans, to do what? Watch me sit on the couch?"

She rested her palm against the back of my neck. "You feel warm. I'll get the thermometer."

I grabbed her hand, halting her as she tried to climb off the sofa. I softened my voice. "Please. I want you and Conal to go out. I'll be fine. I promise." It was their anniversary. I didn't want them spending it sitting here with me.

She stopped pulling away and instead, snuggled closer to me. "You promise?"

"I want you two to go out and have a nice dinner," I said softly.

"You really are very sweet." She kissed my cheek.

"So, are we going?" Conal was making his way down the steps. He entered the living room.

"Whoa, Conal, you look nice," I said, and he did. He wore black jeans and a silky black button-down shirt with a leather jacket over it. Not his usual beat-up jacket. This one looked to be super soft.

"He does, doesn't he?" Solle was giving her mate a look that was hot and hungry.

"See? You've got to go. Your man cleaned up for you," I teased.

Solle got to her feet. She was clad in a form-fitting dress the color of her golden skin with glittery threads throughout. "She says that she'll call if she starts feeling bad."

I nodded and watched my friend head to the coat closet.

"Issa will see to you," Conal said.

"It'll be okay." I wasn't going to ruin their night.

"THIS IS VERY GOOD." Issa lifted her bowl of macaroni and cheese.

"It's extra cheesy," I said as I scooped another spoonful into my mouth. "That's my own special recipe."

"Before you came here, you cooked for yourself? Every night?"

The Lycan guard was fascinated by my life. "Well, not every night," I admitted. "Sometimes, I got home late and would have a bowl of cereal, but I like to cook."

She placed her empty bowl on the coffee table. "I don't know if the Laird would allow you to help in the cafeteria." She gave me a serious look. "For Articles, it's an honor to prepare the food for us."

"I don't want to step on anybody's toes," I rushed to tell her.

The pink-haired beauty looked at me questioningly.

"What I mean is, if that is an important job to the Pack and the members, I don't want to insert myself." Even those considered young at almost three hundred didn't understand my references.

"It is well-received that you help with the young." She gave me an approving nod.

"I don't do that much, unless you count holding the cranky toddlers." I smiled at the thought of my afternoon job helping out at Solle's office.

"You must do it well. The women were discussing you during the Zumba." Issa looked back over her shoulder toward the kitchen.

I motioned with my head. "There's more."

"You did not eat much." She took my still partially-full bowl, along with her empty one to the kitchen.

I wasn't very hungry. I felt a little unsettled. I

137

uncurled my leg and sat with both feet on the floor as Issa returned with a heaping full bowl. "It's Zumba, Issa, not 'the' Zumba."

"I don't care what it is called. I like it." She smiled.

"I can't believe your dancers had never heard of it." I shrugged.

Apparently, dancing was very important to their culture. Brian, who was a medical assistant at Solle's office, was the Pack's champion. We'd been in one of the aisles of the file room around quitting time, and I was feeling silly so after I shoved the folder into its proper spaces, I gripped his hands, put them on my hips, and started to Conga down the aisle. Even with the stupid boot on my foot, I did okay. I don't know who was more surprised—Brian, myself, or the rest of the staff. From that point on, Brian danced with me a little every time we worked. I mentioned that the others could join in, doing some of the steps I'd learned in a Zumba class and within moments, they were all looking up Zumba on the internet.

So, once a week, a group of us met at the community center downtown. The Lycan dancers had built on what they'd seen on the internet, and now, some of the steps were outrageously syncopated. Those sessions were two hours where I could laugh, chat, and forget that I was so different, when my ankle healed, I could join in.

"I am glad you are here, Theodora," my guard said.

"Thanks, Issa." I got to my feet. I moved to the front window and shifted the drape aside to gaze at the moon. Tonight, it was full. I sighed and dropped the curtain. I walked back to the table and picked up her bowl. "Want anything else to eat?"

"No, thank you." Issa followed me into the kitchen.

I rinsed the bowls and loaded them into the dishwasher. I wiped the counters and the sink.

"You should rest." Issa was studying me.

I washed and dried my hands. "I feel kind of twitchy, like I have extra energy."

"Should I call Solle?" She reached for her phone.

"No," I spoke loudly. "Please." I softened my tone. "I feel like going for a walk. Can we go out for a walk?" I spoke rapidly. I turned and headed to the steps that led to the finished basement. "Come on, Issa," I urged.

"I don't know." She followed me. "You are acting oddly."

I tried not to feel the wave of frustration that swept over me at having a babysitter. I headed to the floor-to-ceiling windows that overlooked the deck and pool. I leaned my forehead against the cool glass and stared outside at the velvety night. Tomorrow, I would have to clean the glass. I wanted to go out. It was like I was being pulled. Suddenly, I needed to feel the cool grass between my toes. I started to kick off my slippers.

"What are you doing?"

"I want to feel the earth," I think I said. I was too busy looking out the window. Spring was coming slowly this year. The grass had turned green, but the temperature was still in the low-fifties during the sunny days. "Come on. Let's go outside," I said, but I didn't make any move toward the handle. I knew she would make it there before I could open the door.

"You are acting strangely. I do not understand." Issa moved closer to me.

I looked at our reflections in the window. I was dressed in a white thermal shirt and yoga pants. She wore an aqua T-shirt over leggings that were in a pastel

139

tie-dye. We looked like an odd couple, but I liked my guard, and I trusted her...to an extent. "I need to get outside, Issa," I confided softly. Maybe this was how they felt when their wolf wanted to take over.

"It is dark. What can *you* do out there?"

"I don't know." I closed my eyes briefly as I tried to keep from bouncing on the balls of my feet. "I just need to." I said it with a little more push in my voice. I met her gaze and let her see the need.

"I will make a call." She pulled her phone from her pocket. "Do not move, Theodora," she cautioned.

I nodded once. I didn't want to make trouble. I just needed to go out.

She stepped away and spoke softly into her phone.

The decisions that governed my life were made by Black. Conal and Onyx had input, but his decisions were final.

"The Laird is coming," Issa said.

"Jesus." I sighed and tried to tamp down my nerves. That man, he...he affected me. When he was near, I sensed things, too many things. It made me uneasy and at the same time, a part of me liked the power I felt. "I hope that this didn't interrupt his evening." I dropped my gaze.

"He said, 'Should be interesting.'"

"Great." I did an internal eye roll. I was his entertainment. I moved to the wall outside of the basement bathroom, where a multitude of jackets hung. I selected a navy hoodie and pulled it on.

I returned to my place at the window. Now, I didn't feel as jumpy, as though my need understood that soon I'd be outside.

"The Laird is here."

I'd learned that Lycans could hear vehicles approach long before my ears picked up a sound. I pulled up the sleeve on the hoodie and my thermal to display my brand. Although I had seen the Laird earlier, since he was making time for this outing tonight, I would offer to show my brand again as a sign of gratitude.

His boots scraped on the stairs. *Only because he wants you to know he is here*, the thought entered my head. Which was true, even the huge males were exceedingly quiet. I was still getting used to turning and, suddenly, having one or more of the pack standing right beside me. I moved to the bottom of the stairs.

Black entered the open basement room. "Seer," he greeted evenly.

I rested my forearm in my other hand as I dropped my head far enough that my hair fell around my face. "You honor me, Laird."

"Your guard states that you wish to go out into the night." His eyes moved lower over my body, taking too much time, as if he was memorizing my curves.

I forced myself not to move. He owned me so he could inspect me. I pasted a neutral look on my face and ignored, or tried to overlook, the prickle of awareness I felt whenever he was near. It was like my gift recognized his strength, and it reacted. I felt like a Fourth of July sparkler that suddenly burned brighter. "Yes, very much." My voice sounded huskier. I cleared my throat. "I need to go out..." I looked toward the window and finished weakly, "there."

One side of his mouth tilted upward. "All right. I will escort you."

I turned around quickly because I wasn't sure I could hide my rolling eyes. *Everything was such a production with these wolves.* I headed to the door and unlocked it. The second I stepped through it, I felt freer. I took three, maybe five, steps onto the deck, and I paused.

"Where to Seer?" He stood so close I felt his breath shift my hair.

The weird thing was that his closeness didn't unnerve me. In fact, I wanted to relax and lean into him. I took a half-step away. "I'm not sure." I looked around. *God, I had no clue what to do.*

"Over here." Black moved to the picnic table and lifted the bench off of the top of the table where it rested during the winter.

I sat down and tried to find a position that didn't make me look uneasy, but I was. Issa wasn't with us. I didn't know if I should make conversation.

"Close your eyes and try to calm your nerves." This wasn't an order. It sounded more like an instruction that you would give a friend.

I didn't know if I could close my eyes when he was this near. Not that I would ever see him coming if he made an aggressive move, but my survival instinct was screaming. I took in several deep breaths and slowly let them out. My flight instinct calmed, and I pulled up my knees to my chest. I tried to feel the atmosphere around me. I pictured it in my head acting like sonar. I hoped something would bounce back. I started to my left and tried to use all of my senses, hoping that something would register.

Every time a doubt would enter my mind, I had to start over again. He didn't speak or even move, although I knew he studied me. I was working in the right quadrant when I felt something, like a pull deep in my gut. "There." I got to my feet.

Black was immediately beside me. "I'll follow you."

I moved swiftly to the three steps that led down to the side of the pool, but I didn't take the steps. Instead, I jumped, landing badly, and fell to my knees. Oh My God, it felt so good, touching the ground with my bare hands. I glanced up in amazement. "This is good." I could see clearly. The full moon was bright tonight. I started to giggle. I knew I must look like a fool. I got to my feet and wiped my hands on my thighs. "I think we should walk around a little."

He motioned with his hand for me to lead.

Now, I started to feel awkward. I mean, he was on alert; I could feel his energy. "It feels right, being out here," I began, reaching to find the right words.

"I do understand. If I was given the choice, I would always be outside."

That made sense. I turned my face to the silvery moon, and I couldn't breathe. I think I grabbed his arm in surprise. "I, I, ohhhh Goddd," I moaned. Pain shot through my body, I couldn't even be sure I made a sound as I held onto Black's arm.

The next thing I knew, I was on my hands and knees, shaking my head, trying to form a coherent thought. "Wha-what happened?" I looked up at the Laird who was on his feet.

His head swiveled, and his body tensed. "I don't know."

I knew he rarely uttered those words. Slowly, I got to my feet and looked around. We were in Conal and Solle's backyard, but it wasn't the same. I mean, the deck was there, the pool and the big trees along the rear boundary, but now... I had to blink several times to make sure my eyes were communicating properly with

143

my brain. The colors were different—more vibrant, and in some cases, outlined in neon. I shot Black a questioning look. "Did you give me some acid?" That was the only reasonable explanation I could come up with.

"I gave you nothing." His voice was growly. I could feel that his wolf was fighting for him to change.

I turned in a full circle, taking in the colors. It was beautiful and amazing. I laughed again and, suddenly, I wanted to explore. I wanted to get a better look at the trees. The bright blues, pinks, and greens were hypnotizing.

I knew it was the right thing to do, moving, exploring. I felt light-hearted and exhilarated. This must be what feeling "high" was all about. I started to skip ahead of my escort.

"Theo, don't go too far," he warned.

I turned around to face him as I continued to dance, taking backward steps. "It'll be fine."

"Theo." He reached to grab my arm.

I tried to elude his grasp, but he caught my wrist. *Party Pooper.* I wanted to run and laugh. I was finally having fun.

He pulled me into his big body.

I collided with his chest with an "Oomph."

"Don't run from me."

Jesus, I must be high, because super-imposed over Black's human face was a wolf's. I stared in awe. What was happening? I was too surprised to be afraid. This was beyond anything I could ever have imagined.

His lips crashed down on mine.

I started to struggle. I tasted blood from the impact. He must have wrapped his hand in my hair because I could feel the pull at the back of my head.

Using that hand, he turned my head a little, so that my nose wasn't being crushed and I could taste him. Cinnamon exploded on my tongue. I had to have more. I moved my hands to his thickly muscled shoulders and tried to pull him closer to me.

His tongue was in my mouth, exploring every inch. I opened my jaw wider, giving him greater access. His other hand was now on my breast, and I arched my back. I wanted him to touch me.

I needed to touch him. I wanted to feel his skin under my hands. I reached down and tried to push up his shirt up so that I could run my palms over his body. Christ, he was so warm and strong.

He lifted me off my feet and I wrapped my legs around his waist.

I made a satisfied sound deep in my throat as my pussy rested against his hard cock. I rubbed my core against him.

He went to his knees, still balancing me against him. Then I was on my back beneath him.

This was so good. I continued rubbing, kissing and touching. I felt the pressure build along my spine. For a nano-second, I paused as I tried to identify the feeling. I was going to come from kissing and dry-humping like a freaking teenager.

Black must have sensed my inattention because he gave my nipple a vicious twist, which should have hurt but, instead, made me hotter. I definitely wanted more of that.

When I exploded, he swallowed my cry of his name. I could give him no less. For this moment, this man, this wolf, he owned me.

Suddenly, everything changed. I was falling in slow

145

motion, like those times I'd seen a diver continue somersaulting under the water. I grew disoriented and was unable to stop.

Christ Almighty, the smell. It was like acid in my nasal passages, burning down the back of my throat. It was urine, decomposition, and a few other things I couldn't identify. My stomach roiled as I fought against gagging. I didn't move as I tried to figure out what had happened. One thing I knew instinctively; Black was no longer beside me. Then I heard the agonized screams. They were torn from deep in a body, as if the pain was so bad the person looked for any kind of relief and had to let some of it escape.

I opened my eyes. Wherever I was, it was dark. I blinked several times hoping this was some kind of dream, but the cold seeping into my bones told me I was awake. Casting out my senses, I tried to figure out where I was.

Suddenly the screaming stopped. Nothing...only an eerie silence. Every kidnapping movie I'd ever caught on a Sunday afternoon rushed into my head. Was I in some kind of box? I slowly stretched out my hands in front of me. I touched nothing. Cautiously, I stretched them over my head and, again, encountered nothing.

I sat up and hoped that would assist in helping me think more clearly. But it didn't. I was still frightened and confused. Deciding to move, I crawled five steps forward then ten back, and at last, encountered a stone wall. I followed it for what felt like miles. Of course, the distance couldn't have been that far, but the pitch black was disorienting.

I was tired and thirsty. I wondered what had become of Black. Panic rose up inside me. I didn't like being here and so alone. I pounded on the wall. "Hello?" The stone structure scraped the sides of my palms. "Is anybody there? Hello?"

I did this until my throat hurt and my hands stung. "Please, somebody?" I started to cry. "Why?" I screamed in frustration and fear as I fell to my knees.

"Did you not hear my call?" A disembodied voice thundered all around me.

"Wha…what?" The words came out as a sob.

"My call." This was not the coaxing tone she'd used before on the airstrip. Her voice, now, was full of disapproval.

I licked my dry lips and sank back on my heels. "I didn't know." I looked around helplessly. "I'm sorry."

Silence.

"It's all so new," I tried to explain. "I don't always know what I'm feeling."

Nothing.

"I beg your forgiveness."

A searing pain pierced my brain, feeling like an ice-cold burn. I screamed in agony and grabbed my skull. Why was this happening? I couldn't take the pain. My head felt ready to explode. I fell forward and hoped for relief, death.

FOURTEEN

NOVUS

RAIDER BLACK

I lay on my side in my wolf form with Theodora clutched against my chest. She was out, her breathing deep and slow. I tried to reason through what we'd experienced. When I'd first arrived at the house, I could feel her unease and her power. Our Seer was very strong. I needed to speak with Onyx about her training. I knew he'd been focusing on book work, but these recent events proved she didn't know how to control her power.

We'd traveled to the Goddess' plain. I'd felt the Lady's presence, but at the time, I was more focused on Theo and my need for her.

Someone approached from the house. I sniffed the air. Conal. When he neared, I snarled.

"Okay, okay." My second held up his hands. "Just wanted to check on you both." He headed back inside.

I called to my human form, changing, so that when Theo woke, I could speak more easily. She must have sensed my magic, because she repositioned her lush body against mine, making a purring noise deep in her throat.

Slowly, she opened her eyes. "Hmm, hey."

I wanted to chuckle. She was delectable, all warm and soft. I wouldn't forget the sound she'd made when she came from my kisses. "Theo." Her sweet taste was still on my tongue. I wondered if she tasted of oranges everywhere?

She blinked twice then her eyebrows drew together. "What was that?"

"We visited The Lady's plain."

She shifted away from my chest. "Just like that?"

"Yes." I didn't like that she moved away from me.

Her glance didn't meet mine. "You didn't drug me?"

"Why would you ask that?"

"The colors and... Well, the other...stuff," she finished weakly.

Our sexual attraction made her uncomfortable. She shifted farther away from my body. "You didn't enjoy the other...stuff?" I'd assumed she was a modern woman, one not embarrassed by her sexuality. After all, she'd been involved with a human male.

She sat up and turned her body from me. "I don't want to talk about that."

My wolf didn't like that she was reacting this way. She'd been a most willing participant. I could spend the next ten centuries listening to her come from my touch. "You were with me, and then you..." I struggled to find the words to describe how I knew that her spirit had left behind the shell of her body that I'd held protectively in my arms. "You left."

She dropped her gaze immediately as her forehead furrowed with thought. The speed of her breathing increased.

"Where did you go?"

Her gaze met mine briefly as her tongue darted out and moistened her lips.

She tried to inch further away from me, but I leaned closer. "Tell me," I kept my voice even. My senses were going into hyper-alert. I felt my wolf's growl deep in my gut.

She squeezed her eyes shut and tipped her chin skyward, which caused her head to fall back. "Can't," she gritted out the word.

"Theodora, tell me," I ordered.

I could smell her fear. Her breasts were heaving with each short breath and tears were leaking from her tightly closed eyes.

I leaned over her body, our faces now inches apart. I softened my tone, "Can you tell me why?"

She slowly opened her eyes and again moistened her lips. "It was so dark and c-c-cold."

"You need to tell me." Whatever she'd experienced had terrified her. I waited.

She swallowed so loudly I knew that it had to hurt her throat. "I need to sit up."

I gave her room, but she didn't move farther away. She pulled one knee to her chest, and the other curled around in front of her. She raised her hand to push back her hair from her face.

"What the fuck?" Her hand was swollen and covered in blood. I stilled its movement, taking it gently into mine. "Theo?"

She was staring at her hand in shock. Then she lifted the other, which was in the same state. Her voice was strangled when she spoke, "I was trapped." She looked at me again, helplessly. "Or at least, I think I was."

"Where?" However, the cramping in my stomach

had already begun.

She whispered, "Maybe a cell? There wasn't any light, and I only found one wall. But it was so cold."

I'd spent years in a cell, held captive by an enemy. It had been an impulsive decision to impersonate the prince, one that I'd spent six decades regretting. He was not strong and I was his protector. My grip on her tightened involuntarily, and she winced. Immediately, I loosened my hold.

"She was punishing me." Her body started to shake.

I needed to comfort her. Her pain... I could feel her pain. I pulled her onto my lap and wrapped my arms around her. "The Lady?" I said, hoping she'd say more.

Her bloody hands grabbed onto my shirt. "I was so alone and it was dddark."

I knew how that felt. I'd learned to push those agonizing memories away. Lycan's didn't like to feel trapped and, apparently, neither did our Seer. "Did she speak?"

She nodded. "She said I hadn't answered her call." She was breathing heavily.

"So she punished you?" Our Goddess wasn't always benevolent. Our recorded history had tales of her punishments.

Suddenly, Theo shifted and started frantically running her hands over my body. "Did she—did she hurt you?" Her blue eyes had gone wild.

I stilled her hands. "I'm fine," I assured her.

She relaxed back into my body. "I was so worried about you when...when you weren't with me."

I held her in my arms for some time. However, I was aware that neither Solle nor Conal, had gone to bed. "I need to get you inside and cleaned up."

She gave me the smallest nod.

I smoothly got to my feet and carried the woman to the house.

As we neared the door, Conal threw it open. "Is she okay?"

"She will be." I didn't want to hand her over. I carried her to the stairway. "She needs a shower and her hands attended to," I said to Solle who followed on my heels.

"I'll get my bag." She peeled off in the direction of her small office down the hall from the living room.

I walked through the doorway to Theodora's room. She'd added some personal touches to the guestroom. "Can you stand?"

"Yes," she sighed. Her breath warm against my neck.

I stopped just inside of the small bathroom and placed her on her feet. Once I was certain that she was stable, I let her go.

She immediately walked to the shower and turned on the water. She turned and motioned with her hands for me to move from the doorway. "I need to get undressed."

Her constant need to cover her body amused me. I moved back into her bedroom and stopped at the doorway to the hall. I couldn't stop thinking about a naked Theodora.

"What happened?" Solle approached with a concerned look on her face.

Conal was two steps behind his mate so I told them both, "The Lady called to her and she didn't respond quickly enough."

My Second muttered, "Jesus."

FIFTEEN

NOVUS

THEODORA MORRISSEY

The hot water felt good on my aching body. Traveling to another dimension, or whatever you call it, was hard on a girl. I held my battered hands in front of me. They were bruised, and the skin shredded. I closed my eyes and tried to figure out what to do with what I knew. Those screams of agony had belonged to Black. I didn't think that our leader would like me knowing about his weak and desperate state. This was very dangerous information.

What the hell had happened? We'd kissed, and I'd come. I rested my forehead against the smooth tile of the shower as I tried to remember the last time I'd felt that safe. In the Laird's arms, all of the worries and fears that had plagued me since I'd opened my eyes in the hospital were gone for those few precious moments. I dropped my head back to let the water caress my scalp. When was the last time I'd felt like that? Maybe when I'd first moved into the dorm at Ohio State to start classes?

I was so tired and it took too much energy to recall

what had happened earlier that summer. Over the years I'd tried, but my memory was hazy. I wasn't sure what was a dream and what was real. I'd been in the hospital with a concussion and when I was released, Grandma had decided I should apply for early admission to college. Looking back, it was like she'd wanted me to go away.

"Are you going to stay in there forever?" Black's voice interrupted my thoughts.

"I'm almost done." I guess it was time to get out and face him.

My hope that Solle would take over the treatment of my scrapes and bruises was dashed when, as soon as my nightie dropped over my head, the Laird once again entered my bathroom.

I tried to remember if I'd brought my robe in with me. I wanted another layer of clothes, more of a barrier, between us.

"Grab a seat." He grasped my hips and lifted me with no apparent effort onto the vanity.

I shifted back to make sure I didn't slip off the edge. "I could have done that myself." I wanted. No, I needed…to put distance between us. I was feeling vulnerable, and I didn't like that one bit.

He just gave me a steady look that said he knew exactly what was going on. He started digging in the various drawers, gathering gauze and other medicines. "Hand," he demanded.

I gave him my left one. He focused on cleaning the cuts. Then he wrapped that hand efficiently with gauze and looked at the other one.

You can do this. I sat still and tried to control my breathing, I didn't want him to know how much his closeness affected me. Like he couldn't tell? My nipples were hard and pushed against the low-cut neckline of my gown. When I couldn't handle the silence a second longer, I blurted, "You never really said what you experienced, you know, out there."

He ripped the small piece of tape and secured the end of the gauze around my wrist. He slowly raised his head, and his gray eyes met mine. "You remember."

Shit, damn, fuck. "I do?"

"Oh, yeah, babe, you know." He moved so now he was standing in front of me, and then he slowly folded up the skirt of my gown, exposing my calves, my raw knees, and my thighs. The entire time, he watched me.

I know he heard my breath catch as his warm hands rested on my thighs.

"Need to look at your knees." His voice was quiet. "I don't want you to get an infection."

I felt my body tense as his hand closed on my upper thigh.

"Open up, Theo."

I shivered because his voice caressed the nickname he used. The muscles in my thighs flexed under his palms. God, I needed to get hold of myself. What we did in that other place—that hadn't been real, I told myself. I opened my thighs a little.

He smirked at my reticence. "These are going to be stiff in the morning." He applied a salve to my knees with a surprisingly feather-light touch.

I snickered at his word choice and immediately tried to cut it off.

He shot me a confused look.

"Sorry." I cleared my throat, trying to compose myself. "I think I'm tired and overwhelmed." I didn't know how to act. We'd been intimate and yet he acted like nothing had happened. Not that I wanted him to. Nope.

"You're definitely something, but neither one of those words cover it." He looked pointedly at my hard nipples showing through my nightie and sniffed the air.

Fucking wolves and their hyper-senses. I felt a blush heat my cheeks and my chest. "Sure, whatever." I tried to roll my eyes and act like he didn't affect me.

That damn smirk reappeared telling me he wasn't buying my act.

Luckily, I had to cover my mouth as a yawn hit me.

"You need to go to bed." He helped me to my feet, not hugging me to his body or touching me longer than needed.

I wasn't disappointed. With feigned confidence, I walked to my bed. I ignored the feeling of him watching me as I pulled back the covers, plumped my pillows, and then climbed in, pretending I always got into bed in front of the sexiest man I'd ever met.

"Solle will want to check on you," he said as he moved to the door.

"Laird," I called, stopping him before he walked out of the room.

He paused and turned to face me.

"Thank you for going through that with me." I didn't want to think about it too hard, but I trusted him. How far, I didn't know, but the basic foundation was now laid.

"Of course, Seer. You are mine." He nodded once, solemnly, and left.

"All righty then," I mumbled. I guess that told me all I needed to know. He thought of me as his duty. I didn't have time to examine how I felt about that, because Solle started talking before she crossed the threshold into my room.

"He said you traveled to The Lady's plain." Her brown eyes were huge as she climbed onto the bed facing me.

"Yeah," I sighed and leaned back into my pillows.

"What was it like?" she whispered.

"It was crazy." I smiled recalling what I'd seen and experienced. "The colors were like a neon acid trip."

She rolled her expressive eyes. "Like you've dropped acid."

"I know that I'm not very adventurous," I said, frowning. I sounded a little defensive. So I cleared my throat and continued, "But this was incredibly different, I don't even have the words, Solle. It's like our world, but the colors are brighter, and I felt so free."

"I'm just glad you made it back okay." The doctor glanced at my bandaged hands.

I didn't want to tell her about the rest of what I'd experienced and what I'd seen. I knew Black wouldn't appreciate it. "I'm glad Black was there with me."

"Yeah, about that..." She straightened the light quilt across her lap. "I was a little surprised he took off."

I was too, but I banished that thought. "Well, it's late."

She made a noise in her throat. "I mean, the way he was holding you when he brought you in the house, I figured the two of you would be occupied."

I tilted my head a little as I tried to pretend I didn't understand her.

"Together." She smiled seductively. "You know, in bed, against the wall, in the shower."

"No. That's crazy." *Liar*, my conscience screamed.

"You're single and hot, so why not?" She laughed.

What to say? I mean, she and Conal had probably smelled my arousal, so I didn't want to lie outright. Fuckin' tricky wolves. "It's not like that between us."

The wordless look she gave me screamed that she thought I was pulling her leg.

"Stop giving me that look." I giggled guiltily and bit down on my lip. "Okay, he's the sexiest man I've ever seen, but," I threw up my hands helplessly, "I can't go there."

"God, I'm so glad to hear you say that."

I hadn't realized that she'd moved until she was hugging me.

I slowly pulled away. Lycans didn't mind a lot of physical contact, but Solle took it to an entirely different level. Maybe it was because we were both women, or because she was a doctor, but she touched me often. She walked into my room and bathroom no matter what I was doing. Her body against mine felt...nice. *Focus on her words.* "Why are you glad?" Suddenly, her words stung.

"No honey, I didn't mean it like that." She reached for me again. After another hug, she scooted us down so that we rested on the mattress, side by side. "Plenty have noticed you."

"Right," I murmured disbelievingly.

"What I meant was that, since he's promised to Siobhan Dolan, it wouldn't be fair."

"Fair to the female?"

"Not fair to you." She leaned up on her arm. "But since you're human, and they don't seem to be in any hurry to get together, maybe it would work." Her gaze traveled over my body.

"Solle…" I had to clear my throat before I could

continue. "I am barely holding it all together." I closed my eyes against the feeling that bloomed deep in my belly. Desire was a dangerous thing, and I didn't want any part of it.

"I understand. After seeing you two tonight, the chemistry... You know, he's a really good man." She smoothed back my hair and looped it behind my ear.

"He takes care of me. He's the Laird." I hoped she'd accept my answer. I closed my eyes. Suddenly, I was exhausted.

"Want me to stay with you until you fall asleep?"

How did she know I didn't want to be alone? "Could you?" I said in a little voice.

"Of course." She kissed my cheek. Well, really, it was the corner of my mouth.

I rolled onto my other side, and she curled up behind me. "Poor Conal," I sighed.

"He could join us," she whispered.

Surely, she was joking.

THE LAIRD MUST HAVE MADE another rule because it seemed like a Board member was always around. I tried to ignore their hovering. We were waiting for something to happen. I personally didn't want to miss another call from The Lady, so I was constantly looking for signs.

I circled my head, hoping to relieve some of the tenseness in my shoulders. The day was sunny and too pretty to be cooped up in my office. However, it was a huge pain to ask to go outside. My guard always wanted to know why, where were we going and for how long.

Today, Tex was typing a hundred miles an hour on his keyboard, probably hacking into some foreign government's computers. He alternated between his laptop and two tablets. It was amazing and unsettling to see such speed.

I glanced out the window longingly and let out a sigh.

"Let's go." He closed the lid to his laptop.

"What?" I said, trying to hide my excitement.

"Let's get out of here." His smile was full of mischief.

I put the bookmark into the book I'd been reading and placed it in its protective covering. After securing it in the cabinet that I used for storage, I turned so fast my maxi skirt swirled around my ankles. "I'm so ready."

"What do you want to do?" He had his tech stowed under his arm.

"Don't care. Just want some fresh air." I laughed as I followed him out of my office.

"Darlin', how about I give you a tour?" Tex drawled.

"Only if you crank your stereo." I knew he was into music.

"Goes without sayin'."

I followed him into his office. He stuffed his tech into a computer bag and threw that over his shoulder.

We took the stairs to the parking area. I'd learned that many Lycans didn't like being closed in, so they avoided the elevator. When I was feeling bitchy, I insisted on taking that method. Petty? Absolutely, but I chafed at being so powerless.

Asher sat at the guard's station.

Tex gave him a wave. "I'm taking the Seer out for a ride, and then I'll drop her at Conal's."

"Niiicce," Asher said, smiling.

I guessed he wanted to be out on the gorgeous spring day, too.

I followed Tex to his red pick-up. Internally, I laughed. Boys and their toys. It didn't matter if they grew up on a farm or the suburbs, they liked their trucks shiny, their gun racks filled, and their beer ice-cold. I felt like I knew this man although we'd rarely talked.

He did the gentlemanly thing and opened the door for me. I climbed in and made myself comfortable by rolling down the window as soon as he turned the key in the ignition.

"You gotta buckle up, Seer." He stared pointedly at the seatbelt.

I wrinkled my nose. "Did Solle make everybody promise?" The Lycans never used the safety feature.

"Yup." He laughed as I grumbled.

We headed out of town on the two-lane highway with Chris Stapleton singing about *Tennessee Whiskey*. The music changed to *Cowboy* by Kid Rock, and I curled my leg under me and sang along with the Michigander.

When the song ended, Tex turned down the volume. "Damn girl, you know every word." He gave me an approving look.

"I grew up in the Ohio Valley, that's the place for Rock 'n Roll, Country anthems, and every party always ends with *Freebird*." I rested my head against the seat, enjoying the feel of the sun on my skin.

"Lynard Skynyrd forever," he chuckled.

I nodded. "What's next on the playlist?"

We sang as he drove. He paused to point out land-marks and points of interest. The Pack considered the entire county theirs, but we'd driven east for over an hour, and we were still on Novus land. We'd just finished

163

.38 Specials' *Hold on Loosely* when I started to feel a little light-headed. "Is there anywhere close to get something to drink?"

Tex turned his head to give me a quick look. "In about fifteen minutes, there's a gas station."

"I think I might be a little dehydrated." I licked my dry lips.

"No problem." He gunned the engine.

A few minutes later, my head started to pound. I closed my eyes and considered asking Tex to slow the fuck down. The motion of the truck and the jackhammer attacking my head was making my stomach roil.

"Seer, you with me?" Tex's voice cut through my foggy brain.

"I need you to stop." I had to fight off a heave. "Now, Tex," I said as I covered my mouth.

He did, and I threw the door open, I was going to puke. He unclipped my seatbelt as I practically fell out of the truck. I think I took two staggering steps before I dropped to my knees. I couldn't see, and suddenly, I was falling.

SIXTEEN

RAIDER BLACK

Conal drove us to the remote spot at the far corner of our land. Theodora was sitting with her back propped against the wheel of Tex's truck and her knees drawn against her chest. I approached her cautiously. She clutched a bottle of an orange sports drink and had her eyes closed.

I squatted down beside her. "Nice day to be out," I murmured.

She opened her eyes and focused on me. "Yeah, I thought, 'What can I do to get everybody away from their desks?'"

I looked around, noting that Tex was talking to Conal about fifty yards away, and Glass paced nearby. "Looks like you did a good job."

She dropped her gaze to her hands clutching the plastic bottle. "I guess all of this is true. I'm what you said."

She sounded unnerved and resigned. My wolf

wanted me to comfort her, but I ignored his wish. "Tex said you were unconscious for thirty minutes."

She glanced in the large redhead's direction. "He was freaking out when I…could think again." She frowned. "I'm sorry. I didn't mean to cause so much trouble."

I sighed. "We just want you to be okay." I put my finger under her chin and applied just enough pressure so that she would once again meet my gaze. "Seizures are nothing to mess around with."

She nodded once while pulling what looked like one of Tex's flannel shirts tighter around her shoulders. "Now what?"

I didn't like Tex's scent on her, but I couldn't rip off the shirt. He'd reported that she'd repeatedly puked. "I'd like to take you back to Novus, so that you can tell us what you experienced. Then you can rest."

"I need to clean up," she mumbled weakly. However, she knew we'd be doing this my way.

I got to my feet, bent, and picked up the Seer, cradling her to my chest. "You can use my shower." I glanced in the others' direction. "Let's move."

Conal jogged to the driver's side of the SUV, and Glass opened the back passenger side door.

I climbed in, still holding her. She stiffened and started to slide from my lap to signal that I could let go of her, but I tightened my hold until she stilled.

Conal started the engine. "Tex and Glass will follow and update Onyx."

I made a noise of agreement.

Theo shivered, and I tucked her closer to my body. Within a few minutes, she dozed as the SUV covered the miles.

When we pulled into the drive to the Novus building, she stirred. "Don't carry me in."

I wanted to smile at her feisty spirit. "Why?"

"Because..." Her hand flexed against the skin over my heart. "I can't appear to be weak. If people are going to believe me...*in* me, I can't be weak."

The glimpses of her inner strength always surprised and pleased me. Theo was making every effort to adjust to this life.

SHE ENTERED the conference room wearing a pair of too-big sweatpants and one of my T-shirts. Her wet hair hung to her shoulders. I pulled out the chair to my left. She sat and immediately pulled her legs into her chest. The other Board members filed in and took their places.

I glanced across the table. "Tex, take us through what happened."

He nodded once and began. "We were out, getting air, listening to music, and she," he inclined his head across the table to Theo, "went quiet. A minute or two later, she asked if there was someplace nearby to stop, because she was thirsty."

Theodora gave a small nod.

"About three minutes later, she yelled for me to stop, jumped out as soon as I did, and started puking. When she was done, she passed out."

"And you did what?" Conal asked calmly.

Tex paused for a moment. "First, I made damn sure that she didn't fall into her own mess," he told Conal with an edge to his voice. "She wasn't relaxed like a person is when they pass out. She was stiff. So, I picked her up and started to carry her back to the

167

truck when she had a seizure, so I just sat down and held her."

Onyx raised one finger. "You say she was unconscious, but she was not pliant. Did she say anything?"

"She grunted a couple of times during each seizure," Tex said, his eyebrows lowering. "When they finally stopped, she didn't talk for a few minutes. She just stared up at the sky."

Theo slid her legs to the floor and leaned forward in her chair. "I was trying to figure out what happened." She looked at Tex. "I wasn't sure where I was, or who I was leaning against."

She glanced at me under her lashes.

"She can't scent," Conal reminded everyone as he looked at her. "Sometimes, I forget your senses aren't as strong as ours."

"So, Seer, what did you learn?" Onyx demanded.

I was displeased that he was taking over. I spoke before she could. "First, do you need more to drink?" She was still very pale, and her eyes looked two shades darker, but most importantly, I didn't like that her shoulders were hunched. She seemed rattled, and I didn't like that her vulnerable side was on display.

She glanced at me for a beat. "Thank you for asking, but I am fine." She clasped her hands together tightly on the table in front of her. "I started to feel a little 'off'. I was really warm, and my head felt…foggy. My stomach started to feel upset and we all know what that means." She flashed a half-hearted grin. "I sort of remember getting out of the truck, but I think that was more of a reflex than a conscious action." Her eyebrows drew together, and a crease formed between them. "I felt like I was falling."

"Well, Tex said that you did fall," Onyx used a superior tone.

"This was different," she said quickly. She glanced at me. "I can only compare it to when you jump from a height into water, after you hit the water, that feeling that you're never going to find the bottom."

Glass nodded her head. "I always feel a twinge of panic. My body worries that it won't stop plummeting, yet my brain knows there is a bottom."

Theo flashed the warrior a grateful smile. "I don't even know a word that can describe the feel of it, it's like the air is heavier, and I knew what I was seeing wasn't really happening, but yet, it's very, very real."

Onyx muttered, "Interesting," and began to write on his leather-bound notepad.

Her fists tightened. "Do you guys have anybody driving large equipment, like a combine or maybe a semi?" Her voice was very low, and her eyes were squinting as she stared down at her hands.

I leaned closer. "Why do you ask?" Her change of topic was jarring.

She turned to me again, and I saw the worry etched in the small lines at the corners of her eyes. "I was there. It was like I was viewing things from this…guy's point of view, or I think it was a guy? It was brief."

"Describe the setting," I coaxed. She seemed fragile, and I didn't want to start with a difficult demand.

She again looked straight ahead. "There was a big windshield, and the dash was long." She used her hands to measure a space wider than her shoulder's width. "And his hands were on the steering wheel. It was bigger than normal."

I sensed the others exchanging brief looks.

"Growing up, I rode in the combine with my uncles," she explained slowly as though reliving her experience.

She touched her brand and took in a quick breath. "He had a brand, like mine." Her fingers trailed over hers. "Oh, God, he was human." She started to take short, shallow breaths. "And they killed him."

"What?" I think we all said the word in unison.

She wiped her mouth with one hand and threw her body back into the chair. "He, I'm almost positive, he's a man. White, but his arms are maybe a little tan? His cuff is navy...ribbed like from a sweatshirt. I can see his brand. It's like mine." Her gaze once again met mine. "He's one of us." Her voice shook.

"Tex," I said softly.

"On it." Using his laptop, he'd issue the order for the managers of our current escorts to report in.

Glass moved her chair closer to Theo's and leaned closer to the human. "We need to know the rest, Seer," she murmured close to Theo's ear.

We watched as she took in a deep breath and moistened her lips. "His hands are on the wheel, and he says, 'Hey,' but it sounds like a greeting." She paused and took in two quick breaths. "He sounds surprised, 'What the...?' and I heard the shot. It was loud and then nothing." She looked around the table.

"What do you mean nothing?" Her tutor pressed.

She stared at him for another beat. "I mean, I saw nothing else. The next thing that happened was that I woke up. I knew that somebody was holding me, but I didn't know who it was." She glanced quickly at Tex.

He gave her a smile. "You're breaking my heart."

"Sorry." She gave him a cheeky smile and turned to

Glass. "I pretended to be out while I listened and tried to figure out what had happened."

"Good girl," Glass nodded approvingly. "That is what we discussed during your training."

"At least she listens to you," Onyx added coldly.

The Seer bristled at his comment, but said nothing.

"How do you feel now?" Conal asked as he watched her closely.

"Tired," she admitted. "My head hurts a little, and I feel like I could sleep for a week."

"You can," Conal assured her.

She shook her head. "I just witnessed somebody get killed. Somebody who belongs to Novus...an Article like me." She swallowed loudly. "I won't be able to stop thinking about that for a long time."

I swept a glance around the table. "Tex, as soon as you hear back, I want a full report. Glass, I want a list of everyone that is away from pack lands. Onyx, list every job we're currently contracted for, and Conal—in my office." I stood and glanced down at the Seer. "Theo, I want you to rest."

HOURS LATER, Basil knocked on my door.

"Enter."

"You know, bad news will find you in your bed as easily as it will here," the cheeky wolf said.

"Your point?" I gave him a steely look.

"The word's gone out for everyone to be on high alert. You can't do any more tonight."

"You're free to go, Basil." I glanced at the clock on my computer. It was almost midnight.

"The Seer is still in her office," he said with a pointed look.

I'd figured she'd left hours ago. I got to my feet. "I'll excuse her for the night." Passing my smiling assistant, I walked briskly to her office.

She had on only one lamp and the room was mostly dark. She sat on the sofa, a blanket wrapped around her and her knees drawn to her chest.

I stopped in front of her. "I thought you'd be gone."

"I wish I could tell you more." She dropped her head back against the sofa. "I keep trying to see if there is anything that I missed. Some clue…but I can't."

"You're learning," I said, trying to reassure her.

"I should have looked around, done something more. I knew——" Her voice broke. When she continued it was in a low ragged tone. "I knew it was a vision. I should have done more." She opened her eyes and looked at me.

I took a seat at the other end of her sofa. "Next time, you will."

She gave me a small frown. "Are you trying to cheer me up?"

I shook my head. "No. I'm not that person. That's Conal's job. If your gift will allow you to glean more information, I'm sure that you will."

She gave me a skeptical look, and I think she was ready to argue.

Conal entered the office. "We have three that are unaccounted for." He sat on the chair to Theo's right.

"Three?" she whispered.

I didn't like to hear that any transporters were in the wind, but I didn't keep a tight tether on my people unless they were working on a run. I glanced at the Seer. "Theo, do you know what Novus does?"

She shot me a puzzled glance at the change of topic.

Conal also gave me a sharp look.

"I mean the business that we claim. How we make our money, or a portion of our money?" I'd decided to share more of the Pack's business. Maybe it would help during her next vision.

"Something about security," she answered carefully. At times, her caution rankled. I understood that she knew more than she said. I would also bet that she had more skills than she or Onyx had listed. A part of me understood her restraint, but as the Laird, her secrecy irritated.

"That's right," Conal answered quickly. He obviously didn't want me to tell her more.

I ignored him. "We offer several services in that field. The most lucrative is that we provide escort to and from the west coast."

I could almost hear her thinking, as her gaze sharpened. "What does that mean?"

With a grimace, Conal took over. "When a shipment comes into our area, we travel with it to make sure it safely reaches its destination."

She blinked several times as she reviewed his answer. "But there's more."

I silently applauded that she questioned his simple explanation.

She narrowed her eyes and looked at me. "There has to be more. You said it was lucrative."

Conal's expression grew set. "We get the job done. That's why we get paid."

She stared at him for a long moment then her blue gaze returned to me. "I'm sure that Novus gives fantastic service." She couldn't hide the sarcasm. "If you want me to guess what all that entails, we could be here a long time."

"Why Seer, you make us sound dirty."

I think she mumbled, "Tricky wolves," under her breath. She let out a deep sigh. "I got dropped on you all by a guy who's crooked as hell, so I'm guessing your clients aren't entirely above board."

"We provide a needed service, I said, holding her gaze. "People are willing to pay for that service. That money supports the Pack."

"And me." She rolled her eyes. "Yeah, I get it. In for a penny, in for a pound." She tilted her head slightly to the right as she stared, daring me to tell her more.

My wolf gave his full attention. He never liked being confronted, but this time, he was amused.

"We don't care what is being transported. We simply get it to the destination," Conal explained succinctly.

She blinked twice. "So, it could be guns or drugs," she mused. Her eyes went so big I could clearly see their whites. "Or people." She jumped to her feet. "You traffic humans!"

I, too, was now standing, and so was Conal. The atmosphere in the room was tense. "I protect those who are mine, but I care little for others."

She stared at me in shock, opening and closing her mouth a few times. "So, you prey upon the weak and helpless."

Her accusatory tone caused my back to stiffen. *How dare she judge us?* "We are Lycan. All humans are weak compared to us," I finished with a snarl.

I watched the Seer bite her lip so hard I was sure that I'd smell the copper scent of her blood at any moment. She clamped her jaw closed so that she wouldn't respond. However, her eyes told me plenty.

"You cannot hold us to your human world rules, Theodora," Conal said quietly.

She whirled to face him so quickly her hair fanned out behind her. She gathered herself and straightened her shoulders. "I...I forgot." She turned to me and dropped her chin. "I apologize Laird for my impertinence. I spoke without consideration."

Her formal words stroked my ego, but my wolf knew she didn't mean them. "You're tired. I can feel your exhaustion. Conal, why don't you take her home?" I said the words slowly, needing to keep my own anger in check, but also to let her know I wasn't going to pursue a punishment for her disrespect.

She still looked at the ground. "Thank you, Laird. I would like to go home."

By the heightened color in her cheeks, she was furious, and...I checked the air, disappointed. My anger flared hotter. She needed to learn there was nothing I wasn't willing to sacrifice for the Pack.

"Grab your stuff, babe, and meet me in my office." Conal nodded once in my direction and left us.

She moved very slowly as she folded the blanket she'd been using, as if she sensed that my wolf was awake and closely watching her. Then she backed up two steps as though she didn't trust me enough to turn her back.

"Really?" I lifted one eyebrow mocking her caution.

She let out a loud breath and gave me a shrug. "Well,

when you get all Big Bad Boss, with your wolf waiting to pounce, it's intimidating."

It wasn't until she was in Conal's office that I realized she'd confirmed she knew that my wolf was awake and ready.

SEVENTEEN

NOVUS

THEODORA MORRISSEY

I'd said too much, and, of course, Black hadn't missed a word. So now, he was around all the time. Of course, he wouldn't come out and ask what I'd meant by my comment about his wolf waiting to pounce. *No.* He instead announced that he would supplement my studies. Solle had totally played into his hand by inviting him to join us for dinner, and since I already studied several hours every night, he could work with me then.

Thanks, buddy. She was only trying to help. I did hang out in the basement, so the couple could have some time alone. While they were upstairs, I had the entire three-room basement to myself, and I enjoyed the space. That was until the Lycan lugged a huge desk chair down the stairs and put it right beside mine.

After that, for four nights a week, I tried not to notice how close he sat, how good he looked with stubble on his jaw, and how his cinnamon scent made me want to trace his jawline with my tongue.

I tapped my heels to the floor several times in frustration.

"You're not concentrating tonight," he said, his tone dry.

"Sorry." I shifted a little farther away from him. I don't know what was worse—when he got bossy or when he showed concern. One was exhilarating in a way that both frightened and invigorated me, and the other made me want to rest against his warm, strong body. Both of those things were very bad. "Today was tough."

He leaned back and crossed his ankles, looking relaxed and way too comfortable. I knew he was not only listening to my words, but he was also using his senses to read me. "What happened?"

Why not give him a taste of what it's like to be me? I turned in my chair so I faced him and pulled one knee to my chest. "There's so much I don't know," I started lamely. "I mean, I guess I could live two lifetimes and not figure it all out, right?"

"Did someone upset you? Say something that offended you?" He tilted his head slightly, which I admit was very wolf-like, while never breaking eye contact.

"No. Everybody at Solle's office is nice." I didn't want anyone be on the receiving end of one of his glares. "Today, a mother was talking to me and I could tell she needed...comfort. I didn't know what she was talking about, so I...I didn't know what to say. I couldn't help her."

"They should not ask for more than you are willing to give," he stated in his kingly way.

"Really?" I gave him a long look, wishing I could raise one eyebrow. "I wanted to help. I could tell she needed it from me, the Seer."

178

I felt it, his wolf was with us. Black's other half was always easy to sense. After we'd gone to that other dimension, I could feel the others as well without trying.

I hadn't heard of any other Seer having this ability. I wasn't sure how it would be received, especially by the man beside of me.

"What did she want, Theo?"

Uh oh. He only used the nickname when things were intense between us. Others had heard him use it, but nobody else had picked up on the shortening of my name. It was like he owned that right. "She's worried about her son. He's around sixteen, and he might be ready to change."

"What do you know of that?" His eyes had turned sharp.

"Only what I've overheard," I said quickly. There were certain rites that my gut told me not to ask about.

"We'll need to have that lesson soon."

Okay, wow. I nodded once. I didn't want to show him how that surprised me. Onyx never wanted to share information about Lycan secret ceremonies. I'd argued that withholding knowledge hindered my lessons. "She's worried that her son won't make it. I guess he's had some health problems."

"Caroline Yu spoke to you?"

Although it shocked me that he'd guessed the identity of the woman, I didn't fidget.

"Can you help her son?" he asked casually.

I felt my eyes widen. "Why would you think that?" I stalled. I needed to be very smart with my responses. I wasn't sure I could outthink the man.

He flashed a disarming smile, which caused my

179

internal warning system to blare an alarm. "Theo," he murmured, his voice going low and rumbly.

I was in trouble here. I tried to look innocent as I waited for him to continue.

"You can give me that innocent look all night long, but we both know you can do more with your gift."

Jesus, did the Laird know everything? I tried not to flinch or even blink. When I was sure I could speak, I tried to laugh it off. I dropped my voice. "What kind of things?" Two could play this game.

He chuckled once then cut it off and gave me a look so serious I swear my heart skipped a beat or two. "You can do some kind of communicating with our wolves."

There was no way I could escape him if he jumped on me. Who was I kidding? I couldn't fight him at all. *Stall,* my brain screamed. "Sometimes, I guess right, that's all."

"Liar," his wolf said in his growly way.

I flinched as the black wolf's head superimposed over Black's human skull.

"Theo," he sighed. "Is it everybody's or just mine?"

He didn't seem angry, more like...intrigued. I relaxed a little. "At first, it was only you," I said as I considered whether he'd notice if I inched my chair away from his. *He would.* "So much has been going on that I didn't really figure out that it was happening." I again paused to check his reaction. *No change.* "After we visited that plain, I could feel more, and it was...easier." I nervously licked my lips as I waited for his reaction.

He sighed. "Theo, I'll make you a promise. If the time ever comes that I need to kill you, I'll tell you. I'll give you the chance to fight."

I rolled my eyes in his direction. "I think that would

be more comforting if I actually stood a chance against you."

That was definitely the wrong thing to say. I felt the air in the room change. "Someday, you might, Seer."

I forgot to breathe. If that day ever came, he'd surely kill me.

"Does anyone else know about this skill?" he asked calmly. "Solle, perhaps?"

"I've told no one."

"For now, let's keep this between us." Because he made it sound like a suggestion, I knew how dangerous this revelation was.

I quickly nodded.

He continued smoothly, "But I am curious. Perhaps we should try a few experiments?"

Careful. "I guess." I tried to appear uninterested.

He did that damn eyebrow thing, and I had to admit it looked good on him.

"Whatever you wish," I said, quickly correcting my reaction.

"Thank you, Seer." He nodded his head, but we both knew he'd won this round. He now knew my secret, and I again was reminded that my life was in his hands.

The next night, Black convinced Conal and Solle to go out to dinner. Not that they didn't deserve a night out, alone. But it left the two of us alone in the house. I was uneasy. I knew he had something planned.

"If you're not going to finish your dinner, then let's proceed." He set aside my plate where I'd been playing with my food. "I have something I'd like to try."

Stalling, I carried my plate to the kitchen and returned. I wiped my sweaty palms on my thighs. "So, what do you want me to do?"

"Talk to my wolf."

I wanted to chuckle. "Like it's that easy?" It wasn't a process I followed. It was natural, like breathing.

His look said it all. Somewhere, the Laird had learned he could say more with a look than with words. He ordered me to try.

He took a seat on the sofa and patted the cushion next to him.

I sat stiffly. Suddenly, the room became smaller. I could feel his wolf watching me. I glanced at Black's face to see if he was still in human form. "Are you doing something?" I asked, my voice sounding rough.

"No." His gaze was locked on my face.

I licked my dry lips. "I can feel him. He's watching me…waiting."

"Continue." His voice went low as his eyes narrowed.

I felt a little silly, but I tried to push that to the side. "Wolf? Would you speak with me?" I wasn't sure how to address his other half. I stifled a nervous giggle.

"Human." The deep, rough voice sounded clearly.

My intake of breath was loud in the very quiet room. I glanced at the Laird in alarm.

He continued to watch me, but now I could see his wolf. It was like a filmy overlay encompassing his body.

"Uhm, hello." Questions flooded my head, and I didn't know where to start.

Again, I felt him waiting and watching, but now he was amused at my unease.

I realized I was staring at Black's abs. It always seemed that was the resting place of the animal half. I glanced at their faces. "I don't know what to talk about," I said, feeling stupid.

"Touch me," the wolf's voice urged.

"Wh-what?" But I was already raising my hand. I stopped the movement.

"Female," the wolf again commanded.

I climbed onto my knees and gripped the back of the sofa with one hand for balance as I reached out to touch his stomach.

This time, there was no sensation of falling. Instantly, I was a part of him, and we were running, covering ground efficiently and quickly. I didn't hear the command, but I knew he wanted me to relax. He knew I was with him.

I didn't feel safe, but somehow I knew he didn't want to do harm to me. I tried to relax. I first concentrated on the feel of his body as he ran, the strength of his forelegs stretching out and his strong haunches propelling us forward. And the smells, the mixture of dirt, and something that registered as night, which didn't make any sense, but somehow it did.

DURING OUR EVENING SESSIONS, we worked on developing that skill. Black called our different guards into the room, and I could now "read" whether their wolves were awake or at rest. Also, I could sense their strength, age, and temperament. However, I was never allowed to touch another during these trials, and I only tested this skill with Black present.

Surprisingly, the Laird was a really good teacher. He was patient and focused on my questions and areas of interest. We worked around my inability, at times, to clearly describe what I was experiencing. Where Onyx would've criticized me, Black would listen and allow me to muddle along. We had some kind of a connection and at times, I think that helped him to understand me. I was too cautious to claim that I could do the same with him.

Tonight, he was leaning back in what was now "his" chair with his boots resting on top of my coffee table, and I was taking notes on my ever-present yellow legal pad.

"So, there's a season for when the teens get changed into wolves?" I'd never had the nerve to admit I still found myself relying on what I'd read in paranormal fiction when it came to parts of their lore.

"Spring is the time for rebirth, so it's usually around mid-May."

"So, is it a ceremony, or do they just do it?" I knew from listening closely to Solle's stories that there was a difference between those born Lycan and a human who is changed.

"I suppose this will make sense to you." He gave me that slow perusal that at times infuriated me and other times made my nipples harden. "I can feel their need to change as the time approaches. I wonder if you'll be able to as well."

I dropped my pen and gave him a questioning look. "I thought that a newly changed wolf was super danger-ous. You used the word 'unpredictable.'" The idea of a teenager experiencing all of that power and strength terrified me.

"That is why the newly changed are kept at the Camp."

That was an innocent name for an area at the far northwest corner of the Pack's lands. It was on hundreds of acres and cordoned off with triple fences and surveilled by cameras and alarms. Asher had shared the most info about the place. He'd started out guarding the newest wolves.

"We are kept safe by having them confined to the Camp."

I knew he was plotting something. The Laird had plans. He was constantly weighing the pros and cons. "What happens if they can't learn to control their wolves?" I asked softly.

"I terminate them."

I'd already known the answer. I sometimes tested him, to see if he would tell me the truth. I guess that I secretly wanted to trust him. Not that Conal or Solle lied to me, but, at times, they would soften the realities. Raider Black softened nothing, even though it freaked me out, I liked knowing the entire truth.

I wondered what that was like, having so much responsibility to your people and to the world. Not that I doubted he had a problem killing. From spending time with his wolf, I'd learned that he was decisive and thorough. I didn't know how much of that was the man or his counterpart, but once he had made up his mind, nothing would stop him.

"Does that upset you? Trouble your human sensibilities?"

The needling way he asked and his steady gaze made me wonder if he wanted me to object.

I chose my words carefully. "The death of a child upsets me, certainly." I tucked a strand of hair behind my ear as I tried to frame my next thought. "But, now that I've experienced just a sliver of the power a wolf has...I don't want that running around unchecked."

"Your guards will always keep you safe."

"I'm not thinking about myself, Black. I'm thinking

of anyone in the wolf's path…and ultimately, you." My words trailed off as I looked away quickly.

He grew still. "Do you think I'm too weak to do my duty?"

Careful. "Don't twist my words," I fired back. I hated it when he pulled rank during a discussion, especially when we were talking on a deeper level.

"Do not underestimate me, human." His gray eyes were angry, and his body tense.

My heart rate increased, and adrenaline started pumping through my veins. I took in a breath and slowly let it out. "I never underestimate your kind, Laird." I said through gritted teeth as I tried to calm my urge to flee. "I can't forget that I am and will always be physically weaker." I shifted so I could place one foot on the ground, if only so that I could tap my heel a few times. "I only meant that doing that duty, no matter how necessary, must be difficult."

"Many things are…difficult." He said the word like he was uncomfortable with it.

Yeah, good talk. I tried not to fidget. I knew that master negotiators used the tactic of the watchful stare and silence. Well, this Lycan had it down to an art.

He turned his head toward the stairs. A moment later I heard Conal's boots.

Conal stopped at the bottom step and his gaze locked with Black's. "They brought him in."

Black nodded and got to his feet.

I continued to stay still. I wasn't sure what the announcement meant, but it was important.

He glanced down at me. "You, too."

I had no choice but to stand and follow him to the steps.

Conal gave Black a questioning look.

"She'll be helpful," the Laird said.

His tone made my blood run cold.

I slowly climbed the stairs as I tried to figure out what I was facing.

Solle stood beside the front door. She kissed her husband on the lips then turned to Black, who bent so that she could kiss his cheek. She pointed at me. "Her?" She took my hand. Solle was a nurturer, and her wolf was a protector. She placed her body squarely between the men and me.

"Mate," Conal warned.

I spoke next. My friend was doing what was natural to her. She was worried about me. "It's okay." I attempted a smile. "I think I can help." Why else would the Laird order me to come along?

"The Seer speaks the truth," Black stated as Conal took a step toward his mate.

"I'll let you know when I get back," I promised, although she would hear me. Assuring her was a very human thing to do.

She pulled me into her arms, squeezing me tight. "May The Lady keep you safe."

Only then did she allow me to ease out of her hold. I gave her what I hoped was a confident smile, and I followed the men outside.

Once we were on our way, with Conal driving, I pondered why Solle had used the very formal farewell. The men were unnaturally quiet. I couldn't take it any longer. "Did something bad happen?" I knew the answer, but I hoped that someone would explain.

Conal glanced back at me in the rearview mirror. "Aye. Your vision came true."

I closed my eyes as a wave of sadness rushed through me. "But I thought that you warned everybody," I cried.

"Time passed, and one of our men let down his guard," Conal explained.

I'd failed. I hadn't kept him safe. After so long when nothing had happened, I'd started to hope that what I'd seen was wrong. Onyx had ridiculed me as if he was disappointed that nobody had died. "I'm so sorry."

Instead of heading to the top floor of their head-quarters, Raider led us to the basement. Conal had taken hold of my elbow during this walk. My inner alarm system was going nuts. I relied on Conal. He was protective, yet he also understood that I needed to learn. Right now, his wolf was snarling.

We walked down a long hallway, the men's boots slapping loudly on the tile floor. Compared to the rest of the building, this hallway was stark and utilitarian. The doors were heavy and each had a keypad. It reminded me of a research lab I'd seen on TV, or worse, a high-security prison.

We stopped outside a door. Conal punched in a code, and it opened automatically. I made myself follow the men inside. The room was entirely white, floor and walls. The combination of the bright white and the over-head lights made me squint.

There was a huge chair at the far end of the room. A man was sitting in it. Well, to be honest, he was chained to it. Glass stood beside him, glowering.

She greeted us with one word, "Laird."

I had stopped three steps into the room. Now, I backed up until I rested against the wall. I honestly didn't want to venture any closer.

Conal turned his head as if he was searching for me.

Once he found me, he gave me a nod as if telling me to stay put.

The door clicked and then opened again. A Lycan I didn't recognize entered carrying a tablet. He walked to Black and handed it over. He moved a few steps away and stood at attention.

I watched Black's fingers scroll through the information on the device. When he was finished, he handed it to Conal and approached the prisoner.

"You know who I am." It wasn't a question.

The prisoner stared at Black saying nothing.

"You killed one of my people."

I heard the growl of outrage in his voice.

"A human," the man spat.

"My human."

"He's registered to the Arrevos," Conal said.

I recognized the name of a pack from...was it Arizona or New Mexico?

"Domenico Arrevos ordered the hit?"

Black made it sound like a casual question, but I felt his wolf growl in anger.

Glass slammed her forearm into the back of the man's head, causing his chin to bounce off his collarbone. "Answer the Laird."

The only response was the prisoner spitting on the floor beside Black's foot.

I cringed. I figured that spitting was an insult to any race.

"It's all right, wolf." Black's tone was ice cold. "I don't need your voice to get my answers."

Oh shit, he means me. I slowly pushed off the wall. Basil had explained that Lycans enjoyed pageantry. The Novus Pack might use the newest tech, but deep down they loved the old ways, which meant that this demanded an entrance. I walked to Conal's side and waited for Black's instruction.

"A human? What's she going to do?" the prisoner sneered.

"Give us the truth." Black gave the prisoner a dismissive look.

God, or should I pray, Lady? I hoped I could do this.

"Seer." Black held out his hand.

I looked at it and then studied his face. I needed to see...what? But I couldn't move until I studied his eyes.

In them, I saw anger, violence, and confidence. I hoped that last was for me, for my skill. I took the first step and the second and grasped his hand.

"Make him talk," Black ordered.

My hand was held firmly in his, and through that connection, I felt his wolf pacing and snarling. I knew I needed to touch the stranger, but I paused and looked pointedly at the thick chains that were wrapped around his arms, his legs, and his middle. I glanced back at the Laird.

"Do it." With those words, he made the decree, but there was also an assurance that he would keep me safe.

I moved closer to the chair, using my senses to find a place to touch his skin.

The prisoner snarled at me and showed his teeth.

I knew this was an insult when a Lycan was in human form. I ignored him as the pulse in the air became more noticeable to me. I wasn't in a trance. I knew the others watched me closely, but they stood on the periphery. Now, I could hear the hum of his spirit, his wolf's. I took another step closer and held my hand out, hovering over his shoulder.

There... It was like the puppet popped from the Jack-in-the-box. I knew the best point of connection. I used two fingers to touch the side of his neck, low, almost to his chest. I think my body jerked at his wolf's first attack.

He was jumping at me, but Black was there, giving me strength.

"Settle," he ordered.

I didn't know if it was through our connection or out loud.

The wolf made a few more half-hearted attempts, but he did soon settle.

"Ask," Black told me.

"Your name, wolf?" Amazingly, I wasn't scared. Instead, I sounded confident.

He fought the command.

I drew a deep breath. "I am Theodora, Seer to the Novus Pack. Raider Black uses me, as is his right. *Your name!*"

"Mateo." He shook his head several times. "Mateo Plante."

"Mateo Plante, you are a member of the Arrevos?"

"I was."

"And now, who holds your loyalty?" I don't know how I knew to ask these questions, but they rolled easily from my tongue.

"Fffuuck you," he snarled.

"Wrong answer," Black bit out.

I tried again. "Who is now your leader?"

He shook his head from side to side, putting my wrist too close to his mouth.

"Glass," Black commanded.

She moved behind the man and gripped a handful of hair to hold his head still.

"Your answer," Black demanded.

The man tried to shake his head again.

Glass used her other hand to grasp the side of his face. She dug her index finger into the side of his eye socket with so much force that his eyeball popped free.

I screamed. Being this close to that level of brutality was a shock.

"Drop your hold, Theodora." Black's voice cut through my panic.

"Wha...?" I turned my attention to him.

"Drop your hand, Seer." Although he softened his tone, I could feel the strength of his command.

I did as he said, and he let go of my hand. Surprisingly, I was still able to feel the connections to their wolves.

His hand on my shoulder guided me to stand back, and he took over my position next to the chair. "Now, Mateo, I'd like to know what happened."

"No," the man cried.

"No problem, boy. You see, I don't need your voice to hear your words." Black used his supernatural speed. One moment he was standing by the chair, and the next, one hand was forcing the prisoner's mouth open. He jerked the man's tongue out of his mouth and dropped it onto the floor.

Blood sprayed through the air, coating the man, the floor, and me. I cringed at the viciousness.

"Seer," Black growled.

Rallying, I commanded, "Show me what happened."

It started out in slow motion, but as I got used to the feeling, things sped up. Raider asked questions, and the prisoner answered through our connection. I saw it all, felt the excitement of the hunt for the human, and, finally, the satisfaction Mateo felt after taking a life.

I was crying. I could feel the tears streaming down my face, but I continued to hold the connection. I would do this for as long as Black needed. It wasn't only my job, but I owed it to the one who'd lost his life. I heard Black's wolf decree, "Retribution."

Yes. I felt that desire heat the blood in my veins.

Holding the connection was becoming more difficult. I was tiring. *Have to concentrate.*

Black stood in front of me, yelling into my face. "Theodora, stop. I order you to break the connection."

I did and, again, backed up to my place against the wall. I wanted to leave, but I didn't know how to open the door. So instead, I pressed my back against the cinder block wall and slid to the floor.

Glass began to unhook the prisoner's chain, and Conal joined her. Although it appeared like they were freeing the Lycan, I knew that wasn't true. They lifted him to his feet.

Black stood in front of him: "Fight me for your life, Mateo Plante," he sneered.

The prisoner was gathering his energy, or perhaps he was considering the best method for attack, when Black grabbed his wrist and tore his arm from his body.

I think it took a moment for my brain to comprehend what I'd just witnessed. Blood arced through the air as Black beat the man with his own arm. When the bones were so broken that the appendage was slack, he threw it away.

It landed almost on top of me.

But I didn't scream. I bit my bottom lip so hard I

tasted blood, but I couldn't scream. I didn't want their attention. I didn't know what might happen.

Every time the prisoner fell to the ground, Conal or Glass picked him up. The man had stopped making those terrifying noises a while ago. Finally, it ended when Black wrenched the man's head from his body.

I was numb. I'd watched the entire beating. Something inside me wouldn't let me turn away.

Glass approached, her clothes and exposed skin were covered in blood. She leaned over to grasp my upper arm. "Come, Theodora Morrissey." She pulled me to my feet.

I didn't fight her. Her hold was firm but not bruising. Her wolf was satisfied, and I didn't feel any bloodlust or aggression. I stood still, watching her punch numbers into the keypad.

The door opened, and I followed her into the corridor. After she heard the heavy door slam shut, she looked at me. "Come."

I followed her long strides as we walked through a maze of hallways and up a flight of stairs. We were heading toward the gym.

At the door, she paused. "Shower."

I nodded and followed her into the large locker room.

She immediately began to strip off her blood-soaked clothes.

I was still getting used to all the nudity. I'd shared the showers with her before after my self-defense lessons, or should I say beat downs. I was hopeless against her strength and speed. I walked like a zombie to the row of showers and turned on the hot water at the first faucet, and then continued to the farthest.

She entered as I had just finished adjusting the temperature. "You need to bathe."

I glanced down at my clothes. They were red. Jesus, I was covered in blood. I didn't undress; I just turned and stepped under the hot spray. My brain shut down for a while.

"Seer, are you ever going to finish?" Glass stood near me.

Something broke within me. I started to cry and shake so hard that I dropped to my knees. I didn't want her to see me like this. I screamed at her, "Get out."

Any other time I would have relished the look of shock on the placid woman's face, but tonight, I just wanted to be alone. For a few fucking minutes, I needed to be alone.

"Get out, please." This time the words rumbled from deep in my chest.

She nodded and left the showers.

I FELT him before I saw him. Not that I looked up. His black boots came into view as he sighed, "Theo."

I slowly raised my head. "Laird." I briefly wondered if it was past midnight and did I need to show him my brand?

He sank gracefully to his knees then onto his ass. "You've had a long shower."

I sensed no judgment in his tone. I didn't respond. There were no words. I'd just watched this man tear another, limb from limb until he was dead. I wasn't sure how I felt about that. It was like I was incapable of comprehending it all. Finally, I said the words that I held onto. "He killed one of us."

"He did."

"He had to die." I looked at him again.

"That is our way," he said slowly.

I nodded.

We sat in silence for a while.

"Theo."

I think I'd forgotten that he was still there because for a moment, I just stared. "Yes?"

"Do you hate us?"

I considered my answer. What I'd witnessed shocked me—the controlled anger, the brutality, the blood—but from the time I'd walked into that room, the philosophy of the Novus Pack sounded in my head. I licked my dry lips. "With us or against us," I whispered.

I felt his wolf's approval as the Laird nodded once. "When you're ready, Issa will drive you home."

About a half hour after he left, I stripped out of my clothes. I left them in the shower. After opening my locker, I pulled on a pair of shorts and a T-shirt. I didn't care that I wasn't wearing underwear. I wanted to get out of there. Issa met me at the door and for the first time, she didn't talk at all.

Once I got to my bedroom, I again showered. I wanted to smell the coconut of my shampoo instead of the scent of the prisoner's blood.

EIGHTEEN

NOVUS

CONAL MACGREGOR

I'd gotten home about three hours ago. I checked in with Solle and on Theodora, who was pretending to be sleeping. Black had been firm in his order that we give her space. I'd wanted to give her a ride home, but I'd followed his instructions. I often wondered who knew our Seer best. Solle seemed in tune with her moods and was Theodora's first choice to discuss her concerns about her transition. The human spoke with me at length about Pack politics and the special rules that applied to her. She relied on my counsel, and I enjoyed her sly sense of humor and ability to quickly grasp concepts. However, there was a bond between our leader and the Seer. It was Black to whom she'd turned tonight to verify that she would be safe around the prisoner. She trusted him with her life.

His handling of her wasn't gentle. In fact, he was consistently demanding, always pushing for more. However, he was also protective in a way I'd never seen from him. It was subtle. Perhaps, he didn't realize that more and more often, he checked on her first. A small, petty part of me noticed, that had always been my place, his first concern.

Solle opined that it was Theodora's strength and overwhelming vulnerability that attracted the Laird. The human was actively devoting herself to learning our ways and history while mastering her skills. However, there were times, when she was unguarded, that she was so aware of her frailty we could feel her pain.

I heard her footsteps above my office as she got out of bed and headed to the stairs. For a few minutes, I didn't leave my chair. I didn't want her to think I'd been monitoring her movements. I heard her in the kitchen, so I headed in that direction, because the result was always tasty.

She was making a cup of coffee, so I made sure my steps were heavy enough for her to notice.

"Hey," she said as she turned. "Oh man, you look like you could use this more than me." She handed me the full mug.

"Thanks," I told her gratefully.

I took a seat at the breakfast bar and enjoyed a few sips of the coffee.

She poured another cup and walked to the refrigerator. She stood in front of the open door, studying its contents. "What sounds good?"

I wasn't sure what to make of her mood this morning. She was unsettled, yet she was acting as if last night hadn't happened. "What do you feel like making?"

She looked over her shoulder. "Something with multiple steps. I think I need to be busy this morning."

"Surprise me." I didn't know how to cook. If I got

hungry and no food was prepared, I changed and hunted my own.

She started to unload ingredients onto the counter while facing me. After a few minutes, she began to beat the multiple eggs she'd cracked. "So, did you get any sleep?"

Although she asked casually, I understood she wanted to talk. "No. Solle was asleep, and I didn't want to wake her."

"I tried to sleep." She added salt and pepper to the bowl and continued the quick motions with her hand.

I studied her as she worked, channeling my mate in her doctor-mode. "Do we need to talk about how you're doing?"

She paused her actions and rested the whisk against the side of the bowl. "I think I'm okay." Her eyebrows drew together. "I'm not sure if that should bother me, or if I should feel relieved that I'm not freaking out."

I saw confusion in her eyes. "Babe, I can't promise that you won't be called into something like that again." I needed to prepare her.

Her exhale was sharp. "I get that you're all violent." One side of her mouth lifted. "Brutal."

"Knowing it and seeing it are two very different things." I remembered the first time Solle had watched a challenge. She'd stood frozen in shock, and then had cried for hours later that night.

She noticed that my mug was empty, so she grabbed it and poured me another cup. While her back was turned, she said, "I think it helped that it was the Laird who handled things."

"Black is considered a just and fair leader. We're lucky to have him." I'd pledged my life to protect him.

"I understand that, Conal." She returned the steaming mug to the spot in front of me. "What I mean is that it brings me some comfort that he did it himself. He didn't order one of you to do it." She let out a long sigh.

"The Laird won't ask of us what he wouldn't do himself," I said with some heat.

She again attacked the mixing bowl and added a few more ingredients before she poured the mixture into a rectangular dish and put it into the oven.

I knew that she was working through her thoughts. Theodora turned cautious at times when expressing herself.

She made another cup of coffee and leaned on the counter. "I'm trying to remember that your world is different. Sometimes, I still forget," she said softly, "especially when we do normal things, like talk while I make breakfast."

"Theodora, you're adjusting well. We all think so." I knew Onyx had loftier expectations for the woman, but, in my opinion, she was doing a great job. Last night was amazing.

"Thanks," she said, but it was a reflexive answer. "Do you think he does it because he's the boss, or does... does he like it?"

Her voice had gone very tense. I wanted to answer very carefully. I knew it was important to their relationship and to how she regarded our race. "What do you think?"

She tilted her chin a little and smirked.

I could almost hear her thinking the words, *Tricky wolf*, something she often muttered under her breath.

She narrowed her eyes a little. "I think that he's

violent and brutal. What do they call it? An apex predator."

I shifted on the stool, ready to interrupt her and remind her that, in our world, that wasn't a bad thing.

"But I also believe he's always in control and knows exactly what he wants and has a plan to get it. That's why he's always the most dangerous one in the room." She said these words almost to herself. "He's a good leader, and it seems, I dunno…uhm, I guess you could say that he does the dirty work himself."

After considering her calm expression, I gave a nod. "I think that's a fair summation."

She gave a little shrug. "So, do you want bacon or sausage?"

I wanted to laugh at her change of topic. "Both."

She turned to get the meat.

"Babe," the endearment rolled off of my tongue, "if you want to talk about this some more, we can…later."

She smiled. "I know and thanks."

My phone vibrated.

Black: Have you spoken to the Seer
Me: She's making breakfast

I waited for his response. When one didn't come, I typed: **There will be plenty. You should come by.**

Black: Can she cook

I wanted to laugh at his logical question. **Yes**

Ten minutes later, I heard his bike. I got up and went to the door. As we walked to the breakfast bar, I told Theodora, "There'll be another mouth to feed."

Her back was to us as she made the biscuits. When she turned her head to greet our guest, I saw her eyes flare with interest for a second, before she gave a flustered, "Oh…oh." She rushed to the sink to wash the flour from her hands then formally presented her brand to the Laird. I'd always thought she did it saucily. As if she was saying, "I am wearing your mark, but you don't really own me…yet."

I glanced at my friend, and he was giving her an appreciative smile. He definitely sensed the challenge that she unconsciously sent.

"Theodora, I didn't know that you cooked."

"I haven't told you all of my secrets," she threw over her shoulder as she returned to the dough.

He was watching her ass.

"Coffee?" I interrupted his admiring with a smile.

"Sure." He didn't look upset that I'd caught him mid-act. Of course, he was the Laird, so he could do whatever he liked with whomever. There were more than enough volunteering at every turn to lay with our leader.

NINETEEN

NOVUS

RAIDER BLACK

The Day of Change really took place at night. At dusk, the teens gathered in the square. They stood in a long line as I signaled to Conal which ones would be traveling to the Camp for their first change.

This year, Theodora was three steps ahead of me with Asher. She was calling to their wolves, which made this part of the evening go much more quickly. So far, Conal had recorded seven names. The teens were given time to say goodbye to friends and family before they were transported to our secure facility for the next step.

We were coming to the end of the line. From the corner of my eye, I saw Theo pull up sharply and move a step behind her guard. She was looking ahead to Kenta Yu.

He was small for his age and still resembled a young teen. The only child of Caroline and Akiro Yu was staring boldly at the Seer. It was odd to see one who was so slight stare aggressively at the human. My human. "Seer?"

"That one," she nodded in the boy's direction. "He's ready." Her mask was in place.

After spending so much time with her, I was learning her expressions, and I hated it when she made her face blank.

I bypassed the next two females and came to a stop in front of Kenta. I could feel his wolf. He would be one of the first to change. "The bus will leave in fifteen minutes." The boy stared straight into my eyes, something that few so young dared to do. He slowly turned to focus again on my Seer.

My wolf roared, and Theo moved slowly to stand behind me. Whatever she'd experienced upset her. I felt her hand rest briefly against my back. My wolf was watchful.

I turned my back on the boy and formally offered her my arm. "Seer?"

She looked at my arm, and then at my face, before resting her hand in the crook of my elbow.

I could feel her body trembling as we stood to the side of the gathering. Solle had joined us. She glanced at the group that was slowly making their way to the bus.

"I guessed right except for two." She flashed a satisfied grin.

"Is eight a small group or large?" Theodora usually looked like she was ready to smile, but now, her mouth was set in a straight line.

"It's the biggest I've seen," Solle said.

"We're lucky. The Lady gives us many young." Solle and Conal had explained to her that couples asked to be blessed with a child. We still fucked like humans. If The Lady chose to bless a couple, their sex drives increased until an egg was fertilized. Our Goddess bestowed her blessings as rewards for acts she approved of, or unions she deemed strong. There were packs that were dying because The Lady was unhappy with them. Of course, they would never admit that. They blamed the chemicals in the water or the pollutants in the soil.

Solle studied Theodora. "Are you sure you're ready for this?"

The human straightened her shoulders. "I want to help." I could smell the acidic scent of uncertainty.

"You will help," I said to encourage her.

The teens had boarded the bus, and their families were now heading home to await word of how their child fared. Some didn't survive their first change; more couldn't control their wolves. They had one year to prove they could live safely amongst us.

Mrs. Yu approached our group, walking with purpose. She reached out to touch Theodora's arm. "You'll make sure he survives, won't you?"

Theodora's mask slipped for a moment, and she looked fearful. However, she quickly gathered her composure. "I will do all that I can."

"Kenta, he admires you," the mother told Theodora.

Theodora opened and closed her mouth but didn't respond.

Solle took over. "We will be there, Mrs. Yu, to help in every way we can." Solle placed her hand over Mrs. Yu's and separated her from the Seer. She slowly led the woman away from us.

"His wolf…" Theodora spoke very quietly. "Did you feel anything weird about him?" She looked at me and then dropped her gaze.

"He wants to be freed. I predict he'll be one of the first to change."

She nodded quickly, but I knew that she'd felt something more.

I would have the guards watch him closely.

"Laird," Glass called out. "We should go."

Our group headed to our SUVs. I couldn't speak anymore with Theodora, because she rode with Glass and Tex.

We gathered in the large room at the Camp. The teens were in groups of twos and threes, except for Kenta; he stood off by himself. I waited for Solle to verify that she had everything she needed before the ceremony began.

I'd given specific instructions to Conal that no matter what happened, he was not to leave Theodora's side. If she had to pee, he'd stand over her. She was the most vulnerable person for miles. Newly freed wolves should recognize that she was a gift from The Lady, but I didn't trust their control. She was too valuable, and I wouldn't take the risk of trusting a newly changed.

I was starting to second guess my assigning Conal the task. As a mated male, his first priority would always be Solle. I watched the doctor return to the room and walk directly to Theodora and hug her. I knew that not only would my Second see to the human, but his mate would also.

It was time. I cleared my throat, and the room went silent. Gianni Maslo, who oversaw the Camp, spoke first. He reminded the teens that, once the change began to happen, they were not to interfere with each other in any way.

Suddenly, I decided to change the plan. "Seer, with me." I turned on my heel and headed to the door marked EXIT.

She followed me without hesitation.

Once outside, I moved into the yard where nothing obstructed my view of the full moon.

"You don't need me to do this." Her assertion was almost accusatory as if she thought I was showing off for her.

"Your connection with The Lady will help." I didn't add that I'd fantasized about her following me on her knees. She would do as I bid.

I stopped that line of thinking and refocused my attention on the upcoming event. Before the ceremony began, I needed to know. "What did you sense with that kid, Kenta?"

"Oh." Her shoulders slumped. "I don't think it was anything."

I couldn't keep the growl out of my voice. "I will decide."

I knew she heard it, because she linked her hands in front of her, so that they rested under her breasts in a classic supplicant's pose. "It felt like he was...this is so embarrassing..."

I continued staring at her.

She frowned then lifted her chin. "I felt like he was checking me out. You know, sexually." She blushed.

My wolf growled, and I tried to analyze what she had felt and what it might mean. "You're a beautiful woman."

Her reply was to roll her eyes as she mumbled, "Whatever."

The woman truly had no idea how attractive she was. Conal and Tex spent most of their time chasing off the other men who visited her office too frequently.

I needed to clear my head. I took in a deep breath and held it to the count of five before slowly releasing it.

"Black?"

I opened my eyes to find her standing a few feet in front of me.

"Do I say good luck or something like that? I mean, you know that you're going to have to tell me what to do in there, right? How I can help…because I haven't a clue."

"You are a help to the Pack, Theo. Always."

She nodded again, but her expression was grim.

I closed my eyes and reached for my connection to the moon. I called to The Lady.

I returned to the room with Theo following closely behind me. Conal was waiting by the door and fell into line beside the Seer.

I called to the wolves as their Leader. Immediately, a female started to scream. It had begun.

For those that had an easy time, the hand-picked team talked them through the change, and then the difficult task of transforming back to human form. There were always several who didn't want to change back, and then there were those who became stuck mid-change. Those were the ones that didn't survive.

I hoped that by having Theo here, she might help me control the newly freed wolves and, if possible, help those that were stalled mid-change. So far, we'd had no stalls.

Tex called for me. He was with Kenta. "This one doesn't want to change back." He grunted. The two Camp handlers had already wrestled the wolf to the ground.

"Kenta," I said, using an authoritative tone.

"Fuck off," the wolf snarled.

Tex and I chuckled. There was always one.

"I am your Leader. I command you to change." I used some of my power to keep him focused.

"I want her." Slobber fell from his jowls, and his eyes flashed. "Her, I want her."

"Seer," Tex bellowed.

I watched Theo and Conal make their way to us. She looked pale, but I could tell by her posture that she wouldn't like it if I mentioned the fact.

Conal said quietly, "We didn't warn her about the sounds."

Over time, a Lycan can change instantly, but at first, it's a slow process as joints stretch, skin expands and contracts, and there are certain sounds as our form alters. Now, I understood why she was pale. "Seer, young Kenta needs assistance changing back to his human form."

She glanced at the wolf, who was rigid in his captors' hold, staring at her. "All right," she said, her voice shaking a little. She moved in a semi-circle, studying the newly changed. "Wolf, you need to give up this form."

He snapped at her.

She took a step back. "Come on, you know this is part of the deal." She cajoled in a husky voice. "I'm sure you'll spend the next few weeks in wolf form."

He turned his head, following her every move. "No," he growled.

I was growing tired of his theatrics. I sensed no fear in him, so he was being stubborn. "Change, Kenta," I ordered.

He let out an angry howl.

Theo looked at me helplessly. "I'm going to have to touch him to make it happen."

My wolf didn't want her touching the male. I didn't like it much either, but that couldn't be the reason we didn't try. "Bill, you take his haunches, Tex, grab his upper body, and Malik, you are on the head. Keep him still," I instructed and the men moved to their assigned places.

Conal put his hand on her arm. "Babe, don't fight me. If I have to yank you out of the way, just go with it, yeah?"

"No problem," she said in a serious voice. She didn't savor the closeness with Kenta.

"Do you need me?" I could help bolster her power.

She studied the now snarling Kenta. "First, let me try it alone. If I need more power, I'll let you know."

She knew that if we couldn't get the wolf to change, I would have to terminate him.

I watched her search for the point of connection. Usually, it was the belly, but we'd learned that it could also be the throat or close to the heart. She stilled and looked over her shoulder at Conal as if she was checking to make sure that he could pull her out of harm's way.

Slowly, she extended her hand and made contact with the wolf's throat. "Kenta, Raider Black, the leader of the Novus Pack, has ordered that you change." Her voice was low but insistent.

"Pretty," he growled.

"Kenta, you must do this," she urged him.

I felt the increase in her power, and the wolf growled.

"Change," she gritted out the word. Her hand was shaking.

The fucker attacked. He snapped his head in her direction and knocked Theo to the floor, while he jack-knifed his body with such force the guards went flying. He was half-way over her body by the time Conal pulled her backwards, away from the newly changed.

All hell broke loose. I changed instantly, my wolf intent on stopping Kenta. He had touched Theo. I had the newly changed wolf on his back, my jaw clamped around his throat. Theo was safely in Conal's arms, crying. Solle was running toward them to check on Theo.

Tex and the other guards were on their knees staying still. They didn't want to attract my enraged attention or interfere unless ordered.

I commanded through my locked jaw. "You will change or die. Your choice Kenta Lu."

The boy chose to change, but I didn't loosen my hold until he was again in his human form.

"We can take over from here, Laird," Tex said, his voice calm.

I lifted my head, but I didn't shift off of his body. "No," I growled. We communicated in our wolf form in words but they were garbled and hard to understand, or so I'd been told by Articles. Other Lycans understood perfectly. I made sure the boy felt the full impact of my weight. I probably had four hundred pounds on him in this form. "She is mine," I thundered while I fought the urge to tear off his head. "You dare touch what is mine?"

The boy started to cry.

I changed to my human form and pushed off of the kid. I turned to Tex. "Make sure he is chained. If he disobeys again, I will issue the termination order."

By the increased volume of his crying and the other teens joining in, I knew that I didn't need to spell out the edict. My word was the only law.

I followed Theo's scent. Conal had smartly moved her to the infirmary area. She was sitting on the gurney, and Solle was stitching the back of her arm.

"It isn't that deep," Conal assured me.

I stepped around my Second. I needed to see that Theo was all right.

She was using her other hand to hold an ice pack to her jaw.

Solle stepped away and was doing something on the small table a few steps away from where Theo sat. "The scar will be hard to see." She returned to place a bandage over the area and secured it.

"I'm sure it'll be fine." Theo tried to smile at the doctor.

"I'm sorry. I got her out of there as fast as I could," Conal said.

"I'm fine," Theo said a little loudly.

"That wolf, he's not right," Solle said, her cheeks reddening with anger.

"He's very strong," Theo said, her gaze dropping.

"He could have killed you," Solle insisted, still in protective mode.

"But he didn't," Theo countered. "Thanks to your mate." She gave Solle a brave smile.

It wasn't a real one; her eyes didn't light up.

The muscle at the side of Solle's jaw pulsed. She was still furious.

I grunted. "Why don't you go find a closet and show your man how proud you are of his heroics?"

She made a "humph" sound as she passed me. She knew they were being excused.

Once we were alone, Theo gave me a real smile, and her body finally relaxed a little. "Really? You sent them off to have sex."

I gave her a shrug. "He saved your life; he deserves a reward."

She chuckled and shook her head. "I can't even think of an argument to that."

I liked hearing her laugh. My wolf settled a little. "Are you all right?"

"I won't lie. Tonight was tough." She slumped a little. "He moved so fast." Her voice cracked, and she blinked several times to hold back the tears that threatened to fall.

I stopped fighting my need. I stepped closer to her and hugged her. I didn't know what to say.

"I'm sorry, I didn't mean to break down." she said against my chest.

I could feel her warm breath through my T-shirt.

"Shhh." I made more comforting sounds to quiet her as I tried not to notice how perfect she felt against my body.

TWENTY

NOVUS

THEODORA MORRISSEY

I *am such an idiot.* I told myself as I slowly got to my feet once again. I wiped my damp palms on the seat of my yoga pants and tried not to let my frustration show. I should have kept my big mouth shut, but the dream, or maybe it was a mini-vision, had bothered me so much that I'd asked Glass if there was any way that I, a mere human, could stop a Lycan.

The very next day, the warrior had added more hours of training to my schedule. Training? Who was I kidding? It was two hours of me getting my ass kicked three days a week.

"Are you even trying?" she asked in a monotone.

"Would you believe me if I said yes?" I let out a puff of breath that lifted my sweaty bangs off my forehead.

"Hmph." Clearly, she didn't.

The gym door opened and slammed shut. I knew the Laird had entered the area. I couldn't see him, but I could feel him. This "awareness" had grown since the Night of the Change. I hadn't been alone with him in the intervening week. Something was going on with an escort, so he'd been scarce. Not that I noticed. Nope. I did not miss our tutoring sessions. I could study just fine by myself.

"Again," Glass said with no inflection.

I tried to be ready. I had my weight on the balls of my feet, I attempted to block her advance, but she was too powerful and so fast that I didn't even see her until she was on me. I stayed on my back on the mat, trying to decide which part of my body hurt the most.

Glass was already on her feet and standing over me, frowning. "You weren't ready."

I sat up, still evaluating whether it was my elbow or my ass that hurt worse. "I was too ready, but I don't see you. One second, you're over there, and the next, you're on top of me." I tried to keep the whine out of my voice since he was around, and I'd said this about a hundred times before.

"Let's do it again." She thrust out her hand to help me up.

Once again on my feet, I tried to stretch my back. I would definitely need to stand under the hot shower for an hour when I got home.

This time, I jumped before she moved.

"Concentrate," she ordered.

"I'm trying." I grimaced as I straightened and bent my aching arm.

"I have a suggestion." Black was striding toward us.

"I think I'm hopeless," I said, grimacing. I didn't want to embarrass myself any longer.

"You asked for help," he said, reminding me that his people reported to him. "You did that for a reason."

I looked at my shoes, I didn't want to talk about what

I'd seen and how much it upset me. What had happened with Kenta affected me. His attack was a huge reminder of how vulnerable I was.

"Let's try this. Seer, instead of seeing with your eyes, use your senses," he said as he joined us.

"All right," I said, although I didn't think it would help.

"And instead of trying to stop me, roll with me," he suggested patiently.

Oh fuck, that means he's going to touch me. I took a step backward. "Okay, that's a good idea. Glass, let's try it." I nodded my head several times. Was it wrong that I wondered if I smelled bad? I was so sweaty.

"Theo."

I swear he purred my name. "Right here, Black," I snapped. I didn't want to do this with him.

He chuckled low and deep. "We'll do it three times."

Of course, my mind went *there*. I glanced at him briefly, and his eyes were sparkling with laughter. "Okay, let's get this over with…but if you break me, Solle will be pissed," I warned.

"I'll go slow."

God help me. He was teasing me, and I was letting him. I took in a deep breath, and then slowly let it out. I closed my eyes and tried to find my center. When I'd gotten my emotions under control, I nodded.

"Now, reach out to sense my movement. Maybe you'll feel the air change. Keep your eyes closed and feel."

I did as he instructed, and I felt it. I stiffened in anticipation of impact. He was bigger than Glass and it was going to hurt.

When his arms circled my middle, gently but solidly, my eyes flew open in surprise.

He said close to my ear, "Don't go stiff. Stay relaxed, and just go with me."

Jesus, he sounded seductive. I did as he asked—well, as much I could. He dropped us to the mat. He took most of the impact on his side and rolled on top of me, and I'll admit, I think he rolled me on top of him. We kept going. My body was still stuck on how good it felt having him covering me. He was hard, and I was soft. *Gaaaawwwddd.* I was a mess.

Once I stopped thinking, I realized I was staring down into his face.

"Better?" he asked with a knowing smile.

Damn tricky wolves and their senses. "Much," I said, pumping enthusiasm into my voice and immediately climbed to my feet.

I looked around for Glass.

"She left," he said.

Great, we were alone. "So, I'm supposed to just move with you?" I guess it made sense.

He gave me a cocky grin. "I've always found that it works best that way, for both partners."

I rolled my eyes. I signaled with my hand for him to come at me again.

This time, I used our momentum and went with him, and I ended up on top again. I smiled. "Okay, so now what do I do?"

He was watching my mouth. I became aware that if I shifted just a little, I would be over his cock. My boobs were already crushed to his chest. "Don't answer that," I said shortly. I went to my knees, which definitely put me into contact with his... Jesus, he was hard. I used my hands to push off of his chest.

He laughed at me as he gracefully got to his feet.

This slyly sexy version of Black was too much. I mean, I only had *so* much self-control. I shook off my awareness. "So, I end up on top. Then what? It's not like I can run away or tear their heads off... So, what can I do?"

"You pray that one of your guards is nearby and that you bought yourself enough time for him to pull your ass out of danger."

"Is this hopeless?" I asked honestly. I depended on the Laird for many things but most of all honesty.

He hesitated, and I knew his answer.

I dropped my head. I had known I was much weaker, but now I was utterly defeated.

"Theo," he said quietly.

I didn't raise my head. I was trying to wrap my head around this.

"You are Marked by our Goddess. No Lycan should ever touch you with violence." He paused and frowned. "But there are those who don't follow the rules. Sometimes, they aren't right in the head, or they don't care." His gray eyes lost some of their fierceness. "No human is strong enough to stop a Lycan, especially if they're in their wolf form."

I knew this. I'd seen it in my head.

"What you could do is go for the eyes. They are vulnerable."

"Yeah, I remember the prisoner's screams," I said roughly.

"Stun him and pray." He shrugged once. "One more time."

"Just don't break anything," I groused.

I FELT PRETTY SATISFIED with myself. I'd talked Conal and Solle into going out on another date night, and Issa and I were going through my closet.

"I don't need more clothes," I told the tiny fashionista.

"You don't have one sexy outfit in here." She was shoving my hangers to the right.

"I don't need to be sexy," I argued.

"Oh, honey, we all need to be sexy," she said haughtily.

I wanted to change the topic. "Tell me about that female we saw in the grocery store." We'd been shopping for snacks for later. We'd filled our cart with junk because these damn Lycans could metabolize anything in an hour and were always hungry.

"She was in my sister's Change group. Calista thought she was odd."

I'd noticed the female watching us intently as we shopped the aisles. She didn't have a cart and didn't seem to have any purpose for being there. "Is this the same sister that is mated and living in New Hampshire?"

"Yeah, because Novus was too progressive." Issa frowned at the thought of her highly-opinionated sister. "We monitored Lydia, that female, for a year but saw nothing concerning. She lives with her father on a small farm outside of town."

"Maybe she's shy?" I offered.

"About five years ago, she started to accompany him on escorts." Issa continued going through my closet. "From all reports, she works and keeps to herself."

"In some human families, sometimes, one of the kids never will leave home."

"I don't think she comes into town very often. I was surprised to see her today."

"I'm sure that your snarling will make her want to visit again," I added dryly.

We'd been heading to the checkout line when the female had stepped in front of my cart. "You are her." Her eyes were a very pale blue and her hair was greasy. Her clothes were due for a washing.

It was odd to see an unkempt wolf. Most were fashion conscious and the men who wore long hair or beards appeared to bathe and practice some form of personal grooming. I didn't speak, because Issa had gone into what I secretly called her "guard dog" role.

"Step away, Lydia Bohm," Issa snarled and moved to stand nose-to-nose with the woman.

"I, uh, I..." the woman stammered.

"Move." Issa spat the order.

The woman scurried away.

Confrontation over, Issa had motioned for me to continue on, and I'd complied.

I leaned back on my bed and stretched my legs in front of me. "I feel a little sad for her. Maybe she needs a friend."

Issa stepped outside of my closet. "You have me. That female, she would have nothing to offer you. She doesn't know how to fight or about clothes."

I wanted to laugh. "Iss, we talk about other things."

She gave me a cheeky grin. "We do, but those are my two favorite topics."

That was true. The diminutive guard was obsessed with weaponry and fighting styles. I'd told her about the

MMA, and I was pretty sure she now spent all of her downtime watching matches. That made me think of another female who was obsessed with fighting, "When's Glass supposed to be here with dinner?"

Issa looked at her watch. "In about ten."

We were going to have pizza and watch *Xena, Warrior Princess*. I'd ordered seasons one and two. I couldn't believe they'd never seen it. They were going to love it.

Issa turned her head and held up her hand in a stop sign.

From her suddenly serious expression and tense body, I could tell she was listening for something. I stood still as I tried to hear what had caught her attention.

Issa dropped the hanger she held and started for the hallway.

I followed because…well, for no other reason than I wanted to know what was happening, and she didn't order for me to stay.

We went downstairs quietly and cautiously.

I whispered, "Glass would call before she got here, right?" I was starting to feel uneasy.

"I haven't heard her Range Rover." She sniffed the air.

I watched my guard. Issa was more like a friend than a watcher. Her sudden intensity made me nervous.

We stood at the bottom of the steps for a few minutes until the buzzing of Issa's phone broke the silence. We both sighed and relaxed.

Glass arrived with three boxes of pizza. "I like variety," she said with a shrug.

Conal and Solle had given me the basement as my own space. There was now a leather sectional and a big screen TV. This was where we were going to set up.

I'd served the ladies their drinks, the assorted plates, and napkins when Glass snapped, "Silence."

Both she and Issa listened intently. I glanced at the tall windows that overlooked the in-ground pool and deck. It was dark, so I only saw my own reflection.

Issa got to her feet. "I'll do a perimeter check."

Glass nodded once at the petite guard. I barely heard Issa climb the steps.

Glass pulled her cell phone from her pocket and held it out to me.

I just stared at it for a second before taking it. It felt so odd in my hand. I hadn't held one in months.

"If anything happens, you hit number one on the keyboard, that's the Control Room. Tell them we need help."

"Is something out there?" I asked, my stomach beginning to knot.

"Probably nothing." She started to kill the lights.

I walked to my desk and opened the right side, top drawer. I pulled out a hammer. Conal had laughed, and then quickly sobered, the day I'd helped him put together a trellis for the backyard. After I'd watched him pound some nails, it had occurred to me that the tool would make a good weapon. It was small and light but could do some damage, even when swung by a human.

Glass glanced at my left hand as I returned to stand behind the sectional. "Good thinking."

I watched her pace in front of the windows. I wanted to ask her why she was doing that. I mean, if it was a Lycan out there, they'd be able to see her. Or maybe that was her idea? I started to fidget. My nerves were fraying, and I wondered where Issa was. I was getting ready to ask when something hit the window. It was a hard thud and a scrape against the glass.

I instinctively went into a squat.

Glass changed.

I know, because I felt her magic. I touched the screen on the phone and hit the number one. It rang twice, and a female answered.

"Glass."

"It's Th-theodora," I stumbled over my own name. I wasn't sure what to say. Hell, I'd never called 9-1-1 before. "I mean, it's Theodora Morrissey. I live with Conal and Solle."

"I know who you are," the female told me calmly. "Why do you have Glass's phone?"

"We're at my house and something is outside."

It hit the window again, and Glass answered with a deep growl.

"It's being aggressive," I explained as my voice shook. "Glass has changed. She's in the basement with me, and Issa...she went outside to check. I, uh..." I had to swallow before I could go on because it hit me that it wasn't good that Issa hadn't returned. "Issa hasn't come back."

"I'm sending a patrol and alerting Conal and the Laird."

Whatever was outside started to scratch at the glass.

"Tell them to hurry." I clicked off the phone and shoved it in the back pocket of my jeans. I crawled to the end of the sectional, it blocked me from the view of the glass. "What it that?"

"Wolf," Glass answered in a guttural voice.

I tried to use my senses. I felt the wolf. However, it

was different from any I'd ever encountered. This one was so angry and wild.

It hit the glass again.

"The window won't hold much longer." Glass had moved to stand off to my right, still in clear view of the window. "When it breaks, I'll engage. You use that time to prepare."

"Prepare?" Christ, I didn't even want to know what she was talking about.

"To fight."

I think my brain stopped working for a full minute. I knelt with my mouth open, staring at the warrior.

She pointed at the hammer I still held.

I didn't have time to explain to her that I wasn't ready. I'd picked up the hammer more as a sign of solidarity than with any intent to use it. I started to pray to The Lady. I mean, if I was connected to her, she might be able to offer some kind of help.

The wolf hit the window again, and I jumped.

It howled once and screamed, "*Miiiiine.*"

I knew immediately who it was. "Glass, that's Kenta," I said, my words rushing together.

"The newly changed?" She watched the wolf whose face was pressed against the window.

"How did he get here?" I'd thought the Camp was escape proof.

"Try to talk to him," she instructed.

Slowly, I got to my feet. I took two steps to the side, away from the sofa. I could feel his wolf's madness. "Kenta... Hey." I honestly didn't know what to say. I tried to remember everything I knew about the newly changed. They were incredibly strong and unpredictable. Check and check.

"Mine," he snarled again.

"You have to calm down and, uhm, change back into human…then we can talk." I tried to sound confident, but I was shaking.

"Human weak." He bumped the window again.

I knew he meant his human form. "But I feel more comfortable with that form." I took a step forward.

The warrior protecting me in wolf form blocked my progression, and that infuriated Kenta. The glass shattered. He jumped at Glass but over-estimated the space and, instead, landed behind us.

Glass bumped me as she dove at the wolf. I hit the floor, feeling the glass splinters cut into my skin. Before I could recover, I was wrenched to my feet by Kenta's rough paw. It felt like my arm was being crushed in his hold.

He pulled me into his body. I had lost the hammer during my fall. I fought his hold on my arm. It felt like my bones were being ground into nothingness, and I couldn't think of anything but getting him to loosen his grip.

"Wolf," Glass shouted. "You're hurting her."

She said it two more times, I think.

I screamed, "Let go!" as I scratched at his strong paw.

Glass leaned from side to side, trying to find an angle to attack.

I tried to pull away from him. I needed to get away from him. I was going insane with the pain. I didn't care if he ripped off my arm. I couldn't take the pain a second longer.

She must have read my intent, because she attacked, hitting him in his side.

He released me, and I dropped to my knees, holding my bloody arm.

The sounds. God, they would haunt me until the day I died. The ripping of skin, the snarls, and the smell of blood filled the room.

Somehow, Kenta threw Glass through one of the unbroken windows. Then he let out a deafening howl.

I was on my feet once again, shielding my arm. I didn't run. I simply stared at him, and then I looked at the open space where the window had been. I expected Glass to jump through to continue the battle.

He watched me. We were in a stand-off.

"Mine," he panted.

"No," I said quietly.

"Mine," he repeated, the hideous combination of blood and slobber dripping from his jowls.

"No," I said louder. I was tired of being told I was owned. I'd had no say in this whole Seer thing, and now this... I was done.

He took a step in my direction, panting.

Glass had done some damage, and that made me feel a flash of exhilaration. I knew I was going to die. He couldn't control his strength, and he was insane. However, I was going to get one shot in. Somehow, that thought helped me find a momentary sense of calm. "Kenta, you need to change. Your wolf is too strong. You will do more damage to me."

"No hurt you," he promised as he took another step closer.

I could smell his breath as I let go of my injured arm. I didn't even notice the pain, because I was so focused on his approach. I told myself to aim for the eye. I'd do like Black taught me.

Kenta was so close I could almost touch him, when something hit his back.

It was a black wolf, and he rolled the young wolf over and over until the far wall stopped them.

I couldn't see everything, because they were moving so fast. Suddenly, I realized I should look for my hammer. I saw the edge peeking out from under the sectional. I scurried over to it.

As I squatted down to pick it up, I heard the most awful high-pitched scream, followed by a sound that reminded me of when a rotten pumpkin hits the ground. The thump was wet and juicy.

I watched Black drop the headless body of Kenta to the ground.

I think I blacked out. When next I opened my eyes, I was staring at a man's neck. He was talking, but I didn't understand anything he said. I could feel his words rumble in his chest. I tried to focus on what was going on. "Wha…" I slurred. My voice seemed very loud.

The arms holding me tightened a tiny bit in a comforting way, and he rumbled, "Shhh."

I wanted to close my eyes, but the events were coming back to me. I felt my breathing catch. *Oh, Christ.*

"I think she's in shock, but I'd be able to tell if you'd let me examine her." Solle was furious. Her voice was pitched higher than usual, each word was clipped and angry.

I didn't want my friend to be so mad. She should be out with Conal at dinner and dancing. I shook my head as more memories flooded my mind.

"Give him a moment, Solle," Conal reasoned with his wife, speaking slowly.

I now heard more voices and shouts in the distance. I

shifted a little, the movement sent an excruciating pain up my arm, spreading until it covered my entire left side. I cried out in surprise and agony.

"Babe?" Black was staring at me intently.

"My arm..." I couldn't hold back the sob. "Oh, God, my arm."

Solle was now beside me. "Let me take a look at it."

I glanced down at my left arm. I felt my stomach heave at the sight. I swallowed hard. My arm was blood-soaked and misshapen. I clamped my eyes closed. I felt her fingers gently touch my arm, and I whimpered.

Black asked, "Can't you give her something for the pain?"

"I need to evaluate her level of shock. She's lost blood. I'm sure he fractured both bones," the doctor said.

"But she'll be okay, right?" He sounded a little frazzled.

I shook my head slowly, hoping to clear it.

"She needs to go to the hospital. I need to see the x-ray. She might need surgery." Solle continued her exam. "There's glass embedded in her skin. It looks like she rolled in it."

The word triggered my memory. "Glass, what happened to Glass?" I asked Black.

Conal answered, "She'll be fine."

Solle leaned close to me. "Honey, I'm going to give you a shot. It won't alleviate all of the pain, but it will help." She nodded twice. "Then I'm going to stabilize your arm until we get to the hospital."

"I don't like shots," I admitted. "They hurt."

"Theo, you were staring down a feral wolf. I think you can handle one shot," Black said, his voice gruff.

I stared into his gray eyes. They were darker tonight. "Okay," I whispered. If he thought I could handle it, I would.

I felt the prick of the needle, and within a few seconds, warmth spread through my body. I was starting to relax against the man when I suddenly remembered. I jerked upright in his arms. "Issa?"

Nobody answered me right away.

"What happened to Issa?" I yelled, suddenly angry. I needed to know where my friend was.

"Sshhh, Theodora," Conal said as he reached out to smooth my hair out of my face.

"What happened?" I begged. "Tell me."

"He ripped her open," he said in a calm voice, but his eyes were furious and haunted. "Asher found her in the bushes by the garage."

I started to cry again. The tears poured from my eyes. "Is she dead?" I turned to look at Black. Lycan's were hard to kill; he'd told me that numerous times. They could repair most damage to their bodies by changing into their other form.

"No." That's all he gave me.

"Is she going to be okay?" I asked again. "Black."

"She will be, eventually," Solle answered evasively.

"I don't understand," I said. I needed somebody to tell me what was going on.

"When we got to her, she'd lost a lot of blood. She's too weak to change," Solle said softly.

"So...what?" I needed to know right now.

Solle frowned. "So, she has to heal like a human...with time."

"But she's going to heal, right?" I needed her to be

all right. I couldn't handle somebody being permanently injured because of me.

"In time," Black said gravely.

I stared at him while I tried to figure out what they weren't saying. I noticed that he was injured. "You're bleeding," I accused.

"I can hold her if you want to change." Conal held out his arms for Black to transfer me.

Instead, Black held me a little tighter. "I will do it later."

"It's okay. The shot helped," I murmured. I didn't like the thought that he might be hurting, too.

"Later," he said, using his Laird tone.

TWENTY-ONE

RAIDER BLACK

Things were wrapping up at Conal's house. I still held the Seer to my chest. I wasn't ready to let go of her. In my arms, she would be safe.

For as long as I lived I'd never forget the sight of my human standing like a statue, staring down the feral wolf. She'd looked so brave, and yet, resigned. She'd been prepared to die. I'd recognized that look. I'd seen it many times—right before I killed a transgressor.

Conal returned to where I sat. "She out?"

"For the last twenty minutes." I glanced at her face. She looked so serene during sleep, but I missed her flashing eyes. No matter how blank she made her expression, her eyes would usually communicate her true thoughts.

"I'm done here. They're going to cover the windows until I can get the replacements ordered. I thought I'd go to Kenta Yu's family." Conal's tone was solemn.

"I'll do that after we see to her arm." It was my job to tell the boy's family he hadn't survived.

"Laird," Conal said, addressing me formally, "please allow me to perform that task as your Second."

I started to tell him no, but Theo moved and relaxed again against my chest. I needed to deal with her, and more importantly, I needed time to think.

"Please, I wasn't here to protect her or you. Let me do this," his eyes flashed for an unguarded moment, "for you."

My closest friend and advisor was upset. I knew he felt like he'd let down the Pack. "Conal, if you're willing to handle that responsibility then I thank you."

"I'll go immediately. Will the ceremony be tomorrow?"

"At dusk, yes." I nodded. The ritual would be abbreviated, but Kenta deserved our prayers.

"I'll put out the word after I finish making the notification." Conal walked to the steps.

He met Tex at the bottom of the steps and paused to exchange words. My Second nodded twice and continued upstairs. The redhead strode my way.

I tilted my head at the sleeping woman. I didn't think our voices would wake her, but I knew that in this injured state it was better that she slept.

Tex spoke quietly, "Solle's on her way to the hospital. When you're ready, we'll follow."

"What did Gianni say?" The Camp Manager had much to answer for.

Tex frowned, and his expression turned stony. "They didn't even realize he was missing until I arrived. To be honest, I'm not sure how he got free. I ran the perimeter, both inside the fences and the outside, and found no breach. Tech is reviewing the footage, frame by frame.

My guess is that he climbed the fence, took the electrical shocks, and the cuts."

I considered his findings. "He was crazed when I got here. He threw Glass through the window and crushed her ribs. Issa is so damaged she can't change. In his wolf form, pumped up on adrenaline and on a mission...I can see him taking the risk to get free."

"We can up the voltage, but that might kill a weaker wolf," Tex said, shaking his head.

"I think the answer is more surveillance. We watch them, so they can't get too close to the fencing." I knew that as upset at Tex was, he loved his tech and gadgets.

"I can work up a price estimate by mid-morning." His hazel eyes narrowed as he got busy, shopping in his head.

"Order whatever you require." I trusted his knowledge.

"As you wish, Laird." Tex dropped his chin.

Never Again. Even if Kenta's goal had been to get to Theodora, he wouldn't have stopped there. The blood-lust would have kicked in, and then who knew how many would have died. "Make it happen, Tex."

"Let's get the Seer to the hospital and after that, I'll go to the office." Tex gave me room to stand, and he followed me to the stairs.

Theo woke during the ride. She gently rubbed her cheek against my chest.

"Doing okay?" I asked.

"I'd hoped it was all a dream." She frowned and looked down at her arm that was encased in wraps against a piece of plastic to restrict the movement. "Any updates on Glass and Issa?" Her voice cracked on her personal guard's name.

I knew Tex could hear her, but he pretended that he didn't. "Tex, any new updates?"

"Glass is resting. She should be back in action tomorrow." He tapped his watch-like communicator on his wrist. "No change with Issa."

Her forehead wrinkled, and I wanted to soothe her. "That isn't bad, Theo. She's hanging in there."

She blinked several times and I knew she was fighting off tears. She cared deeply for the petite guard. She again rested her cheek against my chest.

I thought she'd fallen back asleep when she whispered, "Will you please stay with me?"

My wolf growled. We weren't leaving her until I was sure she was safe. "Whatever you need, Theo." Goddess help me, I couldn't tell her no.

THE HUMAN SUFFERED through the x-rays and the setting of her bones. The staff had given her painkillers intravenously. Solle assured me that it helped. I kept checking to see how much discomfort she was experiencing. I knew this procedure was painful, because Solle didn't do it herself. Instead, she stood behind me with her hand resting on my shoulder. I finally relaxed when the cast was applied and Theo slept.

Solle pulled the light blanket higher and tucked it around the human. "Let her rest here for about an hour. Afterward, she can go home."

I nodded.

"You know she'll be fine, right?" the doctor said while giving me a long look.

"I'll see her through this."

"She's special."

"She is," I answered carefully. Something in the way Solle brushed away the hair from Theo's cheek made my warning bells chime. I didn't want to have a talk about emotions with Solle. I didn't even want to have one with myself.

"I don't mean her abilities." She continued to stroke her hair. "I mean her heart." She paused and looked me squarely in the eye. "Have you noticed?"

Again, I was careful with my words. "The Lady has blessed us with a true gift."

Solle dropped her gaze and studied the human. "She's been good for you."

"All of us," I corrected.

Solle let out an aggrieved sigh, communicating that she knew I was being evasive. "I'll be back in a bit to check on her."

"Thank you, Solle." I think I was more grateful that she let the discussion drop.

The doctor was correct. I thought about Theo too often. My wolf wanted her; he had from the beginning. However, he understood tha the contract was signed to mate with the Dolan daughter. My wolf was stubborn and wanted what he wanted, but I was in control of my wolf, my Pack, and my life. Many people counted on me.

The human shifted and groaned. Her eyelids fluttered a few times before they opened. She looked around, and once she saw that I was there, she let out a sigh. "Black?"

"Are you in pain?" I sniffed the air.

"No. I feel kinda floaty, actually." Her voice was low and husky.

"You're drugged." I returned her smile.

"Maybe." She glanced around again. "Thank you," she said quietly. "You saved my life, again." She took in a rough breath. I started to reply, but she shook her head. "Don't talk about duty, or say you were closest. Okay? Just let me say this."

I waited to hear her words.

"I was ready to die." She watched me as the words sank in. "I stood there, and I knew that if I ran, it would be futile. I mean, he threw Glass around like she weighed nothing." Her eyes widened for a moment. "In a way, I felt at peace. I stood at a little bit of an angle, hoping he would grab my broken arm, so that...so I could try to poke him in the eye like you showed me. I wanted to do something to him." She frowned slightly. "I wasn't going to go down easy. I wanted to leave a mark." Her voice had gone rough.

I watched a single tear roll down her cheek. I leaned closer. "You have the heart of a wolf," I told her honestly.

"He said I was his." I saw pain in her eyes. "He kept saying, 'Mine.'"

"You were never his." I didn't try to disguise my growl.

"But he thought so," she pressed.

"He was fixated, or his wolf was. It can happen." It was a sign of instability. "Usually, it's between two newly changed, but it has been recorded that a new wolf pursues someone he's had contact with before the first change."

She let out a deep breath. "I don't understand it. I think I saw him a total of two times. I'm nothing." Her voice had gotten quieter with each word, and then she fell asleep.

I stared at her in astonishment. She honestly believed that.

What was I going to do about her?

TWENTY-TWO

THEODORA MORRISSEY

I was tired of this cast. I'd been a good sport, not complaining about the pain or the itching, but it felt like I'd had it on forever. Solle promised two more weeks. It would be off for my birthday. Lycans did not celebrate the anniversary of their birth, but apparently, *we*, meaning my friends and me, we're going to celebrate mine. Solle was in charge of the plans and had a notebook she kept jotting ideas into.

It had been a month and a half since Kenta died, and I still thought about what had happened every day. I woke late the afternoon after the attack, and everything hurt. Solle decreed I couldn't go out, but I dragged my ass into the shower and with her begrudging help, managed to put on a navy tank dress with an open cardigan to cover most of my bruises. My education hadn't covered this type of event, so I stuck close to Tex, who'd been assigned to me. I couldn't cover my shock when the teen's body was carried to the open field at the far end of town. It seemed like two hundred people participated in the solemn procession. The Laird led the line of mourners, followed closely by Conal and Kenta's family. We walked the mile and gathered in a semi-circle around what I recognized was a pyre. I'd studied cultures in college that had publicly honored their dead by incineration, but to witness it was completely different.

Likely the attendees believed that my injuries and weakened state made it necessary for Tex to hold me up. The truth was that I couldn't watch the flames licking at the pallet. I'd witnessed his decapitation, but I wasn't prepared for this. Watching his skin melt and noting the smell... *Oh God, the smell.* Hearing his mother's agonizing wails tore at my heart.

I felt so much guilt. I'd promised to help her son, but I couldn't. In fact, at the end, I'd wanted to hurt him. I couldn't look at his parents. I kept my head pressed against Tex and closed my eyes.

When we returned to the house, I went directly to my room, crawled into the corner of my closet, and sobbed. I felt so helpless. I cried for the family's loss and the world's. I wept because I didn't understand what was happening. Would I ever feel comfortable in this world? I was so tired and the aches were so deep. I wondered if there would ever be any relief. I hated to admit this, but most of all I cried for Black. He'd had to take a life and then stand in front of his people and speak words of comfort. Who wiped his tears, if he even shed them?

"Is it your arm?" Conal leaned against the entry to the closet, taking up all the room.

"No." I kept my head buried in my arms which were propped on top of my bent knees.

He stayed there for a few minutes. "May I?"

Well, he wasn't going away, and there wasn't a lot of room in here. "I can come out," I said sheepishly as I considered wiping my nose on the hem of my dress. Technically, I probably shouldn't have hidden in the corner, but I didn't think he'd reprimand me tonight.

He reached out his hand and I took it as he gently pulled me to my feet. I walked stiffly to my bed. Conal sat beside me, our thighs almost touching. "Tell me what's weighing so heavily on you."

I considered where to start and how much to share. I liked Conal, I did trust him, but he still had to report what I shared. "I'm not sure where to start."

"Theodora, honey, just talk. I'll listen and try to help you anyway I can." He took my hand in his large one. "I hate seeing you in so much pain."

"Is it always going to be this hard?" I blurted. Immediately, I felt a sense of deep shame at how ungrateful I sounded. "I-I mean..." God, I didn't know what I meant. I ran my casted hand jerkily through my hair, trying to comb it back from my face. When I found that impossible without giving myself another bruise, I gave up with a sigh. "I'm trying Conal, I really am." I closed my swollen eyes for a moment. They burned from all the crying. "Just when I get to the point where I think I'm finding my place..."

"You are the Seer of the Novus Pack. That is your place."

Not helpful. It was a statement made by the pack's Second, not my friend. For a second, I wondered where Solle was. Conal was the Second, and he would always view the world from that position. Perhaps this conversation needed a woman's touch. "I am the Seer. I have accepted that position…but sometimes our differences… they seem so daunting."

"You're thinking like a member of the human world." He studied me with his serious eyes.

"I am human," I reminded him.

He loosened his grip on my hand and moved his lower on my wrist. His index finger lightly brushed over the Novus brand.

My mark tingled.

He used that same finger to lightly brush the space between my eyes and my hairline. "The Lady has given you the ability to see the future, to communicate with our wolves. You're so much more than human."

I swallowed hard to fight back a sob. He was correct. This…my life, was what I was destined for and now I wondered if I could do the job.

He shifted and wrapped his arm around my back and pulled me into his side. "You've been through a lot."

I rested my head on his shoulder. I closed my eyes as I spoke softly, "I wasn't afraid to die."

"You were very brave," he said with his head resting on mine.

"I was terrified," I admitted. "It was like I was so freaked out I didn't even realize how scared I was."

"But you remembered your training," he countered in his low, comforting voice.

"I stood there. I knew I couldn't run, so I just waited for him to attack," I whispered.

"A warrior's decision," he muttered.

"What?"

"An honorable death. When he knows it's inevitable, a warrior faces his opponent and does so with honor."

Conal's voice had gone rough. "When our challenges are to the death, when it's obvious we're bested, a brave wolf cedes victory to his better. In a fight, someone is always the victor, but to choose to die on your own terms...that is honorable."

I slowly lifted my head as I thought about what he described. "I don't feel very honorable. Glass and Issa were hurt because of me and...so was the Laird."

"They were doing their duty. Glass will be fine, pissed that another damaged her. Issa will recover. She will have gained more respect for protecting you with her life. The Laird will reward her."

"He was bleeding."

Conal chuckled. "He's fine. It was a scratch or two."

"I'm supposed to be safe," I whispered.

He pulled me into his arms again, right up against his wide chest. "You are."

Perhaps the Lycan definition was different than mine? I rested my forehead against his chest. "It was awful," I confided. The sounds of battle and seeing Black dump the headless body on the floor. I couldn't get that scene out of my head.

"A Lycan who can't control his wolf, he must be destroyed. Kenta was dead the moment he escaped." Conal stroked my back.

"It's unfair," I cried softly.

"Theo, you saw the damage a feral wolf can do..."

"No, I don't mean that," I rushed to correct him. "I mean..."

I felt his big body tense, or maybe I sensed it? "What are you saying?"

Careful, the warning was going off in my head. I let

245

out a long sigh. "It's so stupid that I don't want to say it out loud."

"I think you should," he urged.

"I feel bad for Black," I said softly.

"You what?" I'd surprised him.

I pulled away and looked down at my hands. I'd spoken from my heart and shown too much.

"Theodora, why do you have these worries for the Laird?"

"It has to be hard to have to do that." I felt so silly even saying it. It was probably heresy for me to consider that our leader might have a weakness.

"It's his duty; it's our duty to protect our race."

"I know that." I glanced at him to see if he looked angry at my bringing up this subject. He simply looked confused. "But it has to be hard to take a life and especially of one so young…someone you've watched grow up…" My voice broke.

"The Laird would not complain."

He didn't understand me. In fact, I wasn't sure I understood me or where I was going with this. "I need to know that it matters, Conal. That he felt it, but that it doesn't scare him." I felt the tears spill down my cheeks. I was to the point where I understood what it meant for a heart to hurt. "Does he enjoy the killing part of his job?"

Conal studied my face and then looked down at his boots. "I have killed many over the years." He told me in a quiet voice. "Black and I met when we were chosen to guard the Council. We survived our training, battles, and challenges. He has killed in order to survive and to become the Leader of Novus." He then looked at me again. "I have pledged my life to serve him. I would not do that for someone that did not value life."

I nodded my head in understanding. "I needed to hear that from you, Second." My voice cracked before I finished saying his title. I could not have these feelings for someone who didn't care.

He tucked his arm under my legs and lifted me easily into his arms as he got to his feet. He carried me into their bedroom.

Solle had a mass of pillows propped up behind her back. "I tried not to listen." She was frowning at me. She got to her knees as Conal circled the bed. "Put her here, honey." She patted the space on her side of the bed.

Conal deposited me gently onto their mattress and Solle hugged me.

"I can't stop crying."

She brushed back my hair. "You're exhausted."

Conal turned out the lights. I felt the mattress depress as he climbed in behind his wife. "She's worried about Black," he murmured.

"Of course, she is," Solle cooed in a comforting voice.

Thank God, she wasn't making a big deal about what her mate had shared.

"You'll sleep with us tonight," Conal said.

"We're here if you need us," Solle told me.

I felt her adjust her soft body against my back. I closed my eyes and felt like I could sleep for a year. I let out another long breath, hoping I wouldn't start crying again.

Solle wrapped her arm around my waist and pulled me closer as Conal added his hand to my waist.

I slept.

SUMMER ARRIVED. On Sundays, the MacGregors hosted pool parties. Friends started showing up around three and stayed until dark. The guys took turns grilling, I made sides, and Tex brought his D.J. equipment and played music. The only problem was that I had to be careful because of the stupid cast. The guests liked to toss one another into the water, so my guard would snarl if anybody got too close.

Black didn't attend these parties. Not that I noticed... Well, of course, I noticed, but it didn't matter. Really.

There were more problems with shipment escorts. I didn't know any of the particulars, but Conal was concerned. There were quickly called meetings, or I'd see people in small groupings, speaking quietly and clearly upset.

I had more dreams, but they were more like impressions than anything that I could identify. Onyx questioned me almost daily and loudly expressed his disappointment. He was preparing to go to some big gathering of uppity-ups. I would have gladly assisted him with his packing because the days he didn't work with me were the good ones.

As promised, Glass recovered and was back at work. I was so happy when she stopped by the house that I hugged her and burst into tears. She was horrified when I blubbered all over her.

"You did not die," she stated the obvious as she tried to disengage from my arms.

"Because of you," I sobbed, but I did let go of her.

"It was because of your training," she said with surety.

"You saved me," I insisted.

"Hmph." She gave me a look that broadcasted she'd had enough. "We'll continue with your training."

Great.

"I will check with Solle to see if there are any restrictions due to your injury." Glass gave my cast a dirty look as if it offended her.

I cradled my wrist. "Whatever you think is best." No, I wasn't looking forward to getting my ass kicked, but what I'd learned had helped save my life. And maybe Black would stop in… I gave my head a hard shake. No more of those thoughts.

Lately, everybody seemed to be busy, but I was tired of studying and was feeling hemmed in. That's what my grandma would have called it. I wanted to do something. So, Solle suggested, no, she decided that they should take me out.

She spent an hour going through her closet trying to find something for me to wear. She also did my hair and makeup. I was now standing by the front door wondering how the hell I'd gotten myself into this.

Conal slowly looked me up and down. "You look hot," he said letting go a low whistle.

"Solle's doing," I grumbled.

One side of his mouth lifted. "I'll probably have to kill somebody tonight."

I smirked at his dramatics.

"The males will be all over you." He didn't look too upset at the task of keeping them away.

Solle and I had very different ideas about what I should

wear to the local club. I'd been thinking jeans, a tight tank, and my one pair of pumps. I was excited, but I wasn't a club kind of girl. I loved to dance but the entire meat market mentality put me off. Just because I danced with a guy didn't mean I wanted to have sex. However, I couldn't say no to Solle when she was so happy and enthusiastic. So, I was wearing a dress that brushed my calves. From the front, I was covered, but my entire back was exposed all the way to my sides. The dress was secured to the edges of my breasts by two-sided tape. I prayed that sweat wouldn't affect the adhesive or my boobs would be flapping for all to see. Although from the stories I'd heard about the club, a little nudity wouldn't matter to the Lycans.

"Remember, if anything upsets you, tell me and we'll leave." Conal glanced at his watch.

"Okay, Dad." I smiled at his protective streak.

Then Solle started down the stairs. She wore a really short dress and if I hadn't seen the tag, I would've thought was one of Conal's wife-beaters. It was white, and she wore a thong under it. That was all.

Already, I could tell this was going to be crazy. I just had to stick close to my group, and all would be fine. Asher was my guard for the night, so he dropped us at the door to the happening place that was really called, "The Club." Maybe Lycans did have a sense of humor?

I was no judge of hot spots. I'd been clubbing maybe three times in my entire life. I didn't like the atmosphere or getting felt up by random hands. Plus, the cover price was usually high and the cost of drinks even more outrageous.

Conal placed his warm hand in the space just above my butt and pressed lightly for me to follow Solle, who was practically dancing to the double doors. "If you're uneasy, stay close, Seer," he said softly.

I was nervous, excited, and curious. I'd heard bits of gossip about what happened when a Lycan cut loose and had fun. I'd seen for myself how physical the play could get at the pool parties. A part of me couldn't wait to see the truth. If Solle's dress was any indication, things got incendiary.

A male greeted us as soon as we cleared the doors. He was tall with a medium-build and elaborately styled hair. So well done it looked like he'd just rolled out of bed and run his fingers through it. He gave Solle an appreciative look. "Ah, Solle, we're honored that you're with us tonight."

"Raul," Conal's voice held a hint of growl. "We have another joining us."

Raul's attention turned to me. His brown eyes studied me from my breasts to my feet, finally returning to my face. "And who do we have here?" His smile promised badness in the best way possible.

The door opened behind us and Asher entered. "She's not your concern," he said, his voice clipped. Since the incident with Kenta, Asher was either with me or at Issa's bedside.

"Asher." Raul stopped leering and stood taller as he addressed my guard.

Conal broke up the staring contest. "We'd like to be seated."

This time, Asher led the way behind Raul. I prepared to have my senses overloaded with sound and color. I was pleasantly surprised to find that the music was loud but not at ear-bleed decibels. There was a light show, but it wasn't strobing, so I could see. We were led

251

up a flight of steps to an elevated platform that over-looked the huge dance floor below. Raul stopped at a large booth. He pulled the table out so we didn't have to scoot into the space. Conal motioned for Solle and I to sit in the middle of the male bookends.

Immediately, a female approached our table. She was dressed in a purple sequin bra and tiny black satin shorts. "I'm Raye and I'll be your server tonight." She stared openly at me.

I gave her a medium-warm smile. Basil and Issa had made me practice my greetings, so I wouldn't be considered aggressive.

"You-you're the human." She stared in wonder.

Asher sat straighter. "She is Theodora Morrissey, Seer to the Novus Pack, so mind your manners, wolf."

Her eyes widened. "I do apologize."

I nodded once and continued smiling. I was used to this.

"My mother says you're a witch," she blurted.

I didn't know if that was a good or a bad thing. "I'm not Wiccan," I started slowly. "But I guess that to some, my psychic ability might cause me to be labeled a witch." I made a mental note to do some research on that. "So, why don't you call me Theodora and leave it at that?"

"She is a gift from The Lady," Conal said in a low voice.

Raye turned pale.

I felt bad for the female, so I tried to throw her a life-line. "Talking about what I am is boring, so let's order."

That made Raye focus, and she turned to Solle. "What would you like?"

Solle's hand went to my thigh under the table and gave a light squeeze.

We placed our orders and Conal leaned back resting his arm behind Solle. "A witch?"

"Now, I know what to dress up as for Halloween." I smiled. "Do you all celebrate Halloween or is it Samhain?" I made another mental entry on my list of things to learn.

Solle snuggled closer to her husband. "The kids dress up, and we usually have a party at the community center."

"She started that," Conal said and smiled at his wife.

Solle shrugged. "It's a reason to party."

Raye returned with our drinks. I tried to relax. From time to time, people would stop by our table to say hello. More drinks were ordered and consumed by the wolves. I knew it took a lot to get a wolf inebriated, and the effects didn't last long. I had switched to tonic water with lime after the first drink. There was no way I could keep up.

Asher wasn't drinking at all. In fact, my guard looked miserable. I'd hit the dance floor twice with Solle and he'd followed us, looking as if it was a terrible fate.

Tex was spinning in the D.J. booth, and Brian, one of the nurses from Solle's office, approached. "There you are." He winked at me.

"I've been waiting for you," I teased. Brian was gay and a great dancer.

"Oh, honey, you are going to get so lucky," he gave me a slow sexy smile.

"If only I could hook the two of you up," Solle told us grumpily.

I turned to my friend. "You know I could never be happy with a man who's prettier than me."

Brian placed his hands on his hips. "Hey. I don't know if I should take that as a compliment or not." He gave me a dramatic frown.

"It was a compliment, pretty boy," I said, giggling, "and the truth."

"Come dance with me, so I can make all of these other wolves jealous." He held out his hand.

I started to shift to once again climb out when I glanced at Asher. "Hey, guys, could you just watch me from the railing?" I was appealing to Conal. "We'll stay right in front of you. That way if I need your help, you can leap over the railing."

Conal looked at the railing while he considered my request.

"I won't let anything happen to Theodora," Brian vowed.

I felt Conal's wolf stir. I shamelessly pouted my lips. "One song? After, we'll check in to see how it's working."

I didn't rush Conal. The muscle at the side of his jaw pulsed once, twice. Suddenly, this was very important to me. I needed a sign that they trusted me enough to give me a little space, that Conal trusted me.

"You," Conal spoke to Brian, "I will show you where to go." Conal got up from our booth.

I'd won.

Brian and I danced, and when that song ended, we turned to face the balcony railing, and Asher gave us a single nod.

I think I stayed on the dance floor for a solid hour. When other males approached, Brian would pull me closer, but soon, we were surrounded by three males who were trying to cut in. Conal and Solle immediately joined us and whatever the Second said made those males scatter.

However, more came. I basically ignored them and their attempts to capture my attention. Solle was plastered against my back as our bodies moved to the beat. Conal was behind her, grinding. I was having a blast with my friends. A dark-skinned male approached our group and tried to grind on me from the front. I mean, the guy didn't even say hello or ask.

Brian pushed him away and a second later Asher was there, with his hand wrapped around the male's throat.

I didn't want to be the center of a scene, so I whispered that I needed a drink. Our group returned to our booth with Brian in tow.

Of course, more drinks arrived and so did Glass with three strangers. Two were beautiful blonde Scandinavian-looking women, and the third was older but still lovely. In human years, I would have guessed her to be in her late forties.

"Glass," Solle yelled.

"Hello." The warrior stood stiffly. She wasn't dressed in revealing club wear. Instead, she was in a black tank and very faded jeans and low-heeled boots.

The elder woman spoke to Glass in a language I didn't understand but, clearly, she wanted an introduction.

Glass frowned. "This is Conal MacGregor, Second in the Novus Pack, his mate, Solle, and our Seer."

Apparently, Brian and Asher didn't matter.

"Margarethe is a member of my birth pack," Glass explained.

I think we were all looking at the two younger women, wondering who they were.

When Glass didn't continue with the introductions, Conal said, "Welcome."

Margarethe smiled charmingly. "And these are my daughters, Elise and Eloise. They are un-mated."

Well, all right. Good to know that pushy mothers were everywhere. I nodded at the younger women but didn't smile. I was trying to recall everything I'd been taught about meeting members of other packs.

"You allow a human to sit with you?" The one, Eloise possibly, sneered down at me.

"Theodora Morrissey is my friend," Glass ground out the words.

"You associate with humans?" the other sister spoke.

Conal cleared his throat, and we all turned our attention to him. "Perhaps you did not hear her title?" He gave the two women a long look.

The mood changed, and I tensed. Conal didn't like what was happening.

Margrethe smiled again, but this time she dipped her chin, "We mean no offense. I don't believe my daughters have ever met a *true* Seer."

I didn't miss the emphasis on the extra word and neither did my pack members.

"Are you questioning her title?" Solle asked with a sweet, confused smile on her face. It made me shiver. I knew she didn't approve of the slight.

"No, the language... Perhaps I chose the wrong word," Margarethe explained as she took one step backwards. "I meant no offense."

Glass looked like she wanted to slap the woman. "We will go to our seats."

256

When they left us, Solle fumed, "What a bitch."

"You would be, too, if you were trying to shop those two girls," Brian added sharply.

"Poor Glass," Conal said before taking a drink of his beer. "They're somehow related by blood. She couldn't put off their visit." He glanced at me. "Duty to blood—it always comes at the worst possible time."

"So, she's stuck with them for the weekend?" Solle brushed her boob into her mate's arm. "That has to suck. That mother is a barracuda."

A slow song came on, and I suggested, "Why don't you two go dance."

"Are you trying to get rid of us?" Solle asked, but she was already scooting to get up.

"Well, you do look hot," I said, and she did.

She looked over her shoulder with a huge smile. "I like that you noticed."

She was such a flirt. Still, I was blushing, and that embarrassed me more.

Brian moved closer to me. "So, do you think that mamma is here to offer her daughters to the Laird?"

"Why?"

"He's supposed to be here tonight. His table's set up." Brian was looking over my shoulder.

I looked around before I could stop myself. The elaborate banquet table in the corner was empty.

"He's not here yet. You'll know when he arrives," my dance partner drawled.

That would give me time to get a handle on my reactions. I would admit to missing him. I liked learning from him. He was a natural teacher, and if I was totally honest, he wasn't hard to look at.

The next half hour my eyes darted to that empty

booth a hundred times. I needed to stop. "Hey, let's go dance," I suggested to Brian.

Asher spoke for the first time in forever, "Solle and Conal return."

Conal and Solle were about five steps from our booth when the lights flashed three times.

Then Tex's voice boomed through the speakers, "Raider Black, Leader of the Novus Pack."

I guess that meant that he'd arrived. I tried not to look around with huge eyes. I wanted to play it cool.

And I failed. As the Laird made his way to the landing, he was stopped numerous times by his people. They were excited that he was out tonight.

I watched Black approach his Second. They exchanged what I called the "bro hug" then Black leaned down to kiss Solle's cheek. After that, his gaze met mine. I felt my mouth go dry as I presented my brand. "Laird." The title came out breathy and low.

"Seer, you honor us with your presence." The corners of his mouth turned up a little.

I felt myself returning his smile. "Hardly." I rolled my eyes and realized that others were watching. "I'm having a good time."

"Are you?" His voice caressed the words.

I swear my nipples hardened. "The people..." I looked at Solle for help. "The music... It's great."

"She's been very popular," Solle said. "Conal had to beat back the males."

He continued to watch me. "Really?"

"No," I said and aimed at glare at Solle.

"In that dress, are you kidding me?" Solle continued.

What the hell was she doing? I didn't want this kind of attention. I tried to communicate that with my eyes.

Why couldn't I have the ability to break into her brain and speak?

Black crossed his muscular arms across his chest. I tried not to notice how his white T-shirt hugged his muscles. "Ah yes, the dress."

Now, I also wished that I had the gift of teleportation because I would be gone. This was ridiculous.

Solle continued, "Turn around, girl. Show him the back."

"No." I tried to shrug off the hand she placed on my arm.

Black motioned with his hand for me to turn around.

I didn't have a choice. I couldn't roll my eyes again. I straightened my shoulders and made sure my boobs were out as I turned slowly, exposing my bare back to his eyes.

Why did it feel so sexual? We were in a room filled with others, but as I turned to show him my back, I felt like we were alone. For one crazy second, I wanted to glance over my shoulder and smile invitingly.

Stop. I finished my circle and faced him again.

"Niiice," he said in a low voice.

Was he picturing how my bared skin would look with marks left from his claws? I couldn't respond. I had no words, but I needed to stop thinking about him.

"Will you join us?" Conal asked.

"For a round." The Laird smiled easily.

Brian made a quick exit, and Asher stood against the railing, watching our table as did two other guards. Black chose the seat beside me.

"Shots," he told Raye when she appeared.

I could do a shot. I didn't want to. Right now, I

wanted to go unnoticed. However, his wolf was aware of me as he shifted a little closer.

He felt so good, his strong thigh now resting against mine, warm and solid.

I should move, but I couldn't, then he'd know that he was affecting me.

They drank three more shots. Luckily for me, when I opted out, nobody objected.

"You've been quiet." Black stroked his finger down my arm.

Tricky, tactile wolf. "It's a lot to take in," I said as I hoped he'd think the goosebumps appearing on my skin were there because I was chilled, not in reaction to his surprisingly gentle touch.

"You doing all right?" he asked but didn't continue touching me.

I didn't miss it, not at all. *Focus.* I knew he meant the Kenta thing. "Trying," I answered and tried to look away.

"Theo."

I saw understanding in his eyes. He was usually so shuttered, his expression giving nothing away. I wanted to rest my hand on his cheek, to give comfort, if only for a moment.

"There you are, Laird." Glass and her group approached our table.

"Oh, yes, Glass mentioned that members of her old pack were visiting." He looked over at the three women and smiled broadly. "Please, join me at my table." He nodded his goodbye to us and led the women to his table.

Solle and I danced some more, and Conal joined us. I was getting tired, so Conal gave Asher a signal, and he met me at the top of the steps. As we passed the Laird's table, I saw something that made me stumble in surprise.

Black had one of the sisters sitting on the table, and he was fucking her. Right there in front of everybody.

I couldn't believe my eyes.

She was resting on the edge of the table, and he was pumping into her. I couldn't stop watching the muscles flex in his arms as he held his body above hers.

Asher took my elbow and urged me forward. "Gifts for the Laird," he said under his breath.

I took my seat and forced myself not to glance in Black's direction. I knew that Lycans liked sex and they had voracious appetites. This shouldn't shock me.

But it did.

I caught myself staring as Black now had the other sister on top of the table. His hips were moving so fast. *Gaw!* I turned to face Asher, "So, I guess that happens a lot?"

He wore his serious expression, although I had seen him laugh many times when we were alone. "I'm not sure what you mean."

I leaned back against the padded seat back and sighed dramatically. "I'm not sure either." Then I laughed at myself. I sounded like a prude.

"It's an honor to have sex with the Laird." Asher glanced in that table's direction.

That wasn't too shocking. Royals had enjoyed that perk since the dawn of time. I once again noted how modern the Novus Pack was, yet they still followed age-old practices.

"And because he and his contracted mate aren't together, families bestow their gifts for goodwill," Asher said, continuing with my history lesson.

I didn't know how I felt about a mother "gifting" her daughters to a Leader, but now wasn't the time to share my concerns.

"I see that our Laird is enjoying his bounty." Conal smirked at Asher as he motioned for Solle to take her seat.

We all stared at the Laird's table where now the Margarethe was sucking off one of the guards, and another was taking a sister doggie—or would it be, wolf-style? Black stood watching and drinking a beer.

Raye appeared to see if we wanted more to drink. I asked for a shot. When it arrived, I threw it back as Conal ordered more.

I tried to chat with my friends and not notice what was happening at the table to my far left.

Solle leaned in, or maybe I was already leaning against her. "Does that bother you?"

"Of course not," I answered too quickly.

"They sort of expect him to do that, you know?" She looped her arm around my shoulders.

"It surprised me, that's all. I mean, I walked right up on them."

"And he didn't ask you to join in?"

My body jerked in surprise. "Whhaaatt?" I think my head was going to explode with the images that appeared. My skin felt tight, and my body temperature rose.

"Oh, come on, you know you're hot." Her gaze was on my breasts. "And he's noticed."

"Stop." I pushed playfully at her shoulder. I missed and hit her boob. I glanced at her face to see how that went over.

"I'd say do that a little softer, but I don't think that you're into P.D.A." Her smile was definitely seductive.

"Conal," I called as I looked in his direction. "It's time to go. Solle's feeling frisky."

"Oh yeah?" He glanced at his beautiful mate.

She pursed her full lips. "I'm thinking we might need to find someone for Theodora."

"What? No." I halted my hand mid-shove. My face heated. A tiny part of me was turned on and wouldn't have minded a sweaty quickie. Damn, these tricky wolves.

Conal was watching me closely, with a small smile playing on his lips. "Are you sure?"

I shook my head several times. "Very." The last thing I'd ever want was Conal being my pimp. That was unthinkable.

"Let's go home," he said.

Asher was already up and on his way to retrieve the SUV.

I tried to prepare myself for having to once again walk past the Laird's table. I giggled at the thought and realized I might be drunk. I tried to focus on keeping my shit together. I didn't want to say or do anything stupid.

The Laird was leaning against the balcony railing as we passed. Apparently, he shared his bounty with his guards, and they appeared to be most appreciative and limber.

Conal stopped our group. He had one arm around my waist and his other around his mate. "We're taking off."

"You could stay for one more drink," Black offered.

"Nah, gotta get the kid to bed." He squeezed my waist.

I giggled and reminded myself to keep quiet.

"Are you making breakfast?" Black asked me.

"Uhm, sure." I always made breakfast on Sunday morning. It was now my thing to do.

He nodded once.

Shit, shit, shit. I didn't need him to be sitting with us after everything I'd seen tonight. Especially, the intense look on the Laird's face as he'd fucked.

I heard him chuckle, and I was convinced he could read my thoughts. I tried to smile pleasantly. "Be there around 9:30, unless you want cold eggs."

This time, he gave me a real smile and toasted me with his beer bottle, "Yes, Ma'am."

TWENTY-THREE

SOLLE MACGREGOR

I didn't mean to upset Theodora by mentioning the attraction between the Seer and our Laird. Anyone with a sense of sight or smell could tell. It was nothing to be embarrassed about. Our Leader was available for a quick tumble or two. When I'd first noticed the mutual attraction, I'd worried that she would not understand that he was promised to another. However, she had proved herself to be rational and accepting of our ways.

Everyone had noticed that she was attractive. She was voluptuous and feminine, plus she didn't realize it, which made it seem even more of a challenge to capture her attention. Who wouldn't want to unwrap that gift? Teach her all about pleasure and know that she would blush and giggle the entire time someone whispered dirty thoughts into her ear.

I thought about it every time she leaned into me. Conal knew her effect on me, and he was into it. Not that he wanted the human. We'd discussed my feelings one morning before she woke. My mate approved of my idea that I try to seduce her, breaking through her nice girl façade. Stroking and tasting her until she went wild.

Maybe tonight was the right time…? He entered our bedroom as I pulled my dress over my head.

"My timing is perfect." His big, calloused hands were on my breasts while he pressed his body against my back.

I pulled back my shoulders, giving him better access.

"I was thinking," I said softly.

"You want her," he finished my thought.

If asked what the best part of being mated was, my answer would be that he knew me. I didn't have to spend time explaining my feelings or desires. Conal always knew.

I twisted my head, so I could look up into his eyes.

"Then why, Mate, are you standing here?" He smiled like a hungry wolf who'd just sighted a deer.

Yeah, he was totally into this. I slipped out of my thong and sauntered to our closet to find my silk robe. I tied the belt around my waist, loose enough so that my breasts showed almost to my nipples.

"You'll need to go in easy," he cautioned.

He'd stripped off his shirt. I loved looking at his body.

"I know what I'm doing," I gave him a cheeky grin. "I caught you, didn't I?"

He pulled me into his arms and kissed me. "You did."

Of course, we both knew that he did all of the pursuing and the catching, although I didn't put up much of a fight.

I made my way quietly to Theodora's room. She was in her bathroom with the water running. "Hey." I knocked on the doorframe. I knew that she liked for us to pretend she had some privacy.

She finished rinsing the cleanser from her face. After drying, she pulled the bright pink headband from her hair. "I'm going to need your help with this tape."

I moved toward her. I slowly started to peel the adhesive from her lower back. After I cleared a section, I smoothed my fingertips over the skin. I did this following the dress' contour over her hips as I moved toward the sides of her breasts.

Theodora's body shivered as she let out a breath.

"I'll have to put some lotion on your skin when I'm done," I murmured.

She didn't speak but nodded slowly as her hands gripped the front of the vanity.

My nose told me she wasn't experiencing discomfort; she was aroused. "All night, I wanted to do this." I ran the tip of my red fingernail over her back in a zig-zag pattern. "To touch this beautiful skin."

"Solle?" she whispered my name.

I heard the need in her tone. I leaned closer and brushed my lips lightly over her shoulder blade as my nimble fingers traveled between the fabric of her dress and her ribs. "So beautiful." The tips of my fingers rested against the side of her breast. "So sexy."

Her hips shifted back, resting lightly against me.

I changed to the other side and after I finished loosening the adhesive, I cupped her heavy breasts in my hands and pulled her against me, so that my silk-covered breasts were against her back. I kissed her neck. "So shy, and yet, so tempting."

She dropped her head onto my shoulder.

I continued kissing her shoulder and the skin that led

to her neck, while lightly kneading her breasts. I loved their softness.

I watched us together in the mirror. Her eyes were closed, but her cheeks were pink with arousal.

She whispered my name again, "Solle?"

I turned my head and captured her lips. I was surprised at their softness. I liked it, and I wanted more.

"What are you doing?" She hadn't pulled away. Her lips were almost touching mine.

"My Mate is seducing you." Conal was leaning against the bathroom doorframe.

I felt Theodora try to break free of my hold. I let her turn her body so that she was now facing me, but our bodies weren't touching.

Conal must have seen her panicked reaction. "Solle wants you," he said, using his softest voice, "and I... I'd like to see that wish come true."

"I'm not sure," Theodora's words sounded confused as she looked from me to Conal.

"Not sure that you want Solle to touch you?" He sounded like he was speaking to a frightened child.

I could almost feel her thinking about her answer.

"I'm not sure about your feelings." She looked directly at my mate.

I loved that Theodora cared about my man. She trusted him and relied on his opinion.

He walked to us. "My sweet girl." He wrapped his arms around us both. "What brings joy to my mate does so to me."

"But..." she whispered as she looked at Conal, her blue eyes were huge.

"And I'd love to watch her make you come." He

growled as he picked us both up in his powerful arms and carried us to our bed.

He dropped us both on the huge mattress, and we giggled. He took the chair in the corner, showing us that he wouldn't be participating. This was my show.

Theodora started to sit up but I placed my hand on her upper thigh. "I'm going to undress you and apply lotion to your back." We would start innocently. She needed to become comfortable with my touch.

She looked down at the dress hanging from her hips. "I need to stand up to take it off."

I liked that she was cooperating. Of course, she could say no, but I didn't want her to.

She rose and unzipped the invisible zipper at the side of the skirt. She shimmied her hips and pushed the dress down until it fell to the ground. We watched it fall. She looked at me as if waiting for my next instruction. God, this was heady stuff.

"Get back on the bed," Conal ordered. "Solle, grab your lotion and attend to her back."

So, he wasn't going to touch, but he was involved. He couldn't help himself. He was always bossy in the bedroom.

Theo climbed back onto our bed, crawled to the middle, and arched her back enticingly before lowering her body slowly to the mattress. *Our girl has watched some porn.* Or maybe, she really was this sensual. If that was the case, I wasn't going to let her out of our bed.

Conal growled, "Mate." Yeah, he'd caught it, too.

I needed to focus. I stretched to reach for the bottle on my nightstand.

"Babe, lose the robe." I could hear the heat in his words. Conal enjoyed watching me move. He liked to fuck—correction—we loved to fuck, but he also liked the seduction. I was one lucky wolf.

I untied the belt and let the silk fall slowly from my shoulder as I watched Conal look at me. I sat back on my heels so that it fell from my body.

I crawled back to Theodora and pressed my lips against her exposed cheek. "I'm going to give you a massage," I said.

She nodded and relaxed her body. Before I moved away, she whispered, "I've never done anything like this."

I loved her. She always blew me away with her absolute honesty and vulnerability at the craziest times. It was disarming and charming. I kissed her again. "Me, neither."

I crawled over her body and straddled her thighs. I opened the top to the lotion and poured some into my hands. I rubbed them together to warm the lotion, and then I touched her skin, running my hands over her. Instinctively, I knew how to touch her.

I leaned closer and kissed a trail down her spine as I traced the tips of my fingers along the sides of her breasts.

"Roll onto your back." Conal's voice seemed loud in the quiet room.

I climbed off of Theodora and helped her roll over, not that she needed encouragement. She was eager, but I wanted to continue touching her, keeping our connection.

When she was on her back with her eyes tightly closed, I leaned over her and captured her mouth. I wanted to taste her again. I pressed my tongue against her lips, and she opened willingly for me.

One of her hands gripped my shoulder while one wound in my hair. I loved that she was responding.

I moved so that I could kiss her neck. She made a noise deep in her throat that made me want more. My hands moved to her breasts. I kneaded their fullness, occasionally plucking her hard nipples. Soon, my mouth followed, and I sucked greedily on the soft skin and the hard point.

Dear God, the sounds she was making made me hungrier. Her thighs were thrown open for me to explore.

"Touch her, Solle."

Conal's voice was rough. This was getting to him. I kissed a trail down her rounded belly. I knew she thought that she was fat. We'd had that discussion several times. Lycan females were rounded, but our curves were from muscles. I thought she was beautiful.

She was still wearing her black silky panties.

"Hand only," he said.

I smiled to myself. I ran my right hand over her mound.

"Solle," Theodora cried, "I...I want."

"Let's take these off." I placed my hands on her hips and gently rolled down the panties.

She helped by digging in her heels and lifting her ass, using one foot to push them down her leg and kick them away. "Are we...you going to...?" Her voice was hoarse, and her eyes a little wild.

"Shh, I know what you need," I said as I ran my index finger over her folds. God, she was so wet. I touched her as I liked to be touched. I circled her clit lightly, and her hips jumped.

"Please," she tried to grip my hand.

271

"Let me," I crooned as I entered her warmth. She was so hot, this was familiar and yet different. I felt her muscles tighten around me as if she wanted to keep my finger inside her.

I added another finger because it would be what I needed. I knew that feeling full would add to her enjoyment.

I finger-fucked her and learned what she liked by her body's reactions. In no time, or it felt that way to me, she was close. Her hips were pumping to my rhythm, and the beautiful girl's hands were on her breasts, pulling on her nipples.

"Oh, God," she panted. "Ohhhh, God." She came. Her body pulsed around my fingers.

"Mate, show me your hand."

I turned to look at Conal. He sat on the edge of the chair. I could see the muscles in his arms flexing as he gripped the armrests.

I slid my fingers free and held up my hand. I started to lick her wetness from my digits.

"Jesus," he growled.

When I finished, I glanced at Theodora and she was sound asleep. I swear there was a tiny smile on her face. "She's out."

"I'll move her to her bed." He got slowly to his feet, picked up the sleeping beauty, and carried her to her room.

I pulled back our duvet and began to climb under the covers, but he was on me, and it was hot and wild.

God, I loved this man.

I loved my life.

Later, I lay wrapped in Conal's arms. "How do you think tomorrow will go?"

"She'll be nervous. We'll show her that everything we shared was beautiful."

"Do you think she'll want to do it again?" I asked slowly.

He grunted. "I think she'll tell herself it was the result of a drunken night. You and I can't pressure her. If it happens again, it'll be because she asks."

I sighed. "Okay." I was disappointed. I wanted to touch her again.

Conal kissed my hair. "She doesn't speak of it, but if you think about it...she has so little control of her life. We can't take any more away from her."

"Do you think she's happy...here...with us?" I asked in a small voice.

"You know she'll only be with us a short time." His voice went deeper. "Even if she lives a very long human life, it'll still be a short time."

"Is this why you don't get involved with humans? The lifespan thing?"

"For much of my life, our kind didn't interact or consider making friends with humans. That has changed and I believe it'll happen more, but yes, losing someone you care about to death is difficult."

I turned my head as if I could see through the wall to Theodora's room. "That makes me sad."

"Solle, enjoy our time with her." He kissed my neck. "That's all that you can do."

TWENTY-FOUR

RAIDER BLACK

I knocked on their front door at nine thirty. Conal greeted me with a grin. He knew the party had gone on and on last night—well, up to about four hours ago. My guards would be happy for days.

"Mornin'," he greeted me, "or have you slept?"

"Is there coffee?" I told him all that he needed to know.

He slapped me once on the back. "This way."

Theo had her back to us, and she was working with something in a deep frying pan.

"Seer," I greeted her.

She looked over her shoulder. "Laird, could you, I mean, may I please have one moment before I present?"

I loved that she always fell into such formal language regarding her brand. "Yes, Theodora."

Her graceful hand was stirring something quickly. She let out a satisfied sigh, "There," and adjusted the knob on the front of the stove. She turned around while pulling the towel from her shoulder and wiping her hands. Then she walked to the breakfast bar and dipped her chin. "Good Morning, Laird."

"Good morning to you." Her consumption of alcohol had been noted by Asher, and he'd sent his report last night after dropping her off. She didn't seem to be showing any ill effects.

"Coffee?"

Her smile didn't reach her expressive blue eyes. Perhaps my first impression was incorrect. "Of course."

She served me and returned to her cooking duties. I enjoyed watching her work. She was efficient and organized. I realized she approached cooking the same way she did her studies.

"I read the most recent report." Conal's tone was grim.

"I don't mind paying off the cops." One escort had been stopped twice during the same trip.

Conal frowned. "It's an anomaly."

"Do you believe someone is leaking our routes, alerting the police?"

"Both stops were for speeding. They didn't show an interest in looking inside the trailers."

"They would need probable cause..." I saw where Conal was going. "However, they would need very little to come up with a reason to search."

"A stop causes inconvenience—the time lost to the stop, the meet up to continue, and a discussion. So, we lose an hour." Conal was thinking out loud.

"If the stop was for more than speeding then the escort riding in front would have to decide how to handle it."

"You can't make a cop disappear." Theo's back was still to us as she spoke. "Not with their body cameras and dashboard cams." She put the baking sheet into the oven before turning around to face us.

"We aren't in the practice of killing officers of the law, Seer." No, we bribed and hacked their systems.

"I don't want to know if you are," she said testily. "Escorting is how the Pack makes money, but more and more cameras are in use."

"So, what do you suggest?" I was curious to learn how much she'd picked up about our business.

"I want to say get out of the business. I don't like it." She took a step closer to the breakfast bar. "In fact, I hate it, because I know what travels along that route. The thought of people trapped in a container makes me sick." She wiped her hands on her thighs. "But those are my personal feelings and if Novus doesn't provide the service, someone else will."

Obviously, we'd discussed many points of business in front of her. She was very talented at making herself invisible, sitting quietly in a corner.

She frowned. "You probably figure that if a human is stupid enough to get caught, then it's his own fault."

"We escort, not capture, Theodora," Conal said coolly.

The line appeared between her eyebrows. "I know I can't win this philosophical discussion. My point is that it's going to be harder and harder to run your routes under the radar."

I tilted my head slightly in agreement.

She pushed a lock of hair behind her ear. "Whoever is causing these disruptions wants to cause inconvenience

only. Let's be honest. If they wanted to really hurt you…
uhm, us…they could do so easily by making a call and
giving a tip."

Conal's eyes had narrowed. "So what are you
saying?"

She stood before us, and I don't think she realized
she was grasping the wrist that carried my brand. "I
think it's someone in the Pack or affiliated with us."

Solle joined us. "No. That's insane. Nobody would
do that," she told Theo bluntly.

Theo dropped her chin, unwilling to engage with her
friend.

"Have you had a vision?" Conal questioned her
sharply. "You didn't say anything."

She shook her head once. "I would report my
visions." She raised her head, and I saw anger in her
eyes. She'd been cooperative. "I've been thinking about
the disruptions for a while. It seems to me that they're
always small things and they don't happen regularly. So,
it makes sense to me that whoever is responsible," she
held up one finger, "knows the routes and schedules."
Then another finger. "The disruption is just large
enough to affect timing, which would be noted by
anybody paying attention." She held up her third finger.
"They don't do it often. Perhaps, only when they absolutely have to."

"You have a scenario in mind?" I saw the logic in her
summation.

She looked at Conal and Solle before returning her
attention to me. "The person is in trouble. They're being
pressured to do these things or share the information
with whoever is pulling the strings." She bit down on her
lip before continuing. "The reason it doesn't happen

often is that they hold off until they absolutely have to spill. They're trying to keep the damage to a minimum, but if this is true, they won't be able to keep stalling much longer."

I studied the human before me. How she'd broken down the psychology of our troublemaker was unexpected. I didn't give her enough credit. She'd surprised me and, more importantly, pleased me.

I should have expected she would see more. Theo's quiet and easy-going demeanor had fooled me and probably my team into believing she wasn't paying attention. She was a quick learner, but we'd overlooked her analytical skills.

"What do you suggest?" I addressed her as I would a member of my Board.

"Ask your techies to delve into your employees' financials. I'd suggest two to three years back. They'd need time to get into trouble, and then come up with a plan."

Conal picked up the thread. "Possibly someone who isn't out on the runs."

Theo closed her eyes and went still. I felt her using her power; it was like a slight vibration against my skin. "No," she opened her eyes. "I think they are out on the road. They want to see what happens. I think..." She closed her eyes again.

We all leaned closer.

She opened her eyes and sighed. "They might believe that if things went badly, they could help." She flipped her hair behind her shoulder. "Look, I know it's all really vague, but I feel that...they're trying to play both sides."

Conal asked, "How much of this is from your gift?"

I watched Theo link her hands tightly together. "My

gift is telling me my theory is correct." She made a stop sign with her right hand. "The problem is I've never done this before, so I don't know how much to trust it." She turned her gaze to me.

"What you say makes some sense." I leaned forward a bit to look over at Conal's mate. "Solle, you know many families. They confide their upsets to you."

Solle had been leaning into Conal's side, but she stood tall as I addressed her. "They do confide in me."

"I don't want to hear every problem. I get enough of that, as it is."

Her body relaxed a little in relief.

Theo spoke before I could continue. "I think the first step is to run through the financials. When that list is compiled, let me talk to anyone who seems to be in trouble."

"No," I said sternly. I didn't want her near anyone who was a threat to the Pack.

"Not one on one." She flashed me a frustrated look. "Maybe when they're getting ready to leave on a job or just getting back. I might be able to pick up on something."

Solle gave Theo a grateful smile. "I know it's my duty to report any threat to the Pack, but I have to be honest, I don't like the idea of turning in my patients."

"We can probably pare down the list before it got to that point, doc," Theo said.

"I'll call Tex." Conal started to get up.

"Hold off," I said, and Theo gave me a look that was filled with hurt. "I want to discuss this in front of the entire Board, tomorrow. I'll present a complete plan."

"Thank you, Laird." She bowed her head, but I saw that she was smiling.

"The Novus Pack is grateful to you, Seer," I responded formally. I wondered if when she was naked, would she be as submissive to me?

The timer made its dinging sound, and she turned to look at it. "Breakfast in three minutes."

TWENTY-FIVE

THEODORA MORRISSEY

I was being a good sport, I told myself as Solle stood behind me in my bathroom. She was running her fingers through my hair for the fifth time. "I love it," she said to my reflection with a smile.

"Basil was so over the top I'm surprised that Kara didn't use her scissors to stab him during my hair appointment." I'd been so uncomfortable being the center of attention at the salon. My hair was short, in a chin-length bob. Every time I moved my head, it swung. I was getting used to it.

"We need to roll," Conal said, peering into my bathroom from the doorway.

"I think we're ready." Solle released me, but not before dropping a quick kiss on my shoulder.

I hadn't shared their bed since *that* night. I'd worried about how things would be between the three of us, but they didn't treat me any differently. Except, Solle touched me even more often, and there was always an implied promise of more to come.

Why was this happening to me? I loved my friends, but I didn't want to fall in love or lust with them as a couple. That would only have one outcome. It would mean heartache for me. Then there was my other problem. *He* haunted my dreams. I told myself three times a day that Black would be a horrible choice for a crush, but I wanted him.

Conal was checking me out. "I'll need to call for two more guards to keep the males off you."

"Nice try." I patted his arm. "It'll only take one glare from you, and they'll scatter." I took one last look in the mirror. Solle had picked out my dress. It was a halter style that was cut very low in the front and to my waist in the back, with a full skirt in a bright crimson. I wouldn't be hard to miss on the dance floor.

"Are you shopping for a male tonight?" Solle asked curiously.

"I don't have time for that," I said honestly. Unfortunately for me, the male I wanted was unavailable. He'd been busy studying the results of the financial searches and checks on the people who worked the escorts. I knew that, so far, nothing had tripped any red flags.

I RODE to the party with Glass, Basil, and Asher. One of the nurses at Solle's practice hosted the special dinner for me at her parent's restaurant. They'd spent two days making my favorite dishes. It was incredible—twenty of us laughing and enjoying the food.

"I wish Issa was here," I told them.

"She is healing," Asher said. The warrior's exact style of speech didn't match the look of loss on his face.

"Do you think she'll want to come back to me when she's better?" I still felt responsible for her injuries.

"Of course." Glass gave me a side-eye look that communicated she thought that was a silly question. "Guarding the Seer is an honor."

Conversations involving emotions were wasted on Glass. Logic ruled her life. "I miss her laugh and her fashion sense," I said more for Asher's benefit. I knew he'd share this conversation on his next visit. I didn't ask about their relationship, but Asher was at the recuperating guard's bedside every day.

He glanced back at me. "She'll be sorry she missed the party."

We were in the middle of the caravan of vehicles making our way to The Club. Tex was going to man the D.J. booth for a couple of hours and had asked for suggestions for the playlist. For a group that didn't celebrate birthdays, they were making a huge effort for mine.

Well, everyone but the Laird. He hadn't attended the dinner. I hadn't asked whether he was invited, although I assumed that he was. I buried the feeling of disappointment. He was off limits.

Think of something else. I turned to Basil. "You look amazing." I touched the sleeve of his suit coat. Only a fashion nut would choose to wear a suit coat on a night when the temperature was still in the nineties.

"It's John Varvotos," he said, stressing the designer's name.

"I'm impressed." I didn't know anything about men's fashion, but I'd learned to listen to Basil's intonation to measure the importance of certain designers' names.

"It took three fittings during my trip to New York."

285

My heart swelled that he'd chosen to wear such an important piece from his closet to my party.

At The Club, we had the entire upper level of booths. It was decorated with streamers and balloons in primary colors. I loved it. At this point, I loved everything. Of course, the Lycans bought me drinks. If the pace kept up, I'd be flat on my ass in an hour. I took small sips and "lost" the glasses quickly. I could've asked Conal or one of my guards to stop the flow, but I didn't want to hurt anyone's feelings.

Luckily, dancing seemed to help burn off the haze. I'd been on the dance floor a few times, and it was a blast. Solle and I had returned to our table when the lights flickered. The Laird had arrived.

Solle's lips brushed my ear as she whispered, "I wonder if he brought you a gift?"

I shot her a questioning look. *A gift?* "You think he would?"

What would Black get me? The question boggled my mind. I waited along with my friends for our Leader to climb the stairs and make his way to our table.

He'd dressed up for the occasion. He wore a black shirt with a tiny blue stripe and black, light-weight wool trousers. I'd thought he was hot in a T-shirt, but business casual on Black was amazing. I checked to make sure I wasn't drooling.

"Theodora." His voice deepening as I presented my brand.

"Laird," I responded in a voice that sounded rough to my ears.

"Happy Birthday," he continued.

"I'm honored that you're here." The formal, correct words rolled easily from my mouth.

His eyes narrowed a tiny bit. "I wonder if you truly are?"

Was he toying with me? "It's a wonderful party." I looked around hoping to gain some control over my emotions.

"I have something for you." He turned to the guard next to him and held out his hand.

"You didn't need to get me anything...really."

"You may not like it." He held a small box in his huge palm.

Slowly, I reached out to take the box. "Thank you, Laird," I told him solemnly as I'd been taught.

"Open it." He moved a little closer to me as if he was cutting me off from the view of the others.

I pulled the ribbon from the white box. After removing the lid, I noticed that my hand was shaking. I gently dug into the tissue paper and removed a ring.

It wasn't just any ring. It had a thick gold band with engravings covering it and a ruby nestled in the middle. The stone was big. I stared at it then up at Black. I felt my mouth open and close twice. I couldn't come up with any words.

"Do you like it?" he asked.

In that moment, I honestly believed that he thought I might say no. I blinked and looked at it again. "It's truly the most beautiful thing I've ever seen." I was in awe. "Thank you," I said breathlessly.

He took the band from my fingers and slid it onto my right middle finger. It was an exact fit.

It looked perfect on my hand. "I don't know what to say..." This felt like so much more than a simple birthday gift, like he was laying another mark of ownership on me for all to see.

"A beautiful woman deserves a worthy gift," he said quietly. "My woman…a superb ring."

I knew my ears weren't playing a trick on me. Suddenly, I couldn't take in any air.

"Let me see," Solle interrupted our moment as she grabbed my hand. "Oh, Black, it's gorgeous."

My gaze met his. "I love it."

"Then I'm pleased," he said as Solle pulled me away to show the others.

The party and club were rocking. I'd managed to avoid most of the alcohol, but I was high on all of the attention. I loved these people.

Brian had arrived with the other members of the Pack's dance team. Oh, yeah, these wolves could dance. They had competitions, and the outcome could erupt in fights. Some of the dancers came to Zumba and were incredible. I knew that Brian danced in competitions with a woman named Valentina. He'd told me that he only liked her when music was playing. I'd seen her once and she was as intimidating as hell, reminding me of a panther, graceful and lithe. Of course, tonight she was with the group.

Somehow, I ended up standing next to her.

"You dance?" She was looking me up and down.

"I have fun." I made sure that I dropped my eyes as I answered. I knew this was an aggressive wolf.

"You enjoy it." She made it sound like a certainty. "You're responsible for the gathering at the Community Center. It is good."

It didn't sound like she was going to punch me. "We laugh, and it's a fun way to see friends." I felt that was a safe explanation.

"My mother attends. She says you're kind to the bumbling ones."

Why wasn't anyone interrupting us? I didn't dare look around for help, but I wanted to. "I'm kind of a bumbler myself," I explained cautiously.

"You are human." She gave a sniff full of disdain.

What could I say to that?

"We will dance tonight. I want to see you move," she announced.

"Oh, no," I shook my head. "That's not necessary." This couldn't be good. I didn't want her attention.

"It will be fun."

I sincerely doubted that.

Luckily, a couple approached. Gary worked at Novus, and I was given an excuse to move away from the intimidating female. He and his intended mate were adorable. They'd met at a multi-pack gathering and were going to ask The Lady for her blessing on their union soon.

Helena was soft spoken. "We were wondering if you'd join us that night?" She added quickly, "If that is asking too much...please forgive me." She lowered her eyes.

I liked them both. "I'm not sure what you want from me, but yeah, I'll come."

"Really?" Gary sounded relieved and thrilled.

"I don't have to get naked or anything, do I?" There was still so much I didn't know, but by my question, I needed to stop my alcohol intake. I made sure I was grinning so that they thought that I was joking.

"They are asking..." Black joined us smoothly. He wrapped his arm around my waist as if he'd done it a hundred times before. "Or rather hoping, that your presence will bring The Lady's answer more swiftly."

I must have been much drunker than I'd realized because I hadn't sensed his approach.

Helena and Gary both looked like statues. The male spoke first. "Laird, we would not impose on the Seer."

"No, it's fine." I smiled at the couple as I leaned into him a little. He was solid. "I'm happy for you, and if you think my being there will help, I'll do all that I can." I nodded hoping Black would see I wanted to do this for them. Gary had been one of the first at Novus to chat regularly with me.

"We will both be there," Black said to the couple and dismissed them with a look.

I slid from his hold. "Is that another thing I need to ask permission to do?" I sounded bratty, but it irritated me that he'd intruded.

"Do you even know what you volunteered for?" He didn't seem angry. In fact, he looked amused.

"I would have asked...before." Okay, he had a good point.

His eyes sparkled.

"I like Gary, he's been friendly—and not in a creepy way. I want to help them," I said, frowning. "It'll be a fun part of my job."

His eyebrows drew together. "Are you keeping some kind of ledger? Measuring the good and the bad, trying to find a way to keep them even?"

I answered quickly, "No." Then I thought about it. "Maybe? You know, some of this I make up as I go along. So yeah, I probably try to make it even." I ended with a dopey smile on my face. Yeah, I was definitely in that fun, drunk place.

He chuckled, and it was low and made my stomach flutter. "You do love us, don't you?"

That made me uncomfortable because I was always looking for hidden messages in his words. I put my hand on my hip and rolled my eyes. "I don't know about all of you…" My smile took the sting out of my words.

"I'd like a copy of your list. To see who is favored and who is not," he drawled with a playful smile, "and where you rank me?"

Fuckin' tricky wolf, taking advantage of a tipsy human.

TWENTY-SIX

NOVUS

RAIDER BLACK

I was watching Brian talking to Theodora. The medical professional stood so close, their heads almost touched. My wolf thought *too close*, but I knew he preferred men. The song ended, and Tex's voice boomed through the hidden speakers.

"Ladies and Gentleman, tonight, we have a dance challenge."

The crowd roared their approval.

"The lovely Valentina…" He held out his hand and the dark-skinned female was pulled onto the elevated stand. "And who are you challenging, darlin'?"

"I pick Brian." She pointed to the spot where Brian stood next to Theodora.

Tex smiled. "Mixing things up a bit, I see. So, who will be your partner tonight?"

"Isaac," she told the crowd and leaped gracefully to the floor.

Tex looked to our upper deck and asked, "Now that you know your competition Brian, who do you choose?"

Brian and Valentina were currently competing together; however, their fights were legendary. They represented our Pack at various events, but I knew a challenge between partners was never good.

Brian grinned confidently and wrapped his arm around Theodora. "The Birthday Girl."

Theodora's jaw sagged a bit, and then she shot Brian a glare.

Tex grinned. "Let the challenge begin."

A short light show played. I guessed that it was so the couples could plan their program.

The first notes of *Batttleflag* poured from the speakers and the dance floor cleared.

I watched as Brian whispered something in Theodora's ear, then he patted her shoulder encouragingly.

Tex made his way up the stairs. He snagged a beer from one of the servers and joined me at the rail. "You ever see her dance?"

I knew he was talking about the Seer. "No."

"She can move." He glanced at the floor. Valentina and her partner were doing some kind of complicated footwork.

I didn't answer. I was waiting to see Theo take the floor.

"This was planned," Tex reassured me. "Valentina and Brian, they talked about this."

I took that to mean the outcome wouldn't end in bloodshed.

The music shifted to the basic notes and the spotlight was on Brian, who held out his hand to his partner. He and Theo did some kind of syncopated walk to the stairs. Theo dropped her ass onto the railing and slid down the flight while Brian leaped to the ground to meet her.

"Nice," Tex mumbled. He was scrutinizing the crowd, gauging their reaction.

I watched, fascinated. One couple relied on complicated, quick footwork, and the other, simple and clean, with Theo giving lots of attitude.

She was...good, not as fast as Valentina, but she made up for that with presence. She flirted shamelessly with Brian and the crowd.

Conal joined us. "It's like she has some Lycan blood."

"Solle could do a search?" Tex suggested. "See if some relative was one of us...?"

"No." I cut that off.

"You don't want another to pack to put in a claim?" Conal was giving me a sideways look.

"She is mine." My tone put an end to that idea. I frowned because I found myself thinking of her belonging to me, in addition to the pack, too often.

The couples were now dancing side by side, and Theo was laughing. Anyone could see she was having a good time.

Tex turned on his mic. "Let's show these dancers your appreciation."

The crowd roared in approval. The wolves lining the edges of the dance floor tossed dollar bills up in the air so they rained down on the couples.

The deal was that the winning couple collected the money and the losers got nothing.

Theo said something to Brian and he gave her a very dramatic frown and nodded.

She broke away from him and bowed her head at the

other couple. Brian stood at her back. They had submitted.

"It looks like Valentina and Isaac are your winners," Tex told the crowd.

The female wolf looked surprised, but her partner rolled her out for her bow to the crowd.

Theo and Brian joined the crowd lining the edge of the floor, clapping to the song's beat. They accepted congratulations from those around them. I was happy to see that the male dancer didn't leave her side.

The Club's crew made their way onto the floor with long push brooms to collect the bills. It appeared the challenge would bring a nice payday to the victors.

Another employee stuffed the money into a white bag and presented it to the winning couple.

Valentina took the bag and sauntered to the spot where Theo stood, now talking to Solle and Glass. The dancer thrust the bag out, clearly signaling for Theo to take it.

The room erupted in cheers.

"That was unexpected," Tex said, his eyebrows rising. "Valentina isn't known for being generous."

I watched Theo sincerely thank the woman, closing with a hug.

Brian escorted her back to our area. He stopped in front of me and, with a nod, left us.

She was tightly gripping the bag. "I don't know what to do with this."

I frowned. "No one would dare touch what is yours." The punishment would be severe.

"I mean, who should I give it to?"

"It's for you. It is customary to split it with your partner."

"Brian said to keep it, but I can't. Everybody has given me so much already. I want to share it with the Pack. So, do you guys have charities I can give this to?"

"You can give it to the hospital or the school." I liked that she was asking me and thinking of others in Novus.

She leaned in a little. "See? I knew you'd give me the best answer." Her smile was warm, and I realized she was a little drunk. "For the kids, that'll be perfect." She handed the bag to me. "Can you take care of that?" She turned away from me, and I wanted to reach out and pull her back.

A couple approached her. As is our custom at a celebration, they offered her a shot.

She seemed to hesitate before smiling her agreement.

My people probably didn't know that a human can't drink as much as we can. She was being friendly to all. I knew she'd have a hard time refusing a drink from any well-wisher.

I moved to her side and wrapped my arm around her waist.

She leaned into me naturally and it felt good. No, it felt effortless and right.

"How are you doing?' I asked her.

"I need to slow down." She gave me a helpless look, and one side of her mouth dipped down. "But I can't refuse, because it would be rude when people are making such an effort for me."

My wolf and I approved. She would sacrifice herself, so that she didn't upset the pack. "Let me help," I offered.

She stiffened for a second. "Don't send them away." She looked away for a few seconds before she spoke again. "I'll be okay."

The Grimes were the next couple to approach with a tray of drinks. They owned the feed store in town and were known to share their opinions with their customers. I watched as Theo flashed a welcoming smile.

"I can't believe you all came out tonight." She gave Mrs. Grimes a short hug and nodded at Jim. "I know you open at the crack of dawn."

"We knew it would be a great party," Mrs. Grimes said.

I took that to mean she didn't want to miss out in case anything gossip-worthy happened.

Jim motioned with the tray of drinks. "I need to get another for you, Laird."

I shook my head slightly. "We'll be fine."

Jim smiled at Theo. "To your health, Seer."

The Grimes and I took the small glasses and I pulled the whisky into my mouth. Then I leaned over Theo and used my free hand to grasp the back of her head and kissed her.

She made a surprised sound as I took her mouth.

I pressed my tongue against her lips, and they opened willingly for me. I shared a small taste of the amber liquid with her and swallowed the rest. I didn't break the kiss. Hell, I never wanted to break the kiss.

She had wrapped one arm around my neck, and the other was tangled in my hair.

The small part of my brain that wasn't focused on the woman plastered against my body heard the cheers. I slowly released her.

God, I wanted to see that look on her face forever. She looked stunned, her cheeks were pink, her eyes a darker blue, and her lips were swollen. *We did that*, my wolf growled.

Another tray was presented, so I took the shot and kissed her again, and again.

Theo used her open palms to push away from my chest. She was giggling. "No more. I can't take it."

That made the people around us laugh.

From the dazed look on her face as she watched me, I thought that might be the truth.

Solle appeared at her side. "Oh, man, good song." She grabbed Theo's arm and pulled her to the stairs, the dance floor her destination.

I watched them head toward the stairs that led to the dance floor. My wolf was energized and focused, and then Theo glanced back over her shoulder at me.

"Cock-blocked by my mate." Conal handed me a cold beer.

I chuckled. "The night isn't over."

He motioned with his head for us to take a seat in the booth. The bag of money still sat untouched in the middle of the table.

I took my seat and leaned back, stretching out my legs, and crossing them at the ankles. I had a clear view of the two women on the floor. The song had a hip-thrusting beat.

"So?" Conal started.

I did not explain my actions to anyone. I was the Laird. I slowly raised my eyebrow.

He held up his hands. "Hey, don't go crazy on me."

"Then don't ask," I snarled. I glanced at the dance floor, again. I couldn't keep my gaze off her. She now had her back to Solle, who was plastered against her, matching her rocking motions with her hips.

"The attraction between the two of you is hard to miss."

I stared at my Second.

Conal raised both eyebrows, his expression innocent. "Your arrangement with the Dolan daughter isn't happening anytime soon, so why not?"

There were so many reasons why I should simply call it a night and go home. I knew Theo was dangerous, and my wolf's attraction to her would only bring problems. I chose my words carefully. "She isn't someone I could easily forget."

Conal gave me a slow smile. "No, she is not."

I let out a breath. "And it would be problematic for the Pack."

"Only if you treat her like she's disposable."

She wouldn't be. That was my dilemma. I took a long pull on my beer. Did he want to hear me say that?

Conal shook his head. "A woman like that isn't disposable. She would love you, all of you—the right-eous and the ugly. She'd embrace the responsibilities and welcome you to her bed every night."

My Second's words were too much. I could picture the life we would have. "Is it fair to her?"

My friend of many centuries said nothing for a while. He leaned onto his thick forearms. "For you to ask tells me much."

I knew I was on the edge. I needed a sign to push me over, to allow me to pursue what I wanted. I turned my attention back to the dance floor. I watched Theo drop her head onto Solle's shoulder and turn her head so that Solle could kiss her lips. The female's hands were under the bodice of Theo's dress on her breasts. I was so surprised I turned my entire body to face my Second. "Is that what you go home to every night?" I glanced back at the women. Solle's fingers were pinching Theo's nipples, stretching them longer as she rested her head on Solle's shoulder.

Conal said nothing.

I tore my eyes from the floor to get an answer.

He gave me a slow smile that told me much. "Solle has been seducing her for weeks. I think it's the human's vulnerability that attracts her. My mate wants to soothe her."

I knew that feeling well. I enjoyed her nimble mind and was thankful she'd embraced her position so easily. However, it was the moments when she leaned on me or shared her worries that I treasured. Solving her problems and shielding her from the pain, that was what I wanted to do. "So, are they together?" I asked, my voice strained as my muscles tensed waiting for his answer.

"Solle is attracted to her. I believe that Theodora finally couldn't put her off. Watching you fuck the sisters affected her."

"What?" I'd forgotten about that night.

"She's had no man since we found her. Many have made their interest known, but she's ignored them all. She waits for you."

I was done with this conversation. I again turned my attention to the women. Solle said something to Theo, took her hand, and led her toward the stairs.

I was on my feet before I'd even completed my thought, heading to meet them at the top of the stairs.

I took Theo's hand from Solle's, and we were once again stopped by more well-wishers.

I took her shot after getting her a bottle of water, explaining that the human needed to hydrate. After I excused us from that group, I pulled her to the balcony railing and leaned in close. "You are going to owe me for taking your drinks."

She gave me a small smile. "I guess we could work something out."

I liked the sound of that.

"What are you thinking?" She was looking at me through lowered lids.

"You must tell me a secret."

That surprised her. Her nose wrinkled as she considered my answer. "What kind of secret?" she asked cautiously.

I grinned wickedly. "One that you've never told anyone before." I wanted to laugh. This was going to be so fun.

She gave me a narrow-eyed glare when a woman I recognized from the hospital approached with shots. I think she mumbled, "Goddamn tricky wolf."

"Theodora, happy anniversary of your birth," the woman said.

I saw the Seer paste a smile on her face. "Hi, Sara." She poked me in my side with her elbow. "Okay."

I explained that I was assisting Theodora with her celebration, not that anyone would dare question me.

I made sure she drank more water as we talked with Solle and Conal. Tex had turned over his duties in the D.J. booth to another and was on the dance floor surrounded by a group of women.

"The next song is for all of the lovely ladies," the D.J. told the crowd.

The song started, and Theo yelled, "I love this song."

Solle listened to a few beats. "Me, too."

Theo turned to me. "I'm going to go dance."

Solle was already reaching for her hand.

Conal and I watched the women head to the dance floor. He asked, "Are we going to stand up here and watch or join them?"

I watched Solle wrap her arm around Theo's waist and pull her back into her body. They were gorgeous together. I envied Conal for the show that he got to watch. "Join them."

The crowd parted for us, one of the perks of being the Leader. I took my position in front of Theo and wrapped my arm around her waist, pulling her away from Solle. The female wolf winked at me and then turned to her mate.

This was the extended version of the song, and the dancers all shouted the famous chorus of *Closer* by Nine Inch Nails. I thought it was most appropriate.

Theo faced me, riding my thigh as we moved to the driving beat. "Okay, I'll tell you."

"It's our secret, only between us," I promised. I knew she was two steps beyond tipsy, so I wondered what she'd say.

She squared her shoulders as if she needed to prepare. "I have to whisper."

So, I leaned closer.

"I've, uhm, I've never come with a man. Not from his cock or his mouth." She dropped her head and tried to pull away. "Only that time with you."

"What?" I raised my voice. That was insane.

Standing still in the middle of a sea of writhing bodies, she looked upset. "Well, you said it had to be something that I'd never told anyone."

I knew she was telling me the truth. I could see her shame. "Baby," I rumbled, "I can definitely help you with that."

Her eyes widened, and I knew she wanted to run.

I didn't hesitate. I knelt and bent over, then put my shoulder into her middle and lifted her over my shoulder. I heard Conal and Solle cheering my name as I carried her off the dance floor.

She was putting up a fight. Not that she could break free, but I didn't want her to hurt herself.

"Black, Stop." She slapped at my back. "Goddammit put me down."

She wasn't going anywhere. I patted her ass reassuringly, since it felt so nice, I gave the softness a squeeze.

"Black, please, put me down." Her tone changed from angry to upset.

I stopped and slowly let her body slide down my front. The second her feet touched the floor, I pushed her back against the wall by the bar.

She put her hands on my chest. She wasn't fighting. It was more like she was holding onto me. "I can't do the upside-down thing."

I nodded in understanding.

"I can walk. Wherever we're going, I can walk." She continued touching me.

My wolf liked that. I took her mouth in a hard kiss. She melted into me. I released her. I wasn't doing this in front of an audience. Not this time. "Come on." I grabbed her hand and pulled her down the hall. I also had an office here as part owner. I pressed my palm to the scanner and the locks disengaged. I pulled her through the door and slammed it behind us. It would lock automatically.

She looked around. "Whose office is this?" She took a few steps away from me.

My wolf didn't like waiting. He wanted her under us.

"Does it matter?" I started to stalk her, matching her step for step as she backed away.

"Kind of."

I moved so fast she probably didn't even see me. I grasped her wrist, pulling her to me. I put one hand on her round ass and picked her up. "It's mine." I laid her out on top of my desk. "All mine." I realized I was breathing heavily.

"Raider," she whispered my name.

I took her breathy word as an invitation, and I kissed her again. I let her feel how much I wanted her. How she affected me. How hungry I was for her.

Raining kisses down her throat and her chest, I then wanted to see her tits, to feel their weight in my hands, and to nip her hard nipples. I was going to be the first man to make her come with my mouth.

My wolf growled, *the only man.*

I made my way down her body, and when my face was over her pussy, I inhaled sharply. She smelled so inviting.

I pushed up her skirt around her waist and tore the tiny panties from her body with one hand. I think it was at that moment she realized what was going to happen.

"Raider?" She tried to sit up, but I pushed her back against the desk.

Lifting her legs so they rested over my shoulders, I used the flat of my tongue to lick her from the bottom to the top of her folds. I did it again and again. I wasn't using any finesse. I needed to taste her.

I have to get her there. I fought for control. I lifted my mouth from her and took in two deep breaths. I traced her outer lips. Using my fingers to expose her sensitive inner lips. I blew on the tissue.

305

Her hips jumped, and she made a pleased sound.

I shifted my hand so that the tip of my index finger was at her opening. I knew she wanted to be filled.

"Please..." she cried.

I circled her entrance with my finger, toying with her.

"Please, oh God. Please, Laird," She choked out the words.

Oh yeah, I liked that. I pushed my finger inside her and pumped. Her body tightened around me.

I covered her clit with my mouth. I exhaled my hot breath on those nerves.

"Raid, oooh." Her hips jumped.

The combination of my two fingers and mouth had her thrashing her head, side to side. I knew she was close. My wolf tensed. *Now.* I used the flat of my tongue on her clit roughly.

She came.

She screamed and I wanted to make her to do it again. Then I would drag her outside and petition The Lady for our Mating.

What the fuck am I thinking? I moved away from her so fast that I ended up with my back connecting with the far wall. I couldn't do that. It was dangerous even to think it. This Marked human... she must have used her magic to put a spell on me. I was in charge of my destiny, and it was for the betterment and security of my pack. I'd given my word.

She was now sitting up, leaning on one arm. "Black?"

I couldn't think of anything to say. I was trying to figure out how we'd gotten here. Why I was having those thoughts of mating with her.

"D-d-did I do something wrong?"

No. She was perfect. That was the problem.

She slid from the desk and got to her feet. She scanned the floor. When she located her panties, she picked them up and balled them in her fist and straightened the bodice of her dress. "I need to get a ride home."

"What?" It was like my brain was on delay. I could only think of one thing, wanting her again.

"I'm going." She edged smoothly around my big desk toward the door. "I'll leave you alone." Never turning her back on me, she edged toward the exit.

"You're going?" She thought she was going to leave me? My wolf screamed in my head, "*Stop her.*"

"Yeah. I guess I should say thank you." She gave me a sad smile.

"Theo." I took a step toward her.

"I'll tell the doorman I need a ride." She was three steps from the door when she turned her back on me.

I pounced. She was not getting away.

She hit the solid wood door with an "Argh."

"Not. Going." My voice was guttural. I was close to losing control. I closed my lips on the space where her shoulder met her neck and sucked hard.

"Raider," she moaned.

I didn't care if she was afraid or was spurring me on. I was going to have all of her.

One time, I promised myself. Then I'd be done with her. I had to have this, just once.

I used my hips to secure her to the door while my hands reached for her breasts. Jesus, they were full and soft. I felt her ragged intake of breath.

I found her nipples and pulled on them as she arched

back against me. She whimpered, which made me want to be buried deep inside her.

I released one tit and unfastened my pants. Somehow, I got the zipper down and worked my trousers down my hips.

She was resting against the door. I could smell her arousal. *I did that*, I thought proudly.

I put my hand between her shoulder blades and pressed her closer to the door as I used my other hand to pull back her hips. I wanted to rip the dress out of my way. She must have read my thoughts, because she was using her hands to lift it up, displaying her strong thighs.

I grabbed my cock and aligned it and pushed my way home.

She arched against me with a strangled moan.

I was large. I'd been told that by countless women over the years. Her body was stretching to accommodate me.

I pulled back my hips until I was nearly out of her.

She pushed back with her hips. *Greedy female.* I laughed to myself.

Again, I pressed deep inside her. I was trying to go easy, but the fire building inside me didn't want easy. It wanted explosive. I pumped hard enough she moved up onto her tiptoes, but she was making encouraging sounds.

I fucked her. I felt her muscles tighten around my cock. I knew I was making her come again. I loved how tight she gripped me.

As I came, I bit down on her shoulder. I pumped my hips then ground them into her ample ass.

We were both breathing heavily. Again, I kissed her neck.

When I was sure my legs would carry me, I pulled free and tucked myself back into my pants.

Theo kept her back to me. She adjusted her dress. She slowly turned around, still trying to tuck her breast into her torn bodice.

"I'll see you home."

She raised her gaze to mine. "That's not necessary."

"Yes, it is." Conal would be furious if I fucked her and then sent her home with a guard.

"I can't go out like this." She motioned to the wrecked top to her dress.

If she'd been anybody else, I wouldn't have cared, but I didn't want the others to see her like this. I walked to the coat tree and grabbed the jacket that went with my pants. I handed it to her.

She took it with a prim, "Thank you."

After she was covered, I grasped her hand and we headed down the back hallway to where I'd parked my SUV.

I opened her door and waited until she had strapped her seatbelt over her chest. Then I walked around and got in. I started up the engine and headed toward Conal's house.

"Where's your guard?" she asked in a small voice.

"Probably with yours, wondering how long to give us."

"I didn't think you were supposed to be without a guard." She never turned to look at me. Instead, she pointedly stared out the window.

"I think I can manage to get you home safely, Theo." I didn't understand why she would want another with us.

"I'd better not get into trouble for this," she mumbled.

TWENTY-SEVEN

NOVUS

THEODORA MORRISSEY

H*old it together.* The ride would last all of fifteen
minutes tops. I stared out the passenger side
window. Who was I kidding? I would never be a hit-it-
and-quit-it kind of woman. Tonight meant something to
me and I was a fool, because he was going to dump me
at the door and bolt.

Only a few more blocks. Then I could go into my bathroom, turn on the water, and cry. Tomorrow, I would
plan on how to break this spell Raider Black held
over me.

I cringed, knowing both Conal and Solle would hear
his huge SUV approach. Their front door was open, so
somebody was prepared for our arrival. He pulled into
the driveway and turned off the engine.

I rushed to unhook my seatbelt. "You don't have to
walk me up." My voice was husky from the force of my
cries earlier.

"I most certainly do."

Great, now he wants to be a gentleman. "Don't pretend, okay?" I said tersely as I threw open the door.

"I'm not pretending anything."

Now he sounded annoyed. I darted a look his way, but his face was hidden in shadows. "Look, we fucked, but I don't need any special treatment. I know how this works." I started to climb down, remembering to allow for that stupid running board, so I didn't scrape the shit out of my shin.

His hand closed around my elbow pulling me back in. "Close the door."

"No." My voice shook. I was going to lose it. The back of my throat burned. I didn't want to cry about this in front of him.

He leaned across me to pull the door shut.

"Raider, please," I whispered, pleading. "I'm not good at this." Why was I using his first name? Nobody called him by it.

He didn't say anything for a long moment then ground out, "I will walk you to the door."

Thank God, no discussion. I opened the door again and stepped down.

He did the same and met me at the edge of the hood. He took my hand as we made our way up the walk and onto the porch.

He didn't let go of my hand as we both faced the glass storm door. "Theo…"

I felt the first and soon the second tear fall as I looked up at him.

"Oh fuck, baby." He pulled me into his arms, and, again, we were kissing.

I needed him, and Goddess help me, I wanted him again.

My back was against the storm door with his hand tangled in my hair.

"Am I interrupting?" Conal's deep voice intruded.

I jerked away from his lips and thumped my head against the door. "Oh, uhm, we were…." I had no idea what we were doing. I gave him a look that begged for him to explain.

"I think that he saw us, babe." Black's smile was that of a man who'd gotten exactly what he'd wanted.

It was devastatingly sexy and I wanted to unbutton his pants right there on the front porch.

"Solle was worried," Conal explained. He glanced at the Laird. "Are you staying or going?"

Fuckin' Conal and his directness. He sounded paternal, except I didn't know of any fathers who invited men in to stay the night with their daughters.

Black's hand was already reaching out to open the door wider. "Staying."

I swear I felt my heart leap with excitement. My common sense told me this wasn't going to end well. But I didn't care. For the first time in my life, I was going to do exactly as I wanted, not take the safest or easiest choice.

Conal locked the door behind us.

Raider broke the silence. "You need to hydrate. Humans can't handle alcohol." He dropped my hand and headed to the kitchen.

Honestly, I didn't know if I wanted to follow him or continue standing there with Conal.

"I can tell him to go if you wish," Conal spoke softly.

Those words held so much weight. Telling his boss to go would be uncomfortable for Conal, but I knew he was letting me know that it didn't matter that Black

313

was the Laird. I didn't have to do anything I didn't want to. He was giving me the tools to make that choice.

"I want him," I said softly.

One side of his lips tipped up. "Well then, I'll return to my mate. Good night."

When he was midway up the stairs, Black returned carrying two bottles of water. I didn't know what he expected to happen. "You know that my room doesn't have a door, right?"

His grin told me he didn't care. "Let's go to bed, Theo."

He took my hand in his again and led the way up the stairs. My heart started to beat faster. We weren't done for the night. When we got to my room, I placed the water on my nightstand and kicked off my shoes. "I need a shower."

"Sounds good."

It occurred to me that he wasn't a regular guy. He was the Laird, and I was under his rule. I didn't know if I could tell him no.

"Unless you don't want me to join you...?"

It took me all of two seconds to picture a naked Black, wet, with my soapy hands exploring his body. "I think there's just enough room." I slid out of his suit jacket and folded it before I hung it over the back of the small loveseat in front of my window. I headed into the bathroom and turned on the taps.

I opened the cabinet to pull out fresh towels. I was doing busy work, suddenly nervous about being naked in front of him. Compared to the female Lycans, I was soft and very rounded. Their curves were all firm, and I... well, he'd seen most of me before, and, by now, he'd felt

314

the rest. I gave an internal shrug and sought the zipper to my destroyed dress.

I hadn't heard him come in, but I caught a glance of him from the corner of my eye and turned. He was naked and glorious. Without speaking a word, I climbed into the shower, and he joined me immediately, pulling the curtain closed. I turned to ask if there was enough room, and he pulled me into his chest and kissed me.

This time his kisses weren't hungry, they were teasing and almost sweet. I pulled back my head to look at him.

"What?" He narrowed his eyes.

"I can't get clean if you're kissing me." I felt pretty proud of that answer.

"Sure, you can. I can wash you while I kiss you," he said with a grin.

I gave a one-shoulder shrug. "You can try."

WELL, I'd score that cleanup attempt an eight out of ten. I was clean, and he'd given me another orgasm. Afterward, he'd wrapped me in a towel and carried me to bed. I kissed him as he lowered me to the mattress. The kiss went from sweet to hungry. My hands stroked over his chest, and then lower. He wouldn't let me get him off in the shower. Every time I tried to touch him, he'd batted my hands away.

Now, I grasped his hard cock. He was big; I had expected that. I mean, I'd already felt him deep inside of my body. I pumped him twice then ran my thumb over the head, smoothing pre-cum over the cap as I lightly toyed with the sensitive underside.

"Can you take me again?" he said, his voice a deep, rumbling growl.

Was he kidding? I didn't care if I couldn't walk straight for a week. "Yes."

"I don't want to hurt you."

Whoa, that admission made me actually use my brain. "Can we go easier this time?" It had been a long time for me, and, as I said, he was big.

"I'll try to be gentle."

My gift flared. Maybe because of the way he said that, like he cared. I ran my hand up his chest, and then I pulled his chin down for another kiss.

This time as he slowly entered me, I could feel the slight burn of my body stretching.

"I don't want to hurt you," he repeated when he was fully seated, deep into my body. Again, we kissed.

But he would. It was inevitable. I didn't need to use my gift to see the future. "Shhh," I said when he stopped kissing me.

He pulled back so slowly that I felt every inch. As he pushed into me, I felt every tiny increment of his cock's journey. It was amazing. I wrapped my leg around his thigh and ran my hand over his strong back.

He continued moving at this incredibly slow pace. He was killing me. I wanted more, but I was already panting and rubbing against his huge body. "Honey, I won't break," I said breathlessly. He was torturing me in a crazy-good way.

"Like this?" He added a grind when he was in deep.

"Yes," I sighed because he hit a good spot.

He increased his speed a little more, but he was still very controlled.

I wanted him to lose control. This masterful Black was hot, but I wanted him to let loose. I wanted him to take everything I was willing to give. "More," I urged him as I used my thigh to pull my body closer to his.

"But…"

"I want you to…" I wrapped my other leg around him. "Enjoy this…me."

His laugh was low. "I'm buried inside of you." He pulled his hips back and pushed into me again. "I'm feeling pretty damn good."

I used my nails and dug into the meat of his shoulder. "Take." My gift stirred, and I swear I felt his wolf.

"Baby, you don't know what you're saying." His voice was rougher, and our gazes met.

"Well, don't kill me." I tried to grin to show him I was kidding, but his hips' extra action made me squeeze my eyes closed. A contented sigh escaped. "Jesus, just do whatever you want." I surrendered. He felt so good.

I had one of my legs around his ass, and I was so close I couldn't believe how good it felt. Every single nerve in my body was on fire. "Raider, please, I want you to come with me."

He dropped a kiss to my clavicle.

"Honey, please." God, my orgasm was coming. I could feel it building, my toes curled in anticipation. I barely had the ability to speak. It was like I could only feel. "Fuck me."

I started to explode. I felt like my skin was going to split open, and an amazing feeling poured though me, like a rainbow of energy. I know that I dug my nails into him. I needed an anchor, because I wasn't sure I could find my way back from this.

He started to pump his hips faster and faster.

I was making noises. I could feel the sounds being

torn from my throat. The only thing I could do was hold on and give.

I think I came two more times, or maybe it was one long ride. I really didn't give a shit. I had his body on top of me, and he was nuzzling my neck. From time to time, he mumbled a word or two that I couldn't make out. I wasn't even sure it was in English.

I ran my hands slowly over his back. I didn't want this moment to end.

He shifted his weight onto his arms and pulled out of me.

I made a sound as my muscles tried to tighten around his cock to delay his exit.

"Shhh," he soothed.

I won't be sad. This had been amazing.

He moved to my side and adjusted his body, so that he lay on his side facing me.

I turned as well. I needed to touch him again. I caught his slight smile right before he kissed me. I didn't want to think about how much I liked his kisses. "Will you let me rest?"

He gave me another quick kiss. "I should."

My giggle was sleepy. I was exhausted, but I didn't want to miss a moment of this. "Should and will are two different things." I giggled again because my words slurred.

"Sleep now, my Theo." I swear I heard those words, but maybe I was dreaming.

TWENTY-EIGHT

NOVUS

RAIDER BLACK

Theo felt right in my arms. The tips of my fingers traced her soft skin. I'd held countless women. For centuries, we slept curled against one another for warmth. However, this morning, I woke with a clear mind. No pressing worries, no endless lists of items that had to be addressed, only the softness of this woman against me.

She stirred and burrowed closer. She'd done this several times in the night and my wolf always gave a satisfied sigh that vibrated through my body.

It was after nine, and Conal was moving around in his room. I heard him open his bedroom door and pad down the hall. My interlude of calm was going to end.

He knocked on the doorframe. "Are you ever going to get up and feed us?" His hair was standing up, and he'd only donned a pair of jeans.

Theo bolted upright and brushed the hair off her face. "Wha?" She shook her head once as if that would clear her foggy brain. She looked at me, and I swear she forgot about Conal for a moment. She smiled at me. "Hey," her voice was soft.

"Food. Can't you see I'm starving?" Conal couldn't keep from grinning.

Theo turned to the door, and then jerked up the sheet to cover her gorgeous bare breasts. "Jesus, Conal." She groaned then glanced at the clock on her nightstand. "Give me a minute."

"Only one." My Second continued to grin like a simpleton before turning away and leaving us. He thought this was hilarious.

I reached for her, I thought we could stretch out the one minute to fifteen or twenty—or maybe an hour.

She scooted away from me. "I need to get dressed." She tried to pull the sheet loose to cover her body.

She really was adorable. This shyness about nudity was foreign to me, but it was entertaining. "He doesn't expect you to start immediately." Most likely my Second could no longer hold off his mate's curiosity or his own.

She jerked the cotton sheet and wrapped it around her body. "I cook on Sundays. You know it's what I do." She opened and closed drawers with jerky motions. She was agitated.

I didn't understand her feelings, so I didn't press her to stay.

She walked to the bathroom turned on the water taps in the sink. In less than four minutes, she passed by me wearing a pair of denim shorts and a black T-shirt that was big enough to be Conal's.

I didn't like seeing her in another man's clothing. It made my blood heat and my wolf awaken. She paused and gave me a very serious look as I lounged in her bed.

Then she gripped her right wrist and presented her brand. "Good morning, Laird."

"Theo," I acknowledged the greeting with a nod of my head.

"I'm sorry I didn't do it earlier." She continued displaying her wrist to me.

Suddenly, the idea of a naked Theo presenting me with my brand on her wrist while riding my cock made me very interested in establishing future etiquette. I stretched out my arm and traced my finger over the scarred skin. "Noted."

She shivered at my touch, and her nipples poked against the offending T-shirt. Maybe she was considering jumping back into bed because she licked her lips slowly, but she blinked. "I-I have to go."

I tried not to grin too big as I nodded a dismissal.

I showered and pulled on my clothes from the night before. I listened to the sounds from the first floor. Solle had joined Conal and Theo after the two had talked for a few minutes.

"So?" Solle had asked as soon as her feet touched the first floor.

"Are pancakes okay?" Theo must have had her back turned, her voice was muffled. "They're fast. I've got bacon and sausage, too."

"You're killing me," Solle cried.

Theo continued cooking. After five minutes, she spoke. "I want to thank you both. That was the best birthday party ever."

Curiosity heightened my senses as I realized the human was avoiding Solle's questions. Was she embarrassed or was her reticence due to her innate modesty. Whatever the reason was, I liked it.

"You two spoil me," Theo said, still not sharing anything about our night.

Conal cleared his throat. "You honor us, Seer."

I could picture her smiling shyly. I headed down the steps, making enough noise so that if Theo was listening, she would hear me.

"Morning," I greeted Solle with a friendly smile and walked through the entrance to the kitchen and straight to Theo. She stood over a flat apparatus watching the pancakes cook. I wrapped my arm around her waist and pulled her to me. I kissed her cheek and said softly, "Is there enough for me?"

She gave me an assessing look as if she wasn't sure what I was doing. "Well, it's their house."

"I was asking you."

I watched her eyes widen, and then narrow as she considered my question. "Of course...Laird."

"I'll just pour myself a cup of coffee." I loosened my hold. She was so cute when she was off-kilter.

She returned to cooking. After I poured my coffee, I took my seat at the breakfast bar.

"Are you hung over today?" Solle asked Theo.

She was using the spatula to expertly flip the pancakes. "No, I drank a lot of water before I went to bed."

Solle turned her head to give me a huge smile and a wink. "Don't you mean before you went to sleep?"

I could see Theo's profile and she was blushing. I changed the subject to give her a little relief. "So, what time is the cookout?"

"Around three," Conal said, sounding confused, "like always."

"Will you be joining us?" Solle asked sweetly.

322

Theo didn't turn nor did she invite me.

"I have a conference call, so that might take some time."

"There will be plenty of food," Solle continued.

Theo set the plate in front of me with a clatter. "Eat these while they're hot."

I grinned at her. "Yes, Ma'am."

The others chuckled.

Theo kept jumping up to refill plates and cups. Solle had stopped making innuendoes about sex and last night, but Theo was still tense.

The time came for me to leave. I needed to prepare for the weekly call from Edinburgh and think about my next move with this woman. I stood and started to gather my dishes.

"I'll do that." Theo got to her feet.

"You've barely eaten," I admonished her. "I can do this." I carried the items into the kitchen and placed them in the sink.

When I returned, she was still standing. I took her hand, and she didn't resist too much. "Conal, Solle, thank you for your hospitality."

Conal lifted his chin. "Anytime, you know that."

"I hope you'll come by later." Solle wasn't giving up.

I gave Theo's hand a gentle tug. "Come with me."

She followed, but she dragged her feet. "Where are we going?"

I quirked an eyebrow. Did she think I meant to drag her back up to bed? "To the door."

She moved a little quicker. At the landing, she braced one hand on the banister. "I hope breakfast was okay...?"

"Theo, baby, relax." I pulled her into my arms and kissed her.

She was stiff for a moment, but then she responded. Her tongue met mine as her hands traveled up my chest to wrap around my neck.

I wanted her again.

She slowly pulled away from me and rested her forehead against my shoulder. "Christ."

I agreed.

THE CALL HAD TAKEN MUCH LONGER than was necessary. The North American Leaders liked to posture and to be difficult. Several would not participate in the call because they abhorred technology. It was two hours of boasting and one hour of business. I revved my bike and rushed to Conal's home. I wanted to see Theo. Hell, I wanted to have her. To see her on her knees in front of me with her hands bound, or sprawled on my bed with a sated smile on her face. I'd had difficulty staying focused during the call.

Conal's driveway was filled with bikes, and the road around his home held trucks and cars parked nose to tail. I stopped in his drive and killed the engine. My guard pulled his SUV into the base of the drive and left it blocking a portion of the street. I could hear the music. Tex was blasting Godsmack. I climbed off my bike and walked around the house to his backyard.

"Laird," Asher greeted me at the gate.

"Asher." I saw Conal standing by his huge grill with a beer in one hand and a huge smile on his face. Solle was in a minuscule bikini, dancing on top of the diving board. Actually, plenty of my pack were dancing. Others were eating, and some were in the pool.

"Black," Conal bellowed.

I headed to the grille.

"Want something to eat?" He pointed to the meat.

"Nah." I tried not to look for her. "But I'll take a beer."

"Joey, get the Laird a beer," Conal barked at one of our newer guards.

The wolf returned with a bottle, then hurried back to his place against the fence.

"You're terrible." I took the opener he handed me.

"The kid has to learn." He took a pull on his bottle. "Besides, compared to what we went through, he's got it easy."

I drank from the icy cold bottle. "A different time my friend." I glanced at the guard and signaled for two more. "We don't need to break a man to remake him."

"You are the progressive leader." Conal tipped his bottle at me in a salute.

The choice had been simple. I needed to attract wolves to my pack that were smart and hungry to advance. I had to offer a different path. "Have to stay current." I took another long pull then stared at the bottle.

"She's in the house, probably the kitchen."

I didn't have to ask who he meant. I hadn't masked my sweep of the area very well. "Good to know."

"She had a meltdown earlier." He frowned as he gave me the update.

"Why?" I kept my expression neutral, but my wolf was awake and listening.

Conal sighed and looked away for a moment. When

he looked at me again, he was frowning. "We pushed her."

I said nothing.

He grimaced. "She told us not to ask her questions about you. We agreed that, if she needed advice, she could come to us."

"I don't know what I'm doing," I admitted to my oldest friend.

Conal grunted. "None of us ever do."

"This," I hated to admit any weakness and my wolf cautioned me to choose my words carefully, "will impact all of us."

He tilted his head a little as he considered the future. "We've proved ourselves to be flexible. We'll do it again. I think she's worth it, I know that you are."

Conal was with me, always. I killed my beer and turned to find the woman.

"Black," Conal called.

I turned to see what else he wanted to say.

"Much luck to you." He gave me a shit-eating grin.

I opened the basement door and followed her scent up one flight of stairs to the kitchen. She was wiping the counter by the refrigerator. She'd changed into a light blue tank top and black pants that fell to her calves. She'd shared that Solle had picked out the dress she'd worn last night, otherwise the woman did not show off her body.

She would save any exhibitionism for me or at my whim.

When she turned, she saw me. "Oh gosh, you scared me." She had her hand over her heart, which I could hear beating wildly. "I hate when you all sneak up on me."

I moved in closer until I'd crowded her into the corner. "What else do you hate?" I asked in a low voice.

She wrinkled her nose. "Cauliflower."

"I'm not much of a vegetable lover myself." I backed her up a little more. "What else?"

"That stupid helmet Solle makes me wear when Conal takes me for a ride on his bike."

I leaned in and pressed my thigh between her legs. "What else?"

She was staring at my lips. "Uhm…"

I nuzzled her neck. She smelled like oranges and sunshine. "Answer me." I caged her in with one hand against the wall by her cheek.

I heard her swallow. "What don't I like?"

I kissed her neck, running my teeth along the sensitive tendon.

She tilted her head to give me greater access.

I gathered one of her hands in mine, gripping her wrist. I easily found the other. "Stop stalling."

"I can't think when you're this close. When you…when you touch me like this."

The scent of the woman's arousal surrounded me. She was practically panting. "You can think of an answer if you try." I was playing with her. I wanted to see how she'd react to my demands.

She licked her lips and I wanted to kiss her, but I waited and watched. "I don't like it when Onyx yells at me."

That surprised me. I pulled back my head so I could concentrate on her words. "He yells at you?"

She opened her mouth and closed it while she considered her response. "He finds me disappointing." She watched me closely.

"I don't." I kissed her. I made a mental note to speak with her tutor regarding his actions.

Too soon, I sensed Solle's approach.

"Oh sorry, I wondered where you'd gotten to."

When she entered the kitchen, Theo took the opportunity to slip from my hold.

"We're going out for a ride," I decided.

Theo turned to me. "I can't."

"Of course, you can," Solle corrected her.

Theo glared at Solle, her gaze boring into the other woman's. "There's a lot to clean up, so no I can't." She turned to me. "You see, I do the cleanup."

"And tonight, you won't," Solle again corrected.

Theo glanced at me. "It's okay, right?"

Solle didn't give me a chance to answer. She grasped Theo's elbow. "Excuse us, Laird. We'll be right back." Her eyes were flashing as she pulled the human out of the kitchen.

I tilted my head to listen in…

"What the fuck?' Theo asked angrily.

"The Laird has invited you," Solle said, her tone firm.

"He could see that I was busy," Theo countered hotly.

The women moved up the stairs.

"He is the Laird," Solle whispered harshly.

I wanted to follow and hear the rest of this conversation. However, I moved to the breakfast bar and took a seat. I knew that my wait would not be long.

TWENTY-NINE

NOVUS

THEODORA MORRISSEY

Solle pulled me up the stairs and into my bedroom like I was a misbehaving toddler. "Solle, slow down," I said through gritted teeth as I tried to delay our progress.

"Sit." She pointed at my bed.

I stood my ground. Why was she acting like this? *Is this some kind of a joke?*

The stern set of her jaw indicated she was serious. I had to hand it to her, if she was playing, then she should look into acting because I couldn't find any glimmer of a smile.

I crossed my arms over my chest to communicate that I wasn't going to sit.

"Now," she barked and took a step toward me.

My gift told me she wasn't messing around and she was angry. I dropped my arms and lifted my chin to show she wasn't intimidating me. It was my choice whether or not to sit. *Ha.*

You'd think after this morning that she'd back off. I'd

made my feelings crystal clear to Conal and Solle. As soon as Black had left, Solle had started in with the questions. Hell, she'd been halfway to planning our wedding. Okay, Lycans don't have a traditional human wedding, but they did have some kind of mating ceremony.

After breakfast, she'd smiled hugely. "I knew it. I just knew it."

"Calm down, chica. You're way too excited about this." I started to clear the plates. I needed to keep my body and my brain busy, otherwise I'd obsess.

"You have no idea how awesome this is." She leaned into her mate, and he wrapped his arm around her. "We're all good friends that makes things...well, easier."

Ignoring her disproportionate excitement, I started running hot water in the sink. "It was one night."

"It's so much more," she corrected me with an arrogant grin.

I turned around to give Conal a look that begged for him to help me. "Can't you do something with her?" I wanted her to drop the subject.

"Black hasn't been this interested in a woman for many years," the blond told us.

"He is promised to another," I said, raising my voice. I fisted my hands in frustration. "You both know that. You know what that means."

"He doesn't want her." Solle pulled away from Conal and flipped her hair over her shoulder. "And she, clearly, isn't into him, or she'd have moved here and claimed him by now."

I didn't want to hear that. I couldn't hold onto any hope. The eventual disappointment would break me. "It was the alcohol and the party." I turned my back on them and started to scrub the pan I'd used to fry the sausage.

"Theodora." Conal's voice held a hint of command.

I didn't rush to turn off the water, but I did eventually. "What Conal?" I sounded shitty. I turned around and met his steady stare.

"Your time is shorter than ours. Their contract might not take effect until years after…" His voice trailed off.

I closed in on the area of the breakfast bar and slammed my palms on the maple surface. "You mean after I'm dead, or when I've cracked up and have to be disposed of?" I hated thinking about my destiny, how I'd be just a blip in their lives. Or worse, my descent into madness recorded by Onyx for history. I could picture him writing every ugly word with a satisfied smile.

Solle looked horrified, and Conal, for once, uncomfortable. Neither knew what to say.

"This won't end well." My voice cracked as I continued, "It can't." I started to sob. Not quietly but with loud, ugly wheezing noises.

Conal dove over the separator to pull me into his arms. Solle hugged my back.

Their concern made me cry harder.

He carried me upstairs to their bed, and they curled around me. Finally, I calmed.

Conal spoke softly, "What can we do?"

Change the past. But I wasn't a fanciful woman; I was a realist. I'd more than proved that during my time here, I'd dealt with whatever was in front of me. "Please don't…" I swallowed hard. "I can't." I tried to gather my thoughts. "Please, let's not talk about this."

"If that is your wish, then we won't," he promised.

I knew he would keep that promise. I wasn't so sure

Solle could help herself. "If I need advice, I'll come to you." My voice sounded stronger as I figured out what I wanted. "This, whatever it is, must stay between Black and me. I don't want it to turn into the topic of every discussion."

Solle's arm tightened around me. "I don't think you can prevent that."

I sighed. "I know."

Conal cleared his throat. "You mean, between us."

"I need..." I reached for the right words to convey what I desired. "I need for you and your home to be my safe place. Where I can think and figure out what to do."

"We'll do that." Conal made it sound like a royal decree.

Now, glancing at Solle's angry expression, I took my seat on the corner of my bed and leaned back on my extended arms. "Well, the promise of a safe place lasted less than a day."

I could almost hear my friend thinking. When she finally spoke, it was in a cold voice. "We've taught you much and you've been a willing student. At the beginning, did you know we were worried that you'd fight us? Resist your destiny?" She raised one eyebrow at me. "You surprised everyone by diving into our culture."

"You did the same thing," I pointed out dryly.

"I was mated. That's different. My immersion was directly tied to my love for Conal."

Okay, so I knew this, but I still didn't like her heavy-handed style.

"Because you were handling things so well, we glossed over certain practices."

That caused my heart to skip a beat. "What do you mean?"

"We agreed to focus on our similarities to the human world. Nobody wanted to frighten you." She sauntered to my closet.

I could hear the hangers slide along the rail. "You gave me the likeable Lycan spin."

"That's a good term." She returned and dropped a pair of jeans on the bed beside me. "Black is the most progressive Laird in the world, but that doesn't mean he doesn't or can't do what other leaders have done since the beginning."

"I'm not in the mood for riddles, Solle. Speak plainly," I snapped.

She went to my chest of drawers and pulled out the bottom drawer. I kept my T-shirts there. She pulled out a long-sleeved, black top then returned to my bedside and placed it on top of the jeans. "If the Leader requests that you attend to him, then you go."

"As simple as that?" Damnit, I wished I could do the eyebrow lift. Instead, I ground my molars so hard that I felt the muscles burn at the corner of my jaw. My eyes were flashing with frustration at my lack of choice.

"Change your clothes."

Her clipped tone made me sit up straight. I pulled my tank over my head.

She pursed her lips as she studied my appearance. "The black bra will be good."

"You're making me feel like a sacrifice," I grumbled as I got to my feet and shimmied out of my capri pants.

She returned with a pair of black panties and handed them to me with a smirk. "Somehow, I don't think tonight will make you feel like a martyr."

I changed underwear and stepped into my jeans.

In the interim, she had brought my brush from the

bathroom and started to brush my hair. "I wish we wore the same size shoes. I have the perfect boot."

"Can I opt out based on my limited footwear?" I flashed a quick smile, so she knew I was joking.

"No, but we can order some tomorrow." She returned from my closet with my white Keds.

After I was fully dressed and my teeth brushed, I stood in front of her for a final inspection. I voiced my greatest fear, "Solle, when this ends, it's going to kill me."

She nodded once, and I saw that her eyes were shiny with unshed tears. "I feel the same way about Conal."

I let out a loud sigh. I needed to get my head straight. Once again, I couldn't veer from the path that lay in front of me. I could only make the most of it. "He's waiting."

My friend immediately understood that I accepted my destiny. A part of me had known it from the start.

She followed me down the stairs and simply waved a good-bye to Black as she continued through the kitchen and to the basement.

We were alone. I felt him studying me. With each step that I took closer to him, I tried to calm my nerves. I stopped a few steps away from him. "Laird, please forgive me." I showed him my brand. "I was wrong to refuse your invitation."

He slowly got to his feet. "And now?"

He was always so much more intimidating when he used that quiet voice. I wet my lips as I prepared my answer. "I am yours."

He grasped the hand that was holding my branded wrist. "Not yet, but you will be." He led me out through the kitchen and into the garage.

I pulled away to fetch my helmet from the shelf in

the garage where it was stored.

"No need," he said, as he continued moving toward his bike.

A helmet was one of the rules I had to live by. Solle had added that one the first time Conal wanted to take me out. I considered reminding him that bikes were dangerous, and I was breakable.

"I'll take care." He promised me and then turned to the guard that was coming around the side of the garage. "I've got this."

The guard stopped and nodded once. He'd been dismissed.

Our gazes met, "Just you and me."

I followed him to his bike.

He started the bike then signaled for me to climb on.

This part always felt wildly intimate to me. My thighs bracketed his, and he wasted no time in reaching behind us with his left arm and pulling me closer so that I was touching his body…everywhere. His hand encircled my forearm and wrapped it around his waist.

My other arm followed without prompting. Honestly, it was no problem to hug him. I pressed my cheek against his back and sighed.

I felt his chest vibrate with a chuckle.

Yeah, I'd failed at masking my feelings around him. Damn wolf.

It felt like we were flying. I loved it. I know we weren't going that fast, but with the wind whipping my hair and the feel of the powerful engine beneath me, riding with Black was an intoxicating experience. Not to mention that every time I tried to loosen my hold on his waist, he took my hand for a moment, before returning it to its correct position.

We slowed as he approached a pull-off situated at the side of the road. The view was picturesque, with trees on each side of a picnic table that overlooked a field of green corn. The sun was slow to set during the summer, so the evening was still light.

I climbed off, and when he joined me, I asked, "So, did you have this arranged for tonight?" I was only partially kidding.

He'd pulled his long hair back into a band and tucked the ponytail into the back of his shirt while we rode. Now he was pulling out the band. Lord, I loved his long, thick hair. On him, the style only added to his dark prince vibe.

"Glad you like it," he said, "but no, even I couldn't pull this together in only a few hours."

I stuffed my hands in my front pockets and headed to the far side of the picnic table. I climbed up and sat on top of the table. He joined me, sitting close but not touching me. I admired the view. "This is really beautiful."

"Does it remind you of Ohio?"

That was an odd question. "I guess." I rarely thought about where I grew up. "The corn is the same."

"You don't speak about that time."

"It wasn't always great." I hoped my vague answer would make him drop the subject.

"Because you were different?"

Okay, so we were going to talk about this. I let out a breath. "Having a mother like mine was confusing and hurtful." I stared straight ahead. I knew he probably had a thick file about me, but if he wanted to hear about my childhood in my own words then I'd give them to him. "She was a habitual runaway and had me really young.

She had mental health issues and addictions. When I was really little, she would go back to the farm to get clean, but she always ended up leaving. Sometimes, she took me with her, other times, she left me with my grandmother and cousins."

"A child should have stability."

I nodded, and my chest began to tighten. I didn't like thinking about those days. "I agree, and so did my grandmother. She got custody of me when I was six, or maybe it was seven." I shrugged. "I lived at the farm and went to school." God, I had hoped my life would become normal then.

"Did that make you happy?"

I started to answer, but I shut my mouth and thought about it a little more. "No, but it did give me relief." I narrowed my eyes as I tried to recall all those old feelings. "I had security and a routine."

"When did you realize you had a gift?"

I looked down at my hands. "That's the really crazy part. I didn't know I was different. I thought everybody knew things like I did." I let out another deep breath. "I was young, maybe five? My mom was there during one of her sober periods, and a neighbor had stopped in. My mother, grandmother, and I walked him out to his truck when he was leaving. He had driven down the driveway, but I kept waving at him."

Black, shifted so he could wrap his arm around my waist. It wasn't really an affectionate gesture. It was comforting. I leaned into him.

"My mom and grandmother had started to walk back into the house when my mom asked why I was still standing there…." I chewed on my lower lip as those old feelings came rushing back. "I told her, 'Mr. Parks is going to die, so I want to say good-bye, now.'"

"I'd never seen my grandmother move so fast. She yanked me around by my arm, slapped me across the face, and then backhanded me for good measure." I realized I was tenderly touching my cheek, so I dropped my hand. "It wasn't like I was a stranger to getting spanked or even getting my face slapped when I smarted off, but this attack was so ferocious it scared me." I recalled. "She screamed in my face, and her spit hit me, 'I won't have another crazy one here. Don't you ever say anything like that again.'"

I wiped my suddenly sweaty palms on my thighs. "I remember looking at my mother for some kind of answer. She looked terrified. She was pale, and she had the most beautiful eyes, they were a lighter blue than mine with these really long lashes." I shook my head at the memory of my poor beautiful mother. "Anyway, she whispered, 'Don't be like me. Don't ever be like me.'" I dropped my head against Black's shoulder. "She had the gift, too and it destroyed her."

"Perhaps hiding her gift contributed to her problems," he offered quietly.

"I still had feelings, but I never said anything out loud again." I closed my eyes tightly for a moment. It was so terribly hard to talk about this, but here in this calm setting with Black, it didn't make me feel ashamed. "I knew the rest of the family watched me, waiting for me to go off the rails like Michelle, my mother. My grandmother would question me every day after I got home from school. She'd also make my teachers give her weekly reports."

"And yet you excelled."

"I'm still trying to find my way," I admitted. I lifted my head from his arm after a few moments when he didn't speak.

He moved his arm from my waist and leaned back on it while staring straight ahead. "That leads me to my next question." He was no longer touching me. "About us…?"

When he didn't continue, I broke the silence. "I don't know what you're asking." I'd never had a conversation like this before.

He made a sound like he was trying not to chuckle. "You aren't going to make this easy, are you?"

"Now, that's a question I can answer," I said, trying to lighten the tone. I hadn't been expecting a talk about this so soon. I was off-balance, so I told the truth. "I can't make this easy, because we both know it's too important for so many reasons." I turned my entire body so that I faced him, putting a little more space between us by tucking one leg under the other.

"I take my responsibilities very seriously."

I didn't know how I felt about being classified as a responsibility. Sometimes, his formal delivery caught me off guard. I had to look deeper to understand. However, I didn't have that luxury right now, so I laid out what I knew. "You're promised to another." I started to tick my points off on my fingers. "I know the Pack will always come first with you, I respect you for that." I touched two of my fingers. Now came the hard part. I knew he could use his darn wolf nose to smell my emotions, but I wanted him to be able to see it in my expression and hear it in my tone. I held his gaze. "From the start, I believe there's been something…an attraction between us."

He nodded slowly in agreement. His odd-colored eyes had gone a shade darker. It was mesmerizing. I would've preferred that he use his words, but I'd take whatever he gave.

"I tried to ignore it. I fought it, but I guess this," I pointed between the two of us, "was inevitable."

He moved so quickly I didn't see his hand until it had captured mine, and he was lifting it to his lips. He pressed a kiss over the ring I wore, his gift.

My eyes started to burn as tears gathered at his sweet demonstration. "This is going to cause us problems. I'm going to cause you problems because I'm not worthy. I'm human." I had to bite down to stop my quivering lip.

"I want you." His voice was rough.

I put my other hand on his chest over his heart. "This is going to turn out bad in the end."

"Have you seen that?" he asked, his voice roughening even further.

I gave him a teary smile. "I don't have to. You're promised to another, I'm either going to die of old age when you're still like this," I dropped my gaze to take in his body, "or I'll get killed by your intended or her people when word spreads to her." I tried to smile. I wouldn't like me either if I was the Dolan princess. "Or, option three, I go insane." Of those three options, the last one caused me the most fear.

"We control a great deal of our destiny, Theo," he said, his voice steady now.

God, I hoped so. I cupped his cheek as he leaned forward to kiss me.

I tried to pull away. I had more to say, but he shifted his hand around the back of my head, cradling my skull, communicating he wasn't done. I pushed against his chest to no avail. So, I spoke against his lips. "Raid, hey, give me a minute." I pressed harder, and he finally released me. *Okay, message received, the kiss ends when he decides.*

"What?" He didn't look pleased, but he immediately replaced that expression with one of interest, his eyes narrowed.

"We have to talk about a few things before things get so..." Dammit, I blushed.

He did the one-eyebrow lift.

My cheeks were hot and I hated my body's reaction that was so telling. "I'm sore from earlier. So, we can't tonight."

Luckily, he understood right away. "Did you talk to Solle?"

"No," I said swiftly, and I blushed even harder. "We're trying to find a balance, regarding what we discuss and what we don't."

"She's your doctor."

"Earlier was not the time," I said with finality.

"If you're hurting, I will talk to her." He started to reach for his phone.

I made a grab for his hand. "You aren't going to talk about my, uh... Just don't ever have that conversation, okay?"

He studied me. I could see that he was trying to figure out why I was so uncomfortable. "I don't understand. Solle is a healer; she would help."

"And she would want to know every dirty detail," I mumbled and wished I could hide. Damn these wolves and their open ways with their bodies.

One side of his mouth lifted in a smirk. "You liked what we did."

Now, my entire body was one huge melty mess. "Well, yeah." I could barely get the words out. I wasn't used to talking about this with my partner.

He did two obvious sniffs of the air. "But you are upset."

"This is new," I told him simply, but I could see he wasn't getting the full meaning of my words, so I began again. "This," I pointed to him and back at me, "I never expected, and I mean, I don't know stuff, and I have questions. I feel overwhelmed, so can you give me a little time to get used to all of this?"

"What questions?" I think he grasped onto what he thought would be the easiest option. "Because if they are about sex, I'd rather show you."

That was worthy of an eye-roll and a mini-glare.

He gave me a teasing grin and a shrug. Then he tilted his head in that very Lycan way, which was my signal to continue.

Jesus, where to start? I combed my fingers through my hair as I tried to rank the importance of my queries. "Well, I guess number one for me is, other partners."

"There will be none." He used what I'd come to think of as his royal tone.

"You mean, for me?" I loved Solle, but what we'd shared was more about comfort.

His eyebrows drew together as he answered. "Unless it is for my entertainment."

I wanted to argue, but I remembered that my lover was also the Laird. He could order me to do anything that he wished. Solle was right; I'd never really explored this concept. I swallowed hard. I needed to mull that over later. "What about you?"

He gave me a look that was befitting the Pack Leader.

I wanted to get my say, so that it was on the record. I needed to make it clear I wasn't challenging his authority. "I'm not good at sharing." I tried to do my own version of a royal stare. Basically, that was me tilting my head a little to the right and hoping he didn't decapitate me.

Finally, the one side of his mouth lifted. "Oh yeah?" he said, his voice huskier now.

I tried not to smile in return because I was melting on the inside. "I really suck at it."

"Possessive?" He made the word sound like it was foreign to him, but I could see his eyes sparkle.

"I probably will be," I answered slowly. I felt both strong and vulnerable at this moment.

He chuckled. The sound was low, and there was an answering quiver deep in my belly. "I might have to try something in order to see what you would do."

I narrowed my eyes in mock consternation. "You've never seen me angry."

"I'm trying to picture it." He continued looking at me.

His eyes were so dark I wanted to lick him all over.

I shrugged. "I try to pick my battles, but when I do get worked up...well, it's not pretty." I think I was puffing out my chest a little. I giggled at myself. "I'm an ender. I don't mess around. I just put an end to it."

He laughed. "I'm sure you are." Clearly, he didn't believe me.

"You'll see," I warned.

He nodded respectfully. "What else is on your mind?"

"Do we have to tell everybody?" It sounded wrong once I'd said it.

"You want this," he repeated my finger pointing between the two of us, "to be a secret."

I could read his tone. He didn't like that one bit. "I didn't word that the right way. What I meant is, there's no public announcement or anything, is there? You know how you all like to make a big deal out of things."

"You mean you don't want the parade and three-day party?"

I think I stopped breathing. "*What?*"

He pulled me closer to him. "No, baby, I was teasing you."

I closed my eyes and let out a long breath. I returned my hands to rest on his chest. "I want us to figure this out, work through the basics before others get involved."

He started to speak.

I cut him off by pressing a finger over his mouth. "Raider, you know they'll try to interfere." I paused, and hopefully, what I said sunk in. "Some won't approve."

"Who do you mean?" he asked slowly. "I can tell you already have a list."

I carefully considered my answer. I'd learned that criticizing a member of the Board wasn't acceptable. "I'm human and weak. Some will think you could do better, that I'm not enough." Was I? Could I be?

He gave a dismissive shake of his head. "Some may have concerns, but they don't know you."

That gave me hope. He respected me. I'd tried not to preen the times when he'd asked and then listened for my opinion. Plus, he had presented my idea to investigate the escorts to the Board based upon my reasoning, not a vision.

"Are you speaking of Onyx?"

Damn tricky wolf. I thought about changing the subject or running my hand over the bulge in his jeans so he'd drop this, but I needed to be smart. We were having a serious and pretty damn open talk, I needed to speak. "I didn't want to single him out." I smoothed his T-shirt over his strong chest. "He's made no secret that he's disappointed in my abilities."

"He's the only one, Theodora," he said with some heat.

"He has high expectations, and I, well, I questioned his plans. He, of course, didn't like that, and now…" I shook my head once and tried to look like this wasn't a big deal. "Don't worry, I can handle it." I had to, because I couldn't use this new relationship to ask for a major change. It would be wrong, but more importantly, it would look wrong to the Pack and the rest of the Board. I could never let them think I was influencing the Laird for personal gain.

He made a low growly sound. "I will not have you upset. I am Laird, and I picked you. They will respect my decision," he said with finality ringing in voice.

WE RETURNED to Conal's and Black followed me to my room. When we were naked and in bed, I asked, "How may I serve you, Laird?"

He was lying on his back, while I was leaning on his chest. His eyes glinted. "Perhaps, I should serve you. Show you my appreciation for you agreeing to be mine."

My gift flared to life. I knew he was speaking the truth. He was happy. "Well, if my Laird wishes…" I slid off of his chest and rolled to my back with a giggle.

THIRTY

RAIDER BLACK

It was still dark outside when I heard the messenger's bike pull into Conal's driveway. My Second woke and left his bed. I glanced at the clock; it was ten after four. Theo was sound asleep as I slid my arms from around her. I donned my jeans and went downstairs.

Conal was in the process of closing the door. He held the locked messenger bag and motioned with his head for me to follow him to the kitchen.

Once there, he unlocked the bag and pulled out several pieces of paper and handed them to me.

I scanned the message. "Lore is bringing someone in."

"Interesting." Conal rocked back on his heels.

Lorenzo Barducci was considered a problem wolf by most. When he'd applied to join Novus, I'd received no less than three calls from Edinburgh, warning me about the rebellious wolf. However, I'd found that he fit in nicely with our group. I gave him space, and he gave Novus, and me, his allegiance. He was the wolf I sent out when I needed answers and didn't particularly care how he came by them. The Lore, as he was known, could be like a ghost, or he could be very messy when I needed everyone to know he'd completed the job. I grew tense, it was unheard of that he would bring in someone without me stating that particular request. "Round up the Board," I told Conal. It was time for a meeting.

Conal pulled out his phone and began typing. "What about the Seer?"

It was his blasé tone that caught my attention. "Who's outside?"

"Wale is on duty." Conal didn't look up from his typing.

"When she wakes, he can tell her I was called away."

"Or," Conal lifted his head, "you could tell her your-self." His phone buzzed with an incoming text. "Human women like that kind of thing—checking in, they call it."

I gave him a mock-glare. "Are you going to give me advice now?"

He didn't raise his head, but I saw him grin. "Only when you need it."

"Shit." I ran my hand through my hair and turned to head upstairs to the sleeping woman.

Theo had shifted during my absence. Now, she sprawled diagonally across the bed. Her naked back was exposed to me as I entered the room. I wanted to run my hand down that soft skin and over her well-rounded ass. Instead, I circled the bed to the side she faced. I sat down and smoothed back her hair from her face. "Babe," I said softly. I didn't want to frighten her.

She turned her cheek so that it filled my palm, "Hmmm." She didn't open her eyes.

"Babe," I repeated. Being human, she wouldn't sense me invading her space.

She made another sleepy sound and her eyelids fluttered then opened. "Wha?"

"Something's come up, and I need to go into the office."

She pushed up her upper half on her arm. "Do you need me to come, too?"

"No, I just wanted to tell you, so that you knew why I wasn't here when you woke."

Her smile was happy. "That's nice of you. Thank you." She reached for me.

I kissed her. Conal had been right.

"Check in with me when you get to the office."

"Okay."

The smile she flashed was full of promise.

"Go back to sleep." I pressed my palm against her shoulder, and she lay down and closed her eyes.

"Stay safe." Her eyes were already closed.

So sweet, how was I ever going to let her go?

I SWEAR my wolf sensed Theodora's nearness before I caught her scent. I was on what seemed to be a never-ending conference call with the Pack Leader in Seattle. I'd instructed Basil to allow her entrance to my office at any time. She opened my door slowly and walked in.

I motioned her to come to me.

She looked relieved that I welcomed her. She approached my desk as I pushed back my chair. She presented her brand.

After I acknowledged her offering with a nod, I held

349

out my hand, and when she gave me hers, I pulled her onto my lap.

She made a small surprised sound but settled easily against me.

I wrapped my arm around her back and pulled her into my chest. "I get what you're saying Wen, but I look at it differently. The Pack's businesses support the Pack, and the members support the businesses." I winked at Theo. I knew she could hear Wen's reply.

I listened patiently for four more minutes, then I told my caller, "I'll consider your points, but honestly, I can't support a mandatory tax on each member and Article." I listened to the man's outraged screech in my ear. "You are correct. I'm different, and as long as I'm the Leader of Novus, I won't see my people ground down." I clicked off and removed my headset.

"That didn't sound fun." She rubbed her hand over my T-shirt, tracing the outline of my pec.

"Some don't want to change."

"Some of you do or have had to." A line appeared between her brows. "They have to do it in order to survive and to fit in."

"I want to live with the human world. With camera phones and surveillance technology taking over, I know that one day we'll have to make our race known."

She looked away, and I could feel her thinking. From our tutoring sessions, I'd learned that Theo was very good at seeing the big picture. Her intelligence made her easy to talk to. I looked forward to hearing her opinions.

She let out a breath. "I wish I could say that'll go smoothly, but I know history. It doesn't bode well for either side."

I agreed with her, and I had plans in place.

350

However, I didn't want to discuss that now, so I changed the topic. "What do you have planned for today?"

She wrinkled her nose. "Class with Onyx. After lunch, I'll go see Issa. Then at three, a session with Glass."

"And dinner with me?" I added to her list.

She circled a finger on my chest. "Would you like for me to make you dinner?"

"I would, but not tonight, let's eat here in my dining room, and then go to your home."

"I changed the sheets before I left this morning," she said shyly.

"I've been staying with you because I thought it would make you more comfortable, but would you like to stay with me one night?"

"Does your bedroom have a door?"

Her chuckle was deep, I knew she was thinking about how she'd held back last night while I'd gone down on her.

"My bedroom and my living quarters," I said, "so you can be as loud as you like."

"Or you could."

"You think you could make me scream, little girl?" I asked as I dropped a kiss on her neck.

"I could try." She flashed me a challenging look. "Like right now."

"What do you have in mind?" I was more than willing to offer a few suggestions.

"I want to taste you." She threaded her hand in my hair and pulled it to guide my lips to hers.

I liked that idea very much. I let her take the lead, curious to see what she would do.

351

"Can you take off your shirt?" She leaned away from me to give me room.

I grasped the back of my T-shirt and pulled it over my head.

She kissed the indentation at the base of my throat, then wasted no time in traveling lower down my chest. She made a line of kisses to my sternum and traced that path upward with her tongue. Each time she went a little lower, toying with me.

"Enough." I grasped her hair at the back of her head, pulling her away from my body.

She climbed from my lap as I unbuttoned and unzipped my fly. Her hands joined mine to pull down my jeans.

As my hard cock sprang free, she made a sound deep in her throat and dropped to her knees.

Jesus, she was beautiful like that, her eyes huge, and her lips wet. "Suck me."

She smiled as she dropped her face to my groin. Using her hand at my root, she took me into her hot mouth.

I'd expected her to start slowly with tentative kisses, but she sucked me with cheek-hollowing pressure. I slid my ass to the edge of my chair so that she could have easier access.

She took me deep and then pulled back until just the head was between her tight lips. The hand that had been holding me was now lightly stroking my balls.

I wanted to tell her she needn't be so cautious, but I found I didn't have the air to speak. I wrapped my hand again in her hair. I loved that she never fought this. She accepted my dominance and I don't think she even realized it.

She fucking took me into her throat.

I gave into her desire for my response, growling low and deep. It was almost like a purr.

She did it twice more and I felt the base of my spine begin to burn. I wanted to hold off, to see what other skills she possessed.

She took me deep again. I knew I couldn't fight my desire. I moved my hand to cover her throat. "Take all of it. Don't you dare spill a drop."

I exploded, streams of cum filling her throat. She took it all then sat back on her heels as she licked her lips one more time. She was watching me as if gauging my reaction.

I wasn't gentle as I grabbed her and pulled her to my chest, forcing her to straddle my thighs. "I want to taste my cum on your lips." I took her mouth.

If Basil hadn't phoned, I would've taken her on the desk or in the chair. Well, there was always tomorrow— or later this afternoon.

I grabbed the receiver. "What?" I growled into the mouthpiece.

"Sir, I apologize, but Onyx has been here twice asking about the Seer's availability."

I knew Basil was unhappy that he'd been forced to call. This wasn't my assistant's fault, it was the tutor's. "She'll be along shortly," I snapped.

"Thank you, Laird."

When I lowered my phone, I frowned. "Your tutor is most insistent that you begin your lesson," I said, barely containing my anger.

She looked at the clock on my wall. "I'm late." She tried to climb down, but I held her firmly. She wasn't excused until I decided to let her go. "You are with the Laird. He serves me."

She kneaded my shoulder as she framed her sentence. "Let me handle this."

"Theo…"

"If I fail, then you can go all hot and growly with him." She gave me a pleading look with her eyes.

"Hot and growly?" I couldn't help but smile at her description. She was going to be a threat to my ability to concentrate. She was so adorable. "Do not allow him to disrespect you," I cautioned.

She looked away for a second, and that told me much. "My relationship with Onyx is difficult. This thing is going to make matters worse. I'm trying to minimize the damage."

"You are the Seer. He should treat you with respect." My voice came out low, and dammit, there was a hint of a growl. "When I name you my Consort, his slight could result in death."

"Can we hold off on killing people…until we figure this relationship out?" She looked a little panicked.

"I gave you my word we would move slowly. Today, you may deal with your tutor," I held back my growl as I granted her wish.

"Thank you." The tenseness in her body softened

"I am feeling generous after that blowjob," I said, "but Theodora, don't think that you will always get your way."

"I-I understand." She shook her head. "And thank you."

With that decided, I demanded, "Kiss me again."

"Yes, Laird."

THIRTY-ONE

THEODORA MORRISSEY

I knew Onyx was going to be an ass. Even so, I stalled the inevitable. I stopped off in Black's private bathroom to check my make-up, before I left to hunt for my tutor. I opened my purse and pulled out my brush. After I ran it through my hair, I applied more lipstick. Basically, I carried a purse to haul my make-up and my notebook. The notebook was for questions or things that came up that I needed to research. I didn't have driving privileges, so no need for keys. I wasn't allowed a phone, and since they'd confiscated my wallet when they'd found me, I never bothered to ask for it back. I already knew what the answer would be.

I looked pretty good. My eyes were shining with excitement, or maybe it was lust. My nipples were poking through my red top, and the crotch of my panties was wet. I wanted to make an adjustment to the silky material, but since I couldn't close the door, it didn't seem proper. Of course, the Lycan on the other side of the wall would probably flash that devilish grin, knowing he was the cause of this situation.

I stopped stalling and headed out to deal with what I knew would be an awful class. Lately, I'd taken to ignoring him and speaking only when I had to. He now referred to me as "human," and I had several adjectives in my head for him. I was sure that word had spread about what had happened at The Club, and if anybody had noticed that I'd left the party on the back of the Laird's bike last night, well, I was screwed.

I found the tutor standing in my office, staring out the window. I was certain he'd chosen that pose so that anyone walking past would admire the cut of his suit. If they had studied him for a moment, they would see the scowl on his face.

Terrific.

I didn't rush into my space. Instead, I entered at a casual pace. "Onyx, I apologize for being late."

"You were with the Laird."

His hard tone made it sound like an accusation. I pulled out my office chair and put my purse in the bottom drawer. I grabbed my yellow pad, a handful of different colored pens and headed to my sofa.

Onyx turned to glare at me. "His time is very valuable."

"I *know* the Laird is very busy," I said, trying not to sound defensive.

He covered the ten steps to the chair to the left of where I sat. He moved beautifully, gracefully. "You think you're important now?"

I didn't respond. I flipped through some of the pages of notes I'd had taken on Thursday.

"You believe that your position has improved, now that he has bedded you," he continued.

I decided to stay quiet. Maybe this way, he would talk himself out, and we could get on with the lesson.

"Explain yourself, human," he demanded with a snarl.

"Onyx," I said, making sure my tone was even, not sarcastic or angry, "I am the Seer to the Novus Pack." I was nothing more.

"He is contracted to another. He will never break that promise," he continued in his sneering, superior voice.

I slowly put down my pad on the cushion beside me. I wanted to only say this once, so I needed to choreograph my movements to work in concert with my words. I looked up at the tall man perched on the edge of the wing chair and called to my gift. "From this day forward, I will not listen to you discuss my personal life. Your duty is to educate me about Lycan history. We will continue to meet three days a week for two hours." My voice sounded confident and strong, with a touch of power. I knew he was going to blow at any moment, and that could be very bad for me. "There will be no conversations or lectures about what I do, unless it is adversely affecting Novus, and you have been designated by the Laird or the Board to speak to me."

"Or what?" he scoffed. "You'll run to your lover?" His face screwed up in an ugly snarl.

"No, Onyx. I will, as you say, run to the Board and advise them of your behavior, in direct violation of my stated wishes. I will ask that you be reprimanded and removed from having contact with me."

"Like they will take your side," he taunted.

I was tired of his tactics. I'd treated him politely. We didn't have to be best friends, but I was done being disrespected. I smiled sweetly at the male. "Did it ever cross your mind that a happier Seer might become more productive?"

"Are you saying that I'm stunting your ability?" The vein at his left temple was now standing out.

"I think it is something to consider." I drew my eyebrows together as if I was studying that angle. "I'll ask The Lady the next time I talk with her."

His face reddened with his frustration. "You will not waste that opportunity asking such…such idiotic questions."

I shrugged once and returned to reviewing my notes. The wolf was jealous that I'd talked with The Lady, and that Black had witnessed it, proving the incident wasn't a hallucination or a story that I'd made up.

He continued seething for about ten more minutes then commenced questioning me about last week's work.

I WAS SUPPOSED to meet Black for dinner in his private dining room at seven. I didn't even know that such a place existed. I wondered if I had enough time to go home and change clothes. I should have insisted I stop on my way back from my visit with Issa at the hospital.

I saw my guard often. I usually stayed an hour, reading and talking to her the entire time. We would finish the third *Harry Potter* on my next visit. She was in an induced coma state, and it looked like she was asleep, but I still found myself watching for a sign that she was waking up. Solle promised me that she was improving, but I missed her crazy fashion sense and her wit. I could only imagine how she would've squealed over the news about Black and me. She would've peppered me with videos of sexual feats.

I was feeling uneasy, probably due to the tension between Onyx and me. During my workout with Glass, I had trouble focusing.

"Theodora, concentrate." The warrior stood with her hands on her hips, her eyebrows drawn together.

"I'm trying, I swear." I scratched the back of my left shoulder then my right forearm. I felt like my skin was too tight. "I'm..." I didn't know how to explain how I felt. "Maybe I need to work out harder. I feel like I can't stay still," I admitted as I used my left foot to itch my right calf.

For the rest of the session, she kicked my ass, so I got exactly what I'd asked for. I spent forever under the shower, hoping the hot water would soothe my aches and pains.

Once again in my office, I waited for my guard to escort me to dinner. I tried to study, but I couldn't remember the line I'd just read. I tossed my notes aside, got to my feet and started to pace. I moved to my window. It didn't get dark until well after nine, so I could see the grounds clearly. There were still cars in the lot. I knew that if I walked down the hall I'd find several wolves at their stations.

"Seer." Mal, who was a guard assigned exclusively to the Laird, stood in my doorway.

"Good evening, Malachi." The man appeared to be in his mid-twenties, but I knew he was eight centuries old.

"The Laird requests that you join him."

Typically, the older the wolf the more formal their speech. Maybe Mal thought he had to try harder. "Thank you." I followed him down the hallway.

"Elevator?" he asked.

"Yes." My body had yet to recover from my workout.

The elevator doors opened a few seconds after the call button was pressed. He inserted a card into a slot that I'd never paid much attention to before. The car began to move.

When the door opened, Malachi motioned for me to disembark. "Have a good evening, Seer."

I stepped off of the elevator and tried to figure out where I was to go. I followed the walkway and passed several closed doors. My adrenaline was pumping. I was considering calling out when the Laird stepped out from one of the doorways in front of me. I flinched in surprise.

"Theo," he greeted me with only a half-smile.

"Don't do that."

"What's wrong?"

"Nothing, not a thing," I spoke too fast. I'd over-reacted.

"Babe?" Now, he frowned as he studied me.

I was screwing this up. "It's been a long day."

"What does that mean?"

He'd arranged something special, but I needed to alter the plan. "I'm not sure, but I think I need to go out in the moonlight tonight."

"You're uneasy." Not a question. By his steady look, he understood.

"I can't stay still. Um, my mind and my body." I started to circle the gold bangle that I wore, around and around my wrist.

"We can do that as soon as the sun sets."

"If you're too busy…"

"Theo, I'll go with you." His word was final.

That was a relief. The possibility of traveling to The Lady's plain alone frightened me.

"Are you able to eat?" He stepped aside, so that I could look into the room.

The dining room was dark wood, burgundy linens, and candlelight. "Of course," I said. Even if I didn't have much of an appetite, I'd eat, because he and the staff had taken the time to do this.

Black didn't mention that I hadn't eaten much. He simply asked if he could have a taste or ten of mine. He was a charming dinner companion, who shared stories of dinners he'd attended at gatherings. My mind marveled at the wealth the Leaders displayed.

He'd been talking about one particular Pack, when I said, "I can't imagine what it would be like to live like that…so cut off from everything."

"They don't adjust to change," he said it in a way that I could tell he didn't get along with their Leader. "The Leader's half-brother is his Second. I deal only with Bredon."

I leaned back in my cushioned chair and stared into my wine glass. "I never really thought about it…how lucky I am that I ended up here."

"The idea of living in a castle doesn't appeal to you?" He tilted his head inquiringly, as held his glass of whisky.

"I'm not very good at roughing it while camping, so to have to step back in time—no, that's not for me." I tried to stop my finger from tapping against the side of my glass.

"I must admit, I like the amenities of this era."

"What's it like to know you'll live forever?" I blurted the question that had been on my mind for months.

He didn't respond immediately. "I don't really think about it." He must have seen my frown because he continued. "Solle might be the one to discuss this with. She hasn't forgotten what it was like to be human."

I knew he was brushing me off, but I let it go. I wanted to get up and move. I shifted again and gripped the arms of the chair.

"Are you ready to go?" He was already on his feet.

"Was I that obvious?"

He did the gentlemanly thing and pulled back my chair. Then he slipped his hand under my elbow and guided me to my feet. "My wolf doesn't like it that you're unsettled."

I saw Wale as we neared the elevator. He inserted a card, and the doors opened so we didn't have to wait. The three of us rode directly to the garage.

Black surprised me by getting into the back seat of the SUV beside of me. There, he took my hand in his. "Wale, windows down, tonight."

I tried to concentrate on the feel of the breeze on my face. The sun was setting and that seemed to help calm my mind, but my body was now vibrating with energy.

We pulled into Conal's driveway, and Black led me around the house. Our guard didn't follow closely.

"I'm going to send Conal a text. I'll tell him that we'll be in later."

I shifted my weight from foot to foot as I watched him type.

He unhooked the gate and took my hand as he led

me to the steps that led to the deck. He took a seat and started to remove his boots.

I'd kicked off my sandals while watching him.

"I like these boots," he explained and removed his socks.

My understanding of how they changed and were clad in clothes was hazy. The explanations I'd been given were vague, and I concluded, purposely so. There was an entry in my notebook about this. Maybe someday, I would ask again. "Can you find your way back from... wherever it is we go?"

"I don't know," he said easily as if he wasn't concerned.

I licked my dry lips. "Are you sure you want to go with me?"

He wrapped an arm around my waist and pulled me forward. "Are you worried about me?"

"Yes," I blurted. "I don't want anything to happen to you."

His hand found my brand. He brushed his finger over the raised skin. "You are mine. I would never send you there alone."

He was going to protect his Seer, not me. I tried to tell myself that it was good to know where I stood.

He wrapped his hand around my wrist and raised my hand to his mouth. He placed an open-mouthed kiss in the middle of my palm. "And if I had my way, I would never let you out of my sight."

Need flared deep in my belly. I think I moaned.

"I enjoyed our last visit. I'd be an idiot not to go again." He gave me a dazzling smile.

I wanted to tear off his clothes and ride him on the grass.

His laugh was low, and I was sure he knew exactly what I wanted. "Call to The Lady, Theo."

I let out a long breath and started to walk toward the back section of the yard. The grass felt good under my feet, as did his warm hand in mine. I wasn't sure how to contact the goddess. I paused when we were in an open space with a clear view of the full moon. "Goddess?" I felt like an idiot. I glanced at Black, and he gave me an encouraging wink. "Goddess, it's me, um, Theodora. I'm with the Leader of the Novus Pack." I hoped that Conal wasn't watching from the window because I felt a little foolish. "I felt your call."

And that quickly, it happened. I was dizzy. It felt like my stomach lurched, and, suddenly, my spirit was pulled from my body. I jerked on Black's hand, and he held on tightly.

I was on my stomach. I pushed up to all fours, and when the ringing in my ears dissipated, I sat back on my heels. I felt Black behind me. His hand caressed my shoulder soothingly.

"My child and Leader," the powerful voice greeted us.

"Goddess," Black responded.

It was like last time. The yard was Conal's, but the colors were not Earth's. I took in a few breaths to get my bearings.

"You have joined."

His hand shifted an inch closer to my neck in a possessive hold. "We have."

"That pleases me."

I couldn't hide my surprise as I turned my head to look at Black.

He seemed calm as if he was awaiting an order.

"She is strong, Leader. She will be beneficial to your people."

"Thank you, Goddess." He bowed his head.

"And a good match for you."

I felt my eyes widen in surprise.

"She will not bow to you."

Black nodded and kept his chin lowered. I could see that he was trying not to grin.

"I don't feel very strong," I mumbled. Hell, right now my legs wouldn't support me.

"Explain yourself, daughter," she commanded.

Oh shit, oh shit, oh shit. "I meant no disrespect, Goddess. I only meant that by my being human, I'm not as physically strong as a Lycan. We, er, he must be careful with my body," I added weakly. *Did I just try to discuss our sex life with a goddess?*

Black gave my neck a comforting squeeze. "I could break her, Goddess." Apparently, he had no problem doing so.

"So, she should be physically stronger." This was not a question.

"Uh," I started. Suddenly, I was very afraid.

"That will be remedied," the goddess spoke.

There was no warning. Suddenly, I was hit with so much pain I don't think my brain could comprehend what was happening. I felt my muscles tense, freezing me in place. I couldn't breathe, but I couldn't figure out why. The tension vanished, and then I felt like I was being burned alive, while being torn apart. I tried to scream but was incapable of crying out. I tried to use my gift to reach out to Black. I needed him to anchor me because I was breaking apart.

THIRTY-TWO

RAIDER BLACK

M y heart thundered. I'd never heard anyone make noises like that. Theo was in so much pain I thought she should be dead, and yet I could feel her heart beating. I couldn't make myself remove my hand from her chest; the steady rhythm reassured me.

The Goddess had done something to her. I'd felt the energy. It raced up my arm through my connection to her body. Suddenly, a thousand bees were stinging me. My wolf fought to change, but I needed my hands to catch Theo as she wilted to her side.

Next, the convulsions began. I wrapped my body around hers. Not impeding her movement, but I wanted to keep touching her, hoping that it brought her some level of comfort.

The next time I opened my eyes, we were back in Conal's yard. Theo was screaming while writhing in pain. That brought Wale, Conal, and Solle running.

"Hurts," she wailed, as she stayed in a ball on the grass, her knees pulled closely to her chest. A moment later, she unwrapped and straightened her body, her legs bicycling in the air. Her lips were pulled back into a grimace and the worst part was her eyes were open, but not registering anything but the pain she was experiencing.

"What the fuck?" Conal slid on the grass as he stopped.

"What's happening?" Wale brandished his gun.

I knelt beside her and tried to pull her to me.

She shrieked. If she was trying to use words, they didn't sound like anything I could decipher.

Conal looked at Solle. "Do something," he shouted.

The doctor didn't move. "I don't know what to do." She threw up her hands.

Theo began to roll from side to side in a jerking motion. "Ba-a-a," she choked out. Then, "Black," she called and threw out her arm as if she was trying to find me.

I crawled closer to her and wedged my knees against her side as I captured her arm in my hand. "Right here, baby."

She was panting. "Black?" She opened and closed her mouth as though she couldn't form the words.

"I'm fine, Theo," I rasped, figuring that was her question.

She closed her eyes and panted a few more times. "Guh."

She stayed on her back, but her legs were bending and straightening. "Hurts."

I leaned over her. "Tell me what to do, Theo."

"Hurts," she said louder.

My wolf roared his anger as he watched her in pain. "I don't know what to do."

Her body bowed toward the sky as she screamed,
"Please."

WHEN THE WORST HAD PASSED, Solle ordered
Wale to go, and for Conal to crank up the hot tub. Theo
had either passed out or fallen into an exhausted sleep in
my arms.

It was then I told Solle everything that had
happened.

She looked like she was going to cry. "I don't think I
can do anything for her." She smoothed Theo's sweat-
soaked hair from her face. "The hot tub will help with
her muscle aches, but I don't know how to treat a
Goddess's intervention."

So, I spent two hours boiling in their hot tub. I
wouldn't relinquish Theo to Conal or Solle. I couldn't.

IT WAS after three the next afternoon when Basil
buzzed. "Theodora's guard is on the line, and she says
the Seer would like to speak with you."

"Put her through," I said quickly.

"Laird," Theo's voice was hoarse.

"I was trying to tie up a few things, and then I was
coming to check on you." I hadn't wanted to leave her
this morning, but my duty called.

"I'm better. Still sore and stiff, but I think I'm okay."

"Did Solle examine you?" I'd left explicit orders
that the doctor was to make sure she was going to
be fine.

"She did. I guess you all were worried about the
seizures, but I don't even have a headache today." Theo

cleared her throat and continued, "I don't think I'll ever complain after a session with Glass, again."

"Tonight, I want you to stay with me. I'll pick you up as soon as I can leave."

"I'm going to Zumba. I'll be done around eight. Can you pick me up there?" she asked slowly. "I need to do the normal stuff, Black."

I looked at my ceiling. I could overrule her wish. It would be so easy to tell her I didn't want her out in her weakened state. "You'll take it easy?"

"I will. Solle agrees that moving is going to help with the aches..." Her voice trailed off. "Thank you for allowing me to go."

She twisted me up in knots. I was tired. I hadn't slept last night. I'd stripped her of her clothes in the hot tub and when it was time, I'd carried her to bed. I spent the night listening to her breathing and monitoring the beat of her heart. "I'll see you when you are done."

"Later, Black."

"Later." I chuckled as I hung up the receiver.

I ARRIVED at the Community Center with Conal. Tonight, I would see this popular event Theo had organized. The parking lot was full and the bass was thumping loudly as we neared the front door.

"Solle says it's very popular." Conal opened the door for me.

"Just to dance?"

"All ages and levels can do it. Plus, it's a gathering." Conal followed me inside the large room.

There was a lot going on. Tex was in the corner in

charge of the music; Brian, the nurse from Solle's office, was on an elevated platform, wearing a wireless headset and counting as he danced. It took me about twenty seconds to locate the Seer. She was leading a line of kids who looked to be around six or seven, dancing along the edge of the floor. The others were dancing or standing in groups talking.

There were well over a hundred members of Novus taking part. The mood was happy, and many were wearing smiles on their faces.

Theo and her group drew near us. She held up her hand and made a signal. The kids started to march in place. She showed me her brand.

"Seer." I moved closer to her.

She held out her hand. "Join us, Laird." There was a teasing challenge in her eyes.

"Think I can keep up?" I took her hand, and she made room for me to cut in behind her. She put my hands on her waist and made another gesture. Small hands gripped my waist from behind, and we began to move. It was six steps forward and two back. The little boy behind me was laughing like this was the most fun he'd had in ages. As we reached the corner, Theo turned her head and said, "Bridge."

I had no idea what she meant, but she took my hand and guided me so that I was standing, facing her, and we held our hands out until they met in the middle as the kids passed under our bridge. I couldn't help but smile. This was fun.

The song ended, and she said, "Stay out here. This next routine is really easy."

"Are you joining our class, Laird?" asked Mildred, who was a teacher at the school.

"Glad to see another man here." Jim, who owned the feed store, slapped me on the back.

"Time to cool down," Tex's voice rang out over the sounds of Pitbull.

"Take my hand," Theo didn't wait, she took hold of mine. "We start to the right, then back to the left, forward and back."

I caught on pretty easily, and with Theo leading me, I could concentrate on the mood of my Pack. They were enjoying themselves. I laughed when I turned too early and bumped into her.

She giggled while winking at me.

The music stopped, and Tex reminded everybody to come back next week. We were surrounded by participants, asking if I was going to attend more sessions.

Finally, Conal and Tex broke up the group so that we could leave.

Solle had wrapped a towel around her neck. "You know she did all of this, right?"

I nodded. I'd given my approval. However, I didn't advertise how closely I monitored my human.

"I thought a few would come out, basically to see her, but more come every week." She used the edge of the towel to pat her chest.

"I was surprised to see so many young."

"She's great with them. At first in the office, parents were cautious, but now, I think some set up appointments just so their kids can play with her." Solle smiled.

I raised an eyebrow. "So, your point is what, Solle?"

"She's good for the Pack in many ways, not just because of her gift." Solle looked around.

I lowered my voice. "How is she today?"

"She slept deeply until two, then she ate. She said

that her muscles were sore, but I think by her ease of movement tonight, the lactic acid has worked its way out of her body." Solle glanced at her friend as she teasingly bumped Brian with her shoulder. "She seems fine."

I nodded.

"She said she's going to Packhouse, tonight," Solle said, fishing.

"She's never been there." I felt for the protective doctor. She wanted her questions answered, but she'd promised Theo not to pry. "Don't worry. I promise to take good care of her."

Conal joined us, wrapping his arm around his mate. "We know that." He spoke for the two of them. "Last night was jolting. I've never seen anyone in so much pain."

I hadn't either, which made it even more amazing that she was dancing and laughing tonight.

"I hope The Lady knows what she's doing," Solle said, shaking her head.

Theo joined us, her gaze scanning us. "Hey, sorry about all of that." She was trying to figure out the mood of our group. I felt her use her gift. She was doing that more often, I didn't think she even realized she was doing it.

"You have quite an event here." Just thinking about the many smiling faces, I was proud of her.

"You all like to party," she said with a shrug.

"Babe, I'm starving. Let's go home," Conal said to his mate, giving us all an excuse to leave.

As we walked out of the building, I noticed Theo put enough distance between our bodies so that it didn't appear we were together. I'd address this later. When she was uncertain, she turned cautious. I opened the door to my SUV for her and sat beside her. I gave the order to my guard to drive once she was settled.

She glanced out the window, "I'm excited about finally seeing the Packhouse."

"Why's that?"

"I hear you have a dungeon and that it's haunted." Her body was turned toward me, and she leaned against the door.

"Who told you that silliness?"

"It's not true?" She sounded disappointed.

"Sweetheart, the house was built in the nineteen-fifties. It hasn't been there long enough to gather ghosts."

"Okay... But is there a dungeon?"

Her bloodthirstiness always surprised me. "There are cells in the basement."

Her forehead wrinkled as she turned serious. "How do you determine who stays in the cells and who is brought directly to Novus?"

"Good question." One I preferred not to answer, but I felt her attention become more focused. "Traditionally, the Packhouse always had space to hold those who had threatened the pack and any feral wolves we located. It's well-lit and clean."

Her hand found its way to my thigh. "If you don't want to talk about this, we don't have to," she said in a gentle voice.

"It was a very long time ago." I rested my palm on top of her hand. I could grow used to her compassion, but I wondered how much she knew about my own imprisonment, and who had told her?

"So, at your Packhouse, you use the cells for a found wolf, whose threat level has yet to be determined or you already know it but you are delaying the inevitable."

"That is simplistic but correct."

"And nobody leaves Novus custody alive," she added in a sober tone.

"I will not tolerate a threat to my Pack."

"That's one of the reasons why the pack is so loyal." She sounded like she was talking to herself. "I doubt they know how much you do to keep them safe, but on some level, they must."

"My goals are simple. Provide security for those who have sworn allegiance to Novus, so that they can live a good life."

"They love you."

"They respect me," I corrected her.

"They do. Didn't you feel the mood shift tonight when you came through the door? They loved that you were participating."

"Are you trying to make a point?"

"Would you be open to hearing it?" she asked respectfully, but she was smiling.

I shook my head. "You are so much trouble."

"But I'm cute." She flashed me a sexy smile and shined her fingernails over her tits.

"Speak your mind, Seer." I tried to sound uninterested, but I was curious about what she had to say.

"Black, you work hard. You have many responsibilities and little free time. I know you go out, like to The Club, but you're surrounded by guards. I understand that's part of the deal." She started to roll her eyes but stopped. "Why don't you mix with the pack more often? Like, host a party or even a huge potluck picnic? The Pack can gather, but it's casual. They can bring their kids, and you can hang out in a relaxed atmosphere."

"Are you looking for something to do once Conal

closes the pool?" I teased, although the suggestion had merit.

"I don't want you to be lonely."

"You think that I am...lonely?"

"Maybe," she said quietly, "a little."

"And you're going to help with that." She was going to turn my life upside down. Hell, she already had.

"I'm going to try," she promised.

We pulled into the long drive leading to my large home. Packhouse was made up of three sections: my private quarters, the large gathering space, and guest suites for visiting dignitaries. Thankfully, the days of easy travel were upon us. No more housing guests for months as they recovered from a long journey.

She stared out her window. "It's huge."

"Novus is steadily growing." I was proud that Lycans wanted to join my Pack.

At the front door, she insisted, "Tour."

"You're very demanding tonight," I teased as I opened the door. I had arranged for the guards to patrol the exterior only. Knowing she was a modest human, I didn't want her to feel like we were being watched.

"I'll make it up to you later, after the tour." She turned in a circle looking at the foyer.

"Laird." Clifton, the Majordomo of the house, approached on quiet feet.

Theo jerked to a stop and slid closer to me. I don't think she even realized she'd sought my protection from the stranger.

I reached for her hand but captured her wrist. "Theodora Morrissey, Seer to the Novus Pack, this is Clifton, the wolf in charge of Packhouse."

Clifton dropped his chin in deference to meeting a Marked. "Seer, welcome."

"Thank you, sir," she said, her voice infused with warmth. "The Laird has promised me a tour of this beautiful house."

She'd said the perfect thing to the man. If Clifton got the opportunity, he'd lecture her about one of the paintings or the antique crystal.

He wore a small smile. "If I can be of any help, please ask." Then he turned to me. "Sire, Titus has called three times for you. He claims it to be most important."

"It always is with him," I grumbled.

Clifton nodded and disappeared.

With a sigh, I turned to her. "I'm sorry. I've got to make a call. He's a representative of the Clayton Pack." He was a gossipy gnat who caused many problems, but I couldn't continue to ignore him. "It won't take long."

"I understand." She turned away from me. "Can I look around?"

I headed to my office. "Sure."

THIRTY-THREE

NOVUS

THEODORA MORRISSEY

For a bunch of wolves that rode bikes and lived in jeans and T-shirts, this place was refined and posh. The art on the walls looked expensive and the rugs were thick and soft. They did like their comforts.

I'd been through five rooms, but I was growing impatient. I wanted to see the basement. Damn Issa for telling that story. I'd have to come up with something really scary to tell her on my next visit. She'd like that, and one day soon, we'd laugh over it. I felt a twinge of pain in my chest and tried not to think about my friend lying in that hospital bed so very still.

I opened the door at the end of the hall. There were metal steps leading to the floor below. I thought about it for a second, glanced around guiltily, and then started down. Black could track me by my scent, so when he was finished, he would find me easily.

I didn't rush down the stairs; I wasn't reckless. I listened hard and heard nothing. I reached the bottom step and glanced around. It was brightly lit, and although I saw a cell with bars to my left, it was empty. I was just going to peek inside, and then I'd sit on the steps until Black caught up with me.

I stood in the doorway of the cell that was basically a concrete floor and bars, when, suddenly, I knew someone, or something, was beside me. Slowly, I turned my head to see what had found me.

"Well, hello pretty." He was too close, but I guessed he knew that by the grin he flashed, showing me his very large white teeth.

"Hello, Wolf." I was going to handle this one with strength. I knew he was testing me.

He leaned closer and sniffed.

My flinch wasn't too obvious. However, I did give him a haughty stare.

"Human," he decided, "yet not." He narrowed his eyes as he studied me for a moment. What the fuck did that mean? I took the opportunity to look at his face. He was beautiful in a masculine way. If I was an artist, I would be reaching for my sketch pad. He had a strong jaw and great cheekbones with striking gold eyes that stood out against his olive skin. His black hair was cut short, but it was still long enough on top that a lover could run their fingers through it.

"The Laird has honored me with a gift." His smile communicated seduction and something else, a cruelness.

I took a step away. "I don't know about that." I measured the distance to the stairs, not that I could ever outrun a Lycan.

"You do not find me attractive?" He took a step toward me.

I backed up a few more steps. "I think you are

mistaken." I passed another empty cell. Where was Black? He hardly ever let me out of his sight. Where were my guards? I hadn't seen one since we were dropped off at the front door.

"I've returned from a job, and a beautiful woman appears before me. How is that not a gift?" He had a trace of an accent that made his words sound almost musical.

I was starting to become afraid. I knew he sensed that because he showed me his teeth again. Where the fuck was Black? I wanted to yell for him, but I knew that was a sign of true weakness. Then the wolf would pounce. I needed to keep stalling. "I'm the Seer. I'm not some reward."

He scoffed. "I'm to believe that Raider Black allows a Goddess's Marked to wander to the cells unattended?"

I cursed my rare moment of adventuring. The last time had been when I was sixteen, and that afternoon had ended with me in the hospital. I tried to sound carefree. "I got bored waiting," I said as I continued my backward journey.

"That is very unfortunate for you." A different voice sounded too close to my ear.

I couldn't even concentrate on his guttural voice and words, because he stunk. So badly, I wondered whether he'd ever bathed or wiped himself. I couldn't gag, because a thick arm was wrapped around my throat, crushing me against the bars.

At that moment, all hell broke loose. I tried to pull his arm loose, which was pointless. He was a fucking Lycan and I wasn't strong enough. As well, the dark-haired man was yelling and trying to loosen the man's hold.

It was like the animal was trying to pull me through the space between the bars. The problem was that I was pressed flat against them, and even if I was able to turn sideways, I wouldn't fit. Besides, I *did not want* to be alone with this guy. Glass's training kicked in, and I tried to poke at the guy's eye over my shoulder.

"Release her!" the beautiful man screamed at my captor.

Grayness was starting to form around the edges of what I could see. My panic sky-rocketed, because once I was out, who knew what these two men would do to me. I tried to yell for Black, but it was more of a rumble in my throat.

Suddenly, there was an explosion of sound, and the arm was gone.

I fell to the floor and as soon as my body could cooperate, I got to all fours and tried to take in a full breath.

I lifted my head and saw Black stuff a huge handgun into the back of his jeans.

He turned to the black-haired man and roared, "What the fuck just happened?"

I had to give the new guy credit, he was either incredibly brave or stupid. He glanced at the prisoner who was now on the floor of his cell. "You shot him," he accused the Laird, "after I brought him back alive."

"Why was he touching her?" Black took a threatening step toward the man.

"I thought she was a reward." He did not cower.

Yes, he must have a death wish. Black's expression turned ferocious, "You *what?*"

I might have I peed myself a little. I could feel Black's anger and his wolf was ready to kill. I must have made a noise because the Laird looked in my direction.

"And you," he started to make his way to me, "just what the fuck were you thinking, wandering off?"

I lost it. Too much had happened in a too short period. I'd been in so much pain last night that I thought I was being torn apart. Now, I'd done something stupid, and I'd almost died—again. I couldn't take it. I crawled to him and wrapped my arms around his leg, resting my face against his thigh, craving his solidness. I swallowed twice, trying to control my tears. "I just wanted to see. I didn't know anyone was down here."

He rested his hand on the top of my head. "You could have died."

"I know." I held on tighter.

"She said she is the Seer." The man had moved closer to us.

"Lore, meet Theodora Morrissey, our Seer, who seems to have a death wish," Black said, his voice deepening.

I lifted my head to look at the man I'd heard about. He was some kind of spy. Mostly, the other guards whispered his name.

"I am Lorenzo Barducci." He dipped his chin and then continued looking at me. "I apologize for earlier."

I wasn't sure if he meant his pursuit or the scuffle. "Neither one of us will ever forget our first meeting."

Lore turned his attention to Black. "She jokes about being choked. Has she gone mad so soon?"

Black combed his fingers through my hair a little roughly, "No, she is sound. However, I am considering locking her away, so she doesn't get into any more trouble."

"Many packs do," Lore said with certainty.

"I'm sorry," I whispered. I didn't want to be locked away. I promised myself I'd try to do better.

"I know, baby." Black picked me up as easily as he would a toddler and held me to his chest. He looked back at the prisoner. "How long do you think it will take him to recover?"

"A day or two?" Lore seemed to be studying the motionless body on the floor. "Depends on how much damage that bullet did."

"Keep me updated," Black ordered and turned toward the stairs.

I was shaking, probably in shock. I grasped his T-shirt in my fist and tried to get closer to his chest. I was so cold. "That, that was a big gun." I couldn't seem to express my thoughts in complex words.

I think he chuckled, or it might have been a growl. "I meant to do the maximum damage."

"Thank you," I repeated.

"He was going to kill you, Theo," he said heatedly.

"I'm sorry." I started to cry again.

"And ending up with Lore wouldn't have been much better," he cautioned.

"I'm so sorry." I tried to say the words clearly, but my teeth were chattering.

I didn't pay attention to the route he took, but soon, we were in his bathroom. It was even nicer than the one at Novus. It was done in a dark marble with a golden vein. The shower was huge, there was a double-sink vanity that spanned one wall. The hardware matched the marble's vein.

He placed me on top of the vanity and started the water in the shower. Once that was done, he returned and grabbed the front of my tank top with one hand while resting his other hand on my shoulder. He ripped the shirt from my body with a tug.

"I can get undressed," I announced because I hated that I had again messed up and needed him to save me.

"You can't even stand up on your own, but I like that you're feeling feisty." He continued undressing me but didn't shred any more of my clothes.

When he was naked, he lifted me into his arms again and stepped into his shower.

Later, I was finally warm and very sleepy in Black's huge bed. He'd never bothered to turn on the lights and I had no idea what his private lair looked like. I was resting against his chest. "I really am sorry," I told him for the hundredth time.

"I could have lost you," he said in his rumbling voice while running his big hand up and down my spine.

"I'll do better," I promised.

"You have to, Theo."

That didn't sound like an order from the Laird but more like a lover's entreaty.

I was so screwed.

I COULDN'T BREATHE. I struggled, but the arm around me didn't loosen. I was going to die.

I didn't want to die. *Help me. Somebody, help me.* I started to kick my legs, but I couldn't get free. Somehow, I found enough air to scream, "Black!"

"Theo." Hands were shaking me. "Baby, wake up."

I tried to slap away the hands. I needed to escape.

"Theodora," his voice cut through the lingering effects of my dream.

I couldn't see anything. The room was dark, but I felt

his hands loosen their grip on my shoulders. "Bad dream," I panted in explanation.

"Okay, you're okay," he assured me.

I turned to him and scooted closer to his bulk and warmth. After a minute, I said, "It was about earlier."

"I got that," he said in a low voice.

"I'm sorry I woke you up."

"It's not that late or early."

"How do you know? It's so dark in here." I lifted my head from his chest. "You don't even have a clock."

"I can tell. I think it's the pull of the moon," he explained. "It's midnight."

I wasn't going to fall back to sleep. Now, I was wide awake. "Did you eat anything after I fell asleep?" I wouldn't have known if a parade had marched through the room.

"I didn't leave you."

Oh. When he was gentle and thoughtful, it made me feel funny. I wasn't used to this side of him. I liked it. "Aren't you starving?" A Lycan ate a lot and often.

"I could eat," he said calmly.

"Where's the kitchen? I'll make you something." I pulled away from him.

"Are you sure you're up to that?"

"I'm a little hungry myself," I admitted.

I felt him climb out of the bed.

"Can you turn on a light? I can't see anything in here."

"Yeah, give me a sec."

The next moment, the room was illuminated in a soft golden light. I looked around. I'd figured out the bed was huge, but honestly, the entire room was designed for a giant. The bed could easily hold four men the size of

Black. The furniture was a dark cherry wood, and it was all tall. The chest of drawers had to be close to six feet. The walls were a cream color, and the sheets were a mix of cream and burgundy. It was definitely a man's room.

"Here," he tossed something on the bed beside me. "Nobody should intrude, but you'll be covered in case they do."

I touched the cotton T-shirt. "I brought a bag." I'd left it in his SUV.

"Put on my shirt, Theo." Now, that did sound like an order.

I pulled it over my head and climbed out of bed. I made a quick stop in the bathroom, keeping the door halfway open per the rules. I hated this part, so I flushed continuously.

I washed my hands and took a long look at my appearance in the mirror. "Black," I yelled.

He was behind me in two seconds. "What?" He was now wearing jeans but no shirt.

I pointed to my throat. "Look."

He didn't waste time looking at my reflection. He turned me to face him and used one finger to lift my chin. "What am I supposed to be seeing?"

"That's the problem." I turned to look in the mirror again. "There are no marks." I cleared my throat and swallowed hard. "And my throat doesn't hurt at all." I glanced over my shoulder at him.

He pulled up the back of the T-shirt and ran his fingers over my shoulder blades and spine. "No bruising here, either."

I felt my stomach drop. The Lady...she'd changed me.

He pulled down my T-shirt and our gazes met in the

mirror. "Three hours ago, you were bruised, and your voice was hoarse."

"I don't want to do any weird experiments." I grabbed onto his arm. "Black, don't make me go through that." I pictured Onyx gleefully breaking my fingers in order to see how quickly they would heal.

I could feel him thinking, considering the different outcomes.

"Black?" My voice cracked. The thought of their tests terrified me.

"For now, we'll keep this development between us."

It wasn't the assurance I wanted, but I'd take it. "What about Lorenzo? Will he tell what happened?"

I sensed that he wanted to chuckle. "Few willingly interact with Lore. I don't think he'll share how he endangered the Seer."

"Why is that?" My damn curiosity made my mouth run, again.

"Feed me, and I'll tell you a little about my spy." He took my hand and led me out of his bedroom.

His kitchen was fantastic. I could create in this work-space. Everything was top of the line. "Let me get this straight. You don't cook, ever, and yet, all of this is yours?" I looked up from cutting the tender brisket I'd found in the huge two-door refrigerator.

He flashed a toothy grin. "I can hunt for my food."

"So, all of this food," I motioned to the pantry and the fridge, "is for when you have an overnight guest?" Okay, that sounded like I was fishing, but I was wanted to know about how he lived.

He tweaked my nose like I was a toddler. "Are you feeling jealous? Keeping the questions vague, when you really want to know about the other women I've had here?" He was giving me a closed-lip smile, like he was feeling smug.

I put down the knife with a clatter. "I'd say that it's about ten percent wondering about other women. I want to understand how things work." I picked up the knife again, but before I started to cut another slice, I pointed it at him. "And if there have been hundreds in that huge bed, then you'd better arrange to get a new mattress, mister, because that's just gross." I crinkled my nose.

He chuckled and reached for a bit of meat. "I think I like your jealous streak."

I stopped again. "Really? I'm holding a knife."

"That wouldn't do any real damage, Theo." He took another piece.

I frowned because we both knew I could never surprise him. I moved the remaining meat onto the china plate and pushed it toward him.

He hopped up and plunked his jean-clad ass on the counter top. "We should talk about earlier."

I sighed. I knew the lecture was coming, so I started cleaning up. I wasn't hungry after seeing what the Goddess's latest gift had done. "I guess I thought that since you were here, I'd be safe." I covered the roast and returned the platter to the refrigerator.

"You don't think."

I told myself to not get upset. "It's hard to prepare for the unknown."

"Are you trying to push blame onto me?" he asked slowly.

"No." I returned to the counter space near him. "I let my curiosity get the better of me." I swallowed because I hated this part. However, the Laird seemed to think I learned best when I had to list my transgressions.

"I didn't have a guard with me. I knew you were tied up with Council business. I should have been more cautious. You are right, I didn't think."

He stuffed the last of the meat into his mouth and chewed.

The other thing he did very well. He would make you wait for his answer or comment. The pause was designed to be nerve-wracking. I simply watched the muscle at his jaw's hinge flex. "You do that so well, my Seer."

That didn't sound very complimentary. I narrowed my eyes as I asked, "What?"

"Your list. It flows from your tongue so easily." He gave me an appraising look.

My stomach muscles tensed.

"I'm starting to think we must explore another form of punishment."

I tried to sense where he was going with that thought. He was angry, but he was also teasing, I could see the sparkle in his eyes. Damn tricky wolf. "I made the list as I was getting the life choked out of me," I muttered flippantly. It rankled that he was right about me not considering the outcome of my actions.

"I should paddle your ass for that," he said, while sliding gracefully to the floor from his perch.

I know my eyes widened, but it wasn't from fear. I was turned on, and he'd noticed. I tucked my hair behind my ear. "Okay...but you should know I'm not into any of the 'Daddy' shit." I gave him a small, challenging smile.

His eyebrows drew together. "What the hell are you talking about?" He shook his head once. "Are you trying to get me off track?"

"No." *Maybe*, I tried to look innocent. "I wouldn't be opposed to a little spanking." I took a step away from him, in case he decided to reach for me. "But I don't have Daddy issues, and I refuse to play like I do."

"Why do you keep talking about Daddy?"

Jesus, I really was going to have to try to explain. "Some men get off on it when their chick calls them 'Daddy,' and sometimes, they want them to dress up like little girls." I scrunched my nose. "That's way too weird for me."

"It does not sound appealing," he said in a very serious voice.

He cracked me up, but I didn't laugh. I was still wide awake, and there was that huge bed to try out. I moved back to stand in front of him. "So," I said, my hands moving to his hips, "about that punishment?"

His hand was under my T-shirt to cup my ass. "Somehow, I don't think you're going to think of it that way."

I wrapped my arm around his neck and pulled him down for a kiss.

HE WAS TOYING WITH ME. Black had carried me over his shoulder to the bedroom. He sat on the edge of the bed and shifted me so that I was face down over his thighs.

I was giggling, I knew he was into this. His hard cock was rubbing against my hip.

The open palm slaps weren't that bad. I think he was trying more for noise than sting. I played along, trying to slide off and wiggling. After the third slap, he ran his finger along my wet slit. "You like this." He pressed his index finger inside of me.

"I like you." It came out as a sigh.

He fingered me and continued with my punishment. He then picked me up and tossed me into the middle of the bed.

I landed with a splat. I tried to push my upper half up, but his hand was at the back of my neck.

His other arm encircled my hips and brought me up to my knees.

I heard the rasp of his zipper. Jesus, he wasn't going to undress, and that made me wetter. He entered me in one stroke.

"Jesus Christ," I swore, not because I was uncomfortable, but because I was so full and I loved it.

Black wasn't going easy on me. He pulled back until only his head was inside and slid back into me.

I pushed my ass back to meet him.

He slapped the side of my ass again. This time it hurt.

"Yeow!" I pushed up enough to look back over my shoulder.

"You were irresponsible." Then he grunted as he pushed forward with enough force I slid forward on the soft sheets.

I was now on my knees with my breasts pressed against the headboard. Black was plastered to my back with his mouth at my ear. "I almost lost you." His tongue swiped over the sensitive shell.

"I know." I loosened my hold on the frame, found his hand, and covered it.

He immediately twisted his wrist so that now his

hand covered mine and our interlocked fingers held the strong wooden frame.

As he ground against my ass, and I wanted to come, but every time I got close, he stilled.

"I'm sorry." I told him again. I took in more air as I tried to drop my head back onto his shoulder. I loved that he surrounded me. "Raider, please," I begged in a groan.

He moved his hands again, this time to my breasts. He wasn't gentle as he squeezed them. I pushed back again, as he pressed harder into me.

"I can't lose you." His teeth closed over my earlobe.

"You won't, Raider. I promise." God, I never wanted to leave him.

I swear I heard him growl, *Mine*—right before he bit down on my shoulder. I came hard, and one stroke later, so did he.

I smiled to myself as I fell asleep. I shouldn't be able to walk for a week.

THIRTY-FOUR

NOVUS

RAIDER BLACK

S he was awake. It wasn't like she moved or started talking. I knew because her breathing changed. She probably had no idea what time it was. I'd have to arrange for some kind of lighting, her human eyes couldn't see in the dark.

She slowly turned, so that she faced me.

I didn't move. I wanted to see what she would do.

She whispered, "I am really sorry."

"Show me."

She started to push away from me, but I caged her with my arms.

"Present your brand, Theodora. Ask your Laird for forgiveness for scaring the shit out of him."

"What?" She raised her upper body up on one arm.

"Show me," I commanded, keeping all emotion from my voice.

"Here?"

"Are you refusing a direct command from your Laird?" I needed to assert my power over her this morning. I'd said too much last night and I needed to re-establish my domination.

"No, sir." She got to her knees and slowly lifted her leg to straddle my hips. She shook her hair out of her eyes and presented her brand. "Laird." She bowed her head.

She did this so prettily. If I wasn't already hard, I would have been, instantly. She held her exposed wrist so gracefully, but there was a tilt to her lips that intrigued me. It was always part invitation and part challenge as if she was biding her time before she tested me.

Fighting dirty wasn't in her nature. No, taking a circular route was more her style. Like last night, when she'd diffused some of my anger by admitting her interest in getting spanked.

"I want a show." I pushed another pillow behind my head so that I was propped up.

"A show?" She bit her lip.

I knew she wasn't acting. My bold Seer was sexually bashful. "Show me what you like," I coaxed. "Touch yourself."

Her eyebrows rose. "Now?"

I was growing tired of her stalling. "Do it in the dark, like you did when you first explored your body. Talk me through what you feel."

Her chest expanded and contracted as she considered my wish. Then she closed her eyes and ran one hand through her hair. Her hand lightly traveled over her full lips, then down her neck to her collarbone. "My skin is so soft, but the sensation is better when you touch me. I like your callouses."

Oh yeah, her words in that husky morning voice... I fucking loved this.

She cupped her tits. She stroked in circles and finally, pulled on her nipples, stretching them.

"Pinch them," I ordered.

She followed my command immediately and moaned as her fingers closed on the hard tips.

She was beautiful, giving me this without thinking, only reacting.

Her hand traveled lower.

I raised my knees so she could rest her back against them. "Show me," I whispered.

She didn't hesitate. She shifted her weight back, drew her knees forward, and then splayed them open. I could see her slick folds. She used her index and middle fingers to hold her outer lips open so that I could see her better.

She was enjoying this, giving me this show under the cloak of darkness.

Her musky scent was getting stronger. A low rumble sounded deep in my chest.

She pressed two fingers into her channel. "Not as thick as you, Laird," she whispered.

"Add another. I want to see you stretched wide."

She did so, and I watched as her thighs contracted as she slowly entered her body. "So good."

On the third stroke, she slid a finger over her clit.

My hand went to her hip. I wanted to fill her completely. I traced my finger over her wet folds, making sure that they were coated for easy entry. I ran my hand over her ass and down her crack.

"What?" She froze mid-stroke.

"Shh, keep going," I said in a low voice. I stroked my fingers back up.

"What are you doing?" She was totally focused on my finger's path.

"I'll make it good," I promised.

"No." She tightened her ass.

"No?" I cajoled.

"That's a firm one, Black. Don't." She started to shift, to close her thighs.

I knew she meant it, so I retreated, this time. I returned my hand to her hip and stroked her smooth skin. "Don't stop. I won't touch you there." I promised for now.

"I mean it. Don't go there." She hadn't resumed her play, so I ran my finger over her sensitive clit.

"I want to watch you come from your own hand, and then if you can take it, from my cock."

She didn't move for a few seconds.

I kept stroking her lightly, hoping she would continue.

She nodded and closed her eyes.

I reached out and cupped her left breast. "I can help." I circled her nipple with my fingernail.

"Oh, God." She shivered and pushed her tits forward. She wasn't afraid of a little pain. I filed that away for later.

I played with her tits, watching her face for every tiny reaction.

She was so close, riding her fingers.

"Come for me," I told her.

As she let go, she said my name.

After she caught her breath, I flipped her onto her back and held her hands over her head, gathering her wrists in a secure hold.

"Yes," she whispered, "God, yes."

As I entered her, I planned on taking advantage of

the Lady's gift. If Theo could take it, I wasn't going to hold back. Jesus, she felt so hot and tight.

She'd already come twice and I was close, but this time, I wanted to mark her in a different way. I felt the pressure build until my balls ached. I pulled out and came all over her belly and pussy. I wanted her to wear my cum all day.

I let go of her wrists. She'd only tried to break free once. I loved that she accepted my dominance.

She surprised me when both of her hands went to her belly and she started to massage the streams into her skin. Moving her hands upward and painted her breasts, paying special attention to her nipples. She bent her head sharply while pushing her tit upward and took her nipple into her mouth to suck.

"Holy fuck," I breathed. I'd never seen anything sexier.

She released her nipple and looked at me. "I wanted to taste you on me."

"Damn." I fell back on top of her, kissing her hard, my tongue tracing the inner recesses of her mouth.

I fucked her again in the shower. What could I say? Now that I knew she could take it, I wasn't going to deny myself anything, or her. She'd said her ass was off-limits, but I knew that I'd have her. She'd learn to love anything I gave her.

A FEW HOURS LATER, I was sitting behind my desk with Conal sprawled in the wing chair across from me. Most of my Pack dressed like bikers. I wanted to be comfortable. When I traveled to a Gathering in Edinburgh, I wore a suit, but I hadn't put on a tie since the 1980s. Conal was in a faded Harley T-shirt, and his jeans had holes at the knees. Currently, the big blond was smirking at me.

"Just say your piece so we can get down to work," I grumbled. The ass was enjoying this.

"I was going to say that you look well…" he dragged out his pause for about six beats as I frowned at him, adding, "rested."

"I would have been in earlier, but it takes her a while to get ready." I tried to frown.

His eyebrows waggled. "But it's worth it."

I had to agree. She wore a pink lace bra under her navy dress. I was going to be thinking about that all day.

"A word of advice," he said, grinning, "if she ever asks if she looks all right, always tell her yes."

"I will not." I rested my forearms on the desk. "If she reveals too much, I'll order her to change."

"Brother, if you're planning on doing that, then I wish you good luck." Conal chuckled.

"My…my," I wasn't sure what to call her, so I settled on the easiest description, "woman will not be provocative."

"Yeah, I don't think you have to worry about that with Theodora. Any revealing clothes that she's worn, she's done so because Solle pressured her."

"Order your mate to stop."

That made him laugh loudly. "I think I'll leave that conversation to you."

"Lore met Theodora last night and has offered to work with her," I said.

That made my Second sit up straight and turn serious. "And you approve?"

"His mother was Marked and a Seer. I'm curious to learn what he thinks about mine."

Conal ran his hand over his scruffy chin. "She mentioned that Onyx told her she was a disappointment."

That irritated me. "I shared Onyx's opinion with Lore and he said something very interesting. He believes Theo is strong for just having come into her power. The way he explained it was that it could kill her to have all her power freed at one time."

"So, it will grow over time?" Conal pursed his lips. "That makes sense after witnessing what happens when The Lady gives a human a boost."

I never wanted to see her in that much pain again. "Too much, too fast could also account for some going insane."

"She's too level-headed to lose it," Conal announced with surety, but I knew his assertion was based on hope.

"She's blood-thirsty and trouble." I finally gave into a slight smile.

"That keeps it exciting." Again, Conal laughed.

"I'm interested to learn what he thinks." I tried to get us back on track.

"I wonder how they'll do together. He rarely speaks."

"She'll pull him in with her vulnerability, charm him with her goodness, and then she'll use her brain. In three days, she'll be leading him around by his dick just like the rest of us."

"You complaining?" He gave me a searching look, and slowly, a grin formed.

I smirked. "Hell, no." Part of my fascination with her was that she was so complex and unexpected. Plus, the sex. I couldn't forget the sex.

"How are you going to handle his being around her?"

"He knows she's mine."

"He might see that as a challenge. She isn't mated or deemed your Consort, so..." Conal tilted his head a little.

"She is mine." I showed my teeth.

Conal raised his hands in surrender. "I'm clear. I just hope that he is."

THIRTY-FIVE

NOVUS

THEODORA MORRISSEY

I was in my favorite spot in my office on the floor, with my desk shielding me from prying eyes. The Burke Pack in Texas had been this week's subject, and I thought they were terrible. One family had ruled them for years, and they seemed rather reclusive and suffocating to their people. I was bored out of my head learning about these North American Packs, but in the spirit of cooperation, I kept that opinion to myself.

Suddenly, there was a pair of olive-green, cargo-pant-clad legs in front of me. I followed the legs higher to find Lorenzo holding a bouquet of mixed wildflowers.

"Good morning, Seer," he greeted me with a formal bow. "Please accept my apology for my behavior last night." He held out the bouquet.

"Oh, thank you." I started to get to my feet, and he held out his hand to assist. I gave it a long look before I decided to take it.

He didn't interpret my caution as a snub. He simply

helped me to my feet and then backed away, giving me room to move.

"I need to find a vase for these," I said, looking at the flowers, and feeling a little off-center that someone with Lore's reputation had brought them. The Laird had never gotten around to telling me about his spy last night. The hot sex had intervened.

"I'll do that." He turned and left abruptly.

"Okay," I said to the empty room. Some of these Lycans were an odd mix of formal, antiquated, and current. I pegged Lorenzo to be formal and very old-school.

He returned in five minutes with a crystal vase filled with water.

I unwrapped the paper from the flowers and arranged them in the vase.

"I see no ill effects from last night," he observed.

I said nothing as I continued to arrange the flowers.

"You heal quickly for a human. Even a Marked human would have bruises here." He ran his hand under his chin, "And you are moving easily. Your ribs and back should be sore."

I used my gift to see if I could learn anything about why he was here. He felt like a friend. *How can that be? I just met him.*

"What does your gift tell you, Seer?" he asked casually.

My voice came out softly, "You know when I use my gift?"

"Like knows like," he told me mysteriously.

I think I blinked several times as I tried to comprehend what he was telling me. Finally, I gave up and showed my ignorance. "I don't mean to be rude, sir, but I don't know what that means."

"Perhaps we should sit. My story is long." He motioned toward the sofa.

I took a seat on my sofa and watched as he chose the chair.

"My mother was like you, Marked by The Lady."

"Oh," I said as I tried to guess his age. He acted like an ancient, but I knew he was a spy, so I guessed he knew many tricks.

"She was a Seer. Back then, my father had sent out search parties throughout our lands to hunt for any Marked. He always said that he knew The Lady would bestow one upon our Pack."

"So, your mother and the Packleader..." I couldn't continue, this was too close to home.

"I am the eighth child, the fourth son. My father's contracted mate died in childbirth with my sister. After many centuries, my mother was located and became Consort to the King."

"Was she changed?" I had a million questions running through my head. This was the kind of information I craved and Onyx withheld.

"No, my father wouldn't chance her gift being diminished."

"But I thought the offspring of a Lycan and human match is a physically weaker wolf." That was what Solle had told me when she explained about how Lycans procreated.

"Ah, that." Lore looked down at his hands. "I might be responsible for that rumor."

"What?" I gasped. That belief was firmly held by every Lycan.

"I was smarter than several of my older brothers and I knew that if they considered me a threat to their position then, eventually, so would my father. I pretended to be slower and physically weaker. I could never be a victor in a Challenge."

"Obviously, it worked." I looked away for a moment as I tried to fathom how this one man's actions became fact to an entire race. "I can't believe no one has ever questioned that belief," I said almost to myself.

"At that time, it was rare for the different races to mate and breed." He shrugged.

"I'm a little overwhelmed, meeting someone who has first-hand knowledge of a Seer," I admitted, hoping he would continue to share.

"You are very new." He was staring at me intently, but he was doing something more.

It felt like a light buzzing against my skin, like a fly was near. "Are you Marked?" I asked quietly.

He shook his head. "No, but I did inherit some of my mother's gift."

I slid forward on the sofa cushion. "Really?" I breathed the word.

"In today's world, it might be called intuition. My gift tells me when I'm on the right track."

"I could do that sometimes, before I came here." I hoped that by sharing some of my own story that he would continue.

"As I said, like knows like."

I wasn't sure how I felt about us being alike. "May I ask, what happened to your mother?" Damn it, Onyx's stupid family tree lessons would have come in handy now.

"She is long dead."

"I'm very sorry to hear that, for you and your birth pack." *And me.*

"It was a very long time ago," he said simply.

From his tone, I guessed that she went insane, or maybe fell out of favor with the Leader.

"She was murdered."

"No," I cried as I reached out to pat his arm, but I stopped the movement. I didn't know him well enough. "That's horrible."

"We were at war with another pack."

That had to have been centuries ago. At one time, Lycan wars were much more common. Now, issues were worked out diplomatically through the Council.

"She was avenged."

Something in his tone made me pay closer attention to him. Alarm bells rang inside me. My door was open, but did anyone know he was here with me? And where the fuck was my tutor? This would be the one day he was late. "By your father?"

"No. Eventually, his army made its way to the fortress, but everyone was dead." He looked so relaxed as he recounted this story. It was chilling how calm he looked. "I kept the Leader, and of course the man who committed the actual murder alive. A quick death was too good for them." He smiled conspiringly as if I'd understand.

I felt the goose bumps rise all over my body. "You, alone, killed an entire Pack?" I asked slowly as I tried to comprehend what that meant. Why was nobody stopping in? Any other day, ten wolves would have been by.

"I asked The Lady for assistance. She poisoned the dinner so that most were disabled. I took care of the rest," he recounted serenely.

Now, I was officially freaked out. An entire Pack! I wanted to ask if Black knew. But, of course, he did. Hell, Lore had probably told him the story over a beer and a cigar. "I, ah, I thought it was against Lycan Law to hurt a Marked?"

"Seer, it will do you well to always remember..." He shifted closer to the edge of the chair and to me. "We are always surrounded by those who will turn on us."

I felt the truth of his words through my gift. "Do you mean here, within Novus?" I asked carefully.

"Certainly," he said, with a curt nod. "You were right to study my hand before taking it. You don't know yet if I am friend or foe."

I used my gift again, and nothing felt amiss. "I believe you are friend, but I'm not sure the word means the same thing to you as it does to me."

"You are very bright." He nodded approvingly.

I made a face. "I think my tutor would disagree."

"Sir Onyx has overseen your training. Tell me, what have you studied?" He pointed at the pile of pads on my desk and the various books strewn around the room.

"We've focused on Pack histories, family trees, and their geographical holdings."

"Ridiculous." He frowned, and his golden eyes flashed in irritation.

Again, I noted how truly striking he was.

"He should be teaching you about your gift."

"He's disappointed. I don't, um, do very much," I admitted uncomfortably.

"Bullshit." The word sounded so odd coming from Lore.

"I don't understand."

"Perhaps, I chose the incorrect word. I don't always keep up with conversant words."

I let out a laugh, and it sounded a little strangled. "No, I got the part where you don't agree with Onyx. What I don't understand is why you think I have more talent than I do."

"I know, because I learned from Lady Octavia. My mother was the most powerful Seer of all time." He nodded once as if he needed to press that point. "I feel…" he touched his hand to his gut, "the same about you."

I was speechless.

"I'll take over your training and evaluate your strength. I'll design a plan for your studies." He said it in the same tone the Laird decreed action to be taken. Of course, he was technically a prince. "Pack histories…" he waved a dismissive hand, "that's only important so that you learn who wishes to do damage to you."

"Almost everybody can," I admitted.

"Seer, you watched the Laird spread a man's cranium around a room with one shot for touching you. You are protected."

"Yeah, but I don't have a gun." I couldn't even pee in privacy, so I seriously doubted anyone was going to hand me a real weapon. "I must depend on others."

He seemed surprised by my answer. "You don't have a blade?"

I shook my head.

"Our lessons will begin there." He stood and motioned for me to do the same. "We'll start with blades. I always thought they were the perfect weapon for a female." He took my hand.

I stopped. "I need to check in with the Laird. I'm not

sure he's going to approve of weapons and all." What I really wanted to know was if he knew that Lore had basically taken over my studies.

The wolf laughed. "Again, you please me."

I'm sure my baffled expression gave me away.

"You don't follow me willingly. You're right to ask the Laird. Very good, Seer."

Jesus, he was a tricky wolf, but the weird thing was, I felt comfortable with him and I could learn from him.

I WAS a Goddamn idiot to go along with this. I was starting to think that Lore might very well be insane. After Basil waved me through into Black's office, I asked formally whether Onyx had been replaced.

"Let's not use that word. It's more of a sabbatical," the damn man told me.

"And Lore is taking over?"

"She's very cautious. Someone was right to instill that into her." The spy had slipped in without me even realizing the door had opened.

Black moved in close to me and tucked a lock of hair behind my ear. "He has first-hand knowledge, babe. I think he'll be good for you."

I was caught off guard by his easy touch and endearment in front of a Pack member. I glanced quickly at Lore, who was smiling at us. "He told me about Lady Octavia."

"Then you agree he will be helpful?" he asked, his expression bland.

"Did you know he wants to teach me how to use a knife?" How dare he act like he had no clue why I was questioning all of this. They were his fucking rules…and my life!

"And a gun," Lore added helpfully.

Black paused before answering. "After last night, I see the merit in his ideas."

We were so going to revisit the entire pee in privacy thing tonight. "So, you're okay with me having a gun?" I wanted him to be clear.

"As long as you don't use it on me," he said, his eyes sparkling.

"Don't be so sure," I muttered under my breath, but I knew he could hear me.

Black laughed loudly. He turned to my new teacher. "She must be at Solle's medical office at one."

I was almost out of Black's office when he called my name. I turned around.

"Tell your guard to bring you to Packhouse tonight."

"Okay, but I need to stop and get clothes for tomorrow." My stomach flipped in anticipation of being alone with him.

"Pack much, Theo."

I gave him a cheeky smile. "Yes, Laird."

Half an hour later, I was trying to throw a knife at a newly erected target in the gym. Every single time somebody walked in, Lore would growl—an actual, bared-teeth growl. My grandma used to say, "Them's fighting words." Yet, nobody approached him.

"This time, I want you to use your gift to help you guide the blade." My instructor adjusted my shoulder.

I felt like an idiot as I tried to clear my mind and concentrate on my lower stomach. That's where I, too, felt like my gift resided. That was the place that stirred when I used it, though it was also the part of my body that always somersaulted when Black gave me a hungry look or dropped his voice, so it went two octaves deeper.

To the middle! I let go of the blade and, I shit you not, it went directly to the middle of the target. "Whoa." I dumbly stared at the circles within circles.

Lore handed me another blade. "Again."

I spent the next two hours throwing different kinds of knives and hitting the center more times than I didn't. My shoulder was numb, and I'd managed to nick my fingers a few times.

"Tomorrow, we'll work on incorporating your blade-throwing into situations," he said as he put several of the knives into a case.

"Okay, first knives then guns. When do I get to work with explosives?" I teased.

"Would you like that?"

Holy moly, he thought I was serious. "No," I corrected him before he went into his pocket and pulled out some C-4 and blew our asses up.

He continued wiping each blade and putting it into its compartment. "I think our time would be better spent on poisons."

I shook my head. "You do realize I'm always with a Novus member. I mean, it's either a guard or a high-ranking Pack member. I don't feel like I'm in that much danger." Learning that my gift could help me control a knife was cool, but I doubted I'd ever use it.

"The daughter of my mother's most trusted friend gave her killer entrance to her private quarters," Lore said solemnly.

"But with your heightened senses, couldn't you tell if someone was plotting against you or me?"

"Like humans, we get lazy around the familiar.

Odella had served my mother since she was a teen. Nobody ever suspected that she'd contemplate a traitorous act."

"Why did she?"

"She was to be contracted to the Second of another pack. She didn't want to leave our lands. She believed that in the chaos of the discovery of my mother's body that she could escape." He closed the case and stood.

"Did she make her escape?"

"For a time, but she died. The Lady is vengeful when her children are mistreated."

I locked gazes with him. "I hope her death was slow and painful."

He smiled as if I'd just given the correct answer on a quiz. "It was most unpleasant and lasted for years." He motioned for me to follow him. "Now, you must be fed, and you are to travel to the healer's office."

"I work there two or three days a week."

"You are trained in healing?" He opened the gym door for me and nodded approvingly as I waited for him to check the hallway.

"No, I file records away and help out with the kids."

He frowned. "I don't understand. Surely, you don't need the money."

I hadn't thought about money in weeks. "I don't do it for money. In the beginning, it was a good way for me to meet the members of the Pack, and I like the kids. Sometimes, I can soothe the ones who are in pain or crying."

"Again, you use your gift, and you don't even realize it. The Lady has truly granted Novus a great honor."

I smiled as we walked down the hallway. I hoped I could help the Pack.

THIRTY-SIX

RAIDER BLACK

It was the third night that Theodora had spent in my bed. I heard my cell vibrate with an incoming text. I let go of her waist and rolled over, reaching for the phone.

Control Room: Prisoner Awake

I glanced at the clock on my screen and responded, **1 hour. Contact Board**

Control Room: 10-4

I put down the phone and sat on the side of the bed.

"What's going on?" She sounded only half awake.

"The prisoner is conscious, so I need to go in." I leaned back and onto my side to press a kiss to her shoulder.

She started to roll to the far side of the bed. "I'll get dressed. There probably isn't enough time to shower, is there?"

She turned on the light atop what I now thought of as her nightstand.

I started to tell her she didn't need to go, but I stopped myself. "Is your gift telling you to come with me?"

She was bent over the bag she'd packed with her clothes. "Good question." She straightened and pulled on a pair of black panties. "Lore says it's all about asking the right question." She pulled on a pair of jeans.

I needed to get dressed, but I couldn't tear my eyes from her. "Then answer me, Theodora."

She paused while pulling a black lace bra up her arms. "I don't know. I'd call it more of a feeling."

In the very short time that she had worked with Lore, I'd seen a major change in her. She spoke more about her intuition and how she was trying to identify the different indicators. It seemed that my spy reassured and praised her work, where Onyx had only demanded and was disappointed. Yesterday, I saw Lore laugh for the first time in my life. As I'd predicted, she had him wrapped around her finger, and she didn't even know it.

She passed me on her way to the bathroom. "If your Board didn't know we were sleeping together, they will now. Your scent is all over me."

Like I had a problem with that. "They all know but are being polite by not mentioning it."

"Except for Conal, I imagine." She stuck her head out of the bathroom. "He probably gives you shit constantly."

I opened my drawer and pulled out a red shirt. "Sometimes, he throws in a little advice."

"Solle mentioned dinner tomorrow, or I guess it's technically tonight, but I didn't accept. I wanted to talk to you first." She bent over the sink and splashed warm water on her face.

"We can do that if you'd like." I started to brush my hair.

She finished, turned off the water, and reached for the towel on the counter. "I don't want her to ask a million questions." She patted her face with the towel. "Does that make me a bad friend?"

I put down my brush down and kissed her cheek. "You're being protective."

"Of you." She put toothpaste on her brush.

I waited until she was ready to spit out the toothpaste before asking, "You think she'll rattle me?"

She wiped her mouth with the towel. "No, but I think she'll ask us questions we might not have answers for, or that we haven't considered, and it could get...uncomfortable."

I pulled her into my arms. "This is new, and we are new to each other. Of course, there are things we don't know."

"I'm being selfish. I like this time all to ourselves." She dropped her gaze.

"Theo, it's not a bad thing that you like being with me."

"Soon, everybody will know and they'll want to see us out together. To watch how we interact."

"As long as you do as I tell you, all will be fine." I kissed the side of her mouth.

She pushed me away. "So, I'm to kneel beside you with my hands clasped behind my back?"

Why would she assume I'd ever want that—other than we when we were alone and playing? Something in her tone didn't sound right. I turned to her. "Hey..." I pulled her back into my arms. "Does that shit make you unhappy?" She'd never shown me a sign that she was uncomfortable with my being dominant in the bedroom.

"This isn't the time to go into this, Black."

She was trying to avoid my question. "Theo, I need you to be honest with me. You spoke up about the ass play, but if I'm doing something you don't like, I'd like to know." I was getting irritated.

She frowned and looked down at my chest. "I like what we do."

"But," I prompted her.

"We're doing stuff I've never done before." She ran her hand over my heart. "I've read some books with Dominance and submission in them, but I don't know how realistic they are."

"I think you're getting too hung up on this."

"I've never thought of myself as submissive. I mean, I'm quiet at times…"

I raised one eyebrow, she was usually in the center of every group.

"At first," she stressed the words. "With you, sex is different… I'm different."

"I'm Lycan." Of course, it was different.

"You're a fucking alpha, Laird. I don't know how much of me giving you everything is because you demand it, or if it's because the Laird demands it—or because I want to give it."

"Theo…" I brushed a kiss against her temple. "You are thinking too much."

She rested her cheek against my chest. "I'll figure this out."

"We'll figure this out," I promised her.

SHE FOLLOWED me as I headed to the lower floor of the Novus building where the prisoner had been transported.

"You don't have to do this."

"I think I do." She was rubbing her belly.

"Same rules as before."

"Yes, Laird." She stayed close as I keyed in my code and entered the interrogation room. She took her place against the wall near the door.

Lore and Tex were standing over the prisoner.

The male looked directly at Theodora. "Hello, Pretty," he growled. "Why don't you come closer?"

"Eyes on me," I ordered.

"I like her." He ran his tongue over his lips suggestively.

Lore punched him in the mouth. "Enough."

Tex grumbled, "This one is quite the comedian."

I smiled evilly. "We'll see."

The male could take a lot of pain. At almost two hours in, he still hadn't cracked.

"My turn," Theodora's voice cut through the violence.

I looked over my shoulder at her.

"With your permission, Laird?" She hadn't moved from her place.

"All right, Seer." I held out my hand to her. It was covered in blood, but she took it anyway, without pause.

She stood directly in front of the man. As soon as she closed her eyes, I felt the buzzing against my skin increase. She put her hand on the man's chest. "Wolf, I am Theodora, marked by The Lady, Seer to the Novus Pack. You will speak when our Leader commands."

I began the questioning. His wolf didn't want to

cooperate, but Theodora did something that must have caused him great pain because he thrashed in his chair and began to answer.

Slowly the story unfurled. My Seer was shaking with exhaustion, but she made him answer all of my questions. I excused her from the room. She didn't need to see the next part. She didn't argue with my decision and left with Lore.

An hour later, after we'd showered and changed, I called my Seer to join us in my conference room. Glass and Conal had watched the interrogation from the Control Room and also joined us.

"So, it is now substantiated that we have a traitor amongst us," Conal stated coldly.

"How many are employed by Novus?" Theodora asked.

"Too many for you to interview," I said.

"Laird, I can continue my search," Lore offered.

"I feel that your skills are better used here for now." I meant with Theodora. She'd not only used her gift in new ways but very successfully. We'd just witnessed her call the man's wolf without my assistance.

"I can send more of my people on the runs." Glass looked grim. Her trained guards liked action. Sitting in the cab of a truck would not please them.

"I think we're close," Tex began, "and he knows it. He'll do something rash and then we'll have him."

I adjourned the meeting.

Several hours later, Theodora stopped in my office. She was going to the gun range with Glass and Lore.

"Have you handled a handgun before?" I noticed that she hadn't changed out of her jeans and T-shirt from earlier.

"On the farm, I learned to shoot a rifle, but that was to handle scavengers. I never actually had to shoot anything." She shrugged.

"If you like it, we'll go tomorrow," I promised her.

She laughed. "You are so romantic."

I knew she liked the idea. "Go practice, so that I'll be impressed."

"Ass," she said before kissing me.

Two hours later my cell vibrated. The screen showed Glass was calling.

"What's happened?" I knew there was a reason for her call.

"It's the Seer. She's having a seizure."

I was on my feet and heading out of my office. "How long?"

"Two, maybe three minutes." Glass sounded stressed. "Should I call Solle?"

"Are you still at the range?" If I changed, I could be there in twenty minutes, driving in my SUV would take longer.

"Yes, Laird. She was shooting and paused to put down her gun. Then she crumpled to the ground."

"Clear the area. I'll be there as fast as I can."

I handed my phone to the guard who was following me. "Tell Conal I'm heading to the gun range."

I changed and headed west.

I arrived to find Glass on the phone with Solle and Lore was sitting on the ground with Theodora leaning against his side. She had her eyes closed and was holding a half-full bottle of water.

I squatted down in front of her. "Babe, you okay?"

She opened her eyes and nodded slowly. "It was another vision."

"I'll call a meeting." I touched my pocket for my phone but remembered I didn't have it.

"Please, don't." She cried.

"What's going on Theo?" I noticed that her hands were shaking.

"What I saw… I think you should hear it first." She gave me a wide-eyed, pleading look.

"It was about me?"

Her chin quivered as she said, "Yes."

"Okay." I stood. "Let's get you home." I leaned over and she wrapped her arms around my neck as I looped one of mine under her knees.

She tucked her face against my neck and I was shocked to feel how cold she was.

I nodded at Lore. I trusted that he understood he was to stand by.

Conal pulled up just as I made it to the parking lot. I opened the passenger side door as soon as he stopped. "We'll go to your house."

My Second said nothing as he drove us to his home.

Although it was in the high-eighties outside, Theo sat on the basement sofa in a hooded sweatshirt with a blanket wrapped around her. Conal had just finished thrusting a mug of hot tea into her hands.

"I told Solle you were fine except for the headache. I figure we have about forty minutes before she arrives." Conal sat on the loveseat across from us.

"It won't take that long," she said, her voice was shaking.

"Drink your tea. It'll help warm you." The shower had helped a little, but she was still shivering.

She took a sip. "You were driving a truck, a semi. It

was like you were baiting them." She squeezed her eyes closed. "It was sunny, the terrain was flat."

I drew a slow breath and darted a glance at Conal. She had no idea that Conal and I had discussed taking a job in hopes of drawing out the traitor.

"You stopped. I think maybe you were following somebody and they pulled off the road." She paused to take another sip. "Some of this is hard, because I'm interpreting what I saw, trying to fill in the blanks about what I didn't, so I could be wrong."

"Go on. So far, it all makes sense," I said.

She took a deep breath. "You get out. You ask, 'What's up?' and then…" She took in a couple of quick breaths and put her mug on the coffee table in front of her.

"What happened?"

"Your head exploded," she cried. "I saw parts of your skull fly past, Black." She reached for me and I pulled her into my arms.

"I can survive a bullet to the head, baby," I said, trying to calm her.

"No, you don't understand." She gripped my T-shirt in her fist. "Your head was blown off your body."

Conal cleared his voice. "Okay, well you might not be able to come back from that."

I glared at my Second. He wasn't helping.

"What else can you tell us?" I wanted every bit of information I could get.

"Did you hear a voice?" Conal asked.

She shook her head. "Only Black's." She closed her eyes for eyes for a moment. "You were relaxed." Her gaze met mine, and then looked at Conal. "It was somebody you recognized. Your body language was comfortable, and your tone, casual."

"I don't like this." Conal frowned even harder.

"I would recognize any member of my Pack," I said.

"This part is my impression only, but this was somebody you didn't view as a threat. You didn't hesitate. Maybe someone with whom you have more than a passing acquaintance."

I didn't like the idea of a traitor. However, it happened. I would deal with the threat quickly and make sure everyone knew you didn't cross Novus or its Leader.

I heard Solle's car pull into the driveway and two minutes later she hurried down the stairs.

She stopped at the side of Conal's chair, but her attention was focused on the Seer. "How are you?"

"I have a headache, but I'm fine."

The doctor frowned. "They said you seized for almost ten minutes."

"I didn't puke and I don't ache like last time." Theo tried to smile and failed. "I was exhausted after, but now, I feel like if I take a nap, I'll be fine."

Solle turned her attention to me. "Are you done here?"

The doctor wanted to check her friend and put her to bed. "For now."

Conal stood and kissed Solle's cheek. "I'm posting two guards outside while we go to the office."

I turned to Theo. "I'll be back."

"I can go," she whispered.

"No, you need to rest."

She frowned but didn't argue.

ALTHOUGH IT WASN'T SUNDAY, Theo was behind the breakfast bar, pouring coffee for Conal, Solle, and I. We had returned after midnight. Theo had been sound asleep, wearing a silky nightgown. I sensed Solle's hand in that fashion choice. Theo hadn't wakened when I slid under the sheet behind her.

Conal added some sugar to his mug. "Gonna have to find somebody else to man the grille, Solle, or cancel the party."

"Why?" his mate asked sleepily.

"We're going on a run."

Theo whipped around to face us then moved to the breakfast bar quickly and slammed her hands down on the counter, "What?" She stared at Conal, and then at me.

"We are going to make the next run," I said calmly.

"Are you fuckin' crazy?" she shouted.

I kept my expression blank. "Theo, this is the perfect opportunity to draw out the traitors."

Her face went red and her eyes flashed. "They're going to kill you," she shrieked.

"We have safeguards in place," Conal tried to soothe her.

"What if they don't work?" She turned her fury onto Conal. "Are you okay with him dying?" She was breathing hard and her knuckles were white from gripping the edge of the counter.

"He won't die," Conal told her slowly. "I'll be there to make sure of it."

She shook her head so hard her hair fanned out. "No, No, No," she chanted.

I slipped off my stool and moved toward her. "Theo, honey, it'll be fine."

"Don't!" She held up a hand to stop me. "Just don't."

She moved faster than I'd ever seen her do, heading down the back stairs to the basement.

We three stayed quiet for a minute.

Conal cleared his throat. "Well, that went well."

"I'll go talk to her."

"No, don't," Solle said. "She needs some time alone."

"She's upset." I don't recall ever seeing her so angry. My wolf urged me to find her and make her see reason.

Solle sighed loudly and frowned. "She's got a lot to deal with. She's still recovering from the seizures. She sees the man that she luh—" She quickly corrected herself. "*Cares* about get his head blown off." She motioned for me to return to my seat. "You drop the bomb that you're basically going to relive her vision. I sure hope it has a different outcome than what she saw." Solle gave him a glare. "I understand why she's upset. I would be, too."

"The Laird will be safe," Conal said, his voice rising, "because The Lady knows I don't want the damn job."

That was true. Conal was smart and a great leader, but he didn't want to deal with the bullshit. At the monthly settlement hearings, his head tried to explode at least four times. He grew tired of hearing cases regarding wayward chickens and business disputes.

"So, how much time do we give her?" Conal asked his mate.

"It takes me hours to get over a good mad and I have doors I can slam," she said with a grudging smirk. "I'll check on her in a couple of hours if she hasn't come upstairs."

"I'll never understand females," I grumbled.

Solle frowned. "Look, I'm not too happy about this either."

"The difference is that you understand I'm the Laird and my word is law." I didn't want to wait. I wanted to go downstairs and tell Theo she had no right to be upset.

"I do, but in this case, I'm worried." Solle looked at her mate for reassurance.

"She can't stop us," Conal explained reasonably.

"She knows that." Solle turned her coffee mug in a circle before she continued. "I'm guessing she's frustrated and terrified. Frustrated, because she can't stop you, and maybe she feels you aren't giving her vision the respect it deserves."

I cut in. "Because of her vision, we know we can draw this man out."

"That's not going to give her any comfort, not after what she saw." The doctor continued turning the mug round and round. "Keep in mind, she's only beginning to find her place with us. She's happy. However, she might feel like everything could change drastically on a dime." She sighed loudly. "She's done a good job adjusting to this life, but by no means has it been easy. It's unnerving and mentally exhausting. You feel like, for everything you figure out, there are a hundred more mysteries to solve."

I tapped the breakfast bar twice with my index finger. "I'll be back later this afternoon to speak with her." I'd made my decision and got to my feet. The longer I sat there, the more I wanted to go to her.

MY DAY WAS FILLED with meetings and plans. We'd leave tomorrow afternoon. I wasn't worried, but I would

427

be extra cautious. I was no fool. I parked in Conal's drive well after dinner. The last message I'd received from Solle said that Theodora was still in the basement and she'd refused to eat.

I didn't like that she wasn't taking care of herself. I was going to tell her that and then watch her eat a plate of food.

Conal was waiting at the front door. "Everything's in place."

"McGraw is taking off tonight?" Our next scheduled escort would start tomorrow. The driver of the decoy semi wouldn't be available. Conal and I were filling in so we could see how it was going and look for ways to improve our business. That was our cover story. It also explained the extra manpower, Asher, Tex, and Lore.

"When he saw the banded hundreds, he remembered he needed to visit Minneapolis." Conal closed the door behind me.

"Lore questioned him. After that, I imagine the guy was happy to get a break." I shook my head. For many Lycans, finding The Lore at their door would scare the piss out of them. The wolf's reputation was widely known and he could be intimidating.

"You're trusting him with her life," Conal pointed out.

"I trust him with Theo. I know he's loyal." I also knew that if anything happened to me, he would give his life to keep her safe.

"She's still downstairs."

I headed down the stairs, making sure my boots thudded on each step. I wanted her to know I was invading her space.

She sat in the corner of the sectional, staring at the

glass windows. She didn't turn her head to see who was entering her domain.

I walked to the hand-carved bar and pulled out a bottle of water and a beer from the cooler. As I neared the sofa, I spoke softly, "Theo."

"Laird," she said, without glancing my way.

Okay, so she wasn't going to make this easy. "Drink this." I sat down, making sure there was a generous space between us. I held out the plastic bottle.

She didn't take it right away, but I continued holding it out to her. Finally she did take it. "Thank you."

I opened my beer and took a couple of swallows. "Can we discuss this trip without you screaming?"

Her mouth tightened into a line. "I guess it depends on what you plan on discussing."

"We have safeguards in place." I took another drink.

"Will you be wearing a bullet-proof helmet?"

"No."

She pulled her knees up to her chest. "I don't understand."

I could smell her frustration and her sadness.

"Even when Onyx told you I sucked as a Seer, you always believed in me," she said in a low voice.

I didn't know where she was going with this.

"Why are you doing this?" She turned her head and focused on me. "I told you what I saw. I had to relive it over and over while I answered your questions." Her eyes filled with tears. "Do you know how hard that was Black? To watch you die?"

I moved closer, reaching out to touch her, to comfort her.

She smacked my hand away. "Don't."

I didn't like that at all. "Theodora, you had a vision.

We're using that information to draw out the traitor. We know what to look for. You've given us that." Didn't she understand how great her contribution was?

"You could die," she said, raising her voice a little, her control slipping.

"I won't," I said quickly, giving her a confident smile.

"Don't. Don't joke about this." She dropped her head back and stared at the ceiling. "I feel like all of this is a joke, that I'm a joke. That nobody takes me seriously."

"Why?"

"Because, you won't listen to me," she said, getting louder. "You...you're still going off, maybe to die."

I let my frustration with her seep into my tone. "I am the Leader. Someone is committing traitorous acts against my Pack. I won't stand idly by when I can do something."

She shifted until she knelt on the sofa cushion. "Then use your spies to investigate. Send the guards. Why does it have to be you?"

"I am the Laird," I answered simply.

She didn't speak. She simply stayed in that position breathing unsteadily.

"I'm going."

"Even if I ask you not to?" Her voice broke in a sob.

"Yes." It was my duty.

She closed her eyes and took in three breaths. "Then go."

I tried not to smile. I knew she'd see reason.

"I *said* go."

"I heard you," I said.

"I mean *now*. I don't want you here."

"Theo..." I reached for her.

She scampered out of my reach, almost falling over the arm of the sofa. "No." She stood at the corner of the sofa, opening and closing her hands. "I've asked you, now I'm telling you. I want you to go."

"Be reasonable."

She screamed, "Fine! Have it your way, Laird." Then she turned and ran up the steps.

I didn't follow her. I killed my beer, got up, and threw it away. If she didn't understand my duties to the Pack, then it was a good thing I'd learned that now.

I tried to shrug off my disappointment as I trudged up the steps. Neither Conal nor Solle were around, so I let myself out and went home, alone.

THIRTY-SEVEN

NOVUS

THEODORA MORRISSEY

L ast night when I made my way upstairs, I sent up a silent wish that my hosts would leave me alone. I'd washed my face, brushed my teeth, and pulled on one of Black's T-shirts. A knock sounded on my doorframe.

Conal held a plate of food, a bottle of water, and a beer. "It's time you eat something, Theodora." He entered my room.

"Are you here to give me a lecture?" My shoulders slumped as I shifted to sit on the side of my bed.

"No lecture, but I'd like to know your thoughts." He handed me the plate and placed the water on my nightstand.

"I know you heard me, earlier."

He sat next to me and studied the label on the beer bottle. "Which part upsets you most?"

I took a bite of my peanut butter sandwich. I couldn't believe Conal had never tasted peanut butter until I'd moved in. "I'd say that it's a seventy/thirty split."

"Which is which?"

"Want half?" I waved the sandwich in front of him.

"No, I want you to eat it all and to continue." He took a drink from his bottle.

"It feels like he isn't taking it seriously—what I saw, my vision." The salty, rich goodness suddenly tasted like paper. "I know Onyx has told everyone I'm not talented, that you all should be disappointed because your Seer sucks."

"You don't suck, Theodora."

"Lore's taught me more in the last few days about my gift than Onyx has in all of those months. I was feeling a little…" I felt my cheeks heat with embarrassment, "proud. You know, like I was finally contributing." Grandma was right; pride was a terrible vice.

"You've contributed from the start." Conal gave me a sideways look. "Some of it was your gift; the rest is your goodness."

I made a "humph" sound. "I wasn't being very good when I yelled at the Laird," I muttered.

"I think you were yelling at your lover, not the Laird."

Conal was very wise, and he was my friend, but his allegiance would always be to Black. "Is this a mistake?"

"Which part?" One side of his mouth lifted in a half smile.

"The lovers' part." I couldn't look at him, so I glanced down at my plate.

"No, I don't believe so, but as you are learning… well, the both of you are learning, there will be difficult times."

"It's hard to separate the two, you know? If I think about him as the Laird, then I'm powerless."

"The reality of our lives is that he is always the ultimate boss." Conal's voice was gentle but firm.

"So, my vote never counts?" I voiced my fears.

"It counts, but he decides." Conal took my plate from my now shaking hands and put it on the floor. "You are going to have to learn to trust in him." He let out a long sigh. "We're lucky, he's smart and benevolent. Some Leaders are cruel and impetuous, keeping their people in constant fear. Black makes mistakes, but in all the years I've known him, he has never intentionally hurt someone he cared about."

"I know that," I bit out. I sounded angry and defensive, so I paused to adjust my tone. "He's a really good man, er, Lycan."

"I think that's part of the problem. You think of him as a man, but he's more." Conal finished his beer and placed it on top of my plate. "Solle and I ran into the same problem at the beginning."

"I need to be smarter," I admitted.

"I keep forgetting how new you are to all of this. It'll take time." He gave me a sad smile. "Building trust takes time."

My breath caught. "We might not have time."

"You have *now*, Theodora."

I bit my lip. I felt like crying. Instead, I leaned into his side. "Can you keep him safe?"

"Yes," he said, instantly, firmly.

"I hope so, Conal." For all our sakes. I didn't want Solle to lose her mate and I didn't want to lose Black like that. I couldn't imagine Novus without Black and Conal. What would happen to me?

"But…"

His voice went so low I lifted my head to see his lips form the words.

"If anything happens, you go with Lorenzo."

"What?" My body went cold as terror gripped my chest.

"Don't worry about Solle, or anybody else, just go with him."

My eyebrows drew together in confusion. "Conal, what are you saying?"

"That's your Plan B. Well, technically it's Black's Plan B for you."

I couldn't speak. I nodded slowly as I tried to make sense of what he communicated without using words. The Laird had listened and made contingencies.

BLACK STAYED AWAY ALL NIGHT. A part of me was disappointed he hadn't come back. It was the first night we'd spent apart since my birthday. I missed his warmth and waking up feeling safe in his arms.

The pool party was canceled. I stayed in my room so Conal and Solle could have time alone. Around five, Conal called me downstairs.

"I'm heading out."

I jumped from the last step and hugged him tightly. "The Lady will watch over Novus."

"Thank you." His arms tightened around me.

He stepped back and gave his mate another long kiss.

As he was just about to walk through the door to the garage, I called out, "Conal?"

He paused and turned around.

I couldn't think of the right words. "Come back."

His smile was easy, but his eyes were dark and serious.

Solle and I stood side by side as we listened to his bike pull out of the driveway and head down the road.

Solle shifted away from me. "I'm going for a swim. Wanna come with me?"

"In a bit." I was hoping Black would stop by.

I waited in the living room, straining my ears to hear a vehicle. After an hour and a half, Solle came in, and I knew he wasn't coming.

She wore her bikini top and a pair of cutoffs that were super short. "What do you want for dinner?"

"I'm not really hungry." I hadn't been since yesterday.

"Do you want me to go all doctorly on you?" Solle put a hand on her hip. "'Cause you know I will."

She would. Deep down, Solle loved to nag. She did it in a charming way, but she didn't give up. "Okay, but it needs to be something light."

"We could have a salad," she offered with an enticing smile.

"You? Eat a salad for dinner?" That was unheard of for a Lycan. Every time I ate lettuce, Conal looked horrified.

Her smile widened. "Well, it might have some chicken on it."

I got to my feet. "You mean yours will be a lot of chicken with a tiny bit of green."

"But it still counts."

My friend tried to keep the conversation light. I knew she was worried about Conal and being apart. Plus, she was trying to gauge my mood.

I'd done the dishes and wiped down the counters. I

didn't want to sit around and try to make more conversation, so I told her I was going upstairs to read.

That was a mistake. Within twenty minutes, the voices in my head were talking. They told me that Black thought I was a failure. They pointed out that he hadn't come by, because he didn't care about me. I couldn't concentrate on my book, so I simply stared off into space.

There was a rumbling outside. I sat up straighter and listened as Solle opened the door. I heard a muffled, "She's upstairs."

My heart pounded as I watched the doorway to my room.

He filled it. Sometimes, I forgot how masculine he was—tall and strong with his long hair falling below his shoulders. "I'm heading out."

My throat felt like someone had tightened a hand around it. I nodded.

"I wanted…" He glanced at his boots and looked unsure for a single moment. "I wanted to say good-bye."

So, there it was. I cleared my throat, but my voice still came out rough, "Okay."

He continued standing there, looking at me.

He turned around and left.

I listened to his boots on the steps. I heard the door slam shut.

The sob that had been building finally broke free. I wasn't going to let him end it this way. "Black," I yelled and jumped to my feet. I ran to the stairs and rushed down them. I threw open the door so hard it slammed into the wall. "Wait, Black," I yelled as I cut through the yard.

He'd started circling around the truck parked in front of the house, but turned and caught me as I jumped into his arms.

"Raid, Raid," I said against his chest.

"Shhh," he said as his cheek brushed mine.

"I...please, be safe." I kissed him. I didn't care who was watching.

"Babe," he said against my mouth.

"I need you to come back." I rested my forehead against his. I thought I'd better clarify. "I mean alive and whole."

That made his chest rumble with a chuckle. "I will."

We kissed again.

"I'm still mad. I ca-can't help it," I said, because a part of me was. We'd be talking about it, later.

"I know."

"I'm scared," I admitted.

"I know that, too."

"B-but I want you to know that I...I care." That was a huge understatement of how I felt about him.

"When I get back, we will work this out." He turned his head to glance at Conal and Solle who were now standing close by. He kissed me; it was a promise.

He put me down, and I took his hand. I needed to touch him. "Be safe."

"Theo, I got this." He gave me a half-smile.

I prayed to every deity I could think of. I hoped so.

"Conal." I looked at my friend.

"Theodora, I know."

Our gazes met, and I remembered our conversation last night. I gave him a nod, telling him I wouldn't forget.

"Got to hit the road, ladies," Black told us.

I made myself let go of his hand and Solle joined me as we watched our men drive away.

"This is gonna suck," I said.

"It sure will." She wrapped her arm around my waist as we headed back into the house.

THIRTY-EIGHT

NOVUS

RAIDER BLACK

We'd made it to the California coast without a hiccup. I called a meeting with my team in the cheap hotel we used to grab some sleep in actual beds.

"We can't let up," Conal reminded our group.

"That goes without saying, Second." Asher was listening while checking his phone. I was sure he was looking for an Issa update.

I scanned the room. "So, we grab some shut-eye and hit the road at seven."

They got to their feet and left, except for Conal, who was sharing the other bed in the room. I heard him throw the locks on the door.

"Are you going to call your mate?"

"No, hearing her voice makes it harder." He pulled his shirt over his head and dropped it onto the floor. He stretched out on the bed.

I turned out the light after I took off my shirt. I tried to find a comfortable position.

"Do you miss her?"

Apparently, under the cloak of darkness, we were going to have "girl talk." I rolled onto my back and shoved my left arm under the pillow to support my head. "I do."

"You two will get through this."

"Of course we will." Theo would see that I'd survived this run and that her theatrics were unnecessary. Things would go back to the way they'd been before.

"I DON'T SEE anything for miles." Tex was on his bike about fifteen miles ahead of my rig.

"Just because you don't see it, doesn't mean there's no threat," Conal cautioned. He was riding a mile behind me. Lore rode shotgun beside me.

The highway stretched out in front of us for what seemed like forever. I considered calling for a break, so I could stretch. My shoulders were tense, and my ass numb.

"I see something." Tex's voice boomed through my earpiece. "A dark blue Ford F150 on the side of the road. One, possibly female, in primary seat."

I glanced in Lore's direction and noted he was sitting straighter. His attention focused on the road ahead of us as if he was casting out his senses.

"That sounds like our traitor," Conal's voice rumbled in my ear.

"It's showtime," I announced. My adrenaline was pumping and my wolf was ready. This would end today.

Lore climbed into the space behind the seats. It held a small bunk. Our escorts typically drove alone. A Lycan could go two or three days without sleep.

442

A woman stood in the middle of the highway, waiving her arms over her head.

I slowed and pulled to the side of the road.

The female approached my side window with an easy smile. I recognized her as the Bohm daughter, Lydia.

When I rolled down the window and glanced down at her, she paused mid-step but quickly recovered with a welcoming smile. "Laird, I didn't expect…"

"What are you doing out here?" I cut her off.

"Oh?" She looked around with a puzzled expression on her face. "I was visiting a friend and my truck broke down."

"Where's your father?" I was giving my team time to take up positions.

"He-he doesn't really know I'm here." She glanced away.

I didn't need to depend on my nose to tell me that was a lie. Her body language screamed falsehood. "I see."

"It's a male, and well…" She glanced up to see how this information was being received. "Dad can be a little over-protective."

"I'm sure he only wants the best for you." I opened my door and jumped down. "Let me take a look at your truck."

She appeared to climb in behind the wheel as I raised the hood and took my time reattaching the connections to the battery that she'd loosened. This was the difficult part, giving her time to take action. After checking every connection, I squared my shoulders and closed the hood. I noticed that she'd disappeared.

I stopped and cast out my senses. The first bullet

whizzed through the air by my ear. I ducked and ran in the direction from which it came.

The next sliced through my upper arm. I barely noticed it as I tracked Lydia Bohm to her small bunker across the highway.

Conal, in wolf form, had her on the ground with his strong jaws around her throat.

Lore stood with his heavy boot crushing the hand that had pulled the rifle's trigger.

Asher was examining the weapon. When he finished, he tossed it to me.

Theo's vision had been correct. The rounds used could've removed my head.

"Second, if you will allow me to take the traitor?" Lore's intonation was so calm it was chilling.

Conal let out a loud snarl.

"Second, stand down," I ordered.

He did and changed. He looked me up and down, noting the slice on my arm. "Fuck, Theo's going to be so pissed."

That made us all chuckle. Hopefully, the wound would be healed by the time I got home to her.

Asher said, "What do you want us to do with the traitor?"

He wanted the kill order given. They would have torn her body apart here on the side of the road without hesitation.

Hell, I wanted to tear her head from her body, but as I reviewed what I knew about the woman, her actions didn't make any sense. I needed to know more. An interrogation along the side of the highway was too public. "Take her to the Packhouse."

Asher bowed his head. "As you wish, Laird."

The guard, along with Lore and the prisoner, would travel in the SUV that we used as part of the escort. She'd be chained. I wouldn't be upset if Lore began the interrogation early, as long as she was alive enough to answer my questions when she arrived.

Tex bounded to our location in his wolf form. He'd made a complete circle of the area to see if there were more hiding.

"Report," Conal called out.

Tex changed, and after his gaze raked me and he knew I was fine, he answered, "There's no one else."

"Good enough. Let's get on the road." I didn't like standing out in the open anymore. I trusted Tex's report, but the idea that the female was working with another rode my senses.

"I'm with you." Conal moved in at my side as Tex crowded my back.

Conal took over the driving duties, and after about thirty minutes of quiet, he asked. "So, how bad is it?"

"A scratch."

"I sincerely hope so."

I couldn't stop the grin. Conal was worried about my human's reaction and retribution.

"You'd better lose that shirt before she finds it," my Second advised.

"I'm fine."

"That first bullet was too close." He glanced at me and I saw worry in his eyes.

"I never doubted my safety," I told my oldest friend and champion.

"Too close." He let out a loud breath. "I'll say it one more time—it was too close, Black."

Conal would worry about that for years, as was his

way. If he sensed the power that I did in my Seer, he'd be terrified that I slept next to her every night. She was the true threat to my safety, for one day, she might be able to control our wolves.

THIRTY-NINE

NOVUS

THEODORA MORRISSEY

F our days. I didn't even try to go into Novus or Solle's office. I felt like I was half alive. I couldn't sleep for longer than an hour or two, I wasn't hungry, and my brain was mush. Brian from Solle's practice had stopped by last night and threatened to drug me if I didn't try to get some "real" sleep.

The first two days, Solle appeared to be doing fine. She went to work, returned phone calls, and watched over me. Yesterday, she stayed in bed all morning and spent the afternoon on a float in the pool.

Today, we both gave up pretending. We jumped at every sound and she checked her phone twenty times an hour.

"I understand why we aren't getting calls, but I hate it," I complained as I stirred some creamer into my fifth cup of coffee.

"I have to think that no news is good news." Solle was flat on her back on the sofa.

Her phone played "Werewolves of London," and I

swear we both jumped five feet into the air. I spilled my coffee down my shirt and didn't even notice. I rushed to the living room to sit beside her. Conal had made contact.

"What-what does he say?" I asked, so tense I trembled.

She read from the screen. "Job done. Be home late."

"So, they're okay?" I moved closer to read the message myself.

"It doesn't say." She was staring at the screen, too. "But if it was bad, he'd call and start out by saying something like, 'Solle, gotta brace, baby.'"

I let out the breath I'd been holding. "That sounds like him." Suddenly, my vision was clouded. My eyes had filled with tears.

She hopped up. "I need to take a bubble bath and paint my nails."

Conal was going to get a very hot welcome home treat. I wasn't as sure about how Black would receive me. Had my taking a stand ruined our relationship? Could I handle the fact he'd always have the final word?

I took a shower around eight and curled up on the loveseat to watch TV. Solle had a boxed set of some telenovela and even though my Spanish was very limited, she assured me I'd be able to follow the plot.

I fell asleep before the first episode ended.

I was floating in that place between wakefulness and sleep. I heard low voices, but I couldn't make out the words. I considered opening my eyes to see who'd joined us, but I was so comfy I didn't want to.

Then I heard his deep voice. "Theo." Strong arms lifted me and held against a solid, warm chest. We moved up the stairs. I wrapped my leaden arms around my Lycan and nuzzled his neck. He placed me gently on the bed. A boot hit the floor.

"You're okay," I mumbled, trying to force my eyes to stay open.

"I'm beat. Haven't slept in two days and what I did get wasn't great." He pulled his shirt over his head and unfastened his jeans. A moment later, he was beside me in bed, positioning his body to face mine.

"Raider, are you all right?" I needed to hear his answer.

"One bullet grazed me," he admitted.

"Where?" I started to rub my hand over his back.

"Upper arm, left." He grabbed my hand. "It's fine."

"Okay, okay." I told my heart to slow down.

I finally calmed and was appreciating how good it felt to be in his arms. My gift flared. He was upset, sad, devastated. "Do you want to talk about it?"

"Tomorrow," he said quietly.

"I'm sorry."

"I am, too."

Whoever the traitor was, he'd deeply upset the Laird.

FORTY

NOVUS

RAIDER BLACK

W e slept most of the day. Close to dinnertime, I finally woke up. Theodora was curled around me, her front to my back. I took her hand in mine and raised it to my lips, kissing her palm first then the spot above my ring.

"You're awake." Her warm breath brushed against my shoulder.

"Yeah, we drove straight through so that we could get back."

She was quiet for a few moments. Then she asked, "What's next?"

I turned to face her. "We need to talk."

I not only saw but felt her body tense. "Oh. I meant about the traitor, but if you want to talk about the other thing now, I guess we can."

I'd address the traitor tomorrow, publicly, as was our way. While on the road, I'd had plenty of time to think about Theodora's response to my decision. I'd also asked Conal for advice. I was going to try it his way first. "I respect your abilities as a Seer. No, they might not be like those that are recorded, but I've witnessed first-hand your strength. With you, I've traveled to the Plain and I've heard you talk with The Lady." I rolled over onto my back. "I know that, in time, your gift will become stronger."

She repositioned so that she leaned her head on her hand, watching me. "I needed to hear that. Thank you for pairing Lore with me. He's helped. His mother taught him much, he understands what I'm going through."

"He doesn't make you uncomfortable?"

"No," She shook her head. I could tell from her scent that she was being honest.

"Most find him...odd." Of course, that could be because of his reputation as a mass-murderer or as a spy.

"I feel comfortable with him." She seemed to relax a little.

"Not too comfortable, I hope?" I was half teasing and a little curious.

She ran her foot along my lower leg. "Never. He's my teacher and protector. It's nothing like when I'm with you." She cleared her throat and said quietly, "That's why I got so upset, Raider."

Now, it was my turn to become tense.

"I care about you. I mean, I wouldn't be here," she said, looking down at the mattress, "with you, like this, if I didn't."

"Go on." She'd chosen her words carefully, but I already knew. My nose told me the truth.

"I was scared and worried. I didn't want you to go because you're my lover." She bit down on her lip as if she was trying to decide if she should share more. "I was also worried about my future, if, um," she swallowed hard then cleared her throat, "something permanent happened to you, or you and Conal."

"Lore would protect you. He would take you to a safe location until the Leader was decided. If he believed that person wasn't suitable, he'd escort you to the Council." I had a firm plan in place. "Conal told you of the plan."

"I was being selfish and I was afraid for myself," she confessed.

"I'll always take care of you."

Her eyes flashed. "I know you want to…and I hope you'll be able to understand, even with your vow, I sometimes feel vulnerable."

My wolf snarled deep in my belly. Of course, we'd take care of her. She was ours. However, I again followed Conal's counseling. I thought about things from her perspective. "I do see your point."

"I thought I'd share the vision, and Conal would convince you to stay far away from the trucks." She tried to smile. "I guess I don't know you as well as I thought I did."

Now, it was time for me to be honest. "Theo, I think you know a part of me that I've never shared with another."

Her eyes rounded, and I knew I'd shocked her with my honesty and my admission.

"But I am and will always be the Leader of Novus, first. My decisions start and end with the Pack."

"I thought I understood but…I don't think I truly do." She dropped her head so that it was lying flat on the pillow and she spoke to the ceiling. "I wanted to rebel against the Laird, to…to make you feel my pain and my anger." She ran her hand over her face. "I know that was wrong. You've always been honest about our priorities…" She let out a long sigh and continued looking up at the ceiling. "I need to reconcile the two parts of you."

"It's three. Don't forget my wolf." I said this because she still thought of me as a human male.

She closed her eyes for a moment as if she was trying to comprehend everything. When she opened her eyes, she whispered, "I'm glad you came back to me, here."

"No place else I'd rather be." I wrapped my hand around her neck to bring her mouth to mine. She was learning.

"Hey, are you two ever going to get up?" Solle's voice interrupted. It sounded as though she was calling from the bottom of the stairs.

"Do you need us?" I asked.

"Yeah, we're trying to figure out dinner." Conal was definitely at the foot of the stairs.

Theo stirred and got out of bed. "Be down in a minute."

WE WERE SITTING around the table on the deck. Conal had grilled dinner for us and now the plates had been pushed to the side as I suggested my plan for the night.

"You want to go out, tonight?" Theo didn't hide her distaste.

"As I explained, we need to be seen out, enjoying ourselves."

Conal leaned forward. "We need to be seen, so it appears the attack was a small incident."

"So, what?" Theo said, frowning. "Do we have a

454

script to follow? 'Laugh now, Theo.' Conal dances two dances with his mate then grabs a beer." Sarcasm filled her tone.

Solle tried to calm her friend. "It'll be fun. We can get dressed up, have some drinks, dance."

Theo looked at me. "After everything…wouldn't you rather stay in?"

I eyed her steadily. "We already cleared everything up." Why was she arguing? She understood that I was the Leader, her Laird, and my word was law.

She crossed her arms under her breasts. "We most certainly did not."

I gave her a look that communicated the topic was closed.

"What if I don't want to go out?" she asked stubbornly.

"Theodora…" Solle cautioned.

She was testing me and I wasn't going to have another fight. "Then don't come." I pushed back my chair and stood. "And if you change your mind, tell your guard to bring you." I turned to Solle. "How long will it take you to get ready?"

Solle shrugged. "Not long."

Conal rolled his eyes. "At least an hour."

"Fine, I'll meet you at The Club." I left.

I KNEW Solle probably spent half of that hour, while she was getting ready, trying to convince Theo to change her mind. When I arrived, Conal met me by the stairs and said one word, "Stubborn."

I grunted. "We'll see."

The Seer was angry and frustrated. I'd learned from

our prior conversation that when she was in this state, stubborn. I was wagering that she'd show. After cooling down, she'd come. I was giving her time to figure that out.

Eventually, I made my way to my booth and as I took my seat, our server appeared to take our order. Soon, she returned with our drinks and two females who were visiting our land approached my table.

The redhead asked, "Is there going to be another private party after your Samhain celebration, Sir?"

I'd hosted a special party here at The Club that had turned into a free-for-all last year. I ignored her. Neither she nor her friend interested me.

Conal cleared his throat. "I don't believe there's anything planned this year."

The other female spoke up, "We could plan it. I mean, it was crazy good last year."

Solle gave the females a harsh look. "Only Novus plans events on Novus land."

The women continued to try to make conversation, which I ignored.

I knew the moment Theo walked through the doors with her guard. I tried to guess her mood as I watched the stairs for my first glimpse of her.

She didn't disappoint. Her hair was slicked back from her face and she wore dark red lipstick. The color made her eyes appear a deeper blue. Her clothes weren't flashy. Instead, they were subtly sexy. A black tank, with her red bra straps showing at her shoulders, faded jeans that showed her curves, and red high heels. She looked confident and ready for a throw down.

She approached our table and greeted me first, presenting her wrist. "Laird."

"Theodora," I nodded.

The two females gave her unfriendly looks.

She glanced at the females then back at me. "I see you started without me."

"No baby, I was waiting for you."

"Charmer," she said with a sly smile. She turned her attention to the females, and her smile vanished. "Are they important?" She watched me closely, waiting for my answer.

I shrugged and leaned against the padded booth, resting my arms along the back. "Not really." I wanted to see what she would do.

She turned her attention to our entire table and asked, "Really? I'm going to have to deal with them?"

I played along. "You kept me waiting."

She winked at me. "Don't worry, you'll be exhausted by the time I get through with you."

I laughed. She was probably right.

The redhead stared at Theo. "Hang on, are you saying you and the Packleader...?"

Theo lifted her shoulders. "Well, I hadn't gotten around to saying it because it would sound like I was bragging, but yeah." The look she gave was so perfect, not a challenge but a clear statement.

The other woman looked her up and down and raised her eyebrows. "But you're a human."

"I may look human. I might smell human, but girls," she leaned a little closer to them, "I'm so much more." She flashed a cold smile that would've made any wolf proud and my cock went hard.

I felt the energy gather around us. This time, it raised the hairs on my arms. She was calling to our wolves with just enough power to cause them to stir.

Mine chuckled approvingly at her rare display of skill.

"What are you?" the redhead asked with a dumbfounded look on her face.

"Marked by a Goddess." She moved around the other female and crawled on the booth's cushions on all fours. When she was right beside me, she knelt on her knees. "I'm his gift and his weapon."

I wanted to fuck her on top of the table. "Mine." I growled the word.

She put her hand on my shoulder to steady her body as she stretched out her leg and straddled my lap. She kissed me. It was a statement to the visitors, but also to everyone in the room.

Oh, yeah, I liked this Theo very much. My hands went to her ass and I pulled her closer to my hard cock. My chuckle broke us apart. "That was some show."

She traced my lips with her finger, probably to wipe away any transfer from her lips. "You think so?" Her smile was cheeky, but I saw the question in her eyes.

"We'll figure it out, Theo."

She leaned closer so that her mouth was close to my ear. "I want to, I really do."

"Then we will," I decreed.

Conal cleared his throat, and Theo twisted her head sharply to look to my left. I think she'd forgotten that we weren't alone. "Want to expound on that thing you just did?"

The interlopers were gone. They'd probably hugged the wall as they'd scurried to the exit.

She leaned away from me so that her back was resting against the table. "Oh, that?" She flashed a guilty look my way before answering. "I was showing off."

"You wanted to run those females off," Solle corrected her.

She gave me a small smile. "I might have a few tools of my own."

Conal wasn't done. "You've been holding out."

She started to climb off my lap.

I lifted her easily and put her between Solle and myself. She looked to her left then her right, as if she wished our server would appear. She finally answered. "I wouldn't call it holding out." She drew her eyebrows together. "Lore has helped me understand some of what I'm feeling and what I can do with it. How to harness my power, so that the next time Onyx questions my abilities, well, he might be surprised."

Solle eyebrows shot upward. "You actually like Lore?"

Theo sat a little straighter, her snapping eyes defensive. "He's brilliant, and he's been very generous with his time, working with me."

"But there are so many stories about him." Solle glanced at her mate, looking for an assist.

"He told me about avenging his mother's death, the massacre." Theo gave Solle a challenging look.

"He doesn't scare you?" Solle asked carefully.

Theo laughed ruefully. "I'm scared most of the time. I mean, I'm always the weakest in the room. But I'm learning how to use my gift to figure out intent. Lore has no ill intent. He wants to help. I think working with me reminds him of a happier time, and I don't think he's felt any happiness in years."

"Do I scare you?" Conal asked with a smirk, trying to lighten the mood.

She gave him a sly smile. "You? Not at all."

Solle joined in. "What about me?"

Theo's smile slowly disappeared. "Are we being serious?"

"Yeah, sure." The doctor watched her expectantly.

I knew Theo was thinking about her answer as she gave Solle an easy smile.

"I love you. You were my first friend when I came here, but yes, there have been moments where you've set off my internal alarms."

Solle sat back in the booth. "Really?" She scrunched her nose, but I knew she liked what Theo had said.

"What about the male sitting next to you?" Conal was now instigating.

She went still. I think she stopped breathing.

My wolf woke and waited for her answer.

"He has always terrified me," she said quietly. She might have been answering Conal, but she was speaking to me. "From the beginning, I felt things for him, with him, I didn't want to even try to understand." She checked on each of us to see how we were receiving this information. "There's so much I don't know, but I can feel his power all the time. I know he's the most dangerous Lycan in the room and that scares the shit out of me, but at the same time, it attracts me like the strongest magnet."

Solle's eyes had gone wide. Conal appeared to be studying every word she'd shared.

On some level, I knew we had chemistry. I'd thought it was the novelty of owning a Seer, but after the first trip to the Plain, it was more. I didn't want to make her have to explain anymore. This was information that should only be spoken between us. I took her hand. "Let's dance."

CONAL DROVE the four us back to his home. I'd chosen to sit in the back seat with Theo, so I could run my hands over her body. She'd been teasing me all night, seducing me with hungry looks and sly promises.

"I like it when the Laird calls you Theo." Solle leaned to her left, so she could see us both. "It fits you."

"You can use it," she told her friend.

"Theodora is a beautiful name, but that woman should wear a robe and wander around with her head in the clouds. You're real and more like us than I'd ever imagined," Solle said.

"I don't know if that is a good thing?" Theo laughed. "Okay, Conal. Can you send out a memo, telling everybody about the name change?"

"I'll prepare it as soon as we get home, Seer." He smiled in the rearview mirror.

He wouldn't have the time. I had something much more fun in mind.

We followed Solle into her home. Conal was shooting me questioning looks. He sensed something was up.

Solle leaned against her mate. "I'm not tired. I'm thinking about going for a swim."

"I have an idea," I announced, "a contest."

"What kind of contest?" Theo had kicked off her high heels as soon as we got into the house and was now holding them in her hand.

"One that you will like…ultimately." I watched her narrow her eyes at me.

Conal chuckled, "What are the rules, Laird?"

"This will be between the females."

Solle gave me a tiny smile. She was catching on. Theo looked as if she was considering the distance to the door in order to escape.

"What do we have to do?" Solle asked.

"And what's the prize?" Theo's suspicion came through clearly.

"It's easy. Solle, how fast do you think you can make Theo come?" I asked casually.

"What?" Theo took an involuntary step backward.

"Three minutes," Solle said, tilting her chin.

Theo was giving Solle, and then me, a wide-eyed look. "Ha-ha, not funny."

"If you can catch her, strip her, and make her come in four minutes, I'll send you and Conal to that resort you liked so much in Belize."

Conal's smile was wide. "We did have fun there."

"I'm in." Solle bent to unhook her sandals.

"Do I get a vote?" Theo asked, one hand raised.

"No," I told her. "Either way, you'll win."

"Can I fight back?" she asked with a little flash of attitude.

"You can try," Solle said with a saucy smile.

Conal suggested, "Perhaps the basement would be a better setting?"

I nodded, and he led us downstairs.

Theo was last, and she paused at the second to last step to survey the room. Under her breath, she muttered, "I am so fucked."

"Not yet babe, but you will be," I said.

She rolled her eyes as she lifted on her toes and then rolled back to her heels.

"Solle you start in the corner, and Theo, you pick

your position. I'll count down from three, and it will begin."

Theo went to the center of the room, watching Solle the entire time. My wolf stirred. He approved of her taking this seriously. She could have refused or thrown a fit.

"I'm ready Laird," Solle said as she stretched from side to side.

"Theo?" I asked.

"Ready, Raid."

By using my name, she told me that she understood I wasn't ordering her to participate. I wondered if she even realized that she was the only one to use it as our bond grew stronger. "Three, two, one...go."

Solle jogged from her corner and went airborne, diving at Theo.

The human had watched her friend's approach, and at the very last second, she twisted out of the way.

"Whoa," Conal grunted, "that's new."

Theo took the opportunity to climb over the sofa. No, it wasn't graceful, but it put space between the women. She was looking around the room.

Solle jumped onto the sofa seat and then over Theo so that she was caged in from two sides. "You could do a striptease on your own... Give the guys a show." The suggestion was made with an enticing smile.

"They're already getting a show," Theo said breathlessly.

Solle lunged and grabbed a handful of Theo's tank, which she tore from her body.

Theo dodged to her left and then went right.

Solle fell for the fake, but caught up in five steps.

Solle again grabbed for Theo and caught her arm.

Theo went with the motion and that surprised Solle, who had loosened her grip enough that Theo was free.

"Take her, Solle," Conal urged.

Solle did as her mate wished and jumped onto Theo's back, knocking her to her knees on the soft carpet.

The human went down and started to fight. She had no chance.

Solle tore off Theo's clothes and tumbled her onto her back. Then she lowered her body against Theo's and kissed the human.

Theo's hands were pushing against Solle's chest, not surrendering.

Solle continued her attack on Theo's mouth.

I motioned to Conal, and we moved closer to the women. I knelt above Theo's head and grasped her wrists, pulling them above her head.

Perhaps I flattered myself that it was my touch, but she moaned against Solle's lips. Theo opened her eyes and glared up at me.

Conal had his hand under Solle's dress tearing off her panties.

Solle shifted her position so that her mate could finish undressing her by tearing her dress from her body.

I understood why Conal had enjoyed watching the women together. As Solle covered her, her lithe frame pressed against Theo's curves, caramel skin against cream.

Then she moved to Theo's breasts. As she sucked the hard nipple into her mouth, Theo sought my gaze.

"Clock's ticking, Solle," I warned.

"Two minutes," Conal said as he ran his hand over the curve of his mate's ass.

Solle moved down Theo's body.

Theo was cooperating as Solle settled lower with her face an inch from her delicate folds. Her body jerked, and she hissed, "Jesus."

I leaned close to her ear. "Are you going to fight her or help your friends go on a vacation?"

She squeezed her eyes shut.

"Should I tell her to use her teeth?" I teased.

"Nooo," Theo cried.

"How many of her fingers will it take to fill you, babe? Three, four, all five?"

"Raider," she moaned.

"Come for her, my beauty," I whispered.

She did, but she repeated my name as her body tensed.

Conal pulled his wife from between the human's thighs and smacked her ass. "Too slow, mate."

"What?" The Latina asked as he positioned her against the wall, undid his jeans, and buried himself inside of her.

I was only a beat or two behind him. Theo was wet, and I fucked her hard. She chanted my name as she came, again.

I'd fucked her twice after Solle had made her come. She lay across my chest as I held her on the sofa.

Solle was making her way to the stairs when Conal wrapped his arm around her waist and forced her to her knees. "Not done," he grunted.

Solle pushed her ass up into the air.

Conal ran his hand over her offering, laughing low.

Conal pulled her cheeks apart and spit into the crevice.

"Watch babe," I told Theo. "Watch your friend take Conal's cock up her ass."

I felt her shift so that she could check out what was happening. The lighting was low, but I knew she could see them clearly.

Conal aligned his cock and entered Solle slowly.

Solle pushed back, clearly wanting more.

Her mate started slowly, but soon, he was taking her fast. Solle was chanting, "Yes, yes, *yes*."

"She likes it?" Theo didn't hide her surprise.

"So does her mate," I told her.

"You want to do that to me?" She turned her head so that she could see my face.

"I want all of you."

"Black. I..." She shook her head. "No. I don't want to do that."

"Shhh," I cut her off. "Just watch." I could wait for a while longer.

"I'm serious, I don't ever want to do that." She sounded definite.

That's the thing with living forever. I'd learned patience.

FORTY-ONE

NOVUS

THEODORA MORRISSEY

I t did not escape my notice that neither man had filled me in on the identity of the traitor. I knew not to ask. The sadness was still weighing heavily on both of them, even though Solle and I kept them occupied. I leaned back into Raider's warmth. Yesterday, he'd given me much to think about. It would have been easy to hold onto my anger, but the Lycan had a way of disarming me by sharing parts of himself that I knew were for me, only.

Plus, he wasn't human. He was a wolf and The Laird. This was new territory for both of us. I'd been in relationships and had a history of only giving a little of myself. With Raider, I would have to give, or he would take.

I was the one who'd have to change to suit his needs. I could never be his equal. I needed to decide if I could live with that. I closed my eyes and tried to imagine my life without this…him. I couldn't.

I let out a deep sigh. I had my answer.

"We're going to be summoned in three minutes." His voice was rough this morning.

"I'll get in the shower."

He joined me, but there was no sex. His expression was grim. I didn't need to use my gift to know that today wasn't going to be bright and cheery.

I dressed in black stretchy leggings and a long tunic in an ocean blue. I didn't think bright colors would be appreciated. The Laird hadn't ordered my attendance, but he didn't tell me to stay home. I headed downstairs as soon as I was dressed. He was waiting for me.

We rode in silence. The guard let us out at the back entrance of the Novus building and I followed Black to our floor. I started to go into my office when he said, "With me."

I noticed that Basil was at his station, and he too was dressed in somber colors.

Soon, we were joined by the other Board members as well as Asher and Lore. No one spoke as they took their places, with the latter two men standing. Black cleared his throat, and all attention was focused on him. "The notice will go out in forty-five minutes. We'll gather in three hours. Seer, your services may be called upon."

I nodded.

"Lore, you stick to her. Asher, you are point." The Laird assigned their tasks.

Lore cleared his throat to get my attention. "Seer, if you would follow me?" He walked to the door and waited for me to follow him. He'd worded it as a request, but it was an order.

I glanced at Black to see if he had any more instructions, when he didn't say a thing, I did as commanded.

In my office, Lore closed the door with Asher posted outside of it. This was highly irregular. I could only name two other times that the door had been closed, and they'd involved sex with the Laird. I felt my stress level triple.

"Here are your rules for today," Lore said in a cold voice.

"What's happening?"

"The traitor will answer to the charges. She will be dealt with."

"She?" That fit in with my visions. "How?" I knew that ultimately, this day would end in death. It was the part in between that I feared.

"We'll gather in the open field a few miles west of the Packhouse property. Everyone who is able will come; the list of charges will be read. She can answer to the charges, and then she can make her choice." He recited this information in a calm voice, as though he was planning a regular day of training and teaching.

"Her choice?" My mouth had gone dry.

"If she agrees to cooperate, her death will be swift, and if not…"

"That's where I come in, right?"

"The Laird may require your assistance." His eyes flashed with excitement. He wanted violence.

I could feel his anticipation.

He studied me for a moment. "We're not human." He made this reminder in a kinder tone. "Don't judge what is going to happen by your human standards."

My heart was racing with anxiety. I nodded to show I understood he was cautioning me and preparing me for what might happen.

"The Laird will lead you through your duties if needed."

The reality hit me and I got a pain in my stomach. "But everybody will see me draw out her wolf."

He gave me a perplexed look. His mouth frowned, and his eyes narrowed. "So?"

"They'll look at me differently." It might scare the shit out of them, if they considered that, this early, I was able to call their wolf. What if later, I could do more?

"You are marked by The Lady. You serve Novus and Raider Black. Does it matter?"

Now, he was watching me closely and it was unsettling. I felt like prey. How could I explain my concern to a man who was a true loner? Who probably couldn't remember a time when he wasn't whispered about? "What if a member gets freaked out and decides I'm too powerful for a human?" I'd never had the courage to even begin to mention the possibility of this skill developing further. It could certainly mean my death.

He went so still that the back of my neck prickled in warning. My inner voice was screaming, *Careful.*

"If you ever do become a threat, the Laird will decide your fate, as is his duty and right."

Black's message from much earlier sounded in my head about how he would give me a fighting chance if he ever decided to kill me. "I serve the Laird." I swallowed the rock in my throat. "I understand." Black would kill me if he ever deemed me a threat to Novus, or more importantly, to him. Of that, I had no doubt.

He nodded approvingly.

I needed to prepare. This would be violent, and I couldn't show shock or despair. I was the Seer and a part of the Pack. I trusted the Laird, and believed in him. I was a weapon of his will, standing beside him in all things. Those words were repeated over and over in my head.

WE WERE at the front of the procession. Black led us, followed by Conal and the members of the Board. Asher walked on my left and Lore on my right. The traitor was behind us, secured on a cart that was pulled by two huge black horses.

Pack members joined the silent procession as we walked to the field. Hundreds of members formed a circle, and into the middle, the traitor was led by Wale and Glass.

Black entered the circle followed by Conal, Tex, and Onyx. He stared at the woman who looked to be no older than twenty. She was on the small side and wore ripped jeans and a gray T-shirt. "Lydia Bohm, you have been charged with treason, the attempted murder of your Leader, and an additional murder. What say you?"

She was shaking and sobbing. "I'm sorry."

"Did you work alone?"

She paused before tripping over her answer, "Yes."

I didn't need to use my gift to know she was lying.

"You dare lie to your Leader?" Black's voice boomed and I felt his power.

She shook her head from side to side. "I-I can't tell you."

"Your sentence is death. Now is the time to decide if you want to meet The Lady with a clear conscience." Black stared at her with so much rage I involuntarily took a step back.

Lore's hand was on my elbow as he anchored me to his side. "Easy."

"I can't," Lydia screamed hysterically.

He continued staring at her for a few beats. He was so powerful and intimidating that I found it hard to breathe.

The woman fell to her knees.

"Then I will make you." Black's voice boomed as he turned in my direction. "Seer."

I didn't wait for Lore to tell me to go to the Laird. I felt like I was outside of my body as his power pulled me toward him. I walked to the center. "Laird." I displayed my brand. "How may I serve you and Novus?"

"Call her." His power swept over my body. It was as if warmth surrounded me. I swear I could feel the blood pump through my body with each beat of my heart.

I turned to the woman and studied her. A part of me wanted to hurt her for trying to kill Black, and another part grieved for one about to die.

I pushed those thoughts aside and closed my eyes as I used my gift to locate her wolf's spirit. I know I made a surprised sound; her wolf was terrified. I'd never experienced that before. "Save us," the wolf whined. "Tell him."

"Speak, Wolf." My voice sounded deeper. I felt so much power strumming through my body. I could feel my heart pound in my chest with each rhythmic beat. "You are in the presence of Raider Black, Leader of Novus."

Scenes flooded my brain. Some I couldn't make out, but the few I could were gruesome. I had to open my eyes and it took me a minute to gather myself. I gasped

472

as I fought to find my center. "I am ready, Laird." I knew I could reconnect immediately.

"Wolf, who do you work with?"

"Her father," the wolf answered immediately. "He made her. He hurt us and made promises that, if we did as he bid, he would stop."

"Anyone else?"

"Her father made all deals. She...she tried to stop them, but...he...did so much damage to us, that she had to." The wolf hated the woman's father.

"She's lying," A man's angry voice came from the crowd. "That cow doesn't know anything."

I knew this was the father. I'd seen and heard him in her memories.

"Ezra Bohm, you have been named as a traitor to the Novus Pack," Onyx recited in a deep, booming voice.

The crowd moved away from the man. He spat on the ground by his boots and took a step closer with bravado.

I felt the magic as he started to change. Before I could scream a warning, he ran toward Black, who was already in wolf form.

I think I shrieked as an arm wrapped around my middle and moved me out of the circle. I was safe, but I couldn't take my gaze off the two wolves fighting. So much was happening at once. The female prisoner screamed, "No," at the fighters, but she didn't move.

It didn't take Black long to injure the other wolf. I didn't know very much about how wolves battled, but it seemed that Black placed his blows strategically. He finally stood over the inert body of the father and asked in that strange, growly wolf voice, "Do you submit?"

"Fuck you."

I felt the Pack's anger and excitement.

"Seer!" Black in his wolf form commanded.

I didn't want to enter that circle with the two Lycan prisoners. Even severely injured, a wolf could still kill me. I hadn't noticed that Lore had been holding my waist the entire time.

He released me, but then tugged on my elbow. "This way, my lady."

We entered the circle. Lore picked a stopping point but he continued to hold my arm. I closed my eyes and searched for the male's wolf. "He is ready, Laird." I bowed my head.

"Who are you working with?"

The wolf growled.

I used more power. It was like turning up the burner on a gas range.

The growl increased in volume.

"Answer," Black demanded.

The wolf snarled, "Peters."

The man who dumped me here? I refocused and strengthened my hold.

"What did you receive for your treasonous acts?"

The wolf fought against my power, but I was stronger. "Cash and…"

"Speak, wolf," Black ordered.

"A human female, so I could mate," he spat.

"What?" Lydia started to get to her feet. "You promised."

The wolf turned his gaze to his daughter. "I want young."

"No more. You promised me, no more," the woman screamed even more hysterically.

The scenes flooded my brain—young women, screaming, a dead body ripped to shreds, digging graves. I whispered, "Murderer."

"What?" Black's voice turned ice cold.

I turned to Lydia. "How many?"

Again, she fell to her knees and dropped her forehead to the hard-packed earth.

"How many human females did he kill?" I added a push to my voice.

"Seven," her wolf answered. Then Lydia screamed, "Seven because I couldn't give him a baby." She made a keening moan. "I begged The Lady to let me have a child. He said I wasn't good enough…that I was weak." She pointed her finger at her father. "I gave him everything."

My knees went to jelly. I was breathing through my mouth. Lore caught me with an arm around my waist.

"Shut up, you filthy whore," the father yelled at his daughter.

"You touched your daughter?" Black roared.

"She's mine, ain't she?" the father responded defensively.

Black changed into his human form, wearing all black. "As leader of the Novus Pack, I, Raider Black, sentence you to death." He wrapped his hands around the man's neck and twisted his head and continued until it tore free of the spine. The Laird tossed the head to the ground. Then he lifted his booted foot and crushed it into the earth.

Lydia screamed, "No," and tried to run toward them.

Conal caught her around the waist.

"Lydia Bohm, I sentence you to death," our Laird thundered.

She struggled inside Conal's arms, shrieking, "Daddy? Nooo, daddy."

I felt the vomit build in my stomach; I fought to swallow it down.

"It's almost over," Lore whispered.

Black walked to the woman and tore her head from her body. As her head rolled across the grass, he said, "May The Lady have pity on your soul, Lydia Bohm."

The crowd was completely silent. Finally, guards moved in to collect the remains and the eerie silence ended.

"Lore," I whispered. "Lore, there are bodies buried on his land. I saw them."

"When you were linked?"

His grip around my waist tightened. I think he was holding me up. "Yes."

"Laird," Lore shouted over the sounds of the crowd.

Conal and Black crowded around us. "Seer?"

I wanted to fall into Black's arms, but he wasn't showing me any signs that would be welcome. I licked my dry lips. "When we were linked," I rasped, "I saw him kill those human women and bury their bodies on his property. He has a farm, right?"

Conal spoke first, "He did."

"They're on his property, you're sure?" Black's asked abruptly.

"Yes."

The Laird turned to Conal. "Raze the farm. Let our wolves take whatever they want and burn it to the ground."

"As you wish," Conal responded and jogged to the

cart. He vaulted onto it and made the announcement. An answering roar came from the crowd.

Black looked at me again. "Novus thanks you for your service." He excused me easily, with a nod.

It would be easier to go home, bury myself under the covers, and try to forget this day. However, I was a member of the Pack. I was with Black. If he was going to the farm, then so was I. "Thank you, Laird, but I wish to see this through to the end." I met his hard gaze.

"As you wish." He turned to Lore. "Arrange a ride."

Lore pulled out his cell and made a call.

I watched as Conal and Black changed and took off running in their wolf forms.

THE BOHM FARM wasn't much. There was a falling-down, two-story house, a barn, and a chicken coop. When Lore and I arrived, pack members were carrying items from the house, and others were chasing chickens.

Soon, the wagon arrived carrying the bodies. The guards worked quickly and created a pyre with pieces of wood and siding pried by hand from the buildings. Everyone seemed to be in a frenzy.

Black lit the match that ignited the fire. We all watched as the bodies were engulfed in flames. I stood behind him so that he could partially block my view. However, I couldn't turn off my senses and all the emotions were overwhelming.

I took a step closer to him and placed my hand in the center of his back. I felt the muscles tense against my palm. He didn't move away, so I moved in closer. I needed him.

When the flames died down and the crowd began to

disperse, the Laird turned abruptly. "Now is the time for you to go."

I didn't try to shield the hurt from my eyes. "What are you going to do?"

"Take the keys and go." It was an order.

Lore held out the SUV keys, and I looked at them skeptically. I hadn't driven since I'd been dumped. It was against the rules.

"Go," Black barked savagely.

Lore moved toward me. "I'll see you to your ride." He grasped my elbow and prepared to lead me away.

I looked at Black for some kind of explanation, but he gave none. I didn't have a choice; I went with Lore.

It was weird driving again. I didn't go over twenty. I came to a complete stop at the intersection. If I turned left, I'd go to Conal's, right to the Packhouse, and if I continued straight, I could travel away from Novus land. I didn't hesitate, I turned right.

It took me much too long to arrive at the house. I was being overly cautious, I didn't trust my reflexes. I left the SUV at the front door with the keys in the ignition. I went directly to Black's private rooms and sat at the dining room table, waiting for him to come to me.

FORTY-TWO

NOVUS

RAIDER BLACK

I'd watched Theo pause at the crossroads, curious to see which direction she would choose. As always, she surprised me. I was sure she would go to her sanctuary at Conal's or try to escape us by driving straight out of town. Instead, she turned to go to my home.

Conal's deep growl had kept the others away from me as I watched the fire burn. Novus would deal with Peters. I would personally kill him, and with great pleasure. The world would know not to strike at my Pack.

Ezra had fucked his daughter. I couldn't wrap my head around it. Each child was a true gift from The Lady, and he'd used his like that. It disgusted me so much I wanted to kill him again.

I needed to run, to hurt somebody, to be brutal. The need to do damage was strong. I wasn't safe to be around, especially for Theo. She needed to go back to Conal's or to her office with the door barred, someplace far, because even though she was miles away, I felt the pull of our attraction.

I turned to my Second. "Go to your Mate."

"You good?"

"No." How could I be?

"Your woman will help."

I changed subjects. "Tomorrow, we'll meet and plan our move against the human."

"As you wish, Laird." Conal nodded and took off.

I did the same, telling myself that I'd stop in at the house and send Theo to Conal's. After that, I'd work this anger and anguish from my system.

At the main door, I changed into my human form and followed her scent to my rooms. I opened the door and found her sitting at the table. She had her knees pulled to her chest, staring off into space.

"Hey," she greeted me cautiously.

I pulled out the chair at the opposite end of the table, turned it around, and sat down. "It would be best if you spent the night at Conal's."

"Why?" She dropped her feet to the floor and leaned her forearms onto the table.

Why couldn't she do as I said without a discussion? "I'm angry, and it's not safe for you."

"I think we're all angry." She tucked her hair behind her ear but made no move to leave.

"I'm not in control tonight."

She looked me up and down.

"I might injure you," I warned.

She frowned at me and slowly countered. "You won't."

She was being stubborn. She needed to go. My wolf growled; we could make her.

"You shouldn't be alone." She squared her shoulders.

"I wasn't planning on…being alone."

Her eyes flared wide in surprise before she sputtered, "What's that supposed to mean?"

"I need to work this anger out of my system. I know only one way, and it's to inflict pain on another."

"So, you're going to fight?" Her forehead creased with worry.

"I'll probably do a little of that."

She blinked twice and let out a sigh as her shoulders slumped. "And then what, Black? Find a couple of wolves to fuck?"

I knew the realization hurt. Her scent changed immediately. "I need certain things."

"And doing it with another is better?" she asked snottily. She was not moving toward the door or making any indication that she planned to do so.

I was losing patience. I'd asked her politely to go, and yet, she was still in the chair arguing. If she wanted to know what was on my mind then I'd share. "Do you think me weak?"

She let out a frustrated sound. "Why would you ask that?" She sounded confused. "No, my answer is no."

"You rested your hand on my back during the fire, as if you thought I needed *your* support." Each word came out tersely as I accused her of this transgression. I felt my wolf push to be freed. He would show her our strength.

Her eyebrows shot upward. "Because I touched you?"

"I don't need your support or coddling. I am not weak. I am the Laird."

"Yes, I am well aware that—you are the Laird. It's your answer to everything." She got out of her chair. "Well, Laird, let me tell you something. I have never thought that you, personally, needed any emotional support from me. But today, I needed you." Her voice cracked. "I saw things." She wiped a hand over her mouth. "Things I can't get out of my head. I needed some of your strength, Raider Black. *Laird.*" She spat the last word. "I needed an anchor, those scenes were pulling me under." She shoved her chair to the table. "So, now you know. I needed *you* because you are strong, I've always been able to count on you. Maybe you can think about that while you're out fighting and fucking." She moved swiftly to the door. "Don't bother coming to me after you've been with others. I won't want you." She opened the door and left.

My wolf reacted to her admission of pain and weakness. He forced me to my feet. I was in pursuit before I realized I was no longer in the chair. I saw her ahead of me. She must have heard me coming. She tried to increase her speed as she headed to the grand staircase.

She almost lost her footing once, but she grabbed onto the railing and righted herself. She sprinted across the polished marble floor to the front door.

I leaped, covering the space between us, and tackled her body against the thick, steel-reinforced door.

"Get off of me," she gritted out the words as she struggled.

"Stop fighting," I ordered her. Her fighting and running to escape excited my wolf. I was struggling for control.

She stopped struggling and turned around to face me. Her eyes were bright blue with her hurt and anger. "You wanted me gone, so let me go."

"Explain yourself." I growled in her face. "What you meant."

"Forget it." She tried to turn back around.

I stopped her and pressed her into the door with my hips. "You saw what happened with that family?"

She went still. "Yes."

"How long have you been able to pull memories, Theo?"

"Today was the first time," she whispered.

"Your gift is growing."

"Well, she can take this part back anytime." She held her body stiffly as if she was enduring my touch.

"I won't ask you about them tonight."

"Good, because I don't think I can talk about them right now." She sighed loudly. "Can I go now, Laird?"

She was upset and hurting. I could see it and smell her turmoil. "You turned to me for help, and I didn't even realize it."

"I thought that was part of our deal, but apparently, that was only when it's convenient for you."

"I need to inflict pain tonight." I laid it out for her. I was trying to protect her.

Her gaze swept over my face. "Use me," she said, her voice cracking.

"Theo," I tried to caution her. She didn't know what she was saying…what I could do to her.

"Let me be the one that brings you peace," she urged, speaking quickly.

My wolf howled his approval at her offering. "I'll hurt you," I warned.

"I'm stronger than you think with The Lady's gift."

We would see.

"I could use a safe word…?" she suggested cautiously.

I leaned in closer to her ear. "Do I look like I would stop at the utterance of a word?"

She dropped her gaze as she considered my statement. "No, you're the type who's going to take until you're satisfied."

I approved of her answer. My wolf believed it was a challenge he would strive to meet.

Her voice shook as she continued, "*Because* I will give until I have no more."

I studied her eyes and her fierce expression. I lifted my nose and sniffed. She didn't know that what she was offering could be her life. "I could kill you."

"You won't." She slowly ran her palm down my chest, then lower over my hard cock, teasing me through the denim.

My brain stopped working. "You're sure?"

"Yours," she pledged.

I growled as my hand caught her head. I turned it at a sharp angle to capture her mouth. The kiss was hard and possessive.

She ran her nails down my chest through my T-shirt.

I looped my arm under her knees and picked her up. I started up the staircase at a run, using my Lycan speed. Instead of turning to the left to my private quarters, I turned to the right and went down the hall to the last room. I punched the code into the keypad and opened the door.

As soon as I crossed the threshold, I placed Theo on her feet and slammed the door closed. It seemed to echo in the silence as the two locks fell into place.

"What is this?" She was looking around. The day was overcast and the room was cloaked in shadows.

"This is where I come to play." When I brought a

partner home, this is where we would go, not my private quarters.

Her eyes got big, and I knew she understood what tonight would entail.

"Strip."

She stood a little straighter before her shaking hands moved to her top, and she lifted it over her head. She rolled her pants and panties down her thighs lastly, she unhooked her bra. Then she knelt and neatly folded her clothes. When she'd finished, she sat back on her heels with her head bowed.

"Are you playing a role or are you feeling it?" I demanded the truth. I was still learning her appetites.

She slowly raised her head and met my gaze. "Feeling it."

I stepped forward until I was towering over here. "Suck my cock."

Her hands went to my fly without hesitation. Soon, her lips were around my cock and pulling hard.

I kept my hand at the back of her skull, forcing her mouth close to my root, allowing her little breaks to get a lungful of air. I was in charge, even of her breathing.

She took me deep and made a humming sound.

Jesus, the woman loved giving head. "Touch yourself. I want to hear your fingers wet from your juices while you fuck yourself."

Her scent filled the room, rich and heady. She was losing her rhythm from time to time on my cock. "Don't you dare come," I warned her.

She squeezed her eyes shut. She'd been ready to be fucked when I took her mouth downstairs. I pulled hard enough on her hair that she let go of my cock. I repositioned my hand around her throat, like a collar. I pressed her backwards until she couldn't balance. I wrapped my other hand around her waist to lift her up enough so that I could plant her on her ass on the floor.

I went to my knees over her prone body. "Hands above your head."

She complied immediately, but I noticed that her hips were lifting, trying to entice me.

I slapped her hip. "I decide when I fuck you."

"Ooooh," she moaned as she stretched, her tits pushing upward.

I fell on her. My mouth closed on her hard nipple. I sucked it into my mouth.

She pressed her wet pussy against me.

I switched to her other tit, taking as much as I could into my mouth.

"Please, please," she chanted.

"Please, what?" I taunted her.

"I need..." Her hips ground upward. "I need to come. Please."

"Laird, you know to address me by my title," I growled.

"Oh, God." She tossed back her head. "Please, Laird, fuck me. If you wish. Please, please fuck me."

So damn pretty. I gripped my aching cock, lined it up with her entrance, and pushed inside.

I didn't ride her as hard as I could. We needed to work up to that. I gripped her right leg and looped it over my hip, and she moved her left. That allowed me to go deeper and Goddess, she got wetter.

"Please," she moaned.

"Not yet." I wanted to make her suffer. She'd asked for this. I moved in short, fast strokes.

"Laird." She ground her heels into my ass.

"Not yet, Theo." I grasped her wrists and forced them over her head.

"Can't," she panted, "need to."

I felt her muscles tighten around my cock. I laughed evilly and knew what my next move would be.

"Damn you," she cried as she tightened around me. Her pleasure had her mewing beneath me.

I followed her and then collapsed on top of her. "You know that I'll have to punish you for coming without my permission."

She opened one eye. "Yeah, I figured."

"And it just increased." I was enjoying this. She was taking the edge off my anger.

I let her rest for a few minutes. Then I got to my feet and carried her to the large chair in the corner of the room. I sat and twisted her relaxed body, so that she was lying face down over my lap. I dipped my fingers in her slit and lightly brushed her clit.

She wrapped her hands around my ankles as if she needed to connect to me.

"This is your first punishment of the night." I dropped two hard smacks on her round ass. I ran my hand over the heat. I loved watching the ivory skin pinken. I continued until her ass was completely pink. When I slid my fingers into her again, she was wetter than before.

I ran my palm over the soft, heated skin. My wet fingers started to trace her ass crack. I didn't go in deeply.

She raised her head. I made a low growling sound, and she said nothing.

I dipped my fingers into her and traced a path from her slit along the crack.

Her body was tense, but she wasn't fighting me. She was waiting to see what I was going to do, although I knew she was fighting against the impulse to deny me.

I paddled her ass again. Then I picked her up and put her on the elevated mat in the corner. It was the closest thing to a bed in the entire room. She lay on her stomach, and I pulled her up on all fours. I climbed on the mat behind her and took her with no preamble or warning. I filled her completely, covering her back. My teeth closed on her upper shoulder. I bit down hard and her blood was sweet on my tongue.

"Ahhh," she cried as her head tilted away from my mouth.

"Mine," I told her.

I swear she shifted her ass so that I could go deeper into her pussy.

I fucked her, not holding back. The only sounds in the room were my balls slapping against her and her pussy making its wet noises.

I was close. I slid my arm under her left arm so that that it went across her chest. My hand once again collared her throat. I pulled her against me as I sat back on my heels. Again, I pressed up into her.

"Oh God, Laird." She was breathing through her mouth as she dropped her head back against my chest.

I tightened my grip around her throat, and she started to struggle. "I decide if you breathe because you are mine," I ground out. I stilled my hips.

It must have been so hard for her, overriding her natural instinct to fight me, all the while knowing she could never win. She pressed her head harder into my shoulder, but she stopped squirming.

I resumed fucking her as her reward.

FORTY-THREE

NOVUS

THEODORA MORRISSEY

I think we'd just finished round number five. I'd lost count of the how many times I'd come. He seemed to be focused on punishing me but making me come. At one point, I'd tried to scramble away from him because I couldn't take the teasing. His hands had changed into paws, and he'd raked my hips with his claws. He then held my hips tightly, digging those sharp nails in deeply as if he wanted to leave permanent marks. I was so tired that I had to strain to remember his last command.

I was on my stomach with some kind of foam pillow under my hips, making my fat ass rest high in the air. I knew what was coming. Hell, I'd known when I'd insisted on letting him use me tonight. He'd been teasing me for hours, running his hands over my ass or sliding his finger along my crack, teasing those sensitive nerves.

He ran his hand up my calf to my thigh. "Still with me?"

"Hmmm." I tried to focus.

"Theodora? Are you still with me?" His voice was louder this time.

I tried to raise my head and look back over my shoulder, it was so hard. "Yesss, Laird."

"I'm going to tie you down then I'm going to take you." His hand rested along the back of my thigh. "All of you, Theo. I will own all of you." His voice had growled. His wolf was very much a part of this.

This isn't a big deal. We watched Conal and Solle do it. You can do this. I tried to relax my body.

He attached some kind of leather wrap around my ankle and then harnessed the other. They weren't spread too far apart, but they were wider than I would have held them. He moved around this platform and lifted my right hand, warming it between his two. Lulled by this moment of gentle handling, I didn't complain when he attached a leather wrap around my wrist that was secured by a chain. He pulled on it so that I knew it had some give.

"That's so that you can rest on your elbows if I deem it necessary." His voice was calm as if he was instructing me on the gun range. He did the same for my other wrist.

I was trying to take deep breaths, to stay calm. I pulled my arms down and rested my forehead on them, hiding my face. I needed time to get control over my anxiety. He knew I was fearful and I sensed that his wolf enjoyed this.

He moved again, he was straddling my thighs. His hand rested on my ass cheek. "So warm."

I probably wouldn't be able to sit for a few days or with my ability to heal, maybe I would? I was surprised my body had been able to keep up with him tonight. My

490

brain had been overloaded with sensations. *Don't think about what is coming.* His fingers were inside of me again, stroking and filling me. I couldn't believe it. My body wanted more of him. I think I heard him chuckle.

"So needy." His voice was deeper and had more of a growl.

His finger was again following the line of my ass crack. I squeezed my eyes closed. "Talk to me," I begged.

"Feeling nervous, my little female?"

His wolf was speaking. "Please," my voice came out in a wheeze. I'd fallen into the submissive role easily, but now, I needed to know that Raider was still with me. He could be a vicious lover. I needed to feel our connection because being at the mercy of his wolf was alarming. One of my arms tested the chains strength. I couldn't help it.

"Do you want me to tell you what I'm going to do to you? How I'm going to fill your body as you scream? You can fight me—in fact, I hope you do." His inhuman sounding laughter held a cruel edge.

I squeezed my eyes tightly shut and tried to find a safe place in my head. At that moment, something inside me clicked. *Oh God, no!*

I was back in Grandma's barn. It was one of those days in late July, where it was sizzling hot and humid. I was done with my chores and wanted to read. Grandma didn't understand my love of books. She was a doer. To sit quietly was foreign to her. I had closed the kitchen door quietly and stuck to the exterior of the farmhouse until I was out of her sight.

I'd used the side door of the barn that was closest to the stalls. We didn't have any horses, so the space was used for storage. I'd set up my hiding place with an old woven chair, a couple of pillows, and my books. I was walking carefully when I turned the corner and ran right into Uncle Doug.

He was the oldest of grandma's children and had never married. He stayed in a trailer a few hundred yards from the house. He was greasy. His hair, clothes, the dirt under his too long nails—all of it repelled me. I tried to avoid him whenever possible.

He gripped my upper arms. "What do we have here?" His mouth was filled with chewing tobacco and some juice fell down the corner of his chin.

"Nothin'," I answered immediately as any fifteen-year-old would.

"Yer Gramma know you're out here sneakin' around?"

I tried to draw back. His breath was terrible. "Yes," I mumbled, which was a total lie.

"Did you come out here to spy on me?" He narrowed his eyes in suspicion.

"No." Why would I want to do that? I did everything within my power to avoid the man.

He turned his head sharply and spit a stream. "Wanna play, little Teddy Bear?"

"No." I shook my head, my instincts screaming for me to get away from this odd man. "I just remembered. I need to do some laundry."

His grip on my arms tightened. "Later." He dragged me toward the back office that he used.

"Uncle Doug, I really need to go." I tried to go stiff, so I'd be harder to propel forward, but this man was used to dealing with cattle. My one hundred-fifty pounds was nothing to him.

"Later." We didn't go into his office. We went into the tack room and he threw me against the wall.

I lost my balance and hit the concrete-block wall headfirst. That stunned me for a few seconds.

He closed the space between us and grabbed my chin, forcing my head back so that our eyes met. "I'm going to like this."

I tried to break free again, and he slapped my face, which banged my head against the wall again. "No," I cried.

He said nothing as he closed in and balled his fist, preparing to throw a punch.

When I opened my eyes, I didn't know where I was. My arms were suspended over my head, chained to a pulley. I shook my head a few times to try to stop the pain, hoping this would make some kind of sense.

"That didn't take long," Doug's hand went to my breast, he squeezed hard.

"Ouch," I screeched as I tried to move away from him.

"I like it when you scream," he said to me as he switched to my other breast. He was the first to man to touch me there.

His hand dropped to my stretchy, elastic-waist shorts. He pulled them down over my wide hips.

I tried to kick him but I could only touch the floor with my tiptoes. I couldn't do any real damage

His hand was at the back of my bikini panties, and he ripped them from my body. His hand covered my hip. "I don't mind meaty."

I dropped my head in shame. I was the fattest girl in my class. I was embarrassed by my body.

"You ever fuck a guy?" he asked as his hand tried to burrow between my thighs.

I clamped them together immediately, fighting off the invasion. I kept thinking about his filthy nails. "No." I was quiet and kept to myself.

He said in a sing-song voice, "Don't worry. I won't pop your cherry. I'll keep you a virgin." He leered at me. "Until next time, then you'll beg me for it."

"No, Uncle Doug, please." I tried to fight him, kicking and swinging. I was screaming and fighting like a feral cat. Since it was so hot, my body became slick with sweat, so he was having problems holding onto me.

He let go of me and undid his jeans. He pulled out his cock and stroked it.

It was the first cock on a man that I'd ever seen. I begged, "Don't, please."

He grabbed me by my waist and stuck his fingers between my butt cheeks. He dug into my back hole.

I howled in shock and pain. "Help," I screamed. I didn't stop screaming even as my hole was stretched by his filthy hand.

"Get away from that girl." My grandmother was standing in the doorway holding a shotgun.

"She wanted it," Doug told her. "She begged me, ma."

"No, no." My throat hurt from screaming. I blacked out.

I knew I wasn't in the barn, but I could smell the feed and feel the heat from that day. "Noooo." I drew the word out like a howl. I tried to twist my body so I could lie on back to protect my ass.

"Don't fight me." Doug? Or was it Black? I didn't know. I couldn't tell.

I fought, bucking and screaming. The smell of the barn was still in my nostrils and the back of my throat. "Uncle Doug, stop. Don't hurt me. *Noooo. Stooopppp.*"

"Who's Doug?" Black demanded, halting his exploration.

I shook my head while yelling. "Stop, please. I don't want this." God, that smell, I hated it.

"Who Is Doug?" His voice was like thunder.

"I don't want this." I cried hysterically. "Uncle Doug stop. Oh God, please stop."

"Theodora?" That wasn't Uncle Doug's voice. This one was deep and so powerful that I felt my body vibrate.

"I can't do it." I cried. "I can't. Please, please don't make me. I don't want this."

He said nothing as he climbed off me. He unhooked my legs and moved around to unhook my arms. I rolled to my side, and then into a ball. I was sobbing. Oh God, I'd kept that day buried away for years. I felt so much anger...shame...terror...and helplessness. My own uncle tried to rape me.

"That is why you have denied your Laird?" His face was right next to mine. His wolf's voice deceptively quiet. I could feel his anger pulsing against my body.

I shook my head back and forth trying to clear it and focus on what was happening now, in this room. I tried to form the words. I didn't know what to say, how to explain. "I, I ca-can't do that."

"Who do you belong to?" His wolf thundered.

I had to take in several breaths before I could answer. "You." I tried to use my gift to sense his emotions, but I couldn't. I was too upset to focus.

"Who?" the wolf demanded in a louder voice.

"You, Raider Black." I promised him.

He grabbed my wrists and rolled me onto my back. "Tell me who this Doug is, and why you speak of him now."

"What?" Did he think I was speaking another lover's name? I tried to sit up, but he pushed me back with a hand collaring my throat.

"Tell your Laird," his voice wolf's voice thundered, "why you speak another man's name while you are naked with me?"

I tried to push him off. I was making sounds that weren't human. They were part cries and part grunts as I fought against him. A part of my brain knew he and his wolf didn't understand what was happening. They only knew I'd refused him and said another man's name. Oh Dear Goddess, he might kill me for that. "Please. Raid... Please don't hurt me." I screamed the last word.

He stilled. He was still holding my body down, but he was watching me closely. Anger radiated from his body.

"Just, just listen. Please Laird." I didn't care that I was begging. "Raider? You're scaring me." I admitted, hoping he would pull back and stop looking at me like I only had seconds to live.

"You should be scared. I told you I was a scary moth-erfucker, but you wanted to see the monster." He, too, was breathing hard.

Why the fuck hadn't I paid more attention in psychology? Oh yeah, because your freshman course didn't cover how to deal with a Lycan predator. "I need to explain." I tried to sound calm, but my voice shook. "I must have buried those memories." I wanted to close my eyes, but I was too scared to break contact with his. "When you...

touched me...there." I had to stop and clear my throat because I choked on the word, "It all came back...what he did to me."

He didn't respond in any way. Not a blink or a sound.

Was he going to kill me?

He kept looking into my eyes.

I ran my tongue over my dry lips. "I was fifteen, okay?" I stumbled over the words. I'd never told anyone this story, except my grandma, and she hadn't wanted to believe me. I'd buried it for so long, so that I could go on. "He, he hurt me." I felt the tears roll from the corners of my eyes and into my sweat-soaked hair. "I told him no. I didn't want that, or him," I sobbed. "He strung me up and...and he tried to..." I couldn't finish. I closed my eyes trying to block the memory. I had to force them open so I could watch my captor.

He still hadn't moved. His motionlessness frightened me. I don't think his heart beat, or that he took a breath. It was terrifying, he was more wolf than man at this moment.

"I tried to fight, but I couldn't... I tried so hard, Raid. I didn't want him to touch me." I closed my eyes and cried. I was so tired from the day's emotions, the ugliness, and now this. I couldn't take anymore. My body went limp. I surrendered. He could do whatever he wanted to me, with me.

He understood. After a bit, he carried me into his rooms, straight into the shower. I couldn't stand. My arms were so weak I couldn't hang onto him. He placed me gently on the built-in bench at the rear of the shower and cleaned himself. He then slowly bathed me, telling me where he was going to touch me before he did.

I was exhausted when he carried me to bed, but my soul hurt too much to fall asleep. I didn't understand what had happened or what would happen. I honestly thought that his wolf wanted me dead.

"His name is Doug?" His breath was hot against my shoulder. He was curled around me, with my back to his chest.

I swallowed hard. "My uncle. My mother's oldest brother."

"He raped you?"

I felt the tears burn my eyes. I wasn't embarrassed. I was furious with him and at my helplessness. "With his fingers." I swallowed so hard my throat stung. My grandmother had made a great production of telling me how it wasn't so bad because it was only his hand. His fucking, filthy hand. "Grandma found me before…he could do more. But his fingernails, they were always so dirty." I hated that they had been inside of my body. I shivered involuntarily at the revolting memory.

"He hurt you." He said it as a statement, cutting me off. "You were young, and he hurt you."

"He was always odd," I explained. "That's how people referred to him." I cleared my throat and tried to keep to the basic facts. "I was fifteen. He caught me sneaking into the barn to read one afternoon."

"Your own kin?" This was a different kind of fury. He was cold and calculating now, and I wasn't sure if it was worse than the growly, snappy kind.

"He would have done more," I continued, "but my grandmother heard me screaming."

"She protected you."

"In a manner of speaking, she managed to get the high school to allow me to graduate early. I was enrolled in college that fall. She sent me away, and Doug got to stay with her. He's still there on the farm today," I finished bitterly.

"You believe she sent you away to protect her son?"

"Didn't she?" I countered. My hurt and anger seeped into my tone.

"I think she made a rational decision for all the parties."

I considered his answer.

"You weren't meant for the farming life. She knew, eventually, you'd go off to college. She couldn't see her son jailed, so she sent you away to start your new life and kept him close so she could watch him."

"I've never thought about it that way." I let out a sigh. "He's in charge of the farm now. He doesn't have any kids, but my cousins do. Do you think that he hurts them, or was I a onetime deal, an opportunity too good to pass up?" Dear God, this was terrible...remembering it all and what it could mean.

"I'll send Lore out tomorrow to kill him for hurting you," Black said.

"Don't."

"I'll do it myself."

I turned in his arms so I could face him. "Please don't." I didn't want another death marked on his soul and not for me.

"He hurt you."

"I don't want you to do that for me."

"You think I can't kill a human male?"

"Of course, you can." Of that, I had no doubt. "I don't want you to kill for me."

"Because you will kill him yourself?" He sounded intrigued and excited at the thought.

"If I found out that he'd touched another child, then yes." I knew immediately that I would do it.

He chuckled and traced the bones along my spine. "My woman is so bloodthirsty."

I was quiet for a long time as I thought about his words. "I refused you…"

"I now understand," he said in a clipped tone.

"But do you understand that I kept those memories buried for years?" My voice cracked, and I swallowed and squeezed my eyes shut, hoping to cut off the tears before they began. "I wanted to please you...to help."

"You do, Theo. You are too generous, with your body and your…caring."

"Raider," I gripped his chest, my nails digging in, "I want to give you whatever you need."

"My sweet girl, you do." He kissed me.

That way, you won't forget me when I'm gone.

I felt him get up and heard the shower start. He did not invite me to join him and I was too tired to ask. I closed my eyes and dozed some more.

I felt the bed depress, and his lips were on my cheek. "I'm needed at the office."

I opened my eyes and raised my hand to run it through his still wet hair. "Do you need me to go with you?"

"I need to address what we learned yesterday."

I started to sit up again.

"Babe, if I find that you are needed, I will call, but I think you need to rest today."

I relaxed back against my soft pillows. "I need to go to Conal's. I'm out of clothes and the ones I need are there." It was hard living out of suitcases. I never seemed to have the right clean clothes when or where I needed them.

"I'll pick you up there, later." He kissed the side of my mouth. "It's time that you stop keeping your things at Conal's."

I wasn't ready for that conversation. It was too soon. "Lore will be disappointed when I don't come in for training."

"He might be on his way to Ohio."

"No, please." I gripped his forearm. "I want to forget that. I need to in order to move on."

The muscle at the side of his jaw pulsed.

"Please, I-I'm begging you. Please don't do anything."

"I make no promises, Theo," he said, his tone grave, "but I'll issue no order today."

I closed my eyes and nodded as relief made me feel dizzy. "Thank you, Laird."

SOLLE WAS home when I arrived. She looked tired. I know that I was. "What's up, Doc?" I tried to tease my friend.

"I'm sitting here feeling guilty about not going in today." She had a coffee mug in front of her.

"I'm sure you aren't the only one. Black gave me the day off." I was in a pair of his sweats and a T-shirt. I wanted to change into my own clothes—after a long soak in the hot tub.

She sniffed the air. "Why do I smell blood?" She was now giving me a narrowed eyed look. "Did he hurt you?" She got to her feet and moved toward me.

"No," I defended him immediately.

She sniffed the air again and softened her tone. "Perhaps, it was an accident?"

Thank God, an easy excuse. "Yes." Although I wasn't sure she believed me.

"What's going on?" She switched into doctor mode.

"Things got intense." I headed down the steps to the basement with Solle close on my heels.

She followed me outside to the deck and we uncovered the hot tub without any more conversation.

I stripped out of the too-large clothes.

Solle stopped me from getting into the bubbling water with a gentle hand on my arm. "Those look deep."

I glanced down at my body. The marks hadn't healed. They were bleeding in places.

"They might scar."

I moved away from her and walked around the tub, trying to put some space between us. "Then I'll carry his marks on my body." I held her gaze the entire time as I entered the tub.

"As you wish." She stripped and joined me in the rapidly warming water.

We settled ourselves on the benches, I rested my head back and closed my eyes.

"You used the word intense."

I opened my eyes and sat up straighter. Of course, she wouldn't let this go.

Her brown eyes had turned almost black. "In what way?"

I tried to ease into my explanation. "He warned me that he was...in a dark place."

"He kept you with him?" she said, her voice rising.

"I insisted, Solle." I hoped that would calm her down, hearing it was my choice. "It was all me."

"Why?" She gave me a look that communicated I'd made a crazy decision. She then sighed deeply and frowned. "You don't have to tell me, I already know."

I jutted my chin. "He was going to end up with another."

"And you couldn't handle that?"

"Of course not," I said hotly.

"You love him," she stated with finality.

I refused to use that word or even think it. I looked away and stared out at their yard. I needed to talk about this, but I was having trouble finding the courage. Saying it would make it truer, more real. "I shouldn't."

"I don't believe that." She moved closer to me and gripped my hand. "You two are meant to be together."

"It won't last," I reminded her and myself. "It can't."

"Does that…make you not want to be with him?"

Oh, Christ. I knew the answer. I responded honestly. "No, I need him, like…like I need air." It felt good to be able to say it aloud.

She let out a relieved bark of laughter. "That bad, huh?" She flashed me a huge smile.

I smiled, and then I grew serious. I was going to share my greatest fear. "I don't want him to forget me," I whispered the words, "you know, over time…he might. You might."

"Oh." Solle looked away suddenly. Her face screwed up, and she blinked quickly several times. "Oh, honey." She pulled me into her arms, hugging me close. "We won't…can't… None of us ever will."

FORTY-FOUR

NOVUS

RAIDER BLACK

I didn't know what to do with all the information Theo had revealed last night. My wolf wanted to head to Ohio and not return until Uncle Doug had paid for his treachery.

Lore had stopped in my office earlier. "How is she?"

His concern for my female didn't upset my wolf. He and the Seer had bonded in a way that I understood, Conal and I shared the same ties. He would protect her with his life and she trusted him completely. "She's exhausted."

"We are truly blessed. She may become stronger than the Lady Octavia." He dropped his chin.

The new ability to retrieve memories would be a very helpful tool.

"Her gift is growing rapidly," Lore murmured.

Our gazes met, and I knew it was a warning. "We will do everything to help her." I would monitor her closely. If the time ever came that I felt her powers were a threat, that the Pack was in danger, I would terminate her as it was my duty. My Theo would never want to injure an innocent.

"I will do my part. You have my word, Laird." He was loyal to Novus, but Theo was important to him. The wolf could be in Ohio tomorrow and he would kill the uncle without a thought, upon my order. In fact, he would rush if he knew what had been done to Theo.

However, giving the termination order might cause her more pain at this time. She had already been through so much. I had not promised to never kill the man, so I had time.

Two hours later, Conal stuck his head in my door. "I'm getting nothing done. I'm heading home."

I dropped my tablet onto my desk. "Can I catch a ride?"

Our females were sitting on the sectional sofa in the basement, watching a TV show on the big screen. They looked relaxed and comfortable. Conal immediately went to his mate, sat down, drew her onto his lap, and kissed her.

Theo pushed to her feet and grasped her wrist. "Laird."

I moved to her and pulled her into my arms. "You okay?"

"I'm fine. I've done nothing all day but rest."

I let her go so I could study her eyes. "But you're good?" I meant physically and emotionally.

She looked to the side instead of answering me immediately.

"Need to talk," I told our friends and started to walk toward the steps, taking her with me.

"Okay." She started to giggle. "Don't be so pushy."

We climbed the two flights to her room.

"Wouldn't that be pulley?" I quipped. "Since I was pulling you along?" I dropped onto her bed and leaned back on my elbows.

"Quite the jokester today, I see." She smiled and leaned against the dresser.

I noticed she hadn't packed her things as I'd mentioned this morning. I wasn't irritated. It might be fun trying to convince her, but I wanted to know the reason why. "I meant what I said this morning."

She gripped her hands in front of her. "About that…"

"I want you with me, Theo."

"I don't know what that means." Her blue eyes were huge as she whispered those words.

I held out my hand to her and she took it automatically. I pulled her down beside me. "It means that I want to go to sleep with you in my arms every night and wake to your body burrowed into mine every morning."

"It's too soon." Her blue eyes were huge.

"Are you mine?" I felt a trickle of sweat run down my back. I was nervous about her answer.

"You know that I am."

We both knew this was an important moment.

"Then be with me, Theodora," I urged her by wrapping my arm around her waist.

"Raider, what if…*she* decides that she's ready?"

I knew she was talking about my contracted mate. "You please me. I want you. I will have you," I said, making sure she heard the certainty in my voice.

"And then what? Have you thought about that?"

"I will not be denied because of something that may not happen for centuries." She started to reply, but I cut her off. "I have you now, Theo. I want you to be with me. I want this, us." The admission was unplanned, but it was true. "I need you." And then I said the word I'd never said as Laird. Not to a single soul. "Please?"

One beat, two, three, and then she smiled, tremulously. "Yes."

My heart skipped then pounded inside my chest. "You'll move in?"

"Yes, I'll move in."

"And…" I prompted. I wanted to hear her promise.

"I'll be with you."

"You please me, Theo." I kissed her.

"I want to Raider, for as long as I can."

I was happy for the first time in…forever. When I'd been given the charter for Novus, I'd felt a deep sense of satisfaction, but this was totally different. I felt light and hopeful. She'd made me that way, my beautiful Seer, my Theo. Mine.

THE END FOR NOW.

FEEL ME-- BOOK 2 in the Novus Pack Series is in the works.

PLAYLIST FOR SEE ME

Chapter 1 *In the End* by Linkin Park
Chapter 2 *More Human Than Human* by White Zombie
Chapter 3 *Man in the Box* by Alice in Chains
Chapter 4 *Take Me to the River* by The Talking Heads
Chapter 5 *Paradise City* by Gun 'N Roses
Chapter 6 *Smells Like Teen Spirit* by Nirvana
Chapter 7 *Voo Doo* by Godsmack
Jesus Just Left Chicago by ZZ Top
Chapter 8 *Rocky Mountain Way* by Joe Walsh
Chapter 9 *Seven Nation Army* by The White Stripes
Chapter 10 *Truly Madly Deeply* by Savage Garden
Chapter 11 *Black Sheep* by Gin Wigmore
Chapter 12 *Suit and Jacket* by Judah & The Lion
Chapter 13 *Here is Gone* by The Goo Goo Dolls
Chapter 14 *Burning House* by Cam
Chapter 15 *Tennessee Whiskey* by Chris Stapleton
Cowboy by Kid Rock
Chapter 16 *Set Fire to the Rain* by Adele
Chapter 17 *Bodies* by Drowning Pool

ABOUT THE AUTHOR

M. Jayne doesn't know what she wants to be when and if she ever grows up. She's worked retail, recorded hearings in a Federal Courtroom, worked behind the scenes with security at a casino and currently she is living her dream writing Romance.

She plots and plans from her farm in central Indiana that she shares with her husband and two mastiffs, Ginger and Duncan Keith. When she isn't creating she can be found watching sports, searching for the perfect mascara and reading. She also loves questionable TV-Any Real Housewives, The Steve Wilkos Show and Live PD. Plus she is addicted to the TMZ app on her phone.

M. Jayne loves to meet readers. She attends many conferences and signings. Please take a moment and introduce yourself and tell her what you are reading.

facebook.com/ReadMelanieJayne

twitter.com/1MelanieJayne

instagram.com/ReadMelanieJayne

goodreads.com/ReadMelanieJayne

bookbub.com/profile/m-jayne

amazon.com/author/ReadMelanieJayne

Made in the USA
Monee, IL
07 October 2023

44120232R00286